"Jean Johnson's writing is fabulo[...] and wildly entertaining. Terrific—fast, sexy, charming, and utterly engaging. I loved it!" —Jayne Ann Krentz, *New York Times* bestselling author

"Cursed brothers, fated mates, prophecies, yum! A fresh new voice in fantasy romance, Jean Johnson spins an intriguing tale of destiny and magic." —Robin D. Owens, RITA Award–winning author

"What a debut! I have to say it is a must-read for those who enjoy fantasy and romance . . . Jean Johnson can't write them fast enough for me!"
—*The Best Reviews*

"A paranormal adventure series that will appeal to fantasy and historical fans, plus time-travel lovers as well . . . It's like *Alice in Wonderland* meets the Knights of the Round Table and you're never quite sure what's going to happen next. Delightful entertainment." —*Romance Junkies*

"An intriguing new fantasy romance series . . . Cunning . . . Creative . . . Lovers of magic and fantasy will enjoy this fun, fresh, and very romantic offering." —*Time Travel Romance Writers*

"A must-read." —*Romance Reviews Today*

"An intriguing world . . . An enjoyable showcase for an inventive new author. Jean Johnson brings a welcome voice to the romance genre." —*The Romance Reader*

"An intriguing and entertaining tale of another dimension . . . Quite entertaining." —*Fresh Fiction*

Titles by Jean Johnson

SHIFTING PLAINS
BEDTIME STORIES
FINDING DESTINY
THE SHIFTER

The Sons of Destiny
THE SWORD
THE WOLF
THE MASTER
THE SONG
THE CAT
THE STORM
THE FLAME
THE MAGE

The Guardians of Destiny
THE TOWER
THE GROVE
THE GUILD

Theirs Not to Reason Why
A SOLDIER'S DUTY
AN OFFICER'S DUTY
HELLFIRE

The GUILD

JEAN JOHNSON

BERKLEY SENSATION, NEW YORK

THE BERKLEY PUBLISHING GROUP
Published by the Penguin Group
Penguin Group (USA) LLC
375 Hudson Street, New York, New York 10014

USA • Canada • UK • Ireland • Australia • New Zealand • India • South Africa • China

penguin.com

A Penguin Random House Company

This book is an original publication of The Berkley Publishing Group.

Library of Congress Cataloging-in-Publication Data

Johnson, Jean, 1972–
The Guild / Jean Johnson.—Berkley Sensation trade paperback edition.
pages cm.—(Guardians of Destiny ; 3)
ISBN 978-0-425-26226-9 (paperback)
I. Title.
PS3610.O355G85 2014
813'.6—dc23   2013051059

PUBLISHING HISTORY
Berkley Sensation trade paperback edition / May 2014

PRINTED IN THE UNITED STATES OF AMERICA

10 9 8 7 6 5 4 3 2 1

Cover art by Don Sipley.
Cover design by George Long.

The GUILD

ONE

Cult's awareness, it shall rise:
Hidden people, gather now;
Fight the demons, fight your doubt.
Gearman's strength shall then endow,
When Guilds' defender casts them out.

I f it weren't for the way the silvery web covering his jaw prevented him from casting spells, Torven Shel Von would have immediately freed himself and transformed his captors into little insects, the kind that were easily squished.

It wasn't possible, though. He couldn't even curse them verbally, let alone magically. The silencing web spell had been applied thickly enough to prevent even plain speech, though the captured mage knew there was an intermediary version that allowed the one while still cutting off the other. Strapped onto a table while fighting off the effects of what felt like a long-applied sleep spell, he could only breathe. That, and contemplate two important things.

One, he *was* going to get free and kill whoever had betrayed him and the Healer strapped to the other table in this dark, unpleasant, heavily carved chamber. And two . . . he was going to need a refreshing room soon. There might be some vengeance to be found in relieving himself straight into the faces of his captors, but they had yet to remove his clothing. The fact that they hadn't was a mixed blessing; it was late winter, and the low-burning braziers in the four corners of the room weren't doing much to either heat or light the place, so at least his clothes were keeping him warm. But oh, how he wanted vengeance.

The sounds of someone approaching turned his head to the side, toward the door. A slender figure entered the chamber, dressed in a dark brown, lumpy-woven tunic with a black, felted cap pulled low over his head. The youth lugged something up to the first brazier, set it down, then furtively looked at the door and approached the still-unconscious Crastus. Fishing a strip of something out of the pouch hung at the front of his belt—knitting, that was what the lumpy fabric was, Torven realized—the knitting-clad, knitting-carrying lad laid it across the Healer's brow.

More bodies approached. The youth quickly snatched the piece of intricately knitted yarn off the Healer-mage's forehead and stuffed it into his sleeve, then realized Torven was watching him. The youth gave the mage an impudent stare and returned to the brazier. Torven couldn't even ask him what that was all about; his mouth was still bound by the enspelled webbing.

Two figures, dressed in high-quality velvet robes embroidered with symbols of gears and esoteric runes, entered the chamber. The stone walls of this place were a dull shade of gray, and the robes were rich dark reds and purples, but the carvings and the embroidery matched. Priests of Mekha, God of Engineering and Patron Deity of Mekhana, making this a temple to Mekha.

May He rot in Heaven.

Torven had learned what to look for, or rather, what to look out for, regarding this particular deity. It had long been known in Arbra that the fate of mages caught by the priesthood of this land was an ugly thing, and the natives there had warned him and the others in his group. To have one's magic, one's essential superiority over all common souls, siphoned and stolen away without consent was an ugly theft. But the fact that he and Crastus alone had been taken captive and brought here while their whole group had slept in a barn set with warding spells meant someone had betrayed the two of them.

Perhaps it was the Arbran farmer who owned the barn and whose permission they hadn't sought since it had been snowing, though most Arbrans hated Mekhanans with a passion. The farmer would have been able to penetrate the subtle shields Torven had laid on the structure, since it was his property and Torven hadn't intended to block out the owner. But perhaps—and more likely—it had been one of the others. That lock picker, Unsial, was at the top of his list. She'd trade her own grandmother for a bag of gold, in his view. Not that he'd seen her do so literally, but she had that kind of attitude about her.

Possibly Barric and Kellida. Those two had been getting rather chummy, Torven recalled, watching the priests warily. He couldn't disguise the fact he was still awake, but he could watch them as they first looked over him and the Healer, then eyed the boy working to refuel the braziers with black lumps. Coal, Torven realized. *Oh, I have a spell or two I could use on those braziers that could damage this lot . . . but this stupid web spell is blocking even the most basic and intrinsic of cantrips from working. And somehow I doubt they're going to wait to deal with me long enough for the webbing to dry up and crumble. If they were going to wait that long, they'd have used anti-magic shackles.*

The taller of the two priests leaned over Torven. Unlike the other, who was short, rotund, and had solidly gray hair and a neatly trimmed beard to match, this fellow had a smooth, shaved head and a white-streaked dark brown beard a full handspan in length. He reached down and pried one of the mage's eyes wider, and lifted his brows when Torven angrily pulled his head free. "Don't bother resisting, foreigner. Your magics are very strong, but we are *very* good at holding your kind captive . . . and you'll do very well to feed His hunger, praise Mekha."

"Don't bother, Hansu," the other priest stated, busy examining the still-unconscious Crastus. "He probably doesn't speak a word of Mekhanan. Remember, they were picked up within Arbra, may He smite the Tree Slut's lands," the shorter man stated in a bored tone that suggested it was nothing more than rote repetition to say such things.

Actually, Torven did know the local tongue. In his youth he had run across a description of how to craft Ultra Tongue and had stolen the tiny supply of *myjiin* powder available at the academy where he had trained. That had eventually been uncovered, and he had been forced to flee and give himself a new name so he could start over at a different school . . . with some funds liberated from the previous one during his flight. It wasn't the first time he had had to flee a bad situation. *The trick is to make sure* this *situation isn't my last one. But in order to do that, I need to talk! I can convince people to give me the gold rings off their fingers if I can only talk.*

He had to settle for meeting the first priest's gaze, then rolling his eyes away in expressive, bored dismissal. Hansu frowned, then quirked a brow. "What, you understand Mekhanan?"

Torven raked his gaze over the man's bearded face and bald head, then nodded curtly. He returned his gaze to the ceiling as if the other man's presence were trivial.

"You aren't the least bit scared of your surroundings?" Hansu asked.

Deigning to glance at him, Torven shook his head. The priest snorted. He stroked his beard, pressing it against his velvet-clad throat as he leaned over the Aian mage.

"Clearly, you don't understand what danger you are in. If you did, you'd be begging me for death."

Oh, I know what danger I am in, Torven acknowledged silently. But he gave the priest a pitying look and shook his head slowly.

"What, does he think he knows something we don't?" the other priest scoffed.

Torven nodded curtly, then relaxed back against the table or altar or whatever they had him pinned to, as if whatever happened next didn't concern him in the least. He had a plan, based on a question that had been bothering him ever since being exiled by that short little bastard who dared call himself Master of the Tower. A question of why the God Mekha had to rely upon draining mere mages for power when there were far better sources available.

"I doubt it," Hansu muttered.

His companion glared at the youth. "Aren't you done building up the fires, you lackwit?"

"Sorry, sir," the boy mumbled in a light tenor. "Gotta git more coal." He lugged the empty pail out of the room, head ducked in a servile hunch.

"If he had a lick of magic, I'd have plugged him into the God ages ago. That's all the little fart is good for."

"That's all any of them are good for," Hansu agreed. "The Servers Guild takes in the idiots and foists the worst of them on us, but the magicless are of no use. Still, as long as they're in a guild, *we* don't have to feed and clothe them."

"Heh, or train them. Remember the temple in Bordastowne?" the other priest chuckled. "They thought they could make things cheaper by hiring non-guild orphans. Burned food, stained robes, dust in the corners . . . The archbishop there finally agreed to hire from the Servers Guild again. I'll admit the boy is slow and stupid, but he does the job thoroughly."

Torven rolled his eyes again. *If only I could speak! They're wasting my time with these trivialities.* The taller priest caught that eye twitch. He stroked his beard, then placed his hand over Torven's mouth and muttered something. From the tingle of magic, the Aian mage guessed something had changed, though the web didn't vanish. His guess was confirmed in the next breath.

"I've given you the power to speak normally, though you still will not be able to spellcast, mage," Hansu told him. He poked Torven in the chest with one bony finger. "If you think you have something to tell us to get you out of your predicament, now is your chance to try . . . and I do mean *try*. It would have to be of miraculous proportions to avert your fate. Mekha hungers, and you're next on His plate."

"A fat, juicy pig like that should have an apple in his mouth," the other priest muttered. "And should *not* be allowed to squeal."

Listening to them muttering, Torven suppressed an impatient sigh. Instead, he asked pointedly, "*Why* are you wasting your time siphoning magical energy from mages?"

"Because our God demands it, you fool! Or have those Arbran lackwits you were dallying with not explained it to you?" Hansu scorned.

If Torven had believed in any one particular God, he would have prayed for patience. As it was, he saw Them as nothing more than leeches on the rights of mortal man. Glaring at the bald-pated priest, he clarified himself, using crisp, biting syllables because he didn't have much patience for idiots. "Not *that*, you imbecile. Why are you piddling around with mages when there are far greater sources of power available for your God?"

Hansu scowled at him, and the unnamed gray-haired priest

moved over to frown down at the captive Aian as well. "What do you mean?" Hansu demanded. "There are no other sources! Gods get their powers from mortals, which means the energies *must* come from mortal mages!"

He rolled his eyes. "Gods spare me from the uneducated," Torven muttered. Raising his voice, he countered the older man's arguments. "There are singularity points, commonly called Fountains, which spew masses of energy into the world. Get your hands on one of *those*, and you can make Mekha a God of Gods."

"We're not ignorant of such things," the other priest snapped. "We have none of those within Mekhana's borders, and our neighbors fight with such ferocity, we cannot gain more than a finger length of land in a generation! Your advice is as useless as *you* are. Only your magic is of any value. For as long as it lasts."

"It is not the *only* source of vast power, though it is the easiest, which is why I suggested it first," Torven countered. "If Mekha is a God, then summon up and enslave a demon to Him! The underprinces of the Netherhells have almost as much power as a Fountain—and you can enslave a whole host of the lesser kind to equal that kind of power with a minimum of risk. It's actually easier to summon and bind a demon than to find a Fountain. The only trick lies in binding it thoroughly *and* in knowing how to tap into whatever passes for its life-energy."

Hansu scoffed, folding his velvet-robed arms across his chest. "And I suppose *you* just happen to know how to do this demonic energy stealing?"

"Of course I do. I've made it my life's work to study how to gain vast power in numerous ways." He knew they didn't believe him, could see it in their eyes, but Torven wasn't lying. "Bring me a Truth Stone, and you'll see the pure white of my words for yourselves."

Hansu looked at the other fellow, who sighed and dug into his robes. The gray-haired priest pulled out a white marble disc and pressed it into Torven's hand. "I'm sure you know how they work, foreigner. First a lie, and then a truth."

"I am in love with you," Torven stated.

He uncurled his fingers, but the angle at which he was pinned to the altar didn't allow him to see what color the marble was. From their satisfied looks, the cold stone had been striped in black wherever his flesh had touched it. Waiting a few seconds to let the marks fade, the Aian mage gripped it again.

"I am Torven, a mage of great power and greater knowledge, and I hold the secrets of how to summon, bind, and drain a demon of its magical energies. Mind you, this is a dark form of magic, almost as bad as blood magic," he warned them, pausing to flex his fingers a couple times to show he spoke the truth, "but since you're already stealing life-energies from your own citizens, which is a worse 'sin,' I sincerely doubt you'll quibble at using a demon's energies."

The two stared at the stone in Torven's hand, then retreated to the doorway for a whispered conference. Torven relaxed, knowing that he had at least been given a shot at freeing himself. The distant Threefold God of Fate—well, not so distant, now that he was just two kingdoms away from Fortuna—gave chances and opened doors of opportunity to the wicked and the good alike.

Of course, Torven didn't consider himself all *that* wicked. Selfish, oh yes, quite, but then why shouldn't he be? Every single person in the world was after whatever he or she could get in life, and he was merely determined to be very good at getting whatever he wanted. At the moment, he wanted his freedom. His ultimate goal was always power, however. Stealing the Fountain at the heart of the Tower had been one possibility, but there had been many others buried in the dusty, forgotten tomes of the Tower archives.

Demonic enslavement and power-draining were simply another way to achieve his goal.

Eventually, Hansu and the other priest had to break up their little conversation as the boy came back, cheek smudged with coal dust and arms struggling with the now heavily laden bucket. Letting him pass, the priests waited for him to reach the next brazier and begin tending it, then Hansu led the way back to Torven's altar table.

"If you really can do what you say you can do, we'll presume you want your freedom. For both you and for this other mage?" Hansu asked him, flicking a hand at the still unconscious Healer.

Torven didn't even glance at Crastus. Most Healers tended to be selfless twits who bleated on and on about having some sort of stupid obligation to use one's powers for the good of many. Before their exile from the continent of Aiar, Crastus had been more interested in being paid for his services, as a sensible person should be. After their exile . . . the older mage had expressed occasional doubts, even feelings of remorse, as if a simple bad turn of luck, losing that stupid fight in the banqueting hall and then being tossed out onto another continent to live or die, was some sort of holy wake-up call. Bad luck was simply Fate's way of saying, find another path toward your goals or be stuck in stagnation like an idiot.

"I don't care about him either way, other than that he's a good-enough Healer. But *he* probably won't serve you willingly, so either let him go or drain him dry. As for myself . . ." He tried to smirk, though the silvery web material covering his mouth probably hid the effect. "I want power. Secular and magical power. A position of some rank in your order, a decent amount of money—obscenely decent, by preference—and of course a way to tap into some of the power that'll be raised. And a nice title wouldn't be amiss."

"Of course," the bald, bearded priest drawled. "And naturally you'll escape the moment we set you free. We do realize how powerful you are. We're not idiots."

The gray-haired priest started to say something, then glared at the youth in the dark gray knitted tunic. "Aren't you *done* yet, lackwit? Stop fiddling with the coals, and get out!"

The boy jumped, hastily scooped a few more black lumps onto the glowing orange white ones, and scuttled off, bucket clutched to his chest.

Hansu covered his brow with his palm. "I swear, we're surrounded by inbred idiots . . . You were going to say something, Koler?"

"Swear a mage-oath," the other priest asserted. "Bind unto your powers an oath that you'll serve our holy order and conjure us a demon for power-binding unto Mekha."

Torven narrowed his eyes. "I'm not swearing any oath casually . . . but if you'll let me sit up and fetch pen and paper, perhaps we could draft a version between the three of us that will satisfy both sides. You *know* I know how to conjure and bind a demon for power-draining. A few minutes' delay won't harm anything either way."

Koler, the shorter priest, narrowed his eyes under his bushy, age-salted brows. "If you know how to do it, then why haven't you done it before? You *claim* you crave power and that this is a great source of it."

Torven rolled his eyes. "Because binding a major demon requires a *lot* of participants? If it's one tiny denizen of a Netherhell, that's fine; one mage can do that . . . but the demon's power is piddly, and a mage can bind only one or two personally before they start to threaten his control. A larger demon has exponentially greater energies that can be drained from its vast reserves, but many mages are required to subdue, bind, and control it.

"Most mages whine about how dealing with anything associated with the Netherhells is an abomination against the world," he continued, while the other two considered his offer and mulled over his motives. "They wouldn't touch such a project if their immortal souls depended on it—which they don't. You'd be binding the power for your God to use, not for yourselves. Heaven couldn't touch any of us . . . and They certainly won't touch Mekha, or They'd have done so by now."

"Heaven doesn't give a damn about any of us," Hansu scoffed under his breath. "If They did . . ." He broke off, sighed, and asserted firmly if a bit rotely, "We serve Mekha, and that is our reward. Fetch pen and paper, Koler."

"If this isn't a viable option, you'll be plugged into our God without a second thought," Koler warned Torven before turning toward the door.

"If it isn't a viable option, that will be the fault of *your* colleagues, not mine," Torven told him, clenching his fist as the older priest turned back with a scowl. "Check the Truth Stone still in my hand—I am not going to let any fault of *mine* damage my chances of gaining vast power." He relaxed his fingers, showing what was undoubtedly an unblemished disc. He spoke the truth after all.

Koler grunted and turned toward the door again, and he was almost bowled over as a junior priest ran up the corridor, skidding to a stop in front of the gray-haired man. "Brother Koler!" the youth gasped, panting. "Brother Hansu! He's gone!"

"What do you mean?" Hansu asked. "Who is gone?"

"Mekha! He's gone! Not ten, fifteen minutes ago, He was in the power chamber soaking up everything like normal, then there was suddenly a great, shimmering light in front of Him, like a giant egg. He stood, said, 'Finally!' and . . . was gone! The light took Him, and He vanished, almost like He stepped into nothingness!"

Bound on the table as he still was, Torven couldn't see the young man's face clearly, but he certainly heard the bewilderment in that breathless, cracking voice.

"He just vanished, brothers, and no one knows why! We waited, and we waited, but now . . . now the *symbols* are going, too! 'Scuse me, I have to go tell the others!" A patter of feet took him farther down the hall.

Koler turned to watch the youth go, moving just enough that Torven could see the scowl on his face. It deepened as his gaze shifted to someone else outside the Aian mage's view. "Haven't you moved *on*, boy?"

Hansu frowned and started to say something—then reached out and clutched his fellow priest's shoulder, hard enough to make the older man grunt. His other hand pointed straight at the carvings, and he hissed, "*Look!*"

His shoulder and sleeve blocked part of Torven's awkwardly angled view, but the robe itself revealed more than enough. The runes and the gears, painstakingly stitched on the fabric and carved into the walls, were melting and fading. Vanishing. Being erased, the Aian mage realized, as the phenomenon spread, rippling across the walls and even the ceiling.

As the wave passed Torven's toes, he felt the spells binding him to the altar weaken . . . and the webbing decay. Using a surge of his personal powers, Torven broke the last of the binding spell and quickly sat up, shifting to dangle his legs over the side of the stone table. He didn't move farther than that, since his head pounded from a lack of blood after his sudden change in position, but it was enough to catch the attention of the other two men. Quickly, before they could re-enslave him, he held up one hand, thinking hard and fast.

"I suspect, gentlemen, that you no longer have a Patron Deity. Which means it is no longer necessary for you to bind and drain me. This . . . vanishing," he added, gesturing vaguely at the walls, "matches some old records I have read about old Gods and Goddesses being disbanded. Which is a little odd, because that would normally require the Convocation of Gods and Man, which hasn't been seen since my homeland was an intact empire two centuries ago . . . but it isn't impossible. After all, there is no reason for Mekha *and* His symbols to disappear otherwise . . . and with no detectable traces of magic, I might add."

"If that is true, then this is a disaster," Hansu muttered, swiping his palm over his bare scalp. "Without Mekha to keep the peasants in line, we'll have rioting in the streets! They'll try to attack us— and I can feel that I don't have the great power I once held . . ."

"Then it sounds like you need a powerful ally . . . and that you still need a power *source*," Torven reminded him, ignoring the faint groan from the Healer on the other altar-table. "My point earlier about other mages not wanting to handle such a source is still valid, particularly if you cross-gift the energies so that you are not tapping the creatures you yourself bind, but instead exchange powers with the beings tapped by someone else.

"I am still willing to work with *your* Brotherhood," he reminded them. "It's not as if you have anything to lose at this point, if the peasants will turn on you once they know that the wrath of their vanished God no longer holds them in check. Gather the others in a secure place, lay out these suggestions to all of them, and make up your minds. But do it *quickly*."

"Hansu—the mage-prisoners," the gray-haired priest said, catching his companion's sleeve while Hansu hesitated. "Without Mekha draining them, they *will* start to recover, and then they'll come after *us*. We have bigger problems on our hands!"

Torven rolled his eyes again. Feeling well enough to stand, he pushed off the altar but leaned his hip against it for hidden support. If he had to fight to get out of here, he would need his reserves for battle not for balance. "For the love of a proper education . . . Gentlemen. Set them *free*, apologize to them—even if you have to choke on your bile to do it—and tell them that you were *forced* into doing everything you've done by your former Patron Deity! After all, who can go against the will of their God? Who cares if it's a partial lie or a flat-out fib? With Mekha *gone*, banished from existence itself, you have the perfect scapegoat to blame!

"At the very least, you'll have them pushed outside the temple doors before they know what's happened to them, *and* you'll have a valid excuse to lock those doors behind them," he added archly.

"*Apologize?*" Hansu looked like he was being asked to swallow a manure-covered toad. He checked himself after a moment of thought, albeit with a look of distaste. "I . . . I suppose if we *must* . . ."

Mind no longer fogged by the spells laid on him, Torven had already thought five moves ahead. *I could easily flee or overpower these two . . . but I'd have to go looking for another Fountain to try to take over, and that could take years of searching and careful insinuation. If the shattered remnants of this priesthood can pull their heads out of their collective arses long enough to stay organized, we* might *be able to summon up a vast source of power . . . and* retain positions of power in this land. If they're not idiots.

"Yes, you *must*," he said, barely concealing his impatience. "You have a very rare opportunity, gentlemen. With the removal of Mekha—as evidenced by the loss of His symbols and sigils from everything, even from the embroidery on your robes—you have the opportunity to *create* a God or Goddess of *your* choosing. One with all the power you could want . . . and one completely under your control."

He smiled at them. Not a bland or a pleasant smile, but rather the kind that showed too many teeth. Koler blinked and frowned at him, but the bearded Hansu slowly nodded his head. "Yes . . . Yes. A powerful 'God' of *our* choosing . . ."

"Whatever you have planned, you had best stay here, if you want to see it through, mage. The others don't yet know that you're willing to join us," Koler said, pointing at the Aian. "And they may not yet know that Mekha is gone. If He *is* truly gone."

Torven glanced down at the hand still clutching the Truth Stone, then lifted it. "I have every reason to believe, based on ancient texts I have read regarding similar situations, that the disappearance of Mekha's sigils from your robes and these walls—and His very presence from your 'power room,' whatever that was— means that He has somehow been disbanded and removed from His Patronage of Mekhana."

Turning his palm up, he unfurled his fingers, revealing the unblemished white disc balanced neatly on his palm.

"As you can see, I have every reason to believe this may indeed be the truth." He gave the other two men an arch look. "If you still want to retain some power, magical and governmental, I am willing to work with you on terms favorable to *both* sides."

Again, the stone was white. Sighing heavily, Koler stepped into the hall. "I'll contact the Patriarch and talk with the other temples. This may just be something that is strictly localized, or it may be kingdom-wide. We won't know for sure until we talk to everyone."

Hansu looked at his departing colleague then at the groaning Healer whose mouth-covering web was still in place, and snapped his fingers, knocking out the older foreigner with a wordless cantrip-spell. He stared at the younger mage. "Don't get full of yourself, Aian. We'll see how 'favorable' those terms truly are . . . and you may still have to be oathbound to them."

Torven dipped his head. He was a capable law-sayer when needed, quite able to word rules and oaths just so. Without the power of their God behind them—provided Mekha truly was gone—Torven was fairly confident he could wrest a good deal from these people.

At least they seem to be sensible, practical souls like me, and not a bunch of moralizing imbeciles, hobbling themselves just because they're afraid of the true advantages that lie beyond being mindlessly good all the time.

Torn between wanting to stay in the next prepping chamber over from the two newest prisoners to try to keep eavesdropping on that slimy foreigner, and running to the slave pens to free the mages—if they *were* free—Rexei finally set down the coal bucket she had been clutching to her flat-bound chest and forced herself to think through the thoughts swirling and clashing in her head. It wasn't easy to comprehend, but the blankness of the very walls around her did seem to corroborate the mage's claim. More than that, though, the pervasive, sour, mildew-slimed feel of the place, the way it had pressed in and down upon her inner senses in a blanket of cold, uncaring repression and depression, was now gone.

Mekha . . . gone. Just gone, poof, vanished! It was a giddy, liberating thought, but also a disorienting one. She felt like a mouse that had long been caught under the stare of a cat, only to see it finally move off and vanish. Except she couldn't quite believe it. The background tune—one of a score—that always filled her thoughts hummed louder, cloaking her life-force to further hide her magical signature just in case.

He's gone from this *temple's power room . . . but I know the other major temples around the kingdom also have power rooms, which He occupies simultaneously. I . . . I need to get close to the scrying room and try to overhear. If He is truly gone, the other temples would surely be discussing it with the priest.*

The foreign mage's other claim was quite chilling. *Conjure a demon? Bind its powers for draining? Did I hear him right?* She hoped not. Demons were reputed to be even nastier than Mekha was, and He was loathed by His whole people, save for the priests who profited from His demands. *And yet if the foreigner was telling the truth . . .*

She picked up the coal bucket, since it gave her an excuse to go places, though she didn't yet move from the room she was in. It was winter, and Heiastowne had been built in a broad valley nestled against the foothills of the eastern mountains. The entire temple was crafted from thick stone laid by masons many centuries ago, back when Mekha had been a kinder, less capricious, less insatiable, less insane God. That meant the place required braziers and hearths to keep it warm. The priests weren't going to tend those fires, though; they considered themselves superior to all others.

In all other guilds, from Apothecaries to Chandlers, Masons to Tanners, Vintners, and more, all apprentices were equal to each other. Journeymen were equals, as were masters and grandmasters, each to their own rank. There was a little bit of jockeying among the Guild Masters, but mostly among related groups, such as Goldworks, Silverworks, Brassworks, Ironworks, and the like, though Brassworks and Silverworks were both considered equal to Lumber, even if they didn't always agree between themselves. At least, they were supposed to all be equal save for the Priests Guild, but there was always an argument or three about whose craft was the more skilled, the more valuable, or the more whatever.

Individual elevation and rank were based on merit and ability, a most sensible way to give someone authority and power . . . but not in the priesthood. Their "novices"—apprentices in any other guild—were to be accounted equal with journeymen in other guilds, their priests as masters, their bishops as grandmasters, and their archbishops the equal of any Guild Master. That was supposed to be the highest rank one could attain, for there was only one Guild Master at a time in all branches of that guild. The Patriarch, the Guild Master of the Priests Guild, was supposed to be considered the highest ranking of all, the spiritual leader . . . and the default kingdom leader, because he outranked everyone. A fact that rankled.

The Patriarch's bound to be in a panic, Rexei realized when her thoughts circled around to the highest priest of all. *He might start issuing nasty orders, if he stops to think that this means the people will try to overthrow the stranglehold of the priesthood, once their greatest source of political and magical power is gone.*

I'd hate to be in Mekhastowne, in the heart of the kingdom. As soon as everyone there realizes Mekha is gone, there'll be rioting for sure. Even the Patriarch won't be safe; priests may be able to use their magics unfettered by fear, and they'll know tons more spells than anyone else, but even a strong mage can do only so much in the face of an infuriated, finally free mob.

Another, more disturbing thought crossed her mind, making her hurry faster, taking the stairs two steps at a time. *Oh, Gods—* this *place won't be safe, once people realize what's happened. I need to get out of here! But . . . I need to know if they're actually going to try the demon-conjuring thing. That's far more important . . . isn't it?*

It was not an easy choice. Ever since her family had been torn apart when she was barely ten, forcing her to flee her home and make her way on her own, Rexei had always preferred caution and flight. She wasn't a fighter and didn't want to be one, ever. She had always avoided being drafted into the local Precincts in her guise as a boy by initially pretending to be too young to be drafted whenever questioned about her age—aided by her slim figure and youthful, beardless face—and by vanishing to a new town and a new guild a month or so later, well before she could be considered old and healthy enough to be hauled to the Precinct headquarters for training.

Just like she had fled many other jobs. In fact, she had fled their associated guilds in the beginning as well, though after the first year she tried to make a point of giving the grandmaster of each local guild a feasible reason why she had to leave, and in a hurry.

Often enough, the truth sufficed: *Some of the priests were looking at me funny. I got a bad feeling. I need to go.* But sometimes it was a non-priest who looked at "the boy" funny. At least until her time in the Messenger Guild, which had allowed her to move around quite a lot.

It was through the Messenger Guild that she had met up with the Hydraulics Guild, and that . . . had led her to her position here. A spy in the local priests' stronghold. *Which means . . . which means I have to find out what is going on and report on it. Even if it scares me.*

Or annoys me, Rexei added, feeling the tender spot on her tongue where she had bitten it. The gray-haired priest, Bishop Koler, had startled her with his shouting about her being a useless lackwit. *I'd think after two months of being berated and harangued on a daily basis, I'd have grown used to it . . . but all it does is make me want to stand up tall and proud and claim I'm* not *a boy, I'm an* adult . . . *since technically I'm not a man.*

Unfortunately, she couldn't let either her fear or her irritation show. She was here on behalf of three guilds: as a representative of the Gearmen's Guild, acting on behalf of the Servers Guild, in order to investigate claims of guildmember abuse—that was the legitimate cover story—and the third was the Mages Guild, to see if there was any way of freeing the mages kept somewhere in here.

In two months, she had determined the Servers apprentices were treated with equal doses of disdain and contempt but, otherwise, were treated fairly for their lot. She had not, however, managed to make it into the basement level, though she at least knew which door the priesthood used. Only those bound to Mekha's will—one way or another—were allowed to pass through that particular door.

Keeping her forehead and cheeks relaxed, breathing through her mouth as well as her nose, she carried the coal bucket to the stairs leading up to the second floor. Here were the little offices for each of the priests and the bishops, plus the larger one for the temple archbishop. Koler's study was next to Archbishop Elcarei's, and from the sound of Koler's voice as she approached, it was to his own office that he had gone in order to use his scrying mirror.

Scrying mirrors were far more secure than the talker-boxes, since the messages sent by those could be picked up by anyone else within fifty miles who had a talker-box. Unfortunately, the scrying mirrors required magic to activate, which meant they were a secret reserved for the priesthood alone. No one outside of the priesthood knew how to make them, here in Mekhana . . . but that was okay, because unlike the sound-maker on the talker-box, which had to be held to an individual's ear, mirrors made conversations as easily audible as if the people involved were standing in the same room.

She ducked into the archbishop's empty office and moved to the fireplace. Her gloved hands went to work, pulling the tongs off the edge of the bucket, shifting the glowing embers, adding new lumps of black in a scattered pattern so they would slowly turn white and pale orange, heating up the place. This room didn't have a brazier; it had a hearth, one that shared a thin brick wall with the chamber on the other side. If she strained her ears . . .

Footsteps were her only warning. "Boy! What are *you* doing up here?"

TWO

The shout should have startled her, but the sound of someone approaching had given her two seconds in which to master her surprise. As it was, she had to conceal her growing irritation. *Lad* was an acceptable term for a young man; it conveyed youth but didn't condemn. *Boy*, particularly when spoken with a sneer to someone of her apparent age, was just plain insulting.

Blinking away her ire, Rexei merely turned her head and stared at the "spiritual leader" of Heiastowne, Archbishop Elcarei. She gaped, really, letting her mouth hang slack in a sign of stupidity. Not for nothing had she earned her journeyman status in the Actors Guild. "Holy sir?"

"What are you *doing* up here?" the dark-haired priest repeated, stalking toward her where she knelt in front of the hearth.

"Helping?" she asked, adopting a worried, dull-witted look that skittered around the room as if looking for anything to fasten on but the scowling priest. He always reminded her of the slimy feel of cold saliva spat onto a polished surface—one of the priests took near-weekly pleasure in spitting on the winter-chilled floor in front of her and then demanding she wipe it up with her bare hands. But she didn't dare show revulsion in front of the archbishop himself. "Coals . . . go t' the rooms wi' people innem, sir?"

"I swear to the Gods, you get stupider every time I talk to you," Elcarei muttered under his breath. Snapping his fingers, he pointed at the doorway. "Out!"

She took just enough time to replace the tongs and pick up the bucket, then moved out of his study. Then stopped just past the threshold, her mind racing. Slimy or not, she needed to know what the local priests were going to do, and that meant asking them about the few things she *could* reasonably know about. Like the vanished symbols from stone carvings and embroidered garments. Turning to face him, Rexei asked, "Holy sir? What happened t' the walls, sir? They's gone blank, sir."

The archbishop, about to seat himself behind his desk, stopped and scowled at her. Now that she was standing out in the hall, she could hear what sounded like the priest Koler arguing with someone at the Patriarch's office that he knew what was going on, and the Patriarch had better speak with him immediately, before the whole populace revolted. But it was the archbishop's reply that she waited for, because she wanted to know what the official line would be. Elcarei wouldn't tell a dull-witted Servers Guild apprentice anything more than that.

Archbishop Elcarei eyed her. Leaving his desk, he clasped his hands behind his back as he slowly moved closer and closer to the lanky figure just beyond his door. "What happened? What *happened*? Our God is no longer here. He has removed all Patronage from Mekhana. We are *Godless*, you stupid peasant, and that means that without His Patronage and protection, our neighbors will gleefully invade, and we will be *crushed* beneath their hatred for all things Mekhanan! That is, unless we can come up with a new Patron *quickly.*"

Stopping right in front of her, the archbishop spat his last few words in her face. She blinked at that, lifted the back of a wrist to get a tiny bit of spittle off her cheek, then shrugged. Rexei knew who *she* wanted for a Patron Goddess, but a misogynistic archbishop was not the person to tell. Instead, she just asked, "Need help, sir?"

She looked and sounded earnest, asking that. Her innocent question made the taller man rear back and blink down at her. Once his stunned disbelief faded, though, he chuckled.

"My, my, you *are* an innocent, aren't you?" He studied her for a moment, then sighed. "Come with me, idiot-boy. And set down the damn bucket."

He returned to his desk, so Rexei moved cautiously into the room, wondering what she had just gotten herself into now. She *needed* to stay near enough to overhear Koler's conversation with the Patriarch . . . but the archbishop had given her a command. Personal notice by a priest was *never* a good thing, but disobedience carried the very real threat of the priest doing something horrible to the offender. Ambivalence warred within her.

Nervous, she set the coal bucket by his desk and dropped her gloves on top of it, watching him warily as he fetched out a heavy iron ring laden with many keys. To her inner senses, those keys glowed . . . dark. That was the only word for it. They were darker than they should have been, full of foul magics, and she wanted nothing to do with them.

Thankfully, he didn't hand them over. He did, however, lead her away from the corridors she was familiar with, toward the one door she was forbidden to enter. The door that led down to the dungeons where the non-priest mages were housed. Rexei balked, watching him use one of the keys to unlock the door. It didn't reek of evil, of rot and horror quite so much anymore, but only a mage might have noticed that. A mind-blind drudge like the "boy" she was portraying would still be afraid for other reasons. "I . . . I'm not s'pposed t' go there, Holy sir . . . not s'pposed t' go . . ."

"Stop cowering and *follow* me," Archbishop Elcarei ordered, grabbing Rexei by the shoulder. Contrary to his words, he pushed her through the door and down the steps ahead of him. Mages were prepped in chambers on the ground floor rather than down below, because until they were bound to Mekha's will, it was too dangerous to give them a chance to not only free themselves but possibly free the others as well.

Descending two, three, four flights until they were well below the level of the city's cobbled streets, Rexei found herself pushed aside when the stairwell opened into a long, curving corridor lined with many, many doors. Several oil lamps illuminated the corridor almost as well as daylight would have, making the cracked, white-washed plaster walls look worse than if the lighting had been dim. To her other sense, her mage-sense, each door in those cracked walls was a blot. Not a slime but more like a patch of mold or mildew, something decaying that she didn't want to touch.

Visible signs of rot, Rexei thought, humming hard in the back of her mind. She suspected that, had the Dead God still been around, that rot would have been ten times stronger, but with His departure, everything associated with Him was fading. Prudence demanded extra caution, however, and so she hummed. Her mother had taught her meditation techniques, musically enhanced mind tricks to hide any and all magical traces . . . but she shied away from thoughts of her mother. That was the horror that had started her long flight and lonely, distressed life too many years ago.

Except . . . except she could hear familiar, frightening, rhythmic noises from one of the rooms on her right. Paling, Rexei sagged against the outer curving wall. Fear rose in her mind, dragging her down into memory. The sharp smell of various vegetables and cool, dusty stones in the root cellar. The faintest glimpse through the cracks in the kitchen floorboards overhead, of her mother's form pinned over the worktable, of her limbs glowing with magical shackles, and those sounds . . . *those* sounds . . . as *that* priest had . . . had . . .

Archbishop Elcarei unlocked that room and flung open the door. "Novice Stearlen!" he snapped. "Pull out and pull your pants back up!"

"Wh-what?" the novice stammered. "Holiness—I swear, I *was* given permission to breed—"

"Pull your piston out of the wench and dry it off," the archbishop ordered, stepping inside and vanishing from Rexei's line of view. "Whether or not she's pregnant is no longer any concern of ours . . . unfortunately."

The last word was muttered under his breath, as if to ensure the dullard leaning against the wall couldn't hear. She heard, but she didn't react. Rexei remained outside the room, struggling to shut out the memory of another priest and her mother . . . her poor mum . . .

"If you haven't noticed, *boy*," Elcarei scorned, "all of the God's markings and symbols have vanished in this room. *And* from all the others. Mekha has somehow been vanquished, and if we *don't* set free all the mages and push them out onto the streets, the locals will come *here* to destroy us!"

"But . . . but we have magic—" the novice protested.

"Magic won't stop a weapon aimed at your head when it's a lump of metal flung from a hand-cannon, imbecile. And magic cannot stop the *thousands* of resentful residents who are about to wake up and realize *Mekha is not here anymore*."

A thump of something striking something else—probably the archbishop's boot hitting the novice's backside—preceded the appearance of Novice Stearlen stumbling into view, hands still fumbling to get his velvet trousers buttoned. Elcarei appeared in his wake, forcing the novice to back up farther.

"The only defense we have is to release all the prisoners, shove them out the doors with a fast public apology, and then bolt the doors behind us. *Boy!*" the archbishop shouted. "Come here!"

Rexei jumped, snapping out of her unwanted memories. She scuttled inside when the archbishop snapped his fingers and pointed into the room. It wasn't quite as bad a place as she had feared. An odd section of the ceiling, some sort of glowing crystal as big as the bottom of a chest, brought in clean daylight. The walls were a little less cracked and crumbling, suggesting this place had been plastered and whitewashed more recently than the main hall, and the floor was neatly swept, though since no one in the Servers Guild was allowed to come down here and clean, it had to have been done by the apprentice priests, the novices.

The furniture was very simple. A water-flushed refresher stood in the corner of the room, and a sink next to it, though there were no drying towels. A chair sat under the sunshine-bright patch of crystal with a small table in front of it, and a narrow bed stood in the corner beside the door. On it sprawled a woman with short-cropped hair and vacant, staring eyes; the skirt of her plain gray woolen shift pushed up to her hips. Rexei flinched away from the signs of what the novice had been doing.

The archbishop noticed. "Haven't you ever seen a naked woman, boy?"

Rexei shook her head quickly, looking anywhere but at the pale but breathing living doll lying expressionlessly on the bed. In fact, she shook it fast enough, her felted hat came off, revealing her own dark, short-cropped hair, though hers at least had been cut evenly so that it looked flattering and not butchered haphazardly just to keep it manageable.

"Figures. Beyond innocent . . . You're probably too stupid to know what your piston *is*, let alone how it works," Elcarei muttered. "Listen carefully, both of you," the archbishop stated as Rexei quickly scooped her cap off the floor, pulling it back over her short, dark locks. "Stearlen, you are to fetch your fellow novices and have them unlock all these rooms. Boy . . . Rexal, or whatever your name is . . . you will touch each of these godly sacrifices on the metal collar, and while touching it, order them to walk up the stairs and into the prayer hall, where they are to seat themselves on the benches.

"That goes for the novices, too," Elcarei added as Rexei stared and Stearlen blinked. "I want every last mage upstairs and seated in that hall . . . and then you will get them all to stand up and line up at the temple doors, where I will remove their control collars. Once they're free, they'll be pushed into the streets, where they can fend for themselves. We will all work quickly, as none of us has any idea how long it will take for them to regain their wits . . . and then *you*, boy, will be dismissed along with the other members of the Servers Guild for the day."

Rexei blinked and managed a dull-witted question. "We . . . go home early, Holy sir?"

"*Yes*, you 'go home early,' you delightful dullard," Elcarei mocked. He pointed at the bed. "Touch her collar and get her on her feet. You know the path back to the prayer hall. Go. *Both* of you. And if you see any other servants, tell them to come down here or be spell-whipped for disobedience. I want these mages *out* of this temple in less than an hour."

Novice Stearlen hustled away, his velvet robes once again neatly closed over his shirt and trousers. He felt to her mage-sense like snot from a bad nasal cold, the kind that looked green and yellow, pus-like, as it stained the sufferer's clean-bleached kerchief. Cringing, Rexei turned back to the bed and approached the unmoving, slowly breathing woman, trying not to look at her still-splayed thighs. Rexei reached down and touched the rune-scribed collar around that pale neck. "Uh . . . on yer feet. Get on your feet."

The woman sat up with barely a sound, closed her legs, then

stood. Her shift dropped down around her legs, concealing what had happened to her . . . but the cloth was thin, even though it was wool, and all she had for shoes were the felted slippers keeping her toes warm in the not-quite-cold air found this far underground. Compassion made Rexei snatch up the top wool blanket from the bed and wrap it around the blank-staring mage's shoulders.

"What do you think you're doing?" Elcarei asked, frowning.

"It . . . it be cold upstairs, Holy sir," Rexei managed, flushing. "Can't give 'er burning coal t' hold. Blanket'll keep 'er warm."

That earned her an impatient scowl, but the archbishop didn't correct her decision. He just snapped his fingers and pointed toward the stairwell they had used. Rexei touched the collar and ordered the woman to start walking—and had to order her to turn left as they exited the room to save her from walking straight into the wall opposite. Thankfully, she didn't have to order the woman to actually walk up the steps; the entranced mage managed them just fine. She even picked up the hem of her skirt so that she wouldn't trip as she ascended the long flight.

By the time Rexei got back upstairs to the once forbidden doorway, two more novices were guiding mage-prisoners up the steps. She backed up to let them pass, ears straining to try to hear Koler's conversation, but the priest's office was silent. Two more trips netted a total of twelve novices and five servants, including herself, now working to get all the mages upstairs.

On the fifth trip, which took her to the next level down, she caught a glimpse of what could only be the "power room" of the temple. It was blank walled now, but crystals lined the tiered edges of the chamber and topped the circular rows of stone pillars crowding the main floor, all focused toward a massive, empty throne at the heart. Here, then, was where a fragment of Mekha had been rumored to sit, the same as at every other temple in Mekhana.

To feed Himself, Mekha had been rumored to split into several "chunks" that then sat in the depths of each complex, draining all the mages the local priesthood had managed to catch. No corner of the kingdom was considered free of His hunger, His presence. Even the smallest of temples was rumored to house both a dozen mages at any one time and a piece of the Engineering God's utterly unwanted being.

But this room was empty, and when she came back on her seventh trip and caught a glimpse of the central chamber again, the stones of the throne at the very heart and the matching crystal-tipped pillars around the edges were crumbling. Several tumbled as she snuck a few seconds to look. Not the walls or the ceiling, which was a relief because she didn't want to be trapped underground in a cave-in. No, just the paraphernalia of Mekha's hunger was vanishing.

He really is gone . . .

She couldn't stop to explore in more detail, though. There were signs the mages were beginning to wake up, even with the collars still clasped around their necks. After having escorted over half a dozen of them upstairs, Rexei could see sections where the runes were clearly missing on the metal collars. Whatever had drawn the mages' powers out of them to feed to Mekha was no longer there, and though one and all were still obedient, some semblance of awareness was coming back into their dull, vacant eyes.

They showed some semblance of living, not just of merely being alive; it could be seen in the way their cheeks started turning pink, in the way their breath caught and changed at random moments, instead of just soughing in and out at an even rate. There was even some semblance of thought. As she escorted the ninth and last of her prisoners upstairs, the older man blinked and licked his lips, frowning faintly as he tried to . . . form words?

Did he want to ask a question? Ask for water? Ask for something warmer to wear? He was lucky to have a blanket as well as his felted slippers and woolen shift, but she could understand feeling thirsty and hungry. It was now well past the noon meal and approaching sundown, which meant supper was only a few hours away. Rexei sincerely doubted the priests would go so far as to feed their former prisoners, though. Not if barely half of them had blankets, and not if the archbishop wanted them out of the temple before sundown.

"Right, then. Bishop Koler, make a one-way warding outside the front door. Something that will allow me to address the masses gathering outside without them getting close, and that will allow these former sacrifices to leave," Archbishop Elcarei ordered. "The rest of you, start getting these . . . poor souls . . . on their feet, one bench at a time—no, make that two benches, in two lines. Bishop Halestes, come take half of these collar keys . . ."

Rexei worked with the others, guiding the collar-bound men and women to the temple doors. Most of them were young, a few middle-aged, none truly old. As she worked, she heard bits and snatches of the archbishop's speech wafting in through the doors. "My dear fellow Mekhanans . . ." And, ". . . unexpected sadness, yet an unexpected joy . . ." The outright lie of, ". . . victims of our late God's wrath, just the same as you!" And the one truth, ". . . decided to let these go into your care, with our deepest apologies . . ."

Well, a half-truth. She didn't believe for one instant that the priests of Mekhana were actually sorry about anything they'd done to the men and women captured and forced to have their magic sucked out of them until they died. These velvet-clad men were sorry they no longer had their God's protection, but that was all, and that was not the same thing.

Each time she directed a collared mage up to one of the two priests standing just beyond the front doors, she could see that while a crowd had gathered and that they were somewhat angry . . . they were also concerned about the men and women being pushed through the barrier holding them off. She could even see some of the mages beginning to recover as they stumbled into the arms of the crowd, usually the younger ones.

Hands lifted to the faces of their catchers, their partial rescuers, then fell limp, weak with disuse. Only the priests knew what they'd been fed, how little they'd exercised. Grimly, Rexei fought back the thought of her mother in similar straits and the sting of tears that wanted to accompany that thought.

It won't do any good. It's been over eleven years. She'll have been used up by now. Dead, with who knows how many half sibs popped out and shoved off onto who knows whose hands as girl-orphans, but watched . . . always watched . . . to see if they developed magic. Or kept and coddled and spoiled as boys who might grow up to be privileged priests.

No. She's gone. I can only . . . hope . . . that my brothers and father are still alive and free somewhere, and that she's safely dead.

It was no good. Two tears spilled out, and two more. One of the novices spotted them and mocked Rexei. "Aww, is the little dullwit upset at how these little piggies have been treated? They were feeding your *God*, you greaseless twit!" the young man scorned, arm sweeping up to cuff her head. "Show some respect!"

Rexei ducked most of it, but the blow still made spots dance in front of her eyes. Her mage-prisoner kept walking, though, forcing her to scramble to catch up once her senses cleared. Thankfully, one of the priests scowled and intervened, ordering, "Leave him alone, Novice Jorlei, and keep to your own work. This isn't the time for games."

It wasn't until she moved outside, stopping the mage with a touch and a word, that she realized her cap had been left behind, knocked off with the blow. Rexei realized it only because the temple steps were shrouded in shadow, making her hyperaware of how cold the air was on her short-cropped hair compared to the brazier-heated halls of the temple and how much she had sweated climbing and descending all those stairs. Not even the sun helped; it was shining brightly, but the crisp glow hit the far side of the modest square in front of the temple and not the spell-wrapped top of the steps.

She had to urge the mage through the barrier, but when she turned back to reenter, she found the priests retreating now that the last of the prisoners had been released. Archbishop Elcarei grasped the edges of the double doors, giving one last statement as he backed up into the hall behind him. "My fellow Mekhanans . . . until we have a new Patron Deity, this temple is *closed*."

With that, he shut the doors firmly. They all heard the bolts being shot home . . . and a tingle of energy washed over the door and spread out across the walls, warding the place. Her cap, and the secrets of a possible demonic summoning, were now locked inside. For that matter, so was her winter coat, an oversized, carefully mended garment of sturdy felted wool pieced together from several shades of dark gray, with wooden buttons she had carved herself.

It was winter, specifically winter in Heiastowne, which was attached to the foothills of the southeastern mountains. If she stood in the sunlight, she wouldn't freeze quickly, but as soon as night fell, she'd definitely be in trouble without a cap and a coat. Unfortunately, she found herself with a bigger problem immediately at hand.

"That's *it*?" a burly, wool-coated man growled, his voice ringing across the stunned quiet of the crowd. "Thank you fer letting us suck yer men an' women dry, here's the lot of 'em, an' we're still too high an' mighty t' give you the time of day or a word of *why?*"

"If they can give us back our people, they can give us back our tax monies!" someone else cried out.

Rexei flinched as the crowd grumbled. Though most of them weren't mages, even the least-powerful peasant could hurl pure life-energy at a hated target and have a chance for some of it to stick—usually as a curse, since it was unformed and untrained, but sometimes as a physical sort of blow. She knew it was about to turn ugly, knew they were about to charge the temple with nothing more than whatever they had in their hands . . . and *she* was still on the temple steps, squarely in their path. Quickly, she cried out on instinct in a hard, high voice, *"Enough!"*

It wasn't quite a child's scream, but it was similar enough to stop the pending mob in its tracks. Tugging her knitted sleeves down over her chilled hands, she slowly descended the steps, trying to glare hard at every face that wanted to twist with anger and charge the place.

"We have *bigger* problems on our hands. If you *haven't* noticed," she bit out sharply, "these men and women are nearly naked, and it is winter. There are a hundred and fifty-three of them. They need shelter. They need clothing. They need *food*, and several of them need to visit the Apothecaries," Rexei added sternly, moving into the crowd.

She tried not to shiver as a stray bit of wind started stealing away what warmth she did have inside her knit tunic and the two linen shirts that lay beneath. Her trousers were faring somewhat better; they were felted wool with a linen lining, and she wore stockings that came up just past her knees and long undertrews that came to just below her knees. But somewhat better wasn't perfect, and the wind pushed through the layers with invasive, icy fingers.

At least the others were closing in around her, hiding her from some of the wind as well as the temple, but only somewhat. Unfortunately, her words had to be said, and the responsibilities asserted. "*Every* guild in this square will have to take in two to four of these men and women, just to ensure they are fed and clothed and cared for while they recover from what has been done to them. *That* is our first priority."

The same first man spoke again, his face flushed with anger. "The priests are—"

"The priests aren't going anywhere!" She hated all the eyes on her and hoped that the priests hadn't realized that the dull-witted, soft-spoken Rexei of the Servers Guild was one and the same as the owner of that sharp voice . . . but her back was to the narrow, glazed windows of the temple. She lowered her voice, knowing that what she said next would spread on its own. "Listen to me carefully, and tell everyone what you can see with your own eyes. Mekha. Is. Gone. I was there when the Dread God's images melted from the walls. I *saw* the embroidery vanish from their sleeves.

"Mekha is *gone*, and that means we have to rescue every single prisoner before those ex-priests in there change their minds and decide they *want* to keep draining these poor people. Men and women who can't even remember how to *speak* right now—and mark my words, the priesthood *will* want to keep their power and their prestige. We must deny them that chance. Stow your anger, and go put your energy to *good* use."

The burly, round-faced man lifted his chin at her. "Who are *you* to give us orders? You're just a boy!"

Oh, again *with the "boy" this and the "boy" that! I think I am finally growing tired of being* young *in everyone's eyes . . .*

Rexei dug a hand under the high neckline of her tunic, pulling out a chain necklace and a leather thong. The chain held a single engraved medallion, denoting the Servers Guild, but the thong held a long column of stamped discs. Four of them were larger than the rest, and she sorted out the one on the far right, pulling it up on its own so that he could see for himself the three interlaced gearwheels embossed on its surface.

"I'm a journeyman of the Gearmen's Guild, and *that* means I'm a Sub-Consul with the right to speak on behalf of any Consulate. And it is *not* overstepping my rights as a Sub-Consul to tell you that these men and women need our help *right now*." She lifted her chin and her voice, looking at the others. "*Who* has kept our people safe from the priests all this while? I ask you that, and I tell you that the *guilds* have kept our people safe. The *guilds* have looked out for each other all this time, ensuring that the priests could never take *too* much of our money or our goods or even our *people*. And it is the *guilds* of this land that *must* stand strong.

"Mekha is gone," she repeated, clinging not to that thought but to the tokens of apprenticeships and journeyman ranks she had earned since fleeing her parents' house at the age of ten. Clinging to the memories of all the help she had been given, because the Guild System *worked*. "And Heiastowne will *not* crumble into madness and lawlessness. Put your faith in your guild, each of you! Remember how it gave you a place to work and a trade to learn. Remember how when you had a problem, you could take it to the Consulates—made up of representatives from *every* guild in town—and know that you'd find justice from *our* hands, when the priests would give us none!"

Engines rumbled in the distance, first purring faintly, then growling louder and louder as something approached from the west. Rexei kept talking, because the crowd wasn't quite calmed down yet. That was more important. None of these shift-clad women were her mother, would never be her mother, but each man and woman who had been drained *was* her mother, because they were fellow mages.

"Mekha is gone, and that means we *must* take over the leadership of this town—but *not* as a mindless beast. We are not a mob! We are guildmembers . . . and we have *laws*, and we have *rules*, and we have *responsibilities* that we will not set aside." She panted a little, grateful that the heat of her speech was keeping her warm, though she knew it wouldn't last. "Now . . . take these men and women home. Give them comfort.

"Get the Apothecaries to look at the women, for I promise you, each and every one has been raped repeatedly by the priesthood, and they will need care and compassion—and have them look at the *men*, too. There are bastards in that temple who'd piston a man's bottom as surely as any woman's front," she said bluntly. "As they would've pistoned *mine*, if they didn't have to answer to the Servers Guild for it—as you all know well they still could try! Any one of us could have been one of these mages, save for the grace of distant Fate . . . and many of us have lost kin and friends. It is *our* responsibility to take care of them and make them feel whole once more. If we do not, then it is *we* who will be metaphorically pistoning their bottoms a *second* time. They don't deserve that!"

Her crude words made a few people blink and eye her askance, but Rexei didn't care. The dangerous energy in the crowd had ebbed too low to be easily stirred as they strained and listened, as they passed along in whispers to the rest what they heard. At least, until an odd stirring rippled across the crowd from the west, from where the rumbling of engines was. With the sharp winter sunlight angling in from that direction, it was hard to see what was causing the commotion until the whispers reached her.

". . . militia . . ."

"Precinct men!"

". . . the captain?"

"No, it's th' leftenant . . ."

"The guards are here?"

"I'll not go without a fight . . ."

She had never met the leftenant of Heiastowne and had never wanted to meet him or anyone like him. Not even a mere private, let alone a sergeant or anyone ranked higher. For good reason, too; the military was ruthless, taking in lads of seventeen or older for five years of mandatory service. Not everyone was taken, but criminals were at the top of the conscription list, so staying out of the militia's notice was a necessity. Escaping once one was inducted into the service was extremely difficult and extremely dangerous.

Runaways were hunted down and whipped the first time, flogged heavily the second, and hung on the third failed escape try.

Between her slight frame, beardless cheeks, and careful acting, Rexei had always passed herself off as fifteen to sixteen at most. She had also taken care to heed the laws and cause no trouble, for the Precinct guards were also the town guards, and they drafted the troublemakers first and foremost. Women could serve in the Precincts as auxiliary members—clerks, cleaners, cooks, even as mechanics, helping keep the various machines running—but it was the men who *had* to serve in combat positions.

That was the last thing she could let happen. Guardsmen bathed together, and she was no boy in truth. The one good thing about the approach of the militia was that it would give her a chance to vanish into the crowd. The one bad thing was that she would have to wait until everyone's attention was elsewhere to successfully vanish.

The engines cut off, leaving an odd sort of near-silence in the square.

"By order of the Precinct captain," a strong male baritone called out, "the citizens of Heiastowne are to disperse and return to your homes, shops, and guildhalls. There will be *no* rioting in the streets. No disorder. The Precinct will investigate the claims that the . . . God of Engineering . . . is indeed gone, and we *will* maintain order. Anyone who riots, strikes out in violence, or attempts to loot anything at this point in time will be clapped in irons and dragged off for quarry work at the rate of one month per hour you cause trouble . . . *rounded up.*"

The crowd quickly started dispersing. Rexei turned to follow the nearest clump out of the square, but a heavy hand clamped down on her shoulder. The burly man dragged her around, his deep voice calling out, "Here's yer first troublemaker, Leftenant!"

"Oy!" Gaping in shock, Rexei glared at the man. "I'm not a troublemaker!"

"Shaddup!"

He felt harsh and dry to her senses, like an overbaked cracker, not slimy. Worse, his big hand had a firm grip on the flesh underneath her knitted sweater. He added to it a grab at the waistband of her trousers when she tried to squirm free anyway, hiking them up so that she was forced to walk on her toes while he hustled her west through the rapidly departing crowd. At least the others were taking the spell-shocked, shift-clad mages with them as they moved off. Unfortunately, she couldn't vanish with them, for the burly troublemaker—the real troublemaker, not her, in this matter—marched her on toe-tip right up to the quintet of motorhorses and the pairs of men astride them.

Each man wore an overcoat of metal-plated leather, a metal helm with leather coverings, stiff bracers, and leg guards. Like their armored clothes, the flanks of their motorhorse steeds bore the symbol of the local Precinct militia, a war hammer on a shield. The operators of the motorhorses sat toward the front where their hands could guide the somewhat horse-shaped machines by their steering bars, feet ready to brace the bike when at a standstill like this or to stomp on the galloper pedals to go fast and the stopper pedals to slow down. Their riders sat on raised saddles behind the operators, where they could grip the flank-brown housing with their thighs and operate crossbows and hand-cannons, lariats and lances, whatever tool they needed when chasing down a criminal . . . or a mage who was trying to flee.

Rexei flinched when the muscular man dragged her up to face the second of the two men seated on the lead motorhorse. He was the only one wearing bits of metal at the collar of his overcoat and with studs banding his bracers, and he carried himself with an air of unquestioning command. That, and his slightly long, pointed nose were the only things distinguishing him from the rest, but this was clearly the Precinct leftenant. Swallowing, she quickly dropped herself into the role of a brave, lawful youth who hadn't done wrong—which she hadn't—and was determined to be brave in the face of authority. Which she was.

"I ain't done nothin' wrong." She asserted that much before wincing from the strength of the man's fingers; they dug in hard on her shoulder, bruising to the point where she feared for her collarbone. "I've done nothin' wrong! Leggo a' me!"

"Oh yes, you have!" Burly Man asserted, dropping her to her knees with his grip as he tightened his fingers and pushed her down to hold her in place.

"*Enough.*" The order came from the leftenant. "Release him. You'll not damage the youth any further, or *you* will be judged a troublemaker."

The angry man released Rexei's shoulder with a slight shove, making her gasp with the sudden flush of blood to the bruised region. She was grateful for the release but wished heartily she could run away. Unfortunately, running was a sure sign one had done something wrong, and it was not unknown—rare but not unknown—for Hunter Squads to use motorhorses. Usually, they used regular horses, as it was easier to guide a real horse through rough terrain than a mechanical one.

Not that the Hunter Squads are needed to chase down mages anymore, she tried to reassure herself. *Mekha is no more, His hungers are gone . . . but they might not believe that . . .*

"So," the leftenant stated, shifting his light brown eyes between the two of them. "What are the lad's supposed crimes? Inciting a riot?"

Rexei couldn't let that one stand. "I *stopped* a riot."

"Not *that*," the other man growled. He grabbed at her throat, almost choking her as he pulled free both necklaces. "*This!*"

She quickly pushed to her feet and grabbed at the thong and the chain, not wanting either to break. "Leggo! You'll snap 'em!"

"*This* boy claims t' be a journey-level Gearman," her accuser growled. "But th' lad's clearly not even militia aged, an' yet he's got nigh-on *twenty* Guild coins! He's a *forger*, that's what. *That's* yer troublemakin'," he added, aiming his last words at Rexei, grabbing the youth's shoulder for another shake.

"I said, let go of him." The words were delivered mildly, but they didn't need to be forceful. Two of the other second riders were already dismounting and moving forward in matching martial menace.

The man quickly released Rexei's shoulder. He even backed up a little. The leftenant swung his leg over the rump of the motor-horse, dismounting. Since the leg-shaped shanks connecting the machine to the wheels were shorter than a regular horse, more like a pony's legs, the militia officer managed to do so gracefully. Rexei forced herself to hold her ground. What she wanted, desperately, was to flee. Being noticed by the authorities was nothing but trouble, and trouble could get her killed or . . . *Well, maybe not shackled to the temple, now that Mekha's gone, but I can't let them find out I'm a girl, either. And I don't want to fight anyone!*

It wasn't easy to stand her ground when the leftenant walked right up to her and looked down into her eyes. Without a cap to help shield her gaze, all she could do was try not to flinch, and, keep humming in the back of her mind. Not that she suspected the leftenant of having magic, but it was by now a long-standing habit that kept her outwardly calm in the face of her inner terrors. She was afraid, but mentally humming the tunes her mum had taught her kept her brave.

The leftenant gently lifted the thong-strung medallions on Rexei's flat-bound chest with one of his leather-gloved hands. She hadn't worn all of them—a good dozen or so from her earliest years on the run weren't registered with her current identity—but she had worn eighteen guild tokens. The others were hidden among her things in the bolt-hole she currently called home. She tried not to flinch when he thumbed through them, but at least he didn't pull or yank or say anything derogatory.

She didn't trust the way he narrowed his eyes, studying the four larger coins strung on the thong, the ones representing her journeyman status. The first one was for the Actors Guild, the second for Engravers. The third for Messengers. The fourth was her journeyman Gearman status, gained when she'd earned the one for the Messengers. Shifting the thong aside, he stared at the Servers Guild pendant strung on the silver chain beneath it.

When he spoke, she shivered from more than just being cold. "Rexei Longshanks . . . isn't it?"

Oh Gods . . . he knows my name.

"Y'know who th' boy is?" the burly troublemaker asked.

He dropped her medallions back onto her chest and moved past her. "Walk with me, Longshanks. You," he added to the broad-shouldered man, "you're dismissed. Go about your business, and cause no more trouble."

Taking that for what it was worth, the stout man quickly hurried off. Just like Rexei, he didn't want the attention of the Precinct leftenant upon him, either. She wished she could join him.

Rexei did not want to go anywhere with the leftenant. She stayed where she was, silently amazed at her courage, and asked, "Why should I?"

Surprised, he turned to face her from a few paces away, brows raising. She lifted her chin, fingers balled into fists to keep them warm. It wasn't working.

"I've done nothin' wrong . . . and if you know my name, then you know I'm a Gearman. Sub-C-Consul." She folded her arms quickly, trying to stave off more shivering. "I'd n-no more c-c-cause a problem than c-cut off my own arm. You got no c-cause t' arrest me."

Returning to her, the leftenant leaned in close. "I'm not

arresting you. I'm asking you questions. If you want to stay here and freeze, be my guest, *Sub*-Consul. If you want to be warm, I'd suggest walking and talking. Though I doubt your intelligence, standing here without coat or cap in the dead of winter."

"'S in the bloody t-t-temple," she muttered, shivering. "They sh-shoved us out th' d-d-doors before I c-could g-g-get it."

"Then start walking home. Or better yet, get on the motor-horse. We'll give you a ride there." He stared at her, then flicked his gloved hand impatiently. "The sooner you get home and get warmed up again, the sooner I'll have my questions answered and go."

He was being entirely too reasonable. Too polite for her to pro-test. Tucking her hands under her armpits, Rexei started walking. Behind her, she heard the leftenant give an order that sent most of the others off. She heard the creak of his leathers as he remounted behind his motorhorse operator, and the gruff rumble as the engine was restarted.

There was no way she was going to be sandwiched between two militiamen, where she could be all too easily subdued and hauled off for unwilling service. Or incarcerated for doing nothing wrong but catching the leftenant's eye at the wrong moment in time. That and her bolt-hole was only a few blocks away.

As a member of the Messengers Guild—the longest guild she had spent time in so far, almost two full years—she had learned how to walk at a tireless, long-legged pace. It helped that the melo-dies constantly playing in the back of her mind, hiding all traces of her magical abilities, were usually set at a tempo well suited for walking.

For messages delivered between towns or to a recipient more than a couple miles away, she had learned how to ride a motorhorse, but those were loaned out by the Guild and had to be returned at the end of each ride. Unless it was an emergency, any messages delivered within a town were delivered on foot. The pace she set was brisk enough that some of her chattering eased, though her muscles were still tight from the aching cold.

Within a matter of minutes, she reached the wood and stone tenement building which was her home while in Heiastowne. This one was occupied by tenants from various guilds. Though some apprenticeships came with lodgings, usually in the home of whatever master had been assigned to teach said apprentices, not all of them did. The Servers Guild was one of those that didn't.

It had been decided long ago that no member of that guild would stay overnight in any temple or priest's home, just to be safe. The guild had also raised its members' wages so that they could afford to rent rooms . . . and had withheld all services from all priests when some of those priests had tried to incarcerate their servants on their properties to keep them past their service hours. Peer pressure had forced the release of the maidservants, footmen, housekeepers, and butlers. But while the wages had been raised to pay for lodgings elsewhere, that raise hadn't been much, and her tenement reflected it.

The leftenant dismounted when she started up the external stairs. The operator didn't come with them, though he did shut off his engine. A glance behind showed the leather-armored man settling into the saddle to wait the leftenant's return. It also showed the leftenant moving up behind her, clearly determined to follow her all the way home. Wincing, she moved up the steps. At the fourth floor, she strode along the open balcony. Their boots clomped on the wood, both hers and his.

The only thing that showed almost a dozen Servers lived here was how well the snow had been scraped off the balconies and steps of the whole building compared to the one directly across from it. All of them got together in the mornings and the evenings after a snowfall to keep the balcony and steps clear, since living on the fourth floor meant a very dangerous fall should they slip on an icy surface. It also meant a slight break for them in the cost of living here in winter, if they swept and shoveled.

Fourth floor rooms in winter were usually a bit warmer than ground or first floor ones, and thus were more expensive. Size was another factor. When she unlocked her tenement, there was only one room to it; that was another cost kept down. The right-hand wall was a mass of brick, since every room above and below hers had its own hearth, and they all shared a wall for the chimney spaces. Midday in winter, it could be quite cold if the others were out and about when their hearth fires were either banked or gone out. At midnight, it could be cold, too, but it was now close to supper, and that meant people were coming home and lighting fires, preparing food.

Her breath didn't frost inside her tenement, but it wasn't exactly warm, either. Grabbing her spare coat off one of the pegs by the door, she shrugged quickly into the felted wool and picked up the sparker and oil lamp from the shelf above it. Light came in from the narrow window by her door and the slightly broader window at the back of the somewhat narrow, rectangular room, but she carried the lamp to the table and lit it with a squeeze of the spring-loaded arm that scraped a bit of flint over a coil of steel.

Her teeth still threatened to chatter, though the coat helped somewhat. Unfortunately, it was a summer-weight coat, not winter weight. More heat would be needed. Ignoring the leftenant, she crouched by the hearth in the middle of the wall and used the fire tongs that came with the room to scrape back the ashes, hoping for a couple live coals. Grateful there were a few, she reached for the coal bucket, not the kindling box, and laid sooty black lumps on the glowing orange ones. It would take a while for the room to heat up, but at least she had started the process.

Only after she had washed her hands in the bowl of water by the front door did the leftenant speak. He didn't seat himself on the sole chair in the room nor on the edge of her bed—not that she had invited him to make himself comfortable, but he didn't seem upset at the lack of courtesy. Instead, he got straight to the point.

"I know you were *assigned* to be a Server in the temple, Longshanks," the older man stated without preamble, making her heart skip a beat. She turned to stare at him, absently wiping her hands on the cloth hung on the rod along the side of the washstand, and watched him dip his head to her. "And I know *who* assigned you to watch the priests as well as serve them."

He . . . he works with the mages? She stared at him, wide-eyed and unsure whether to be relieved or afraid.

Taking off his leather helmet, he set it on the table with a sigh, then scrubbed a gloved hand over his short-cropped hair, as if relieving a full-scalp itch. Smoothing the ginger-brown locks back from his face, he wrinkled his nose. "I need to know what happened in there, Longshanks. I need to know if . . . He . . . is actually gone. The only thing keeping this town from going mad is the bitter cold and the shock of disbelief, and I *will not* have Heiastowne overrun and burned down by rioting. So tell me, what did you see in the temple?"

THREE

She honestly did not know if she could trust the man. He was militia, and the militia had special squads sent out by the officers—at the prodding of the priesthood, admittedly—to hunt down and capture mages. But . . . the *purpose* for the Hunter Squads no longer existed, as far as she knew. If she could convince this man of that, then *maybe* word would spread, and the Hunter Squads could be disbanded. That would save a lot of mages' lives.

Hands dry, she slipped on a spare pair of leather gloves, pulled a knitted cap over her head for warmth while the fresh coals slowly caught, and folded her arms across her chest. "I saw two mages brought in . . . and midway through interrogating them, before the priests could bind either one . . . every last cog and gear of Mekha's decorations vanished from the walls and from the priests' embroidered robes. The outlander mage they were interrogating, *he* claimed it meant that Mekha had been dissolved. And then, later . . . they were making us haul all the prisoners up out of the basement rooms, where we weren't supposed to go, before.

"While I was down there . . . I saw Mekha's power room." She shivered, more from the memory than from the cold. Then she shivered again from the chill in the air. What she wanted to do was crawl under the felted-wool blankets on her bed and huddle there until she and her room were both truly warm, but she couldn't.

"And?" Surprisingly, he didn't ask her what the chamber looked like. Nor did he ask her where her accent had gone. If he knew she was Rexei Longshanks, if he knew she was a journeyman of the Actors Guild, then he'd know she could don and doff an accent at will.

"And it was crumbling. Pillars with crystals disintegrating. Some sort of chair-thing at the heart of it, cracking and sloughing off in clumps, like you'd let garden dirt fall from your hands."

"*And?*" he prompted when she fell silent. "I know you're bright enough to have observed far more than that, Longshanks. Give me the details."

She folded her arms across her chest. "That's for my unnamed client to know, and it's time for you to get out of my tenement. I've answered your questions. Now, go."

He stepped close to her. She didn't have anywhere to retreat, since next to the washstand was the table and cupboards where she kept what little food she cooked. Lifting her chin, Rexei tried to stare down the taller man.

"You're brave, I'll give you that. But these are *priests*, lad," he warned her, fooled by her slim frame and ambiguous, youthful face, as everyone had been. "And they now have your cap and your coat. All they need to track you down is a hair plucked from either. They can tuck that into a tracking amulet and *find* you . . . save for one location. If they realize you saw or heard anything you weren't supposed to—if they now know, after watching that blowhard's ploy at making trouble for you, that you *aren't* just a mere Servers apprentice—then they will come for you. And they will try to demand the Precinct's help.

"I am trying to find out if that will happen or not . . . because if Mekha *is* truly gone, the captain and I are *not* giving anyone else to the priests ever again," he finished grimly, moving close enough that she could feel the heat of his breath on her face. "But we don't have any magic to counteract their abilities. And I know you don't have full access to the one place where they cannot find you. Yet. So give me a reason to help you."

She didn't know what to make of him. It was clear he *knew* things . . . and that implied he was one of *them*, too . . . but neither of them could ask each other outright questions. Not here. The sanctuary he alluded to was not in Heiastowne, though it wasn't far by motorhorse. But mentionable or not, he knew who Rexei Long-shanks was—as much as she had let anyone know—and he was the Precinct leftenant.

One thing he was not was slimy feeling. Nor brittle and harsh like a cracker, like the man who had bruised her shoulder and hauled her to the leftenant's side. Instead, the leftenant reminded her more of a fine leather coat. Precise, tailored—a finished product, not rawhide. He was also not a bully like so many other officers she had warily watched in other Precincts, men who would not have hesitated to beat an answer out of her with the back of a hand. This leftenant seemed to actually care about his city. Ambivalence warred within her, between the need to flee far away and establish a new identity elsewhere, and the stacking of subtle facts that said he might be semi-trustworthy.

Mekha is gone, Rexei reminded herself, and shrugged defensively. "I overheard the foreign man—not an Arbran but from somewhere else—telling the priests of . . . an alternate power source. Other than draining you-know-whats dry."

One *thought* of the word *mage* in the kingdom of Mekhana, but one rarely ever said it aloud. It was whispered that priests had ways of tracking the word, spells that could pluck it out of the wind and backtrack it to its source. No one had a spell that could penetrate and reveal the privacy of a person's very thoughts. So while her claim made the leftenant narrow his eyes in wary puzzlement, he only mouthed the forbidden word; he did not say it aloud.

Instead, he said, "What alternate power source?"

Hoping she wasn't making a mistake, Rexei murmured one word, "Demons."

He stumbled back from her, shock widening his light brown eyes. Rexei felt unsettled herself; she had never seen any militia officer so quickly discomposed. They were bastions of power, authority, and in many cases cruelty. This man's composure had been shattered, though. He stared at her, clutched at his head, stared, and turned first toward the door, then back to the rest of the room, then toward the door again, as if unable to decide what to do or where to go.

"Demons," he whispered, no longer even looking at her. "It starts *here* . . . *This* is where it starts!"

It was her turn to frown at him. Eyes narrowed, she opened her mouth to ask—but he interrupted her, snapping his fingers and pointing at the majority of her tenement.

"Start packing!"

"What? I'm not packing!" Rexei argued, though her heart pounded with fear. She *was* going to pack. Her assignment from the Mages Guild be damned; she would only pack as soon as he was gone, make her report, and head for the northern hills—or maybe the southern, head to Sundara in the hopes of escaping everything. But she wasn't about to let *him* know that. "I'm not going anywhere with *you*. I've done nothing wrong!"

He swung back to face her, ending his awkward pacing. "Oh,

you've done nothing wrong, I'll agree. But the moment the *priests* find out you know *that*, your life will be worth *nothing*, lad. There is only one place in this whole kingdom, or what's left of it, where you will be safe. Trust me, their ambitions did *not* end with Mekha," the leftenant warned her, pointing at her face. "And *your* knowledge is needed to save the whole world. Start packing."

"Why?" she demanded.

"I'm taking you to the one place where *both* of us know you'll be safe . . . though neither of us dares say why. It's not like you have that much to pack," he added gruffly, looking at the stark contents of her tenement room. "Now, be quick about it. The faster we get you out of here, the faster we'll have you in the one place where they cannot get a hold of you."

She only had the bits of furniture, such as the table, chair, cupboards, and bed, simply because they came with the room. Most tenements had at least a few basic amenities, thanks to the efforts of the Consulates representing the many, many lessees across Mekhana in negotiations with the Lessors Guild. Even the lamp, the sparker, the coal bucket, and the wood bin were borrowed, but then Rexei didn't own a clothes chest, either; what she owned, minus two of the blankets on her bed, could fit into a single large pack that could be hefted onto her back. With her other coat missing, she could add in one of those blankets.

But she didn't move yet. "How do I know this isn't a trick to impress me into the militia?"

The leftenant frowned at her, then sighed heavily. "Because we'll be headed due east, not west by southwest, and that is *all* I can say. If you're Rexei Longshanks, hired to pose as a Servers Guild apprentice, then you *know* why I cannot say."

West by southwest was the direction of the Precinct headquarters, with its barracks and training yards. East of Heiastowne lay the Heias Dam, in a valley that had been blocked off. Its runoff powered various engines that drove the great presses and extrusion rollers of the Steelworks Guild and others. Eastward . . . was also the Vortex. The one place that could thoroughly confuse active magics and render mages too dizzy to concentrate if they weren't keyed into the spells maintaining that sphere of instabilities.

Some of those spells prevented anyone from even talking about the fact there was more to the Heias Dam than power generation. Yes, she did know what he was talking about, and what he wasn't able to talk about. The spells involved, enriched with generations of paranoia, prevented anything from being even hinted at in the presence of a priest or a priest sympathizer. To be questioned about it by a priest would cause complete amnesia regarding the secrets hidden behind the dam, or so she had been warned.

She didn't know what the leftenant meant by, *It starts here. This is where it starts.* But she did know he was right about the priests' reactions if they ever realized she knew about the demon-summoning thing. Because even without Mekha, they could band together, summon a powerful demon, and use the siphoned energies to power their own magics. If demons truly were superior to mages as a source, then the sheer level of power that could be siphoned from them was not a pleasant thought.

"Fine. But one hint of the wrong direction, and I'll react badly," she threatened, letting the implication sound as if she would attack him or steal his motorhorse and run. She'd run, but the most Rexei would do to him and the other militiaman would be to put them to sleep with a simple spell. A second one to make them forget they had ever met her, and she would be on her way with neither man the wiser. It was an escape plan that she already knew worked on priests, never mind non-mages. She'd been forced to test it on three in the past.

The leftenant flicked his hand at her meager belongings. "Hurry up, then. Don't dawdle."

Edging around him, she crossed to the cupboard built into the wall next to the bed. Pulling out her travel pack as well as her clothes, she stuffed them inside, added in the basket of crocheting needles and soft balls of wool that sat near the hearth, then stuffed in as many blankets as she could.

As she worked, the leftenant crouched in front of her hearth and used the tongs to nudge apart the coals. Once that was done, he replaced the grate. "Your lease will have to expire, but I'll see you're compensated for the refund lost. We don't want rumors that you've fled to get out, so as far as your fellow tenants will know, you'll just vanish."

"If I'm to walk out of town, I should go at night, when I'm less likely to be recognized," Rexei pointed out.

"You won't walk," he countered.

She looked at him. "And being dragged out of here on a militia motorhorse isn't going to cause people to talk?"

"You'll not walk all the way," he amended. "Head for the east gate. As soon as I've dropped off my corporal, I'll come back and pick you up. I should make it back by the time you're less than a quarter-mile from the city."

Crossing back to the cooking cupboards, she pulled out a leather sack and stuffed in her bag of crushed oats for porridge, a waxed round of cheese, a waxed paper packet of dried fruit slices, and a bag of mixed beans. The sausage end she stuffed into a half loaf of bread, wrapped it in a kerchief, and put it into her coat pocket.

"Once we get where we're going, leftenant," Rexei found herself stating as she swung around to face him, "I am going to question you thoroughly about how *you* know about what we are not talking about."

That caused him to quirk one of his brows, but the leftenant merely gave her a slight half-mocking bow. "As you wish, Sub-Consul. Though it will become apparent if you'll simply be quiet and watch."

He headed for the door. Rexei discovered she had one more question. "Hey."

He turned to face her. "Yes?"

"You got a name?" she asked. "Or should I just call you Leftenant? Somehow I don't think they'll be all that friendly toward your title."

"It's my rank, not my title, and they already know about it. But they mostly call me Rogen Tallnose when I'm there. Try to refrain from any jokes about the family name while you're there," he added dryly. "Be a good guest, Longshanks, and you'll be treated well. Remember that."

He walked out the door before she could do more than frown in confusion. The leftenant was roughly average in height, maybe a tiny bit taller, but by no means the tallest man in town. Nor was his nose particularly "tall" in appearance, though it was a little longer and pointier than average. Unable to think of a reason to make fun of his name, Rexei fished out the sausage and bread and gnawed on it, then remembered belatedly to pull out her waterskin and fill it from the keg that fed the washstand. The splashing water competed with the rumble of the motorhorse starting up.

When her uncooked supper was halfway eaten, she wrapped it up and stuffed it back into her pocket, then took herself outside and to the far end of the balcony where the refreshers were located. As she came back, she checked the alleyway. No sign of a motorhorse, so she ducked into her tenement, hefted her packs, and stepped out again. A quick look around showed her an empty balcony and no one in sight across the narrow street, so she placed the key along the upper edge of the doorframe once the room was locked.

With that taken care of, she hefted the pack so it sat more comfortably and headed down the stairs. Choosing a path that would get her out of the north gate of the city, she started walking. After three blocks, though, just as she passed the mouth of an alley, the sudden rumble of a motorhorse coming to life startled her. A quick glance to her right showed the leftenant on the machine, with no sign of the operator from earlier.

Rexei glared at him. Releasing the stopper pedal briefly, he coasted up next to her, then stilled the rumbling mount. "This isn't the way to the east."

"Any fool would head east right away. I know better when expecting pursuit," she shot back.

For a moment, his mouth twisted wryly. Leftenant Tallnose tipped his head at the street she stood on, then at the second saddle position on his motorhorse. "I had a feeling you'd bolt, so I sent the corporal back on foot and picked your most likely route in this maze of streets. Get on. We'll head north, then swing around east."

For a second, she wanted to rest, to enspell him and run. But the Vortex was the safest place for her, and a motorhorse was considerably faster than a shank's mare. Since she didn't want to spend all night marching on foot in an inadequate coat while the temperatures dropped, she moved over to the side of his bike and awkwardly climbed aboard. Not because she was unfamiliar with motorhorses—no one reached journeyman status in the Messengers Guild without learning how to operate one of the machines— but because her belongings coupled with the greater height of the rear seat made climbing into place a bit awkward.

She managed, though. Tucking her gloved hands into his belt for security, she tightened her legs on the machine's flanks and held on, balancing with each turn and twist in their path as they got under way. The last light of the sun glowed peach where it touched the city walls by the time they rumbled out of the north gate. He continued north for a mile, too, but she wasn't too alarmed; in fact, when he slowed the motorhorse at the crossroads and turned right, she relaxed, leaning gently into the curve with him so the wheeled, mechanical beast wouldn't slip or skid.

Once on the road that would connect with others headed

eastward, he shifted a couple of levers and increased the fuel mix in the engine. Rexei wasn't completely sure of how such things worked; the Engines Guild was one of many she had yet to apprentice in, never mind master. She did know just enough to be able to tell the engine sounded like it was in excellent shape. Good enough that the leftenant increased their speed once they were on the straightest stretch of the road, until she was grateful to huddle behind his leather-clad back, though the wind still whipped around him, chilling her where it blew through her felted outer clothes.

The trip by motorhorse took only a fraction of the time it would have taken her to walk the five miles on foot. If it weren't for the heat of the engine seeping through the metal flanks of the motorhorse, she would have been as cold from the wind caused by their speed as she would have been from the longer journey at a shank's mare pace. Even the pack on her back helped somewhat, but her arms were stiff and numb by the time he carefully guided the vehicle up the winding road that mounted the side of the northern hill and turned it onto the crystal-lit curve that formed the top of the Heias Dam. By then, they were so close that the water cascading over the spillway was louder than the motorhorse engine.

The dam was one of the few structures still extant that had been crafted in part by magic. Over three hundred years old—and rumored to be from a time before Mekha had turned rapacious—the runes that imbued it with the power to self-seal any developing cracks drew their power down from the aether via large crystals on the ends of tall iron poles. During thunderstorms, those crystals attracted and transformed lightning into the magic necessary to prevent even a minor failure.

It was also rumored that the priesthood had been considering a similar system in their temples, but storms were difficult to conjure, even more difficult to turn electric, and without magic, they were too unpredictable and infrequent to make such a use practical for anything other than the slowest, most long-term spells. Such as repairing the Heias Dam. Right now, there were no storms in the clouds drifting in patches over the near black sky, and what few stars shone through their gaps could not compete with the glow of the crystals.

They weren't the only source of light. Brother and Sister Moons were riding the night sky, though their light was partially blocked by the clouds. On the northern hillside, Rexei and the leftenant had passed the buildings used by the Steelworks to manufacture the extra-hard, flexible metal for Mekhana's war-machines industry. That guild ran its services every hour of the day, for it was far more difficult to restart the smelting fires from scratch than to keep them going, and too wasteful not to use up all that nighttime heat. On the southern hillside, there were only a few oil lamps and crystal lights, but those were the Guilds that had a mere building or two, not several, and they were usually only worked in the daylight hours.

Some of them were not what she had expected. The first time her work as a messenger had brought her here, Rexei had not expected to see the Tillers' symbol—a scythe crossed with a wheat sheaf—on one of the signboards. She hadn't expected to grow dizzy from the conflux of energies, either, but during her recovery in the outer halls of the Vortex and her subsequent induction into the never-mentioned Mages Guild, she had learned that the Heias Dam had been so well planned, its creators had even included a special set of spells and a sluice that scraped up the silt washed down to the reservoir from farther upstream.

That silt was captured, dried, and bagged by the Tillers Guild for shipment to local farms so it could be mixed in with composted manure and other forms of mulch. The Tillers—the farmers—who worked those fields spread it out to keep the ground fertile. She had grown up in the north, where the land was flat and had few trees and mines, but was rich in good farming soil. Down here near Heiastowne, the valley where the town sat was fertile enough, but most of the landscape was hilly and better suited for growing timber, grapevines, and digging ore.

But they weren't headed for the far side of the valley. At the center point of the broad, long curve, the leftenant guided the motorhorse to the left, along a causeway out over the reservoir waters. It terminated in a roundish, almost castlelike structure. To either side of the causeway, smaller ones led to the open, semi-submerged, pipelike spillways feeding the great turbines powering each of the local buildings, but this one led to the control house.

Moonlight gleamed off the ice that had crusted the edges of the lake, cold and pale blue. Warm yellow light spilled down from the windows of the control house. The leftenant guided his motor-horse into one of the stables set aside for vehicles, but once he parked it and turned it off, once they were both off the saddle-fitted back, he did not lead her toward the nearest door into the stone-walled structure. Instead, he caught her wrist and pulled her toward the back of the parking stable.

Confused, Rexei followed. The tune in her head had changed the moment they drew within sight of the dam. A counterpoint melody wove itself around the first one, stabilizing her inner senses so that the swirling energies of the aether around this place would not disturb her own energies, as they had the first time. As they did to any mage who didn't know the exact key to countering what seemed to be a natural phenomenon, but which she had been told on her first visit was a deliberately exaggerated effect. Priests did not like coming here because of that effect, which was the one thing making the Vortex a safe zone for mages.

The militia officer did something in the darkest corner of the stall . . . and part of the stone wall swung away. Beckoning her to follow, he entered the shadowed passage beyond. Hoping she wasn't making a mistake, clinging to her knowledge that the priests hated coming to the dam and that Mekha was dead, Rexei followed him inside.

The head-sized rectangular stones quickly gave way to the smooth concrete surface that made up most of the dam. A good thing, too, for the passage turned into a spiral staircase that descended down, down, down. She expected the air to turn damp as well as cold, but it didn't; it stayed dry and became warmer. The light coming from below grew brighter, too.

After the third turning, she could see the source, another of those odd, ceiling-embedded crystals like in the forbidden basement of the temple. It wasn't quite as bright as daylight, but it was brighter than three oil lamps put together. It illuminated a table set at the bottom of the stairs and a man who was hastily pulling his feet off the table, replacing them with his book. Behind him lay a longish passage lined with two doors nearby, two farther down, and one at the end; the door behind him and to his right lay open and seemed to look into another curving stairwell leading down.

"Rogen!" the sentry exclaimed, gaining his feet. "Wait . . . who's that?" he demanded, frowning at Rexei. "I don't recognize that one. *He's* not authorized to be here."

"Stow it, Barclei," Rogen Tallnose ordered, or tried.

"Stow it yourself, Tallnose," the other man retorted, lifting his chin. "Your brother may be one of us, but *you're* not, and I don't take orders from you. *Leftenant.*"

Rexei struggled to keep her shock off her face. This man had zero fear of a leftenant of the militia? Or at least so little that he felt he could be rude to the man's face? That was unheard-of, in her experience. Next to the priesthood, the militia was the second-biggest source of authority and power in the kingdom. Even the Consulates, which represented all the guilds, treaded lightly around their local Precinct officers. This man didn't, and that astounded her. The only thing she allowed herself to do was blink; the rest of her face, she kept carefully straight and blank.

"Stow it anyway, and get my brother up here," Tallnose ordered. "There are things going on that *you* are not authorized to know about, but I am. So get him up here. Now."

Barclei eyed Rogen a long moment, then shifted to a small box set in the wall above the edge of the table. Pressing a toggle, he spoke, "Barclei to central, Leftenant Tallnose wishes to see his brother at the control house gate. He has a . . . guest . . . with him."

Releasing the toggle, he straightened. The mesh grille crackled and a tinny voice spoke. *"Central to control house gate, who is the guest?"*

At a lift of the guard's brows, Tallnose gestured at her. "Journeyman Rexei Longshanks. He's already authorized for the outer levels."

Barclei passed that along, though he eyed Rexei as he did so. A few moments passed, then a reply came back. *"He's on his way."*

The longer they waited, the warmer Rexei felt. Even the leftenant started feeling it, for he unbuckled the belt of his riding coat, unfastened the buttons, and pushed the edges aside. Eventually, he removed his helmet, once again revealing flattened, reddish brown curls with the faint start of a receding hairline. His hair reminded Rexei of her father, though her father's hair had been as dark brown as her own. She turned away to hide her reaction, masking the movement by unbuttoning her own coat now that she, too, was finally feeling blessedly warm.

Footsteps made her turn back. A figure bounded up the steps of the second spiral stairway. He had a cap on his head and a scarf wrapped around his throat and chin, though his shirt and trews were lightweight wool at best. Green viewing lenses perched on his nose . . . and there was no doubt that this was the reason why the leftenant had warned her against making fun of the family name. His nose was long vertically like the leftenant's, yes, but it also jutted forward in a sharp point, more nose than most men possessed naturally.

She tried not to stare. Dragging her eyes up to those green lenses, she realized the leftenant's brother was at most only a thumbwidth taller than her, not the length of a finger. It was odd, but she could sense his presence in the aether as easily as if she had been around this newcomer for a good solid week. He felt warm, clean, and well shielded. The redhead looked back at her, looked at his browner-haired brother, and clapped his hands together, rubbing them in an eager motion. His strawberry blond brows rose in an inquiry.

"Right, then, what have you got for me, Leftenant?" the unnamed brother asked. His tone was a lot more polite when using the other man's title than Barclei's had been.

"Tell him what you told me," Rogen directed her.

Licking her lips and wondering how much she dared tell when this shrouded man was *not* the mage she was supposed to report everything to, Rexei finally began with the truth. "I was hired by someone in the uh . . . local guild . . . to investigate Servers Guild claims of abuse by priests. As a Sub-Consul, I could represent the local Consulate in the investigation."

That was her cover story. The cap-and-scarf swathed man nodded, rolling his wrist to get her to move on. "Yes, yes, I know all that. Go on. What do you know about the claims of the Dead God being gone?"

"There was a foreign man—not Arbran, but brought up from beyond the border with another man—and he started negotiating for his freedom," she said. That earned her snorts of disbelief from all three men. "He said, why should they be draining . . . you know, the prisoners . . . when they could be draining demons."

The leftenant's brother's eyes widened behind those green-tinted viewing lenses, but they did not move from her face. His hand moved though. He pointed at Barclei and snapped his fingers. "You, forget you ever heard that." Pointing at his brother next, he said, "You, get back to town, and cover all his tracks; make it seem like Longshanks left town with no notice or future address. I'll give your love to the family." That finger jabbed at her. "You, come with me."

"Why?" Again, Rexei surprised herself, but she stood by the word, lifting her chin a little. "I don't know you from *him*." She poked her thumb at the stairwell sentry. "Why should I go any-where with *you*?"

"Because I need you to give your report in full to some *very* interested parties, and it needs to be done immediately." He reached for her hand.

Rexei backed up. "My orders are to report to Master Julianna Harpshadow. Not to *you*. If you want to know the full-on details, you can ask her after I've given my report. *If* you're authorized to know what *she* requested I learn."

Both the leftenant and his brother stared at her, mouths open but without any sounds coming out. It was Barclei who spoke, pok-ing his thumb at the brother. "Master Harpshadow reports to *him*, you stupid twit. *He's* the Guild Master."

She looked back and forth between the three men. The new-comer wasn't wearing the symbol-stamped gold oval medallion of his guild, so she had no clue which one he headed. Rexei tried a guess. "Hydraulics?"

"The *other* guild," the leftenant's brother said flatly. "If you truly overheard what you say you did, then the priests might want to eliminate you. That means *we* need to know everything that you know. Give my contemporaries and I every scrap of knowledge you have, and we will give you sanctuary. Now, come."

This time, when he held out his hand, Rexei let him clasp hers and pull her into the stairwell he had come from. A last glance over her shoulder showed the leftenant turning to head for the stairwell that led back to the hidden entrance in the motorhorse stables.

"Have you eaten?" the Guild Master asked her.

"Uh . . . somewhat. I've got food for a bit," she added. The left-enant's brother flicked his hand, dismissing her statement. It occurred to her she didn't know his name, and it looked like this was another long stairwell spiraling down to who knew where. "So, uh . . . the Leftenant's name is Rogen Tallnose. If you're his brother, what's yours?"

"Alonnen." He didn't tack on the family name. "And you're Rexei. We're a little bit crowded at the moment; we've taken in several of the mages that were released, but that's all in the outer layers, where you were allowed before. Normally, you'd be quar-tered with them, but right now you're in too much danger. Some of the outer layer guildmembers have been shifted to the mid-layers, so that's overcrowded because of the shift inward . . . and of course some of the mid-levels got bumped into the upper levels.

"So, since you're now an even bigger target than I would be if they knew about me—or maybe on par," the Guild Master half joked, "that means you're going to have to share quarters, since there are no empty rooms left."

She blinked at that and cleared her throat, hoping he would attri-bute her flushed face to the heat of this place and her layers of wool. Sharing was not a good idea. Sharing when she was pretending to be male was never a good idea, because they'd room her with another male. She'd have to do all her changing in the refreshing room and bind her breasts even for sleeping. At least it was winter, so the extra layers would keep her warm. "Uh . . . who am I sharing it with?"

"Me." Pulling his scarf down, he flashed her a smile and opened a door at the bottom of the stairs. Alonnen nodded at yet another person seated at a table. This time, it was a woman, though Rexei could only tell because she had definite curves under her knit tunic. The Guild Master lifted his chin at both of them. "Margei, this is Rexei Longshanks. Rexei's being moved to the inner Vortex.

Rexei, this is Margei, master rank. She's sort of a leftenant type—and much better-looking than my brother," he added, winking at the middle-aged woman.

Margei blushed but gave him a dark look. "And happily married." She turned her green gaze on Rexei. Her brow creased in a frown. "Well, you're a bit tall for an unbearded youth. How old are you, lad? Fifteen?"

"Old enough to know it's none of your business." At the other woman's affronted look, Rexei gave her a pointed one. "You're married, remember?"

"He has you there," Alonnen said. Tugging Rexei past the station, he led her down the hall to the door at the end. He touched the wood rather than the doorknob. She saw the faintest ripple of magic over its surface and stiffened. Sensing her movement, he glanced back at her. "Relax. Everything's disguised by the Vortex. I've even made some progress with mastering that masking spell of yours."

"Funny, I don't remember teaching you," Rexei countered. After her message had been delivered to the Hydraulics Guild, she had been drawn into the Mages Guild to explain just how strong she was—moderately so—and how thoroughly she could mask her abilities. That had led to her being inducted into the Teachers Guild for one month as she strove to train three other mages to replicate the meditation spells her mother had taught her. But that had been two women and a man, and that other man was taller and had possessed a rounded, more broad nose.

"Scrying mirror," the Guild Master explained. "I watched what I could, when I could, and puzzled out the rest on my own. You're a terrible teacher, you know."

"I know. Aside from the Carters Guild, it's the shortest I've ever been apprenticed," she muttered. "I didn't like doing it."

"You'll never make master rank in any discipline if you can't learn how to teach better," he warned her.

"It's the *subject* I don't like. I don't even like saying the *M* word out loud, and I've spent over half my life hiding that such things even exist, never mind that *I'm* one of them. But I taught new carving tricks in the Engravers Guild, and everyone took to the lessons like ducks to water," she countered. Then frowned. Her sense of direction was good. The hallways were still smooth and seamless, broken only by metal-framed doors. "How much of this complex is under the reservoir?"

"The outer layers are on the hillsides above the shoreline, the middle layers under the shoreline. The inner depths of the Vortex are mid-lake. There used to be an island there. It got destroyed when the last Convocation of Gods and Man ended rather abruptly, killing off Mekha. Unfortunately, not permanently. He came back, more hungry than before, which was when everything grew exponentially worse for us."

"That foreign fellow was rather sure Mekha is gone. He swore it was what he believed had happened on a Truth Stone," Rexei offered. "He said he'd heard about such things happening in the ancient days, back when we still had the Convocations. I don't know how it happened *now*, but the embroidery, the carvings, anything directly tied to Him . . . all gone."

"Oh, I know how. And every single one of us who pricked a thumb and bled in the protest books owes a certain Darkhanan priestess a huge thank-you, since she's followed through on her promise."

Using his palm to unlock one last door, he stepped through and pulled her into an astonishing chamber . . . if one could call it that, since it seemed to be both outside and inside at the same time. It was as if a great, multiguild glassworks team had crafted a huge, crystalline bowl and upended it in the reservoir, trapping a vast bubble of air in which a large, multileveled stone building now sat, anchored to what had to be the stub of bedrock left over from the explosion he had alluded to a few moments before.

"Breathtaking, isn't it?" Alonnen asked her, grinning the moment she glanced his way. He removed his cap and green lenses as he did so, revealing kind hazel green eyes and longish strawberry blond curls pulled back into a short tail at the nape of his neck. "Welcome to the safest place for mages in all of Mekhana."

Breathtaking was the word for it. It wasn't just the fishbowl dome—literally, fish were swimming down near the bottom edges, barely visible in the glow from the crystals providing illumination for everything, while thin patches of ice distorted the light of what had to be Brother Moon overhead. It was also the man next to her. Seeing that grin, the welcoming warmth of it, made her feed odd. Nervous, excited, and perched on the edge of something big. Like her first solo ride on a motorhorse at messenger speeds.

"The view's a lot better in the daylight, of course. Fish, plants . . . well, more of the latter in the warmer parts of the year. But the sunlight through the ice can be nice. Oh, don't worry about the lights being seen at night. It's all cloaked under layers and layers of illusions," he dismissed, waiving his free hand. The other had tucked his scarf and cap under his arm, while his spectacles had gone into a clever pocket on the breast of his tunic. He caught her gaze drifting down over his lean chest and shrugged, misinterpreting her curiosity. "I know, I know, I'm not wearing a knitted shirt. Certainly not one I knitted myself.

"Truth be told, lad, I can practically spin wool into gold, it's that fine and slub free, but anything after that point keeps eluding me. Stabbing my fingers with embroidery needles, hopelessly tangling any yarn—oh, speaking of which," Alonnen added, nudging her toward the multistory structure ahead of them. "You were given a scrap of spell-knitting by Master Harpshadow. Do you still have it?"

She put her hand over her pouch. "Yes. I'm lucky I put it back in my pouch, not in my coat pocket, or it'd still be back at the temple, like my coat and my cap."

That checked him mid-stride. Swinging around, he faced her, his cheerfulness gone, along with much of the color in his cheeks. "They have a cap from your head? With your hairs in it?"

Defensively, Rexei touched her chest. "*I* didn't have any choice! One minute, I'm helping get the others out of the priests' clutches, and the next thing I know, they're shoving me out the door with the last of them, right past the bubble-ward! They had the doors locked and shielded before we knew what hit us. *Maybe* they won't realize the cap on the floor is mine, and there's no way they could tell which coat is mine, since there were five other Servers from the guild serving the temple at the time, and they got shoved out without their coats, too.

"I couldn't exactly go knocking on the door asking for it back, either. Not when I was supposed to be playing a half-wit," she added, giving him a hard stare. "I don't care who's signing my pay vouchers. I'm not going to take huge risks for anyone."

"And we won't ask you to," Alonnen stated, touching Rexei's forearm. "It'll be okay. We've had hairs caught in tracking amulets before, and we've always been able to lead them astray once they get near the dam. We'll need a few hairs from your head, but within a day, they'll be convinced you've gone over the eastern mountains into northern Aurul.

"Now calm yourself and get inside," he said, though she suspected the request was as much for his own sake as for hers. "You'll be safe here. *And* well fed. The inner circle of the Vortex is served by a grandmaster chef from the Hospitallers Guild, a journeyman, and three apprentices." He eyed her up and down, and flashed a brief smile. "I'd bet a lad like you could eat a whole chicken in a single sitting, plus have room for veg, bread, and pie. Or rather, I think it's a stuffed rib roast tonight. Come on."

She wasn't hungry until he opened up the nearest door and ushered her into a warm foyer not too dissimilar to what she'd seen in the larger houses attached to farms and workshops. The rich scents of roasting beef, herbed vegetables, fresh-baked bread, and more made her mouth water and made it difficult to struggle out of her pack, her coat, gloves, and knit hat.

A youth came at a call from the Guild Master; he took the bundle of her things and staggered upstairs. When she opened her mouth to protest, Alonnen cut her off with a lift of his free hand and a quick explanation.

"It's Guild policy to check over all belongings for magical traces, in case something's been slipped in by the priests or one of their agents that could help them track this place. That, and it's also a policy that everything gets cleaned. There are spells that recycle the air to keep it fresh, but every little bit helps when trying to keep the air from being manky or stuffy. Among other reasons—just consider it a free laundry service. All your things will be accounted for, so don't worry."

She wanted to worry, but he took her hand and guided her up the steps in the young lad's wake. That took them away from the delicious smells of the ground floor. But where the lad detoured at the third landing, they kept going up.

When they reached the top, Alonnen led Rexei into a wood-paneled room. While he tossed his hat and scarf onto pegs by the door, she looked around. There were three mirrors on the wall with the door along with shelves and cupboards, a woodstove on the other wall flanked by bookshelves, a desk with a vast window to her left, and an even larger set of windows on the right—floor to ceiling windows broken into four giant panes by what she realized were two sliding panels in the middle that could be retracted along grooves.

The windows overlooked a broad stone balcony with a view of the night-lit fishbowl. The crystals in the ceiling were radiating a dim sort of light, but her Messenger-trained mind said she could not possibly be seeing what was just outside the window.

It was impossible, flat-out impossible, for what she saw to have fit into the space. Tugging her hand free, she slowly approached the balcony and the vast window that covered it, trying to make sense of what was out there. Vortex was the right name for it, for it reminded her very much of the swirling funnel formed when one pulled the plug out of the bottom of a large basin of water. But this wasn't water she was seeing.

This was pure magic, and instead of draining down to a point at the base—a bright point of light just a little bit lower than the balcony itself—the Vortex seemed to be spewing upward, infusing the waters of the reservoir almost all the way up to the surface. Except it was also constrained in the whole fishbowl warding sphere at the same time, yet she hadn't *seen* any sign of this from outside the building.

"Illusion," Alonnen stated. She jumped, not having heard him approach close enough to speak into her ear. He shrugged and nodded at the view. "That's what the reservoir truly looks like, that funnel right there. Everything outside this room, it's all cloaked in illusion after illusion. Grandmaster-level magery, and we're damn lucky to have it. The old records say that the previous Guild Master of the Mages Guild had traveled to Aiar to petition for a new God. But we don't know what happened after that. His replacement, she was the one who quickly caged the shattered Portal that had been on the island and wove all the protective illusions on top of all the previous wardings that had been here.

"Unfortunately, she suffered a stroke before she could do more than start to teach her surviving apprentices how to maintain it all properly, though they managed as best they could. The confusion in the aether around the Heias Dam is the result of generations of imperfectly made repairs from before and after the Shattering. My predecessors then figured out how to capitalize on that effect. It's helped us to weed out would-be spies. But then you've already been through that interrogation process, so you know that."

Blushing, Rexei cleared her throat. "I . . . am surprised you're showing this to me. Explaining it."

He clapped her on the back. "That's because you, young man, are now on the front line of a war to help save our entire world. From a demonic, Netherhell-based invasion, no less. And for that much, you have the Guild's undying gratitude. More than that, lad? You're about to have the undying gratitude of some of the most powerful mages in the whole world. This way—oh, you'll probably want to disguise your face and hair as a precaution. I do, and I'm not the only one who does. If you like, I've got a spare scarf and hat on the rack.

"They're very trustworthy, but I have *no* clue whether the priests can spy on scrying mirrors or not, even if this connection goes straight through the Fountainways," he said, confusing her with the unfamiliar word. "It's also been a sort of tradition for all the Guardians of the Vortex to hide their identities over the centuries. Even if Mekha's gone now, I see no reason to stop just yet." Nudging her back over to the door, he redonned his cap and scarf, settled his glasses back on the midpoint of his beaky nose, and offered her a floppy felted cap and a soft lamb's-wool scarf to wrap around her throat and chin.

She took both, but after only a few seconds of wearing it, she had to unwind the scarf. He might only be wearing a woven wool shirt and matching waistcoat, but her knitted tunic lay over two layers of linen and her breast and waist bindings. In fact, she was now uncomfortably warm, for the iron stove across the broad room was keeping the Guild Master's study quite cozy.

"Something wrong?" he asked as she tried to discreetly flap her sweater to cool down a little.

"I'm too hot now," she admitted, grimacing. "The temple doesn't get a lot of heat outside the priests' rooms. I'm not dressed for this."

"Looks like you have a shirt on underneath," Alonnen observed, peering at her clothes. "Strip off the knit and make yourself comfortable. Nobody's going to care what you're wearing so long as you're reasonably decent. Most of the people we'll be talking to don't wear sweaters or other layers to keep warm—in fact, some are downright undressed compared to us, but that's okay; it's just the way they dress in their homeland."

Not quite comfortable, Rexei unbuckled her belt, set it and her pouch on the side table, then pulled the wool tunic over her head. She had tucked her medallions back under her sweater on the walk to her tenement with his brother, but not underneath her undertunics. Not when they had been exposed to the chill winter air. They were still cold but not shockingly so. She had to redon the cap, but this time when she tried the scarf, it wasn't so cloying. Nodding, she looked at him.

"Good—try those blue-tinted lenses, if you want to hide your eyes," he added, nodding at a set of spectacles on the narrow, tablelike side cupboard not far from the pegs on the wall. "Mind the curvature, as it might make you a bit dizzy. I'm mildly farsighted; I need 'em to look at things close-up."

Unsure what the lenses would do, Rexei picked up the glasses and gingerly peered through them. Everything turned blue, and there was indeed a slight sense of distortion . . . but she kind of liked everything faded to blue, so she carefully hooked the wires over her ears and gave him a thumb-out gesture, palm flat to the floor to let him know she was okay with it despite the discomfort.

FOUR

Pleased that the lanky young man was doing alright, Alonnen moved over to one of the three silvered glass mirrors on the wall near the desk. *Boy's not quite so suspicious now. Can't say as I blame him. I do wonder about Harpshadow's choice of Longshanks for playing spy in the heart of a bloody temple though . . .*

Stroking the edge of the mirror, he muttered his activation word and waited for the scrying spells to connect with the Tower far to the west. Blue rippled across the screen for a few moments, only to be replaced by the dark-skinned face of a woman. She smiled wryly at him. "I'm sorry, Guardian Alonnen, but the Master of the Tower is not available at the moment and will be indisposed for another hour. I can record a message for him, if you like."

"Great. Can you connect me to the other Guardians?" Alonnen asked.

"I can certainly try. Is this an emergency?" she asked politely.

That made him pause. Whatever the priests were planning, the fact that Mekha was no more and that other cities would no doubt be on the brink of rioting meant the priesthood would be in turmoil. Which meant the Guardians probably had a little leeway. His brother and the Precinct captain would keep Heiastowne as calm and orderly as possible, but their only concern was for the citizens; looting, fighting, and setting fires were not things one did carelessly in the harsh cold of winter.

"Well, it's not yet life-or-death, but it is more than a bit important," he finally said. "Get who you can on the Fountainways, and record our conversations for the others when they're free."

"Of course, Guardian. The Tower is happy to serve your needs in this matter." She shifted and did something that caused the blue glow to come back, covering the surface of the mirror.

"The Tower?" Rexei asked him.

"Yes, it's . . . um . . ." Alonnen scratched at one ear, trying to figure out how to explain it to a fellow Mekhanan. "It's . . . utterly unlike the Vortex. Pretty much the exact opposite, really. Mages openly flaunting their powers, scrycasting what they can do . . ."

"Scrycasting?" the youth repeated, giving him a dubious look.

"It's like a performance by the Bardic or Actors Guilds. The important thing is, the Master of the Tower, Guardian Kerric, has a special mirror that can peer one year into the future. And in that mirror, he saw . . . ah, hello Guardian Sheren," he interrupted himself, greeting the wrinkled, white-haired woman who appeared on the mirror. A moment later, the image split, with her face sliding to the left and shrinking a bit, and a new face appearing on the right. "And Guardian Keleseth."

"I just woke up," the darker-haired but still elderly woman on the right groused. "What's so important that we have to talk about it right now?"

A third face appeared between them, a man with blue eyes,

short blond hair, and a worried look pinching a line between his brows. "What's the emergency, Guardian Alonnen?"

"Please, gentles, if we can wait until we have everyone who can join this scrying, then I'll answer all the questions all at once and not have to repeat anything," Alonnen stated. He glanced over at Rexei Longshanks, who was hanging back a bit, peering at the mirror in curiosity but clearly not willing to get close to it. "Oh, don't worry, Longshanks. It's not going to hurt you. Come here."

The images split and shrank even more, reducing into a grid of nine. Alonnen taxed his memory to remember all of them. Besides Sheren of Menomon and the grumpy lady, Keleseth of Senod-Gra, they now had Daemon of Pasha; Suela of Fortune's Nave in Fortuna; Sir Vedell of Arbra; the dark-skinned Tuassan of Amaz; the tired-looking, spectacles-wearing Koro of the Scales; the autocratic Ilaiea of the Moonlands; and the woman from the Tower whose name he couldn't remember. He knew her face, but he couldn't remember her name.

"These are all the ones who are answering the call, Guardian Alonnen," she stated. "The rest are either delayed or have messages stating they are out of reach, and the Fountain of Nightfall is completely without communication at the moment thanks to the reconvened Convocation."

Alonnen heard the lad a few paces to his side draw in a sharp breath at that, but the Guardian ignored Rexei's shock. He nodded. "Thank you, dear. This'll do for now."

Nodding, the woman bowed out of the scrycast call, leaving a grid of eight faces on the horizontally hung mirror. Rubbing his hands together, he drew in a deep breath and began.

"Right, then. To get straight to the point, I do believe I know how the foreseen Netherhell invasion begins. Or at least, *where* it begins. Come here, Longshanks," he ordered, tipping his head to summon the youth. Eyes blinking behind the blue lenses, the young man moved closer until Alonnen could pull him into proper viewing distance at his side. "Everyone, this is Longshanks, who was assigned to spy on the priests of Mekha. Several things happened today which are extraordinary and which pertain strongly to *our* current mutual quest.

"Longshanks, these are eight of the Guardians of the world—like me, they protect powerful sources of magic. They are as trustworthy as you could hope to find, and I want you to start from the beginning and tell them whatever you overheard and anything you saw today. Give us your report like you were going to give to Harpshadow. Don't worry about being understood unless it's a term unique to Mekhana. These mirrors are made to automagically translate everything we say. Got it? Good. Go."

Rexei nodded, swallowed, and began at Alonnen's command. "I, uh, was picked because I . . . can hide all traces of . . . of magic from the priests of Mekhana. I was supposed to spy on them, and this morning I saw them bring in a pair of newly captured . . . uh . . . mages . . . hauled all the way up from the Arbran border."

"Wait, you're in Mekhana? You're Mekhanan? A land that devours mages? When were you going to tell us this?" Ilaiea demanded.

"Ilaiea, would you keep your mouth shut?" Alonnen interjected. "It doesn't bloody matter where we live; *we're* not priests of Mekha. Now do have the courtesy to be quiet and listen. Please. Go on, Longshanks."

Rexei cleared her throat before continuing. "Uh . . . right. The two, ah, men—the priests distribute the captives across all the temples, and I think we were overdue. That's what the other Servers Guildmembers said when I joined. I was hoping to find a way to break the binding spells on them and help them get away, but the priests came in early. One of the two managed to convince them to let him talk . . . and he asked them why they were using, uh . . . our kind to feed the God. Mekha."

The men and women in the divided grid of the mirror flinched at Longshanks' words but thankfully stayed quiet.

"Go on," Alonnen encouraged again when Rexei paused. He stayed close to the youth's shoulder, lending support and protection as the Hostess of Senod-Gra scowled.

"There was a bit of name-calling, and then the foreign one—he wasn't from Arbra, but I don't know where—he said they should be stealing energy from *demons* . . . and that *he* knew how to bind and drain 'em."

Noise erupted from the eight Guardians as they all reacted and tried to speak at once. Alonnen subtly braced Rexei, waited for a brief pause in the hubbub, and spoke up sharply. "Oy! With respect? Shut it! He's not done reporting yet."

Longshanks nodded and continued when they fell watchfully quiet. The scarf shifted off the youth's jaw, distracting Alonnen with the dawning realization that for someone as old as Longshanks surely had to be, there was no sign of stubble, let alone the beard-shadow that should have been there on someone with such dark hair. There wasn't much time to contemplate that oddity, however. Alonnen pulled his attention back to the subject at hand when Rexei continued.

"Mind you, I couldn't hear all of it. They kept trying to send me off—I was playing the part of a dumb servant, a lackwit, and had been for two months, so they'd be used to talking more freely around me. But I did hear enough. He, the foreign man, wanted to bargain with them, with Mekha's priests. Set him free and give him access to the power they raised . . . but then a novice came running up with the word that Mekha had disappeared from the power room."

"Power room?" the woman with sun-streaked light brown hair asked.

Alonnen explained that one. "Every temple to Mekha has a set of rooms in the basement level—down where they keep the mage prisoners they drain to feed the Dead God. It's said that Mekha divides . . . or divided . . . Himself into pieces and sent each of those pieces to a temple to be housed, so that He could drain all the locally caught and enslaved mages of their power. The power room is where He is—or was—rumored to sit and sup."

The winces of disgust and disbelief on his fellow Guardians' faces were mollifying to see. Not everyone understood what his fellow countrymen had suffered all along, but these mages were beginning to understand. He nudged Longshanks subtly, who nodded, swallowed, and continued.

"Right . . . So the God-piece in the local temple was summoned by some sort of shimmering light, He apparently said something about it finally being time, whatever that meant, and then vanished. I wasn't there to see any of it, so don't ask me whether the report was accurate," Rexei added quickly as one of the men in the mirror drew in a breath to speak. "You have to understand, the Servers Guild was *forbidden* to go down to the basement level. We always cleaned the public parts of the temple, and the novices cleaned the hidden parts and . . . and took care of the prisoners and their cells.

"But then a short while after Mekha apparently vanished . . . so did everything of His. All the walls were carved with His sigils and signs, and the priests' robes were embroidered with the same sorts of symbols. I watched it all fade from the walls right in front of my eyes, and when I looked at the priests, their robes were bare, without a single stitch of embroidery. And *that* was when the foreign fellow said it was most likely a sign that Mekha had been removed from power. They even used one of their Truth Stones on him."

"*I* know, thanks to our little cross-guardianship conferences, that the Convocation of Gods and Man has been reinstated," Alonnen stated. "So whatever is happening down in Nightfall, even though we cannot get through to Guardian Dominor right now or to Priestess Orana Niel, who pledged to my people for generations that she *would* take our complaints to the Convocation when next it took place . . . I'm pretty damn sure Mekha is gone for good . . . and good riddance, I say.

"Of course, this causes a bunch of other problems for us, things which may impact our ability to stop the Netherhell invasion, but we'll give you our all. Now, back to the lad's report. What else happened?" he asked Rexei.

Licking her lips, Rexei continued. "Well, I'd stashed a spare coal bucket in the next room over, so I could pretend to go get extra for the braziers, and though they kept sending me off, I heard much of it. The foreign man said, to throw off any rioting, something about setting the imprisoned mages free, if they weren't going to be drained by Mekha anymore. And . . . it sounded like the two priests listening to him talk about conjuring powerful demons with their help were going to give it actual thought. But then everything vanished of Mekha's, and one went running off to mirror-call the other temples.

"So I grabbed my bucket and followed to see if he was going to share the offer with the other temples, but before I could hear much, the archbishop—that's the local high priest—he grabbed me and made me go into the basement rooms and start . . . and start bringing up the prisoners."

Alonnen could only imagine what the youth must have seen, for his cheeks flushed and his mouth sealed for a moment in a grim line. Cupping his hands around the youth's shoulders in silent support, he wordlessly urged Rexei to continue.

"The novices and the other servants, we brought up over a hundred and fifty of 'em, sat 'em on benches in the prayer hall. Then we guided them to the door, where the archbishop and a fellow bishop-ranked priest unlocked their spell-slave collars and pushed them out through the wardings. I got pushed out, too, and they said the temple was closed until further notice, and . . . that's it. That's all I know." Rexei shrugged. "I don't know if they're going to take up this foreign fellow's offer on conjuring demons or not, and . . . well, that's all I know."

"Before you all get your various pants wedged up," Alonnen asserted as the others started to speak, cutting them off, "just try to remember *this*: We have no God now. No Patron Deity. Locally, we don't have any problems yet, but that's a very big *yet*. There's no telling what it'll be like here in Mekhana a day or a week from now. Riots, fighting, maybe even an invasion—no offense to any of our neighboring Guardians, such as Sir Vedell, whom I'd trust to be kind, but Guardians aren't the ones who decide whether to make war or not. Now, I've got someone in the local militia who's going to try to keep things calm around here, but there's going to be things falling out all over this land. Power grabs, anger problems, retaliations and counter-retaliations, you name it.

"We do *not* have a lot of resources, training being the foremost. So if things do go sour, before you try accusing me or mine of not acting fast enough or hitting hard enough, or whatever else might or might not happen, try to keep *that* in mind."

"You'll have *my* sympathies, if not theirs," Guardian Daemon stated. "Pasha's being hit by the early stages of a civil war, with the old king's sons and daughters and even a few cousins all fighting for the right to claim the throne. I suspect you're about to have a far-less-organized version of that descend on everyone there, so for what it's worth, *I* at least understand."

Alonnen nodded at the blond mage, thankful for the sympathy, but Keleseth took the bit in her teeth.

"Well, that's all to the well and good, but do try to impress on your people that you have *bigger* problems than the overthrow of a sadistic God," she stated.

"Ha! *That's* a laugh," Guardian Sheren scoffed. "You're the Guardian of the City of Delights, Keleseth. Try to impress anything serious on your *own* people, and we'll see how far you get."

"Oh, and like your Menomonite committees are any more organized or fast acting?" Keleseth shot back.

"Stop it!" The sharp protest came from Rexei. Alonnen lifted his brows but let the youth speak. "This isn't the time or place for . . . for petty quarrels! You'd think you were *apprentices* from different guilds, squabbling like children over whose guild is run better or worse than the other. If a Guardian is anything like a Guild Master, then *set a good example. Is that clear?*"

I think I can believe the lad is indeed a journeyman Gearman. Sub-Consul and all that. Wait . . . Gearman. He shot the youth a quick look, thinking quickly. Squeezing Rexei's shoulders, Alonnen lifted his chin at the faces on his mirror. "As Longshanks so rightfully points out, let's get back on track, shall we? Now, the prophecies Guardian Saleria shared with us before the Convocation have a few things to say about this point in time, and they're quite clear."

"Clear perhaps to you," the brown-faced Tuassan stated, "but we're not Mekhanans. The boy talks about guilds, so that strongly suggests the last line of the third verse. What more can you tell us about any relevancies?"

"Yes," the sandy-haired woman a few frames over agreed. "And the fighting of the demons, that much is clear, based on the suggestion of this outkingdom mage and his bartering with the Mekhanan priests. But of the fighting of one's doubts, maybe the doubts refer to the current instabilities? Maybe you'll have to wrest some sort of new kingdom organization out of the chaos?"

"They could try, but if these priests are so used to the power of their previous God backing them, they're going to want to maintain control any way they can," Guardian Ilaiea stated. She frowned, tugging on her long, pale cream braid. Alonnen had last seen her daughter, Guardian Serina pulling that same trick when she was worried. The mother firmed her look. "Your best bet is to establish a *new* God or Goddess, a Patron Deity to seize control away from the priesthood."

"*Finally* you say something reasonable and calm," the black-haired man with the blue viewing lenses muttered, the one named Koro. The others started to argue, and he quickly held up a hand. "Sorry! Sorry . . . it's just her better-than-us attitude gets on my nerves. She's right, though. Guardian Alonnen, you *need* to select a deity and get everyone to worship whatever that is."

"Guildra."

Alonnen turned his head quickly, staring at the young man on his side of the mirror conference. "Beg pardon?"

"Guildra," Rexei asserted, turning to look at Alonnen. "That's who I've been thinking we should've had for a Patron Deity. A Goddess, kind and gentle, wise and skilled. She'd be the Patron of the Guilds . . . because it's the *guilds* that have consistently given a damn about Mekhanans all this while, when our own so-called Patron and His priesthood clearly have not—and I'll be damned if I'll have another bastard *male* God in charge of this land. Women are the equal of men, and to the Netherhells with the priesthood if they think they can keep us . . . if they can keep us pushing women down any longer.

"No more. By the pricking of *my* thumb, no more," Long-shanks added firmly, invoking the oath virtually every guild member across the land had given when signing their name in their own blood in the books reserved for presentation at the next—now the current—Convocation of the Gods. Which Rexei Longshanks had undoubtedly given multiple times, given how many guilds the youth had clearly joined, based on the sheer number of medallions alone. "There's even a symbol out there that's Hers."

"Well, that's the first *I've* heard of this. What symbol?" Alonnen

asked. Before the youth could answer, a bell chimed from inside
the talker-box mounted on the wall next to the right-hand mirror.
Sighing roughly, he shook his head. "Never mind that. It's something Longshanks and I can discuss off-scrying. The rest of you
can chat amongst yourselves about what we now know. I know it's
not much, but at this point, all we can do here in Mekhana is try to
spy carefully, and try to impose some sort of order locally . . . and
we'll *try* to come up with a good Patron Deity as fast as we can. No
promises other than that we'll try.

"Now, if you'll excuse us, it's suppertime here. I'll leave the dis-
section of what this means in relations to the prophecies to the lot
of you, and I'll review the Tower's recording after we've eaten and
I've had a chance to chat in more depth with Longshanks, here. I
had to share what little we know right now with the rest of
you, because the lad *did* pinpoint where it'll most likely start, but
without a God or Goddess, don't expect any miracles from us just
yet. I'll chat with you all later, so have a good night. Or day, or
whatever time it is where you are."

Tapping the frame of the mirror, he cancelled the connection
spell. In an instant, the image flicked away, leaving him with a
reflection of his long-nosed self and the pale-chinned young man
at his side.

Rexei cleared his throat. "I'm not sure they like me."

The youth said it with a touch of what sounded like self-
deprecating humor. Alonnen patted Rexei on the back. "Bunch of
self-important twiddlers half the time, if you ask me. But they're
good sorts, even if that pale-haired woman is an uppity twit at
times, and the darker-haired elderly one is a grouch, and . . . well,
they all have their plusses and minuses. But they'll back you if they
believe in you, and they're quite literally the most powerful mages
in the whole world.

"Anyway, that bell was for announcing supper," he told Rexei,

dismissing the subject of the Guardians. "Don't worry about finding enough to fill your appetite. There's always plenty. Mind you, we
get any leftovers for luncheon on the morrow, but it's a very rare
day when our chef makes something that's no good reheated."

He helped Rexei put the caps and scarves back on the pegs,
reclaimed his spectacles, and watched the youth blink and stare
several times, trying to refocus. Alonnen grinned. "You look like I
felt, first time the Optics Guild gave me a pair for reading. How's
your vision, lad?"

"Uh . . . just fine, thank you," Longshanks replied politely.

Alonnen clapped Rexei on the back and nudged the youth
toward the stairs. "Come on, five floors down. My quarters and
personal workrooms are on the fourth floor, other bedrooms and
the laundry are on the third, and the second floor is workrooms for
the others. The first floor is kitchen, dining, meeting, and storage
rooms."

Rexei glanced back at him as they descended the steps. "I'm
surprised you let just anybody up here, if the Vortex is such a huge
power source."

Shutting the door firmly behind him, Alonnen shook his head.
"It's not the risk you're thinking. Anyone else opens that door,
they won't even see the balcony, never mind the Vortex. It'll just be
a blank wall covered in maps of Mekhana."

"Wait—you told that boy to take my things somewhere. Third
floor. But you said I'd be staying with you?" Rexei asked.

"I told you, it's standard for anyone coming to live in the Vortex. This is all an enclosed environment, so we need to make sure
there aren't any spying talismans or rank odors. Or, for that matter, fleas and other things. It was a bit before my time, but the
Vortex chronicles mentioned a great plague of fleas one summer.
We try to ensure they get killed off quickly with soap and hot
water. Don't worry; nobody will shrink your woolens while they're

being washed," he added in reassurance. The youth didn't look reassured.

"But . . . my things. I have *private* things in my bag," Rexei protested. "Things I don't want anyone touching or handling. I know it's a bit too late, but . . ."

Alonnen patted the youth on the shoulder. "Relax, lad; they'll treat your things as carefully and circumspectly as they treat mine. And it's to your advantage to have your gear checked over. We might be deficient in many areas of magical knowledge, but the one thing we *do* know how to do is find and disable priestly tracking spells. Anyway, I still have a few more questions. Like, how old are you?"

"Old enough," Rexei replied, still sounding a little distressed over the absence of those belongings.

Alonnen wondered what was in the lad's bag that should distress him so much. *Maybe a crankman? They were originally made for women, but there are plenty of us lads who enjoy the clever little things, too. Maybe if he learns we're not prudes here in the safety of the Vortex, he'll relax a bit? I can tell the poor boy's far too tense by habit, given how hunched his shoulders are even when calm.*

Out loud, Alonnen said, "Yes, but what specific age are you? There are a few rules in the Vortex about how to behave around the ladies and such. And if you're a mage, then you get rationed on anything fermented. So how many years have you lived?"

His pestering earned him a hard sigh from the lad. "I'm twenty-one, alright? Almost twenty-two."

That made Alonnen blink and almost miss a step. Thankfully they had reached one of the landings, or he would have stumbled badly. *Nearly twenty-two? And hardly a sign of a whisker on the boy . . . er, young man? How odd . . . unless he knows one of those cantrip things for plucking whiskers and not just shaving them?* He rubbed his chin thoughtfully. His own beard grew slowly, but it did grow, which left him with a slightly sandstone-rough chin at the end of each day.

"How do you keep your chin whisker free?" he finally asked.

"Spells."

"So, you'll teach me, then?" he pressed.

"I'm a lousy spell teacher, remember?" Longshanks shot back.

Caught in his own honest, unflattering trap, Alonnen chuckled and clapped a hand over the younger man's shoulder. "I can tell we'll get along fine—wait, why are you flinching?"

Rexei pushed his fingers off her shoulder. "Because some bully-man tried to crack my collarbone when I was trying to stop the town from rioting on the temple steps, with *me* between them and the doors. He dragged me off to your brother and tried to get me arrested."

"Oh. Sorry. I apologize for the other hugs, too," Alonnen offered, hoping he hadn't hurt the lad earlier. "I can call in an Apothecary mage if you like, have them look at your shoulder and all."

"No! No, thank you," Rexei added politely on the heels of the quick denial. "It's just . . . the top of my left shoulder is bruised, not the side or the right one or anything. I'll live."

He's got a ways to go before he trusts us, I see, Alonnen realized. *And I'm glad I mostly touched the near shoulder or the side of his arm, before.* Gently clasping the right shoulder, he patted the youth with his fingertips. "I'm sure you will live, too. But you're now a guest of the inner circle . . . and something of an involuntary guest, since until we can figure out how safe it is for you to go outside, you'll probably be stuck here for a while. So you might as well take advantage of all the amenities, eh?"

Rexei shrugged, arms folding defensively across her chest. As they reached the ground floor, the noise of dozens of people engaged in multiple conversations drifted back to them. A few turns this way and that, and they wound up in a large hall a few steps down from the rest of the ground floor, but one with a grand view of the fishbowl in the night through another quartet of floor-to-ceiling windows. It was also crowded with several tables, chairs, and benches, enough that the sea of people surprised Longshanks, making her lift her head and slow her steps.

"Come on, it's not so bad. A bit crowded, but not so bad," Alonnen murmured. Raising his voice, he lifted his right hand. "Oy! Everyone, this is Rexei Longshanks, a journeyman Gearman and my personal guest. Rexei, this is . . . everyone. You'll have a chance to learn names and faces, don't worry. The rest of you, treat him right, or I'll have your ears boxed up for Midwinter Moon! Come on, budge over; make room for two hungry lads!"

He nudged Rexei forward—almost having to push—and maneuvered the two of them over to a spot that opened up on a bench seat. Clean plates and silverware were passed down, thankfully faster than the platters of food, and two mugs of mulled apple cider. One of the women in the hall rose and made her way over to the two of them.

"Oh hey—Rexei, this is my mum, Alsei. Alsei, Rexei," he introduced.

They shook hands, then Alsei rested her palm on her hip. Like many of the women in Mekhana, she no doubt wore baggy knits and trews to work in, but skirts when she wanted to relax. At the moment, she wore a warm skirt in the same dark gray and black wool favored by the locals, though a bit of reddish wool had been knitted into a rolling wave pattern down by the hem of skirt and tunic alike. Or rather, a crocheted tunic and skirt, since that particular pattern required a hook to create, in Rexei's experience.

Alsei eyed Rexei's worn linen shirts and felted dark gray pants, then shook her head. "Al, *where* are you going to put this lad? Sure, he's skinny, but we've got every bed and couch crammed with bodies right now. Every quarter hour that passes, we're getting a new mage or two shipped to us from the other guilds—at least *this* one is cognizant and not crying all the time, but where are you going to put the lad? In a drawer somewhere?"

"He'll be staying with me," Alonnen dismissed, reaching for the roast beef platter passing their way. He snagged a slice for himself, and an extra one for Rexei, who hadn't grabbed a great deal of food. Even at almost-twenty-two, the lad should have hollow legs. Alonnen had certainly had hollow ones at that age.

"Staying with *you*?" his mother repeated, brows lifting. "How long have you known the boy? Is he trustworthy? What kind of family does he come from, and where are they? Why can't he stay with them?"

"I haven't got a family." The unhappy words came from the target of her doubts. Rexei shrugged, shoulders hunching inward a bit. Then she lifted her chin a little. "And I'm a Sub-Consul. If you don't think *that's* trustworthy enough, take it up with your Consulate."

Alonnen suspected there was a whole history behind those few short words. He didn't press, though. "Mind your manners, mum. This young man is the second-most important person in the Guild right at this moment."

"What, are you finally taking up an apprentice?" Alsei asked, brow lifting toward her strawberry and silver curls.

"He's not strong enough for that, from what I've heard. But he *was* spying in the temple when Mekha vanished. As soon as we've fed, I'm taking him back up to my office to write out everything he can remember from his time in there—and he knows enough, the priests would happily grab and torture him, if they don't just kill him outright the moment they find him. So stop pestering him. Frankly, the safest place he can sleep *is* in my suite, under the circumstances. Now sit down, and enjoy your meal."

With a last, doubtful look at her son, Alsei complied. Alonnen sighed. He leaned in close to Rexei, murmuring in the younger man's ear.

"Don't mind her. She doesn't know I've had you under surveillance ever since they told me we had a Gearman with sixteen guild coins show up, only to turn out to be a mage." Picking up knife and fork, he cut into his beef. "She doesn't know much about the prophecy my contemporaries mentioned earlier, but I do. Since it just might be talking about you, I'll get you a copy of it when we're back up top. Go on, eat up. Food's free here . . . though I'm not sure how much longer it'll last, if we keep packing in more people like this," he muttered, eyeing the others crowding around the five long tables.

Head swimming with tiredness, Rexei finally put down the graphite stick she had been given for writing down everything she could remember. She wasn't done recording her thoughts, but she was done for the night. Her notes weren't the most organized, but she had underlined and repeated key words in the left margin so that one could skim the body of the text and pick out a specific topic. With all the food her host had pressed on her, it was a wonder she wasn't fast asleep with full-belly syndrome.

What she wanted now was a hot bath with some mild-scented soft soap and a soft wool-stuffed bed with thick blankets. Of course, the mattresses down here in the southlands weren't nearly as thick as the ones up north, but then up north was where most of the sheep grazed on large stretches of pastureland. But that was there, and this was here, and she was seated across the desk from the Guild Master of all mages. The head of a guild almost no one ever mentioned aloud for fear the priests would somehow hear of it.

Smothering a yawn behind her hand, she glanced at the scroll Alonnen Tallnose had offered to her. *Eight verses of five lines, transcribed from some far-flung language into Mekhanan. The stuff doesn't rhyme in our tongue, but there are notes down the side of what the meter was and which words rhymed together. The Mathematics Guild would claim that the numbers and the countings and the position of things has relevance . . . but all I can think of right now is that the first line of each quintain is paired over the whole simply by rhyme but mainly pertains to the verse it prefaces. And the four lines that follow each cover a specific event.*

Line about me? Maybe. I don't know. She honestly didn't, but she did read over the third verse again.

> *"Cult's Awareness, it shall rise:*
> *Hidden people, gather now;*
> *Fight the demons, fight your doubt.*
> *Gearman's strength shall then endow,*
> *When Guilds' defender casts them out."*

The verses about hidden people and "Guilds' defender" were surely linked. There *was* a Thieves Guild in Mekhana, simply because having a guild structure meant having the safety of like-minded people who would band together to watch each other's backs. Sometimes they were called the Antiquities Guild or the Reclamations Guild. But the line about fighting doubt, that was very much the life of a mage, the doubt that Mekha was truly gone, the doubt that the priests could be overthrown, the doubt that there was a better life just waiting to be somehow seized.

So that's bound to be talking about the Mages Guild, not Thieves. But I have no clue what "Gearman's strength shall then endow" means. I don't have any strength. I've been a bit more brave than usual in the last day, after that horrid feeling of Mekha's mildew and oppression and decay went away, but . . .

Another yawn interrupted her thought. Across from her, Alonnen sighed and set down the papers he was reading.

"You know, your yawns are making *me* sleepy. I can take the hint, though. Off to bed for both of us. Or rather, me to my bed, and you to a nice, broad, well-cushioned couch in my sitting room. I've napped on it a few times, and it's about as good as any bed. Save mine, of course," he added, flashing her another of his engaging grins. "But then mine comes with a feather-stuffed mattress two full handspans in depth. You should see the covers when I'm lying abed. It looks like nobody's even in there; the mattress is all mounded up level with the rest of me."

Deeply grateful she wouldn't literally be sharing a bed with him, Rexei allowed him to shoo her out of his study and down the stairs to the next floor. This part of the building curved a little; now that she knew the Vortex was there, even if hidden, she could see how the floor had been built to curve around the swirling base of the Vortex. They passed a few rooms, which her host dismissed as "workrooms, nothing special unless you're into trying to figure out how to make magic work properly" and guided her into a door at the end.

This turned out to be the promised sitting room. Touching the control rune by the door, he brightened the suncrystals in the ceiling. Squinting against the light, Rexei was glad he had taken the time to explain to her what they were, how they were activated, and how they absorbed real sunlight, transmitting roughly half of it right away and storing the other half for use at night. The shout, however, was unexpected.

"Oy! Turn't off!"

"What the . . . ? Dolon! What the bloody Netherhell are you doing in here?" Alonnen demanded, glaring at the squinting redhead wrapped up in blankets on his divan.

"Got booted out by Grandmaster Parsong an' his wife," the younger man grumbled. "Too many damned people in th' Vortex. Turn it off, already!"

Her host reduced the light coming into the sitting room, but he didn't reduce his glare. "Bloody hell . . . Fine. I guess you'll have to actually share the damned bed with me."

"Oh, good," Dolon mumbled, struggling to sit up. "More room in there."

"Not *you*, you daft twit!" Alonnen argued, pushing Rexei forward to the far door. "This one. *You* snore too much. Not to mention I didn't invite you in here."

"I didn't know you played that way, brother," Dolon quipped, knuckling some of the sleep out of one eye, while surveying Rexei's slender form with the other.

"I *don't*," the Guild Master retorted as Rexei flushed, belatedly catching Dolon's meaning. "But *you* snore like an ore crusher. I'll take my chances with Longshanks, here. At least *he* doesn't have the family nose and all its attendant resonances."

"Fine, whatever. Get the light, will you?" his brother muttered, hunkering down under his bedding.

Alonnen slapped the runes scribed on a metal panel next to the other door, then smacked the ones inside the next room. Muttering under his breath, he shut the door behind Rexei. "I can see I'll have to make more rooms under the mountains to accommodate everybody. Or at this rate, I'll be packed into my own bed with eighteen others. Sorry 'bout that."

"I really shouldn't . . ." she started to protest, trying not to look at the bed in the center of the carpet-strewn chamber. It was a little wider than twice the cot she was used to sleeping on, and maybe a little longer, but that was about it. There was one overstuffed chair by the iron stove, a short padded chest at the foot of the bed, a wardrobe cupboard, and a tall clothes chest. At least someone had built up the fire in the woodstove, but unless she could get her hands on the blankets she had brought, there wasn't anything she could curl up under, other than what lay on the bed.

"Nonsense, it's late, we're both tired, and if I snore, I'll forgive you for trying to smother me with a pillow. If *you* snore, I'll expect you to extend the same forgiveness." A friendly shove pushed her toward one of the other doors. "That's the refreshing room. I'll get you one of my nightshirts.

"Just dump your clothes in the basket in there, in the corner," he directed her, moving over to the chest of drawers. "It'll be taken off and cleaned, and your other things will be back by morning, fresh and ready to wear. The other door's the bathing room, but the tub takes a while to fill, and it's a bit late for that. You can do a sketch-bath with one of the washcloths, if you want, but don't take too long—here, the nightshirt."

Rexei caught the folded fabric, fumbling it before she had it secured in her grasp. Swallowing, she stalled for time. "Uh . . . you go first. I can wait. Promise."

Eyeing her, he shrugged and stepped into the refreshing room. Left alone, Rexei tried to dredge up any excuse for not sharing a bed with her host. With this Guild Master, though, she didn't really feel like a member of his guild, the Mages Guild. Picking her way over to the side of the bed, she investigated the coverlets. A sheet, a wool blanket, a feather-stuffed quilt, and a lightly felted coverlet in a soft dyed gray; the color of the coverlet was too uniform to have been from a naturally gray sheep.

Maybe if she stripped the bottom and top blankets and doubled them up, she might be comfortable enough. As a messenger, sometimes she'd been forced to sleep in the wild. A carpet-strewn floor in a fire-warmed building would be far more comfortable than dossing down on a bedroll inside a low-slung tent made out of an oilcloth tarp tied over the back of her motorhorse for a ridgepole and staked out to one side. Not often, but sometimes she had been forced to camp like that.

The door opened. She glanced at her host—and gasped, stumbling back. Alonnen Tallnose was naked. Completely nude. Hair brushed out and looking like gold and copper fluff around his shoulders, he padded out of the refreshing room on bare feet . . . bare legs, and bare everything else . . . and headed toward the same drawer he had used before. Only to stop and stare at her. "Are you alright?"

Wide-eyed, she shook her head. He looked around the room, then down at himself, clearly puzzled by what was upsetting her. Thankfully his organ was flaccid, but it was still *there*, exposed to the world amid a short thatch of reddish nethercurls. Rexei tried not to stare at it, but she couldn't help backing away from it. She had spent over half of her life avoiding the horrid things, thanks to the memory of what that priest had done to her own mother, and if it so much as twitched, she would run. Except there really wasn't any other place for her that was safe from the priests. Feeling trapped, she tried not to panic.

"What? You're acting like you've never seen another naked man before." Pulling out a second nightshirt, Alonnen padded over to her. She looked anywhere but at him. "Buck up, lad! It's not like you're seeing nothing you yourself don't have, right? . . . *Right?*"

He wasn't going to let the subject go . . . and there was really nowhere left for her to flee. Arms folded across her chest, shoulders hunched, she squeezed her eyes shut. Hoping—praying to any God that would listen—that he was as nice as he seemed, Rexei blurted out, "I'm a *lass*, not a lad!"

FIVE

⧓

"Gods!" Shocked, Alonnen smacked the nightshirt over his groin to hide it, then quickly fumbled his way into it while she still had her face scrunched up and her head averted. "I'm so sorry! I didn't know . . ."

Her confession clarified several things in an instant, the lack of any beard hairs on her chin, her reluctance to share his quarters—not that there was much chance of finding a place for her this late at night—and other little things. "Rexei" was common enough when used for both girls and boys that it was probably her real name, or perhaps one she had chosen to cling to her true self in the midst of her deception.

He couldn't blame her for that deception, though. Everyone in the Mages Guild knew what priests preferred to do to childbearing-aged women, whether or not they were captive mages. No doubt she was mortified by him walking around all but waving his piston in her face. As soon as he had the nightshirt tugged down over his knees, he spoke in hushed tones, hoping to keep her calm. Since she was something of a mage, he had to keep her calm so that she didn't just randomly lash out with her magic. "It's okay. You can relax. I'm all covered now, promise. I *wish* you'd told me a couple hours ago, when I'd have had a chance of finding you a female bunkmate. But it's okay. I promise, you're safe with me."

She unsquinched her eyes a little, but she still looked like she was bracing for some sort of blow. It made him feel worse, that this otherwise brave and rather talented young *woman* could be so patently afraid. Sighing, he raked a hand through his hair, which he had unbound and given a quick brushing while in the refreshing room. She didn't relax much more, just continued to give him a wide, wary stare while he stood there and thought.

"Oh, *do* stop looking at me like that," he groused when Rexei didn't relax. Her fear made him feel like a monster, which he was not. "I'm *not* going to pounce on you. Even if I were so inclined—which I am *not*—I've got my bloody youngest brother in the next room—who would flirt with you if he knew, since he's a bit dense that way—plus our two sisters and our mum and dad all live here in the inner circle. And my elder brother himself would publically flog me 'til I bled to my knees if I tried to harm you. Now, it's late; we're both tired; we're both polite, properly raised adults.

"There are more people crammed into the inner circle than I expected, which means I doubt either of us would find anything for you if we tried looking for another room right now. So we'll just have to put up with things for one night. Go get changed, wash your face and whatever else, and pick a side to sleep on—and don't even suggest sleeping on the floor. The woodstove doesn't burn wood; it burns magic, but the spell's set to drop the temperature once the lights go out, and that means it'll get bloody cold in here. Don't freeze just because you only think you have to be afraid of me. Because you don't."

Her jaw dropped. Alonnen held up a hand, forestalling her argument.

"*Not* for the reason you're thinking. Frankly, you're insulting me with that look on your face and those suspicions in your eyes. The natural state of a man is *not* a rapist, and I'll thank you to remember that. And *I* am certainly not one," he asserted. "I've no urge to assault you. I'm not going to beat you in your sleep, or even bother you, unless I should snore . . . and I can't help the latter, in case you haven't noticed by the size of my rather tall nose. But either way, *nothing* is going to happen between us but a bit of snoring . . . and maybe an elbowing if one of us snores.

"*Have* I harmed you?" he added tartly when she didn't move and didn't speak. "Aside from the shoulder thing? Have I done anything cruel or savage or utterly lacking in self-control? Or even just slightly lacking?"

"No," she admitted reluctantly. Her shoulders were still a little tense, but her arms had relaxed slightly.

Alonnen took that for the positive sign it was, and he flipped a hand at her again. "Well, there you go. You'll be as safe in my bed as my mum would be." Oddly enough, that caused her to wince and tense again. "Or your own mum," he added.

That made her blanch and stare at him. Or rather, through him. Alonnen had the disturbing notion she was seeing very bad memories. Before he could question her, she tightened her arms across her flat chest and mumbled, "She's . . . She was taken. By a priest. She'd be long dead by now. He . . . He . . ."

She didn't finish the sentence, but Alonnen was not ignorant. He could fill in the blanks.

"Taken" had only one meaning in the Mages Guild. It meant her mother was a mage, and if she was female, then she was undoubtedly raped. New priests had to come from somewhere, and that meant boys with magic, which often ran in family bloodlines for a handful of generations or more.

Orphaned girls were dumped on the other guilds all the time once past the weaning stage, and sometimes boys, though the latter usually were raised among the priests until old enough to manifest powers. If they had no magic, they were pushed out of the temples. Often, they made their way to the militia, where they were usually considered arrogant and coldhearted enough to be assigned to the Hunter Squads.

But the women . . . they remained forever under the threat of being taken and force-bred by men, compelled by more than enough magic to enforce their attackers' will and whims. Alonnen gave Rexei a sympathetic look.

"I am sorry that it happened, Longshanks. I wish we'd found a way to break and banish Mekha long, long ago . . . but not even the strongest mage can change the past. We can only move on," he said.

She sniffed and glared off to the side, then gave a tiny, huddled shrug. "'S okay," she muttered. "He's gone *now*. No one else will . . . U-Unless the priests really *do* start . . . summoning demons to regain . . ."

This was entirely too depressing a line of thought. Alonnen stepped forward, slipped his arm gently around her shoulders—steadfastly ignored the way she flinched—and guided the lanky young woman toward the refreshing room.

"Enough of that for now," he ordered gently. "Those kind of thoughts right before bed are enough to give anyone nightmares, and we'll both need a good night's sleep to be fresh minded and ready to tackle all the other problems at hand. Now get in there, wash your face, get yourself changed into your nightshirt, and get ready for bed. You can even borrow my tooth-scrubber if you like. I use a spearmint paste mixed up at one of the apothecary shops in

Heiastowne—you know the one, on the corner of Bladesmith and Seventh Lane? It's the best apothecary in town, in my opinion."

She nodded, and he patted her on her good shoulder.

"Excellent. There's also a bottle of pain drops in there from the same shop, extract of willow, clearly labeled. Take four drops for your shoulder now if you want, or in the morning if it's still bothering you. But if you take it now, use the scrubbing paste after. I find it helps kill the bitter taste. And don't worry when you come back out. Just think of me as a brother. Did you have any brothers?" he asked her as she slowed a little. "Or any sisters? Or were you an only child?"

"Two brothers. Older. A lot older." Her shoulders hunched inward. "They . . . they and our father were out of the house w-when . . ."

He swatted her on the shoulder blade, making her blink and look at him in shock. "Oy! *What* did I say, Apprentice? Stop thinking about the awful bits in life all the time. Start thinking about happy things, and about scrubbing your teeth, and worrying about nothing worse than whether or not I'll snore. I'm told if I sleep just right—on my stomach, not on my back—I don't actually, so that's how I try to sleep at night. You know, I should set you an assignment to see if I really don't snore on my belly, that's what. Go on, wash up," he ordered her, giving her a little push. "Don't take too long. And don't try to hurt me in my sleep, or I swear I'll roll onto my back and keep you awake all night by snoring."

A soft sound escaped her. Alonnen wasn't sure if it qualified as a snort or as a laugh. He took it for what it was worth—something other than fear or distrust—and nudged her the last inch or so into the refreshing room. When she was fully inside, he closed the door between them, and quietly rested his forehead on the panel.

Her mum raped and taken by the priests; family scattered who knows where or what happened to them; she's afraid of men, afraid of priests, afraid of me . . . Gods, I need him—her—*to trust me, and You dump* this *in my lap?*

Praying to all the Gods and Goddesses of the world wouldn't get him very far, though. Not even if They were gathered right now at the resumption of the old Convocations. That was on an island somewhere on the other side of the Sun's Belt, where it was summer instead of winter and where the people hadn't ever had to deal with the murderous hunger of their so-called Patron.

Maybe I should look into this Guildra person he . . . she *mentioned. Gods . . . she certainly* can *pass for a young lad when she tries. Actors Guild, journeyman rank. Yeah, I can see how she earned* that *one, with who knows how many years of pretending to be a boy under her belt.* Pushing away from the door, he crossed to the bed, rapped the control rune for the small crystal mounted on the headboard, then turned off the ceiling-embedded suncrystals. Retreating back to the bed, he picked up the book he had left there the previous night, selected the far side, and climbed under the covers.

It took her several minutes to emerge. When she finally did, he tried his best to ignore how the light from the refreshing room crystals backlit her figure. She looked around the room, then headed warily for the bed. Alonnen did his best to ignore her, save that she just stood there for a long while. Giving up, he sighed and tucked a ribbon between the pages to mark his place.

Instead of putting the book on the nightstand, though, he held it out to her. "Here. It's a book of tales about Painted Warriors. Don't budge my ribbon, please, but you can read as much of it as you like. The runes for the reading light are on the bedposts, there and there," he added, gesturing over either shoulder. "And don't hit me with it if I snore; that'd be too cruel to the book. Goodnight, Longshanks, and sleep well when you get there."

With that, he twisted over, tucked one arm under the small mound of pillows, squirmed to get comfortable, and closed his eyes with a sigh. Several more seconds passed, then he felt her tentatively drawing back the covers. Determined to go to sleep, he focused on first tensing, then relaxing each muscle group. The only way to get her past her understandable fear of men was to be as matter-of-fact as possible. When she finally climbed onto the bed and slowly started turning the pages of the book, he relaxed further, until sleep finally claimed him.

Rexei woke abruptly. Her neck and shoulders ached, and there was a bruise on the side of her breast. It came from the corner of a book, she realized. Blinking, she tried to make sense of where she was. The bedding was far too soft and warm to be her bolt-hole in Heias-towne. The dove gray coverlet topping the layers keeping her toasty and comfortable was vaguely familiar for a moment, then it all came back in a rush: the temple, the mages, the dissolution of Mekha, the freeing of the prisoners, her uncomfortable interrogation by the Precinct leftenant, and the innermost depths of the Vortex.

And Alonnen. Her first post-awake memory of him was the full-on view of his unclothed frontside . . . and the feeling that had lain *beneath* her shocked fear at the sight of her host's naked male body. Beneath the panic . . . *beneath* it, lay that same strange spurt of excitement from the first time he had grinned at her. Heart beating erratically, Rexei lifted her head to look at the other side of the bed.

The only sign he had been there at all was the divot in the feather-stuffed mattress and the rumpled lay of the covers, which he had apparently dragged more or less back into place while she slept. She was still clad in his nightshirt and her underdrawers, her chest wrappings were somewhere in the refreshing room, and aside from the awkward, curled-over angle at which she had slept and the book she had slept on, she felt just fine. Unviolated. Not that he'd . . . or that she'd . . .

Blushing, she admitted to herself that there had been more reasons than the fact she'd been tired to have impelled her into crawling into this bed. She was wary of men—rightfully so, given the things she had heard and seen—but Rexei knew that not *all* men were horrible, brutal creatures who abused authority and were driven by uncaring lusts. In fact, there were plenty of men who were good souls, kind and considerate, polite and proper.

Alonnen Tallnose might be a bit . . . casual . . . about his nudity and relaxed about his body in the presence of what he had thought was a fellow man, but at her confession, he had covered up quickly enough. And he had *continued* to treat her presence in his bedchamber as if she were still Rexei the "lad," with no difference toward Rexei the "lass" aside from the quick donning of his nightshirt.

Once she got over her shock and realized he was honestly trying to go to sleep, she had thought it safe enough to climb into the bed. That was one reason right there. And he had proved himself a gentleman. Another reason was the fact that the longer she had stood there in the borrowed nightshift, the colder the room had grown, making the thick bedding look inviting. It certainly felt deliciously warm and soft this morning, even if a stripe of her back felt cold and a little stiff from having been exposed above the covers in her curled-over position. Wiggling onto her back, she pulled the covers up to her chin and blushed again.

And the third reason—fourth, if you count how tired I was—that I crawled in here . . . was because I wanted to sleep next to him. It . . . it doesn't make me wanton or whatever, she asserted in her mind. *It makes me human. He's so* different *from most men I know. Very open and very accepting. Very friendly and welcoming. Yes, he wants something from me, but it's nothing I'd refuse to give to anyone in this situation, man or woman.*

But she didn't want to think about Netherhells and priests summoning demons. Snuggling under the covers, she let herself inhale the slightly musky smell clinging to the blankets and sheets. The scent of a fully grown male, but not the sort of stench she associated with rancid, stale sweat. Some of the men she had worked alongside had reeked of the stuff—during her brief stint in the Coalminers Guild in particular. No, the head of the Mages Guild was a man who bathed regularly but without drowning himself in perfumes or heavily scented soft soaps.

Rexei knew she couldn't lie abed forever, though. Her stomach insisted it was hungry. Adjusting the pillows, she scooted up against the headboard for support and surveyed the room.

The rest of the room, like the bed, was empty. It was lit by the suncrystals overhead . . . and by the headboard crystal, which she had forgotten to douse before falling asleep last night. At the foot of the bed, on top of the bench-chest, she could see her pack and a stack made from the clothes she had stuffed into it. The sight of a scrap of paper intrigued her enough to abandon the warmth of blankets and quilt.

Tapping the rune to shut off the headboard light, Rexei struggled out of the overly soft bed. Belatedly, she remembered to rescue the book and set it on the nightstand. Moving to the foot of the bed, she saw how neatly everything had been folded and that the scrap of paper held a list. On it was a neat accounting of every last item she owned, including all the spare Guild medallions from her earlier days, and a list of the food she had brought, with the beans and the oats counted by volume, the wheel of cheese by weight, and even the cloth-wrapped bread and sausage, which had apparently been rescued from her summer-weight coat, mentioned at the bottom of the page. But she didn't *see* her food.

What she did see was an extra stack of clothes. She started to set the note aside and realized more had been written on the back. Turning it over, she read the star-tagged notation that her food had been added to the kitchen stores of the inner circle. The rest of the note listed a sweater, undershirt, undertrews, socks, and sheepskin-lined house shoes, which were the extra garments stacked on the bench-like chest. All of that was in one set of handwriting.

A separate hand had scribed a message in tiny, neat writing on the rest of the page. Referencing the starred line above, it clarified that note.

It's an inner circle policy to share food supplies; food is something that can spoil if left alone too long, so it's better to eat now and make it up later in meal-size equivalencies. The clothes are on loan while you're here. You can trade for others to wear, or even buy them outright at fair prices in either labor or coin if you like a particular garment. If you would rather wear a skirt, the person to see about it is Master Tarani Redgriddle, the housekeeper, same for buying clothes or eventually arranging replacement meals for the amount you brought here.

Depending on when you wake up, there might be breakfast, or there might be leftovers of breakfast. When you've eaten, come up to the top floor and knock on my office door. It may take me a few minutes to respond, but don't worry, I will. Do Not Enter without my opening the door first, or you'll literally never see me.

Your task for the day, O Apprentice of the Guild, is to finish writing up your detailed report on the doings in the Heiastowne temple. That and to relax. You're safe here. Feel free to bring up the book.

~Alonnen

There. That right there. That was what he did to her. Touched her somehow with his openness, his honesty, his warm welcome coupled with his pragmatism. She barely knew the man, but she knew that as the head of the Mages Guild he surely could display the greatest of guile in protecting the men and women and even the children of the mages in his care. Yet he clearly didn't feel the need to exercise any guile with her, and had instead spent some of his time in explaining things instead of dissembling or offering a lie.

It wasn't a tender love note of the sort she vaguely recalled from her childhood. Her father had sent them to her mother when his expertise at repairing wagons and wains on the roads they broke down upon had kept him traveling around the countryside. Sometimes there would be a flower carefully pressed and folded into the letter, sometimes a bit of colorful ribbon, but always there were loving words. This note wasn't anything like that—pragmatic, not passionate—but it touched her anyway that he would take the time to explain these things to her.

The warmth engendered by that thought, by that courtesy, warred with her deeply ingrained wariness. His brother Rogen, the leftenant for the Precinct, had made her feel afraid and wary; how odd that Alonnen could make her feel welcomed, even able to relax in spite of her fears. At least, a little.

She needed the refreshing room before breakfast, and with clean borrowed clothes at hand and with the bathing room specifically mentioned last night . . . she wanted a bath. Her tenement didn't have bathing rooms, just refreshing rooms, and it cost to use the public baths. Rexei had money scattered across various guild accounts, but since she was in Heiastowne pretending to be a Servers apprentice, that meant either dipping into her savings or only being able to afford baths once a week.

Back before her world had fallen apart, her family had lived in a house with its very own indoor pump and boiling tank. Baths had to be taken in the kitchen since that was where the plumbing was, but at least the water had been plentiful and hot. After things fell apart, years of being on the run had given her an appreciation for being clean whenever possible. The trick had been finding a moment of complete privacy in which she could be safe.

Scooping up the stack of clean clothes, she added a roll of bandaging from her belongings and headed for the bathing room. After she bathed, she would rewrap her breasts and hope he hadn't told . . . there was a note in the bathing room, too. Folded in half and propped up as a tent, it explained in the Guild Master's neat handwriting how to use the spigots to control the flow of hot and cold water, which were powered by magic instead of the more normal boiling-tank method.

He had taken the time to do this, too. For a moment, Rexei smiled, touched by his helpfulness. Then she frowned in worry. *Is he being nice because he actually* is *nice? Or is this Alonnen Tallnose trying to sweeten me for some purpose? I mean solely for some use he wants out of me. It's obvious he wants something; he wants me to tell him everything I know of what happened in the Heiastowne temple. But is he also being nice because . . . he is nice?*

. . . He doesn't feel slimy to my inner instincts. Too many men and women had, in her past. More men than women, but enough of each to have made her leave twenty-five or so guilds. Like the women in the Actors Guild who had insisted that "the lad" that was Rexei was "horribly shy" and "just needed to be taken in hand." In one case, literally; the woman had tried to shove her hand down Rexei's pants in an effort to grope "his" groin. Everyone knew that women were preyed upon by the priesthood—and certain unscrupulous men in other professions—but it had been a shock to realize that some women were willing to force themselves onto men even in the face of the "young lad" protesting vigorously against the idea.

That had been one of a dozen cases where Rexei had been forced to sleep-spell her attacker. Most had been men. Most had a *feel* to them, what she had come to think of as an aura of intent, that was just wrong. It wasn't always noticeable, particularly when the person was just . . . *being* a person . . . but when they started to plot, to indulge in evil thoughts . . . Reading another mortal's thoughts was impossible, but these were feelings. Intentions, in the sense of the direction of one's focus. The longer she stayed around certain people, the more she could sense it.

Bishop Hansu, oh yes. Bishop Koler, yes. Elcarei, the Archbishop of Heiastowne, yes as well. All in varying degrees from each other, and from the other bishops, priests, and novices of the temple. She had known and worked among them for two months. She wasn't completely sure about that foreign mage, but his words, his suggestions had sounded flat-out wrong, in the sense that they felt wrong in his intentions, however truthful his words.

Alonnen Tallnose had none of that sense about him. In fact, he felt like . . . Rexei blushed. *He feels like that bed behind me. Big and soft and warm, yet fully supportive. A refuge . . . if I can only bring myself to relax fully into it.* She smiled wryly to herself and set her stack of loaned clothing on the small side table in the bathing room. *Instead of staying up stiffly for half the night, reading until I was too tired to do anything but sleep.*

She might not be able to bring herself to fully trust him just yet, but her instincts had kept her alive so far. With Mekha gone, it just might be time for her to start trusting someone, somewhere. *Might as well be here, right? I guess. . . . I mean, if I can't be safe in the midst of the Mages Guild, where can I be safe?*

With a deep breath, she set her mind on the task of trying to trust the men and women around her. It felt weird and awkward. *Too many years of being on my own. But they're under the same threat. We all have a common cause . . . and Alonnen is right*, she thought, blushing a little when her mind strayed in his direction. *We* need *a place where we can accept who and what we are, a safe place to be ourselves.*

To be myself.
A very odd thought, but not an unwelcome one.

If Alonnen had to keep expanding their available rooms like this, no one would be safe in the Mages Guild. The Vortex could only cover and cloak its existence so much. So wide, so high, so deep. Reports were coming in by talker-box from all over the kingdom of the disappearance of Mekha's symbols, of some of the temples disgorging all their mages, of other temples trying to deny their captives' existences . . . and of rioting in certain towns and cities.

Not in Heiastowne, thankfully. Captain Eron Torhammer and his second-in-command, Leftenant Rogen Tallnose, enforced the local laws ruthlessly, even when it meant going against the whims of the priesthood. But those other towns where the mages had been released, those in the know wanted to send them all to the Vortex, "just in case" this was a ruse by Mekha or by the priests. Even warned by Guardian Dominor that the incipient kingdom of Nightfall intended to try to resurrect the long-lost Convocation of Gods and Man, the actual Convocation had happened too quickly for Alonnen to prepare anyone outside the innermost circle of the Mages Guild . . . which included his brother, even though Rogen was no mage himself.

So Heiastowne was more or less prepared to quell rioting. The region was not, however, prepared to house thousands of spellshocked, traumatized mages, many of whom were terrified of being recaptured and drained by the priesthood. Many more were physically damaged, or worse, violated. Not just the women had been raped and bred with bastard children, but some of the men bore signs of being abused by the priests, too.

The Mages Guild didn't have the rooms to house them, they didn't have the food to feed them or the clothes to give them, and they definitely did not have the ability to counsel and help hundreds of mages rebuild their shattered, emptied lives.

When the coded messages came through that shipments of certain vintages of "wine and dried fruits" were being sent toward the Heias region, Alonnen gave up trying to reshape more of the bedrock under the hills flanking the reservoir. *Heias cannot house, feed, clothe, and care for them all. I will not be responsible for something that would completely beggar our resources "just because" the Vortex has a tradition of trying to keep mages safe from the priesthood.*

We literally cannot keep them fed, housed, and all the rest, and so I will not take the blame for it. Swimming out of the Vortex—an odd, dry sort of swimming—he breached the gel-like barrier keeping the water back from the living spaces, dropped lightly onto the balcony, and ducked into his office.

Gabria Springreaver was manning his desk, trying to coordinate in code the shipment of all those mages to the Heias Dam. In the depths of winter, no less. The ash-blonde woman gave him a grateful look when he finished sliding the huge glass pane back into place, sealing off the faint chill of the Vortex chamber from the warmth of his magestove-heated study.

"*Please* tell me you've made eight hundred rooms?" she begged.

Alonnen choked, checking his stride. "Eight *hundred?*"

"Well, at the moment, it's only four hundred and . . . thirty-six more of . . . well, our kind," she admitted, consulting her notes. The talker-box, a thing of brass and wood and steel mesh, squawked, but no one actually spoke through it. Someone had probably hit the receiver-cone that picked up sounds for transmission. Springreaver shrugged when it made no further demands on her. "There's even that Healer-mage fellow from outkingdom staying in the outermost circle. He's making himself very popular by tending to all the traumatized mages."

"I'm glad he's making himself useful," Alonnen allowed.

"Yes, but it's barely an hour past breakfast, and only a handful of cities have relayed their requests. There's bound to be more. Many more, Master Tall. If we can cram four and five to a room, or even sleep them in shifts, eight hundred *might* be enough . . ."

"*Enough?* No. *I've* had enough, that's what." He started to say more, but someone rapped on the door.

Crossing to it, he pressed his palm to the metal plate above the handle. A section of the door turned transparent, like a window. Rexei Longshanks stood there, clad in the fresh clothes he had brought into his bedroom from his sitting room this morning, but still looking more male than female. Opening the door, he gestured her inside.

"In you get," he ordered. She stepped inside, lean and lanky and looking like a nervous young man not yet old enough to shave. Her brown eyes widened when they alighted on Gabria's face at his desk. About to introduce them, Alonnen hesitated, then leaned in close and whispered, "Which would you prefer to be introduced as, a lad all the time, or a lass while you're here and a young man while you're out beyond the dam?"

She blinked and gave him a startled look. Cheeks warming to a charming shade of pink, she ducked her head a little. "I . . . don't know?"

He patted one of the arms holding his book of tales to her chest. "It's okay. We have lots of girls running around with boy names and boy clothes, but they are safe here, and they know it. Nobody's going to blink if you announce three weeks from now that you're not actually a lad . . . and a few will guess it outright, but they won't tell. Come on, I'll introduce you." Nudging her inside, he shut the door and led Rexei over to his desk. "Gabria, this is Rexei Longshanks. Rexei, Gabria Springreaver. Longshanks is a journeyman in the Gearmen's Guild. Springreaver is a master in the Guild Which Is Usually Not Named . . . but which is giving me a bloody headache this morning."

Gabria smiled shyly. "Hello. I think I've heard of you. Something about a . . . melody-chant . . . to hide energy traces?"

Rexei . . . acted like a boy, the kind who was mildly interested in Springreaver as a person but not as a potential flirtation candidate. She looked over the other woman, who was clad in felted gray trousers, a cream and gray knitted sweater—without any breast bindings—and a couple of long pins skewering her golden curls in a knot at the back of her head. Rexei then shrugged diffidently and dipped her own dark, short-haired head. "Yeah. Just something my mum taught me."

"Well, the more you can teach the trick of it to, the more we'll all be grateful," Gabria said, and gave Longshanks a warm smile.

Alonnen felt odd. That half-shy smile was almost flirtatious. Not quite, but it irritated him to think of one of his assistants flirting with the lad . . . who was a lass. The talker-box squawked again. Shaking the feeling off, Alonnen focused on what his guild needed and not on what he was feeling. "Right. Call them all back and cancel the shipments."

Gabria blinked, shocked. "What?"

"We're not taking them."

"But, sir . . ." she tried to protest, flabbergasted.

"We are not taking them in, because we *cannot* take them in. It doesn't matter if I craft eight hundred rooms or eight thousand, Springreaver," Alonnen told her. "We cannot *feed* four hundred, never mind eight hundred or eight thousand, we cannot *clothe* them, and we cannot *tend* to them. Particularly as most will be suffering from various physical, mental, and emotional traumas. A few, we can manage, but not hundreds and thousands.

"Not to mention it's bloody winter. Nobody travels far in winter. If everyone tried to ship them all here, even if they *didn't* freeze to death in transit—which is a chance I'm not willing to take—the priests would know *exactly* where they're headed, and come looking for the Vortex. Two or eight or twenty, we can hide—barely for the latter—but four hundred we cannot, and I *will not* compromise the safety of this place."

Longshanks looked between the two and lifted her chin, looking less like a callow youth and more like a young but mature man. Or a young but mature woman. "He's right," she stated, her low voice somewhere between a tenor and contralto. "There's not much travel in winter. Even the Messenger Guild doesn't go far from a particular town in deep winter, unless it's truly urgent."

"Well, they can't keep the . . . ah, victims . . . where they are," Gabria argued.

"Why not?" Rexei challenged her. "Every single one of those victims came from a guild, or was the child of a guildmember, and it is *that* guild's responsibility to help care for its members and their immediate family members when they are injured beyond their capacity to contribute. That's *why* everyone pays guild dues in the first place. Just because most of these guildmembers haven't been free in years is no excuse for their parent guilds to shirk their oathbound duty to those members."

Her words triggered a memory. Alonnen hurried over to one of the cabinets and started rummaging through it. "If I remember correctly . . . the agreement one of my predecessors . . . no, not this cupboard . . . The agreement one of my predecessors wrested out of the other guilds . . . no, no . . . ah, *this* cabinet . . . was to send a tithe of goods, foods, and coins to *this* Guild in exchange for taking in their mage-born members. And in exchange, we would train them to hide their powers and . . . here it is! It's getting old. We'll have to make a copy of it . . ."

"Train them to hide their powers, and . . . ?" Rexei asked, curiosity in her searching gaze. Both she and Gabria watched Alonnen unroll the parchment farther, crinkling the material as he searched for the exact words he wanted.

"And how to help shelter and protect the others . . . within their original guilds. There! Right there, inked and ratified by a quorum of Guild Masters," he stated, tapping the middle of the scroll he had found and untied. "The assertion that . . . 'the parent guilds shall *remain* responsible for the upkeep of their mage-empowered members.' Right there, plain as can be. Just as a Gearman receives both an income from his current or highest-ranked guild *and* a stipend from the Consulate to which he or she is currently attached, so shall mages be granted all the rights, responsibilities, and privileges due to them by their original guilds as well as this one. Only even more so, as the Consulates do receive a tithe from all guilds within a given jurisdiction, because they act openly, but the Mages Guild *cannot* be acknowledged openly, so the other guilds must take up the slack.

"At least, until now," he said. "Relax, I am *not* going to make the decision to expose ourselves anytime soon," Alonnen added firmly as both Gabria and Rexei flinched. "Gabria, get on the talker-box to everyone and send out a message to hold those shipments in each town for now and to watch over them carefully. Phrase it, oh . . . that they are to be tended carefully so that they'll be in excellent shape for *later* transport at some point after winter has ended. Emphasize that we have *no room* available to store any such shipments, and that they are *required* by guild charter to hold on to and care for that cargo until we send for it."

"And if they ask when, exactly, the 'items' in question can be shipped?" Gabria asked him.

"Stall," he ordered her flatly. "Don't give any exact dates, just point out that shipping anything in the depths of winter has too many hazards at this point in time."

"Don't forget to emphasize how awful early spring weather is, too—wet and cold, with threats of sudden ice storms," Longshanks offered. "Plus muddy conditions if the local Roadworks Guild hasn't been keeping up with repairs, the constant threat of floods . . . all manner of troubles. The only really good season for traveling is summer, and even then, broiling heat and thunderstorms are always a hazard."

Springreaver blinked, then nodded. "Right. I can do that. Thank you for the ideas, Miss Longshanks."

Rexei started and blinked. She looked between Alonnen and the other young woman, visibly taken aback.

Gabria had the grace to blush. Ducking her head, she apologized. "Sorry. I'm used to spotting all the females running around in male clothes. This is the one place where we're safe to *be* females. I don't wear skirts often, but I like to wear them here, sometimes."

"I told you, Longshanks, we have a *lot* of women who try to hide their gender in this guild. Speaking of which," Alonnen added, snapping his fingers and pointing at his assistant, "Springreaver, have you got room for one more in your quarters here? Longshanks could use a spot."

The blonde shook her head. "Sorry. In fact, it's now crammed with seven others, and we're all now on rotation for sharing the bed and the couch. We had forty more from the local lot show up this morning. If you didn't need me in here and if I hadn't already given up my middle-circle quarters, I'd be headed back to the *un*shielded Hydraulics tenements on the north shore. They're probably being filled up, though."

Sighing heavily, Alonnen rubbed the bridge of his nose. "Gods . . . I may have to have you do that anyway. Right. *First* thing, Miss Springreaver, is to get on the talker-box to the Consulate in Heiastowne. Tell them there's going to be an emergency meeting of *all* Heias Guild representatives this evening at sundown. Consuls, Sub-Consuls, grandmasters, and whatever Guild Masters can show up at the Consulate Hall from our nearest neighbors. There are a lot of them around, the Gods know . . .

"Then—politely—request Captain Torhammer to loan us his leftenant as well, since what will be discussed involves the governance of Heiastowne in the wake of the dissolution of Mekha, so-called God of Engineering and *false* Patron of Mekhana."

"I'll pass it along through my friend Marta, sir," Gabria agreed.

Alonnen looked around, but there weren't any actual seats in his office, other than the one Springreaver was currently occupying. He folded his arms across his chest and muttered a curse. Gabria blinked, but Rexei took it in stride. He shrugged and gestured at the chamber. "*This* place isn't exactly set up to be the heart of a new government . . . and it *cannot* become the new heart. But we *are* going to remind all the other guilds that we do still have a government of sorts. And now that the priesthood isn't being backed by the power of an unholy, un-dead God, we—the guilds, all of them—need to step up and take over."

He looked at Rexei, who was slowly nodding, her gaze fixed on something beyond the walls of his study. "The guilds must take the lead. They've been our strength all along."

Nodding as well, Alonnen unfolded his arm and draped one around the young woman's shoulders for a brief, comforting squeeze. As much as she needed protecting, he knew he was going to have to ask a lot of her. Alonnen had never prayed to Mekha for help—no one in the kingdom had for generations, save for the priesthood—but he did have a sense for when someone had been tapped to be an instrument of the Threefold God of Fate. "Come on, let's go back to my sitting room, since it's the only place with more than one seat and more than enough privacy to start talking about this idea you had, about a Patron Goddess of Guilds.

"At least, I *hope* it still has some privacy left," he added, guiding both of them out of his study. "For all I know, my chief housekeeper has shoved my entire family into my quarters by this point, trying to find room for everyone. If I'm not lucky, I'll not only be stuck sleeping with my younger brother and his motorhorse-loud snores, but my father and maybe an uncle or a cousin as well, all crammed into my bed—you did sleep alright, didn't you? Last I saw, you were curled up in an odd position."

She blushed but nodded. "Most of me was warm. And, um, not too uncomfortable."

"Good." He patted her on the back as they reached the fourth floor. Voices could be heard from behind the first three or four doors. "I'd take you to a workroom, but not at this time of the morning. It'll have to be my sitting room. A lot of my workrooms are being used for painstaking experimentation."

"Experimentation?" she asked.

"We sometimes get mage-tomes shipped in from outkingdom, but since we daren't get any living mages for instructors, we have to work out not only the translations for those tomes, but also what their actual meaning is. The inner circle of the Vortex is the only safe place to practice such magics openly, but they still require wardings to contain any accidental explosions or upsets in the aether." Catching a hint of wistfulness in her gaze as they passed one of those doors, Alonnen reassured her. "Don't worry; if you're going to be here for a while, you'll have a chance to enroll in classes as a student-apprentice. In we go . . . and excellent, no one is sleeping in here. Have a seat."

Briefly glancing at him, she studied the collection of leather-padded furniture, then picked an armchair. It was clear she didn't want to sit on the sofa, though Alonnen couldn't be sure if that was because it would have allowed him to sit next to her or because his brother Dolon had lain on it last night. *Either way, it doesn't matter. I'm not going to do anything that'll make her shy and bolt like a scared, half-tamed horse.*

After all, Rexei Longshanks was not the first fearful, gender-hiding apprentice to enter the Mages Guild. Alonnen was fairly confident he could win her trust, even if it had been a few years since he had last gentled and soothed a nervous apprentice. He meant what he had told his mother last night, of course; Rexei Longshanks hadn't nearly enough magic to be apprenticed directly to the Guild Master. But she was still important enough to need handling by him personally. He needed her to trust him.

That meant picking an armchair across from hers rather than the sofa. He went a step further and arranged himself with his back tucked into the corner of the chair and his leg hooked over the opposite arm. Not exactly the most Guild Master-ish of postures, but it did make her relax a bit. Bracing an elbow on the unoccupied armrest, he gestured at her.

"Tell me about this Guildra concept you have. If we're to ensure law and order remains in place across the kingdom, then we need to impose it locally and ensure it spreads. Having the *idea* of a Patron Deity is too deeply ingrained to ignore, particularly now that we have none . . . but nobody will ever want another lying, false deity like Mekha," he acknowledged. "So. How long ago did you first hear of Guildra? Or did you come up with the idea yourself?"

SIX

Still a little off-balance from that friendly hug, Rexei focused on settling her thoughts. Alonnen Tallnose was not the only person here in the heart of the Mages Guild to touch others so casually. Going downstairs to break her fast, she had seen a couple dozen late risers laughing and chatting, and yes, touching each other in friendly, companionable ways. In ways she had not seen since the destruction of her family.

She hadn't realized how much she missed such friendly closeness. It unsettled her even as she longed for it. This whole place unnerved her, even as it made her want to relax—even her habitual mental humming, protective and omnipresent, seemed quieter in the back of her mind here. The place felt warm and cozy to her inner senses. It was hard to uncurl from her protective mental huddle and accept that comfort, when she had been forced to live out in the cold and the damp for so long.

Squirming a little, Rexei slouched in her seat and considered his questions firmly, banishing all other thoughts to the back of her mind. "I came up with it myself. Mostly. I remember . . . when I was young, my father and brothers were talking about this and that, and they got onto the topic of what we'd do if we ever actually *did* get rid of the Dead God. Lundrei, that was the one . . . my eldest brother—half brother, technically—*he* said something about he'd never want another male deity.

"He said Goddesses were almost always more compassionate and caring, and less devoted to war and other violent pursuits—not that we knew for sure if this is true or not," she cautioned. "Even now, we barely have any friendly trade with the Sundarans, and the priesthood constantly comes up with blatant lies about them and everyone else just to keep the wars going on the other three fronts, against Arbra, and Aurul, and the northeastern lands.

"But that was his thought, to long for a gentler ideal to worship. And Father asked, what sort of patronage would a Goddess have of our land? So we all thought about it, and the others offered suggestions. I was a bit young, so I didn't say much, just listened. But I remembered it, and I thought about it from time to time, especially after I had to leave," she said, looking past him at one of the bookcases lining his sitting room. "I remember I was apprenticing with the Coalminers. One of the priests came to oversee the operation.

"He wanted to grope me, just because he saw a young lad with . . . with a pretty bottom." The indrawn hiss of Alonnen's breath reassured her of his sympathy. She continued, clearing her throat. "One of the master miners distracted him, while one of the visiting Carters whisked me away in a coal shipment. Got me a job with the Coopers Guild, making barrels. Just like I'd gotten a job in Brassworks after a Tanner journeyman tried the same thing— he got punished by the local grandmaster, last I heard—and how the Woodrights took me on after my first accidental . . . you know . . . thingy we shouldn't do."

"Spellcasting?" Alonnen asked her, arching one brow.

Rexei nodded. "Yeah. That. It drew attention when I was apprenticed in a Glassworks forge. That's when I realized the *guilds* had always been there for me, even as an orphan." She looked up, meeting Alonnen's gaze. "That's when—in the Coopers Guild—I realized what kind of Goddess we needed, if we could only get rid of Him. A Goddess of Guilds."

Listening to her recite her thoughts, Alonnen almost missed it. Almost, but not quite. As the Guild Master of Mages, he was constantly hyperaware of magical energies. Rexei still appeared to have none, even though he had watched through his scrying mirrors as she had demonstrated how to cast spells while cloaking the power traces. But behind her . . . something shimmered.

"I'd already played around in the Woodwrights with some carvings and drawings, a symbol of all the things I'd done. I was thinking I might go into the Engravers Guild at that point, but I ended up having to flee when my powers showed up again in the woodshop at the wrong moment, and I wound up in the Lumber Guild. I realized a Goddess would need a symbol . . . so I started working it up, perfecting it . . . and then drawing it everywhere I went. All the while thinking about what kind of deity we deserved, instead of the one we suffered."

Alonnen scratched his chin, listening to her rambling reminisces. The faint glow had eased a bit and faded once she stopped talking about the concept of a female Patron Deity. Letting his suspicions simmer in the back of his mind, he focused on her current words. He had seen the extra Guild medallions while setting out the stacks of her freshly laundered things. At the time, he had wondered how it was possible, but with just a few descriptions of her troubles, she had outlined just how one youngish person—male or female—had racked up memberships in roughly thirty guilds.

With that many guild associations under her belt and with her mind attuned to the thought *of a Goddess of Guilds . . . Gods, this young woman might actually be the focus for manifesting an actual, real, tangible Patron Deity. . . .* But he didn't say that out loud.

"I'd think that would be the most dangerous thing you've ever done, marking everywhere you went with the symbol of a new Patron," he said. She gave him a lopsided smile, one reminiscent of Gabria's friend, the one who worked as a clerk in the Precinct his brother served and who rarely smiled fully at anyone or anything. He smiled back equally wryly at Rexei. "So, what's the symbol, and how did you slip it past everyone?"

Rexei tried not to feel too much pride in her cleverness, since part of it was simply because it was a good design. "I didn't work out the final version until I was around fourteen, and by then, I was in the Tailors Guild and ended up chatting with a Brassworks master while filling an order for my master . . . and he realized I knew enough about brassworkings and glassworkings and such, he sponsored me to the local Consulate as a Gearman apprentice." She shrugged, folding her knitting-covered arms over her flat-bound chest. "When I got in, the master Gearman who approved my apprenticeship caught me doodling it one day, asked me about it, and said it was perfect."

"Oh?" Alonnen asked, raising his brows. "How so? What does it look like?"

She shrugged diffidently. "You've probably seen it by now. It's a gear-toothed wheel, but the six spokes are actually made up of three crossed tools," she explained. "A scythe, a hammer, and a paintbrush."

"Yes, I've seen it," Alonnen agreed, nodding slowly. "I remember seeing it a few years back in the Heiastowne Consulate—that was you? I thought the name of the creator was some chap named Targeter."

Rexei sighed. "That was the name I held at the time. The gear stands for our engineering knowledge, the hammer is for craftsmanship, the paintbrush for artistry, and the scythe represents our kingdom's many resources. Master Crathan said it covered all the guilds he could think of and carved a stamp of it to use on all his Consulate paperwork. I think his fellow Consuls saw it, liked it, and started using it as well. By the time I was fifteen, the Masons Guild I had joined was already carving it into the motifs for the Consulate Hall they were renovating."

"So when did you stop being Rexei Targeter?" Alonnen asked, curious. "Or did you have a different first name?"

The question roused a blush to her cheeks. Rexei shrunk down a little in the padded leather chair and tugged on her black woolen sleeves, half hiding her hands. "I had to quit the Actors Guild, so I just picked a new last name when I moved on."

As much as he wanted to respect her privacy, Alonnen could not help the rampant curiosity her shy, embarrassed shrinking evoked. "What happened that had you abandoning a guild you'd gained journey status in?"

Her face heating even more, Rexei mumbled, "Th' women wouldn't leave me 'lone."

For a moment, Alonnen frowned in puzzlement. Then his confusion lifted. "Ahh, right. Randy older actresses, younger cute lad . . . Well, you're quite good at acting. My brother would've given me a sign if he thought you were a young woman instead of a young man. He's good at figuring out that sort of thing, weeding out the women in trousers from the men he's had to conscript, but you still managed to fool him. I can see why you're a journeyman."

He fell silent, thinking. Rexei watched him rubbing at his chin. The sitting room was warm, but she still huddled a bit in her chair, feeling vulnerable instead of chilled. Finally, he sighed.

"Right, then. Can you put yourself together, mentally, so you're back as a boy again?"

She snorted at the question. "I've been a boy for longer than I've been a girl. It's always been safer."

"Well, I'd say 'you're safe now,' except you're not safe *now*, you're just safe *here*," Alonnen shot back. "But the point is, you *should* go back to the temple to ask for your coat and cap. If you were a normal sort of Server apprentice."

Rexei shuddered and shook her head. "I don't know if they were listening or not. I didn't sound like an idiot when I . . . when I stupidly confronted that crowd all but on the temple steps. And I don't *need* the coat. Not if I'm going to stay here."

"That might be so, and you're more than welcome to stay . . . but if *we*, the regular sorts, don't find a Patron Deity fast, the priesthood's going to want to fill it for us. I don't know about you, but *I* don't want whatever they come up with. Odds are, it'll be a demon in disguise, but even if it isn't, they're a group of men that have never hesitated to kidnap, torture, and do many worse things to anyone they wanted."

"You think I don't know that?" Rexei asked, challenging him.

He leveled a look at her. "I know you do. But we have two major problems on our hands. First and foremost, the threat of demon summonings. Now that Mekha is gone, we might have a chance to get some sort of scrying aids planted inside the temples, but to do *that*, we need someone to get inside with focus crystals. There are probably a dozen other things we could use, but I know how to make those. Still, to get past the outer wards, they'll have to be smuggled inside and *then* activated. That takes a mage . . . and you're the only one we've got who they won't *know* is a mage."

Every time he said the *M* word, she shivered. Rexei tried to hide it by sitting up a little more, huddling into her borrowed sweater. "You said, that *you* know how to make them. But weren't we talking last night with a bunch of powerful mages from outkingdom? I'd think they'd know tons of stuff we don't about spying and scrying."

Alonnen hadn't considered that. So used to doing things on his own, of struggling against the local ignorance of his fellow mages, plus the need to hide his actual location and the existence of the Vortex, he had not actually considered that. Blinking, he nodded slowly. "Yes . . . I suppose I could ask them. But that solves only one problem, *if* it can be solved.

"The other thing we need is to make sure the rule of law doesn't break down here in the Heias region. Those laws were decided upon by the Consulate, which means by the representatives of all the many guilds. If we can present the local guild heads with a Patron Deity they can understand, grasp, and focus upon, then we just *might* be able to get one to manifest—and what better Goddess than this Guildra you've been meditating upon?" he asked her.

Rexei wasn't too sure about the word *meditating*, but she supposed it did fit, sort of. Guildra was a concept she had clung to in the hopes that one day, someday, they could be rid of Mekha and lead far less fear-filled lives. Now that Mekha was gone . . .

"For that matter, who better to *explain* the concept of Guildra to the others than you?" Alonnen added, gesturing toward her. "You're practically Her . . . well, not a Patriarch since I don't think anyone would want a system so similar to the last one, but I'm not sure what to call the highest priestess of the new system, if not a Matriarch."

His words stirred unnerving feelings of trepidation within her. She could see his points, but Rexei wasn't so sure she wanted to follow Alonnen's suggestions to their "logical" outcome. Rexei shook her head. "Actually, if we're going to have a Patron Goddess of Guilds, Her priesthood should be arranged exactly like a regular guild. None of this 'superior to you' nonsense the old priests used, and none of their fancy titles. No one guild should be ranked higher than another."

"Rule by committee is a terrible method," Alonnen pointed out. "There is always someone who guides and rules during Consulate meetings. But I don't think the other guilds would care to always be ruled by the Guild Master of the Gearmen's Guild."

"In one of the towns where I stayed, they had three grandmasters of equal rank in the Weavers Guild," Rexei pointed out. "Each one served a term of two years. We could rotate Guild Masters that way."

"Yes, but in what order?" he challenged her. Then sighed. "I suppose we could always call a quorum vote . . . So, what, the highest clergy would be a Guild Master of . . . Priests? Of the Worship Guild? Prayerful Guild? I'm Not A Bastard Meanie Guild?" Alonnen tossed out. It pleased him to see her grin at his silly suggestions, though she did duck her head a little in the effort to hide it. "See, there? That's what we need. A fresh look at everything.

"So, Longshanks . . . will you please come with me to the Consulate meeting this evening and discuss your ideas for a new sort of Patronage with the rest? You can consider it a part of your official duties as a Gearman, and thus a Sub-Consul, a representative of Guilds that cannot make it to the meeting. Only in this case, you're representing a new sort of Guild that doesn't exist yet."

She wasn't quite swayed, but his words did make sense. "I'll think about it. And . . . I might attend the meeting. But I won't go straight to the temple. It'd be smarter to contact one of the other Servers who was working there and ask them to discreetly see if they can find out if the priests know I'm smarter than I pretended to be, while trying to fetch my coat and my cap for me."

"I suppose that could be done instead," Alonnen allowed. "The priests'll have to open up at some point for food supplies, if nothing else. As much as I'd love to get a scrying crystal in there . . . not at the risk of your life, no."

Studying him, Rexei wondered. And then she wondered if he would be offended if she asked. Since she had learned in thirty different apprenticeships that the only way to learn fast and far was to ask, she asked, "What are *you* thinking? About all of this. Mekha vanishing, the kingdom collapsing, a new God or Goddess, Guildra . . . everything."

He raised his brows at the question. Lacing his fingers over his chest, he tapped his pinkie fingers against the brushed-flannel wool of his shirt. "Quite a lot, actually. Even without the threat of demonic invasion, we'd still have to deal with the priesthood somehow. Some *might* be willing to disband and take up other livelihoods . . . but these are, one and all, boys and men who grew up understanding that the priesthood had the greatest power in the land."

"They could take anything, do anything, and they answered to no one but another priest . . . unless it was the combined weight of the guilds. But even then, not even the strongest of Consulates dared resist all that hard," Rexei agreed, letting her head drop against the padded back of the chair. "I got the lectures when I became a Gearman."

"And 'Gearman's strength shall then endow,'" Alonnen murmured, eyeing her speculatively. Her head lifted up off the chair and her brows came down in a wary frown. He flicked a hand partly in dismissal and partly in acknowledgment. "You're definitely mixed up in all this. I can see it."

Her mildly wary look shifted into a much more nervous one. "No, I'm not."

"Yes, you are," he argued lightly.

"No, I'm *not*," Rexei asserted, sitting up a little.

Re-lacing his fingers together, Alonnen shrugged. "Yes, you *are*."

"It's coincidence, nothing more," she tried to dismiss him. That only earned her a chiding look.

"We have exactly *one* kingdom between us and Fortuna, and that's not far enough away to escape the Threefold God's sight. Even nations on the *far* side of the world have heard of Fate and acknowledge Them as the oldest and strongest of all the Gods." Alonnen reminded her, "You *are* the Gearman in question."

"I'm just a journeyman!" Rexei protested, throwing up her hands as she sat forward. She dropped them onto her knees, so used to pretending to be a half-mannered youth that she didn't bother with sitting decorously. "There are hundreds of master-class Gearmen all across Mekhana. Or whatever it is we should start calling ourselves, now. Mekha was nothing more than a False God, propped in place by false priests, refusing to die even though He was struck dead with the collapse of the last Convocation two hundred years ago. I refuse to call myself a Mekhanan now that He is gone. I want nothing to do with Him, not even my nation's name."

"Well, if you believe the guilds should have a Patron Goddess named Guildra, then it only makes sense to call ourselves Guildarans or something, and thus Guildara for the kingdom," Alonnen agreed. Then pointed a finger at her. "And no getting us off the subject. You *are* the Gearman of the prophecy. Which means, if we're going to scrape together enough of what used to be Mekhana to be strong enough to stop demon-summoning priests, we'll need your promised strength."

"That's just it!" Rexei exclaimed, agitated enough to shove to her feet as she spread her arms. "I don't *have* any! Strength implies standing your ground—I *run* from confrontations! Strength is all about facing down your fears. I bolt at the first sign of trouble and pick out a new name and a new life at the drop of a knitted cap! And I'd have done it last night, if there'd been any way to avoid your brother."

Alonnen remained sprawled in his chair, but he did dip his head in acknowledgment. "That's fair. Your plethora of Guild apprenticeships are a clear sign of just how many times you've run. But Rexei, dear," he told her, giving her a pointed, level look, "you've also stood your ground."

"When?" she asked, though even as she spoke, she recalled a few times from the last full day.

"When you questioned me, for one. Admittedly, anyone who actually *knows* I'm a Guild Master wouldn't have dared contradict me or demand answers before obeying—and even now that you do know it, you're still saying *no* to me," he said a touch tartly. He softened it with a wry look. "Not that I'm going to object. It's good to hear a flat-out *No* every once in a while, and several sessions of *Why* per week, for that matter. But from the sound of it, you said you had to stop playing a dull-witted Server on the temple steps so that you could stop a riot. If you truly had no strength to stand your ground, no strength to insist that everyone hold it together and act in a lawful manner, you'd have scuttled off and fled. Right? . . . *Right?*"

Defeated by his logic, she sank back down onto her chair again, elbows braced on her knees. The position always reminded her of how tightly she bound her breasts and of the padding wrapped around her waist. It was comforting, yet restrictive at the same time. Sighing, she scrubbed her fingers through her short-cropped locks. "I don't even have the courage to say the *M* word out loud."

"Well, it's not like *I've* had a choice," Alonnen shot back. At her skeptical look, he rolled so that he slouched on his elbow and his hip instead of his back. That left him angled just enough to give her an earnest look. "I *am* the Guild Master of the Mages Guild, Rexei. I have to be able to say the *M* word, and say it so comfortably and easily that it puts other *M* types at ease," he half teased. "As the Guild Master, I cannot be afraid of who and what I am. Besides, I only ever say words like *mage* and *mages* while I'm *in* the Vortex, within its protections. I'm not a fool. Outside of the dam's vicinity, I'm just the Guild Master of the Lubrication Guild, a subset of the Hydraulics Guild. But if Mekha *is* gone . . ."

"Don't risk it," Rexei found herself ordering. He blinked at her, but she lifted her chin, standing her ground on that point. "If what *you* implied is true, that the Convocation of the Gods was indeed restarted, and that Mekha was . . . I don't know what happened . . . but one hopes by the pricking of our thumbs that He was revealed as a False God and struck down by the other Gods and Goddesses. *If* all of that, then m-mages *might* be safe," she managed to say without tripping too much on the *M* word. "But we also don't know what it takes to bind a demon, or even if they *will* bind a demon. The priests might just go back to snatching up our kind and sucking the energy out of them again, and *you'd* be the juiciest goose in the butcher's shop."

He tipped his head, acknowledging her point. "That may be an actual problem . . . and that may be why not every town with a temple in it has reported seeing its prisoners being released. I could almost wish they *would* turn to demons instead of our fellow mages . . . but Guardian Kerric of the Tower has repeatedly seen prophetic scryings of a Netherhell invasion. Demons fighting warriors and mages and everyone else." He sighed heavily, slumping a little more in his chair. "And I wouldn't wish *that* on anyone else, save that most of the visions seem to have the invasion starting from *here*."

Rexei frowned in thought. She rubbed her forehead, then stroked her palm over her short, dark locks. "That prophecy you gave me to read . . . you mentioned something last night when you handed it over about 'the others.' I presume the Guardians we spoke with think that the demonic problems will spring up in several nations?"

"This one and five more to come, yes," Alonnen said. "The first verse of one of the prophecies seems to have come true in Guardian Kerric's homeland, and we think the second was about Guardian Saleria. She's off at the Convocation of Gods and Man, though, and there's no easy way to chat with either her, Guardian Dominor, Guardian Serina, or Guardian Rydan right now. If we're the third verse, then the fourth of eight will probably be Mendhi, far to the east and south."

"Since the lines mentioned a Painted Lord, yes, that makes even a Mekhanan think of the Painted Warriors of Mendhi," Rexei agreed.

Clasping her hands between her felt-covered knees, she gave him a keen, penetrating look. "If we can send them on their way, if the prophecy is *about* sending these demon-minded priests on their way to their prophesied point of doom . . . then *how* do we go about it? What little I overheard made it sound like they come in different strengths. One mage can hold one or two minor demons, but if they summon a major demon with the aid of many priests—and they're far more trained in magics than we are—then how can *we* stop them?"

The lad—the *lass* was a lot smarter than she looked. Not just educated, but smart, able to cut to the heart of the important questions. Alonnen slipped his right leg off the armrest and pushed his body upright with his left arm. Echoing Longshanks' pose, he rested his elbows on his knees as well. "This has actually come up in some of the discussions the other Guardians and I have been holding over the last few weeks. And oddly enough, *you* just might have the best solution."

"Me?" Rexei touched her flat-bound chest, bemused by his assertion. "If this is more nonsense about me having a Gearman's strength . . ."

He shook his head. "Not that. Not exactly. There are two Guardians in the empire of Fortuna. One of them, Guardian Suela of Fortune's Nave, ransacked some of the oldest libraries outside Mendham. As did Guardian Tipa'thia of the Great Library of Mendham, in Mendhi. And her apprentice, Pelai. They both agreed that the few old records of demonic fighting included the fact that the *priesthoods* of the various afflicted lands were able to turn back the demons as surely as if they'd one and all been mages . . . only not all of them *were* mages. The records said that some quality of being a 'true priest' granted them the power, the ability, to cast demons back into the Netherhells."

She blinked and sat up. "So . . . my thoughts on Guildra, on manifesting ourselves a Patron Deity, might actually be helpful?"

"Yes. But in order to do that, we'll need to *not* be inundated with all these ex-prisoner mages," Alonnen said, sitting back. He crossed one leg over the other, resting his ankle on his knee. "We'll need order instead of chaos. We'll need organization. Because if we're *not* fighting each other, then we'll be able to concentrate as a nation—or whatever corner we can grab of it—on worshipping a manifestation of faith and belief. And I think you've hit the nail on the head squarely with the thought of a Patron of Guilds."

"The Guild System has kept the priests shut out of our lives as much as it can," she agreed. "We all believe in the guilds. But they have to step up and take responsibility for what's happening. No one group, not even the Precinct militia, can impose order on all the others. Every guild stands equal in the Consulates for the laws affects us all. One Guild, one voice, one vote. I've actually had to stand *in* for all the missing Guilds, even the ones I haven't been a member of, for those times in my Messenger days when I'd take some problem to a distant Consulate only to find I'd have to represent those who had sent me when the Consulate had to make a decision based on the information I'd brought."

"Then you'll go to the Consulate meeting tonight," he stated, not making it a question. She drew in a breath to speak, but Alonnen held up his hand. "Not to represent *this* Guild, because I'll be there . . . but because *you* need to represent the new . . . well, the new *holy* Guild that needs to be formed. If we're going to get a new Patron Deity, Longshanks, *someone* is going to have to represent the rest of us and organize our worship and . . . and figure out what sorts of ceremonies there will be, and what sorts of holy days.

"Somehow, I doubt we're going to want to keep celebrating Resurrection Day," he added tartly. "Not if the Dead God is finally *gone*."

"Well, no," she muttered, agreeing with him. "But *me*? Organize a new priesthood? The only things I know about the priesthood come from the nightmares that destroyed my family, and . . .

and what little I observed in the two months I spent spying on the current lot."

"Then you'll know what *not* to put into the new order. More importantly, Longshanks," he stressed, pointing at her, "you're a Gearman who's been at the very least an apprentice in, what, roughly thirty Guilds? I seem to remember about that many medallions among your things. I don't know of anybody who has apprenticed in more than ten."

"That's hardly a qualification, Tallnose," she shot back. "I'm a journeyman in only three of them, and no master of any."

"On the contrary, you're *still* fooling me into thinking you're a male, so you're bound to be master class in the Actors Guild by now. *And* you spent the last two months walking into and out of the Heiastowne temple under the very noses of the priesthood without getting caught," he countered. "That's worthy of a master's rank right there. I'll even put your name up for it, next time I chat with the Grand Master of Actors."

She blushed.

"Rexei, the *real* reason why you're the most qualified to set up a new Holy Guild is *because* you're proposing a Goddess of Guilds, and *you*, lad—lass," he corrected himself, "have personal, firsthand knowledge of all those Guilds. In fact, I'd suggest the first rule you draw up is that no one can *serve* in the new Holy Guild unless they're already an apprentice Gearman at the very least. Because it's a Patron Deity of the *Guilds*, plural, that we need . . . and if you can classify *any* Gearman as holy, then *any* member of the Mages Guild who has served in two other Guilds—and many of them have—can then be considered a member of the Holy Guild."

"So?" Rexei asked.

"So, coupling holy power with mage power has made all the defenders in all past accounts appear to be *three* times as effective at thwarting, banishing, and outright destroying demons as anyone else. Not just twice as effective as holy persons alone or mages alone," he said.

She blinked at him, then sighed heavily, scrubbing at her hair. "Well, I wish you'd *told* me all of this earlier."

He flung up his hands, sitting back. "I only thought of it just now! Forgive me for being mortal."

For a moment, she stared at him . . . then her mouth curved up on one side. Raising her hand, she fluttered it at him. "You're forgiven, young man. Though I'll have to figure out some sort of holy penance for you to perform later."

Chuckling, he relaxed back into his chair. It wasn't just the almost-twenty-two-year-old Rexei calling *him* a young man, when he was nine years her elder. It was the fact that she was willing to make a *joke* about being a priestly type. Shaking his head a little, he smiled at her. "You remind me of me, just now."

"I do?" Rexei asked, giving him a dubious look. "How?"

"It was back when my predecessor, Millanei Tumbledrum, picked me to be her personal apprentice. I was barely ranked a journeyman in the Guild, and I was convinced I wasn't the right person for this job," he confessed, flicking a hand in a dismissive, expressive motion. "Being Guardian, and thus Guild Master, takes a great deal of personal strength. The Vortex can *kill* a weak mage, burn them up like a leaf blown into a glassworks forge. She told me I had the power to be the next Guardian of it.

"*I* pointed out a Guardian needed a lot more experience, like a master or a grandmaster. She countered by stating yes, I was incredibly young for a journeyman mage, barely sixteen, and that I'd likely make master status long before she'd hand over the starter key for this particular motorhorse," he told her. "The same had happened with the other two candidates, Gavros and Storshei, both of them rising up the ranks quickly and early, based on their wits and their magical strengths. There are a few others who were and are strong enough magically, but she told me she picked the three of us because we could *think*, and we could *lead*.

"You can lead," he told Rexei, giving her a frank look. "And it's obvious you can think. Beyond that, what a priest needs—a real one, and not the false bastards we have here in Mekhana—is the ability to *believe*. Which you clearly do. So . . . you'll still need to write down all your observations on what you saw in the temple in the last two months, apprentice *priest*," he admonished, "but I think your biggest task, to be completed before midafternoon, is to write down and organize the rules for the Holy Guild we'll need. At the very least, you'll need something written up before we head off to Heiastowne this evening."

"I suppose you're right," she muttered, rubbing her forehead. "I left all my papers on the temple doings up in your study."

"Set it aside for now. Focus on the new guild. Start with what we're going to call it," he added. "Priesthood has a rather nasty connotation in this kingdom, so we'll want another name for it." She opened her mouth to say something, then shut it. Alonnen raised one brow. "What did you think of just now?"

"I was about to say, why call it anything when your suggestion about making Gearmen into holy guildmembers was a good one, so why not just merge the Gearmens Guild with it . . . but not all Gearmen are the sort I'd trust with something as important as worshipping a new Goddess," she told him. "Some Gearmen have been rather *priestly* in their attitudes."

"In that case, write up some sort of criteria that'll winnow out the unsuitable sorts," he told her. "You've been in enough guilds by now to surely know how to sum up the differences between, say, Silverworks and Blacksmiths?"

"Silverworks Guild crafts in silver and its related alloys, predominantly making jewelry and tableware, but also certain engineering components," she stated promptly. "Blacksmiths primarily fashions the iron and steel tools all the other trades use. And they work at least a little bit in all the various metals, doing the crafting and repair work for things that don't need a true specialist."

"So make up a list of the differences a true Priests Guild needs, and not the false crap Mekha's bootlickers have forced on us all these years," he ordered. Unfolding his limbs from his seat, Alonnen nodded at a side table beyond her. "I've paper and graphite sticks over there, so you can start writing right away. I need to get back up to Springreaver so I can make sure she's got the various Guilds alerted about the big meeting tonight, and then I might have to go yell at a few folks through another talker-box for foisting so many ex-prisoners on us, but I'll be back."

Nodding, Rexei rose as well. She had been an apprentice for too many years not to give respect to someone of master rank or higher whenever they stood to leave a table or a room. Which made her think about the kowtowing and subservient respect the False God's priesthood had demanded of all others. "I'll make sure the new Holy Guild is no more important than any other."

"And no less important," he agreed.

The chugging rumble of a motorcart engine greeted them when Alonnen, Rexei, Gabria, and four more emerged from the back of the motorhorse stalls. Motorhorses were cheaper to run, as they consumed far less of the smelly, difficult to process fuel, but when there were eight people all headed to the same place, it made sense to take a single, larger vessel.

It was just as well Tallnose had ordered the motorcart, too; the great crystals illuminating the thick curve of the Heias Dam also illuminated the tiny white specks drifting down out of the lead gray clouds overhead. While the seven of them climbed into the back and found seats on the padded benches lining the long sides

of the roof-covered motorcart, the guider quickly finished lighting
the oil lamps at the front of the vehicle, then climbed into the
guiding seat. Having rarely had the chance to ride in one of these
machines, Rexei peered over the back of his seat, watching him
crank the engine into starting.

With a shift of three levers, he released the cart brake and sent
the vehicle trundling forward. Instead of guiding posts like a
motorhorse had, sticking out and back from the mechanical beast's
neck, someone had affixed a spoked wheel with short, rounded
knobs along the outer edge. She remembered a long, long time ago
her father, Gorgas Porterhead, sketching out the steering mecha-
nism developed for horseless vessels like these.

Gorgas had told his young, wide-eyed daughter that the "steering wheel" was based on a sailing ship's wheel and that the knobs
helped the helmsman—or the guider—control the vessel with a bit
more leverage and thus without needing that much more strength
in bad conditions. She had never seen a sailing ship, however, not
unless one counted the little toy boats that were carved and set to
float on ponds with little paper sails—hardly the same thing. But
thoughts of toys led her right back to thoughts of her family.

Letting her wool-and-leather covered arm cushion her chin
from the bouncing and jouncing of the seatback, Rexei wished she
knew what had happened to her father and her brothers. *With Mekha
gone . . . if we can stop the priests from drawing upon any source of
power . . . and if we can make this land into its own kingdom, a real kingdom with a real Goddess and not a False God like Mekha was, then maybe
I can find out what happened to them. Maybe, because if the old priesthood
gets disbanded and scattered into powerlessness, then nobody will have to
fear them looking for more mages among the family of the people they've
already taken.*

Warmth leaned against her back and left side. Alonnen's voice murmured in her ear, just loud enough over the motorcart's engine to be heard. "Silver tricoin for your thoughts."

"They're not even worth a copper square," she returned, "but I was thinking of my family. Wherever they are."

She lifted her head a little so she could turn it and speak. That brushed her scarf-wrapped cheek against his. He had left off the tinted viewing glasses since night was about to fall, and that meant she could see little flecks of gold and green in his hazel eyes and the faint hints of laugh lines at their outer edges. His hair wasn't golden copper anymore; instead, he had done something, cast some sort of spell, that made his hair, even down to the brows and lashes, look a plebian shade of brown. It also made the planes of his face appear subtly different, particularly the length of his nose.

It took her a few moments of studying the differences in his face to realize she was actually comfortable with him leaning up against her, and the realization confused her.

Seeing the faint look of worry creep into her gaze, Alonnen righted himself. As he shifted, he used a one-armed hug to scoop her back against his chest and shoulder. *Somewhere along the way, this poor young lady—lad again, now that we're away from the Vortex— lost the right to hold and be held. That's too damn sad not to correct.* "Come on," he murmured. "You'll be warmer leaning against me than against a bunch of wood and metal."

Since he was right, Rexei didn't resist. She did squirm a little, getting a little more comfortable, and adjusted the lie of her messenger bag, which was doing double duty as her crocheting bag, laden with both papers and skeins of wool. A frown creased her brow when he shifted and scooped the other female, Gabria Springreaver, up against his left side. She relaxed after a moment, realizing the three men across from them on the other bench were huddling together. A glance to the front showed the fourth male was hunkering as close to the driver as possible without interfering with the other man's arms and hands.

They weren't moving fast yet, but she know that would change once they got away from the winding road on the hillside flanking the dam. When they cleared the forge buildings, the dark, damp cobblestones gave way to an icy patch that the guider drove carefully over, then that gave way to frosted white pavement. The cement-mortared road was grooved for traction even in wet or icy weather, but only if the snow remained only a few inches deep.

"Looks like the snow's going to stick," one of the men across from them muttered. "Might be smarter to head back, Tall."

Alonnen shook his head. "This meeting is too important. If things get too tough for traveling back, we'll just use the bolt-holes in Heiastowne." Next to him, Rexei snorted. The sound was almost lost under the rumbling of the motorcart picking up speed as they reached a straight stretch, but he heard it. "Something amuses you, Longshanks?"

"You're not laughing at his nickname, are you?" the other fellow asked her. His face wasn't easily seen, now that they were away from the lights around the dam and its many outbuildings, but his tone was thick with disapproval.

"What? No," Rexei denied. "Though I guess it's ironic, you calling him 'Tall' when you're a full head taller. No, I was . . . well, that's what I called my tenement in town. My 'bolt-hole,'" she explained awkwardly. "I just found it funny for a moment."

"Is it a good bolt-hole?" Alonnen asked, curious.

"On a Server's pay? Apprentice grade?" she asked, brows quirking skeptically under her borrowed felt cap. The motorcart trundled around a corner, forcing her to reach up and tug the cap farther down over her ears in the face of the increasing wind. "It's a one-room hole on the fourth floor, with an external refreshing room. The only advantage it has is that it's in the middle of a six-floor building, and that means I got shared heat from the rooms to either side, above and below. Your brother demanded that I clear out, so there's not even a set of blankets left. Coal for the hearth, yes, but nothing else to keep warm, so I hope your own 'bolt-hole' is better off than mine right now."

The three men across from her exchanged looks and chuckled. The young woman on the other side of Alonnen groaned. "Oh, gears . . . you are *not* dragging me to Big Momma's for a 'bolt-hole.' I'd rather walk all the way back through an *ice storm*."

"Big Mom . . . ? *Oh*." Clearing her throat, Rexei realized who, or rather, what the other lass referenced. Big Momma's was short for Big Momma Bertha's Brothel.

Home of the Happy Whores, she mocked silently, rolling her eyes at the establishment's motto. Posing as a young man had given her a broader education—in theory—than she probably would have learned if she'd posed as a young woman. Though at least the local Whores Guild was egalitarian in that there were rumors of male guildmembers working in Big Momma's establishment, too, not just females.

Out loud, she said, "You can always share my bolt-hole. A bucket of coal is bound to be safer for keeping warm than whatever might be offered at Big Momma's."

"It won't get that bad," Alonnen countered firmly. "At least, not down in the flats. The cloud cover isn't that thick, and it's thinning out on the trailing edge. The mountains will get the worst of it, but the guilds always clear the road up to the dam. There are too many shipments going back and forth every single day not to scrape the roads."

That made Rexei think. "Tallnose . . ."

"Yes?" he asked, holding both women a little more closely as the motorcart skidded a little on a bit of ice. *These carts need some sort of safety rope system, so we don't get flung off the benches . . .*

"The priests were the ones ordering all the fighting against our neighbors, right?" she asked, though she didn't wait for confirmation. "Even though the militia received the war machines and munitions, it was by Mekha's will that they tried attacking the borders."

"Yeah, so?"

"So . . . with Mekha gone, do the Steelworks at the Heias Dam *need* to keep producing all those parts for war machines?" she asked. "I know there's a chance the other lands will try to swoop in and claim chunks of Mekhana now that we're Patronless. But do we really want the priests *or* the militia still controlling everything?"

"Lad's got a point," one of the other two men muttered. All three on the bench across from Gabria, Alonnen, and Rexei were there to be bodyguards for the Guild Master, but they were clearly smart as well as muscled. "Leftenant's alright, but the captain's another matter. The Hammer of Heiastowne is strict when it comes to upholding the law, but what if he gets it into his head to *make* the laws? I heard the leftenant declared anyone making trouble would be dragged off to the quarries."

"That's just a rumor," the third man stated.

Rexei shook her head. "No, that's what he threatened. I was there. Captain's orders, a month's work per hour's trouble."

"That's exactly why we need to have all the guild heads meet at the Consulate," Alonnen asserted. "Up until yesterday, Mekha demanded, the priests ordered, the militia enforced, and we all had to obey. But not anymore."

He poked out his thumb sideways. So did the others, though Rexei was the last to move; since the thumb he poked out was the left one, it meant Springreaver's cap-covered head hid the initial action from her view. Alonnen gave her far arm a little squeeze with his free hand.

"That does not mean, however, that we're going to let lawlessness take its place," Alonnen cautioned them. "That's what this meeting is for."

A gust of wind swirled around the side of the trundling motor-cart, sending more snowflakes in through the open sides of the driver's bench and a few in through the open back. The very front had an angled glass wall shielding the guider and his passengers from most of the wind, and a pair of clever sweepers that scraped the snow from the panes when a lever was pulled, and the sidewalls of the cargo section had glazed walls, too, but not the doorways by the front bench nor the very back of the vessel. Alonnen grimaced and shifted his right hand off Rexei's shoulder, swiping at some of the crystals as they smacked into his face and tried to melt on his cheek.

Tugging his scarf a little higher, he switched topics. "We need to start talking with the Caravaners about making these motor-carts more weatherproof. Motorhorses, I can see why they can't be fully enclosed, but these things could be. And should be."

From the enthusiastic nods of the others as they huddled together for warmth against the swirling snow and wind, they agreed.

SEVEN

Torven Shel Von wished he had not been seated at the arch-bishop's right hand. The dining hall had two hearths, one at each end of the long table and both with warm-glowing coals doing their best to heat the space, but there was a draft at his back that pushed half the heat away. At least the food was reasonably good and the wine not bad, if well watered. Allowing mages to get ine-briated was rarely wise.

Still, it was better than the fare found in most inns and taverns, thanks to one of the priests who actively enjoyed cooking. The apprentices roped into assisting him had grumbled, but with all the servants kicked out, no one of lower status had been left to help in the temple kitchen. Torven found it amusing that the apprentices who had complained the most were the ones being fed the thick glop, half stew and half porridge, which had been earmarked for the former prisoners.

He reached for the thigh of the roasted pheasant quarter he had been given for a third course, ready to remove the tender meat. The conversations around him revolved around his lengthy lessons in the exact wording needed for oathbinding demons into obedience. From the gossip, Torven had proved to be a fair, if stern teacher. A few of the novices had ended up with reddened hands from being slapped for their poorly presented oaths, but the elder priests hadn't objected to his use of an Aian-style ruler smacking. Plucking at a bit of still juicy meat, he wondered if he'd been too light on them. Demons rarely played fair with honest mistakes.

The murmur of voices fell quiet at the far end. Into the hall strode the bald priest who had first questioned him, Bishop Hansu. His lips, framed by his long, neatly groomed, dark brown beard, were pulled down in a frown. So were his matching gray-salted brows.

Archbishop Elcarei lifted his own brows. "You have news, Bishop Hansu?"

"Yes, archbishop." He paused at the midway point and bowed. "The Patriarch and over half the priesthoods have voted against our guest's proposal." A slight, ironic dip of his head was aimed at Torven, then he continued. "But six of the nearest ten temples have *agreed* to it. Provided our guest can *prove* his method works, and works safely . . . then they will be with us.

"On another, somewhat related topic . . . from the state of chaos in many of the cities out there, it was strongly urged by our counterparts in the other temples that we get this city under control. Given what the talker-boxes picked up and the fact that it is now sunset," Hansu continued, "I strongly suggest you select someone to go to the Consulate, Holiness."

"Yes, we should remind them that we are the highest-ranked Guild in the land, and thus have a very strong say in the governing of it," Elcarei agreed. He narrowed his eyes thoughtfully. "You said the other towns are rioting?"

Hansu nodded. "Not every temple has reported in via scrying

mirror. It is presumed that, by now, they have been overrun by the local peasants—many of those are the ones that did *not* release their prisoners. Most of those temples which followed our guest's advice have been spared. Not all, but most."

"Thankfully, Captain Torhammer is a stickler for the law. This will work in our favor." At a gesture from the archbishop, Hansu took the remaining empty seat and began dining on the food left around his plate. "I shall go myself in a moment, with a bishop and two priests. Koler, you have served well in our dealings with the Consulate; you shall come with us. Brother Grell and Brother Tanik, you will join us as well."

The three selected priests bowed their heads. Elcarei looked to his right, meeting Torven's mildly bored gaze. "Under Bishop Hansu's supervision, you shall direct the novices to clear the power room of rubble and set it up for a series of test summonings. You will start with one minor demon, demonstrating that you can summon, control, and banish it, then progress to more powerful kinds.

"You may have the assistance of up to three priests and six novices but no more . . . and the *first* thing you shall do once the room is readied is teach everyone here the proper banishment spells, before actually summoning anything."

Torven dipped his head. "I was going to suggest something similar myself, Your Holiness. I am pleased we are so well matched in our thinking."

His flattery was even true, save that Torven had no intention of remaining subservient for long. Banishing a demon was not a problem; even if an enemy banished one, unless that enemy were a higher-ranked priest, the demon could always be resummoned. No, *binding* the demon was where all the true power lay, and he intended to bind the demons summoned to himself as their ultimate master.

"Save dessert for us," Elcarei stated, rising from his seat. "We may be back late."

Everyone else rose as well out of courtesy, giving the archbishop a bow of reverence. Even Torven, though his was not quite as deep. He would not upset this chance at securing a vast power for himself, but neither would he play the bootlicking toad to get it. *They will acknowledge me as an equal, or they will find out the hard way that I am their better.*

Thankfully, the Consulate was warm. Not only had the message for the meeting gone out in plenty of time to stoke the fires, taking the chill out of the air, Heiastowne itself was large enough that there was a permanent Consulate staff. It wasn't the biggest city in Mekhana, but it was in the top ten easily, with many strong guilds and a handful of actual Guild Masters in the Precinct, not just grandmasters or mere masters.

At Alonnen's urging, Rexei had brought all thirty of her Guild tokens, all strung on her silver chain. The other Gearmen of the Consulate had duly examined those thirty, including her trio of larger journeyman-rank medallions, the fourth one that represented her Gearman status—always left uncounted when tallying ranks—and permitted her a seat on the guild bench. Off to one side, of course; she was from out of town as far as they knew, which meant she had the right to speak only for those guilds not represented here in Heias Precinct, or at least not at this meeting.

The discussion hall was packed. All three fireplaces were roaring with the crisp, competing scents of coal, applewood, and oakwood. Even without the fires, she probably would have been warm enough to remove her Vortex-borrowed coat, though she was glad that her current project, a fine, silvery gray wool suitable for summer weight, was now big enough to cover her thighs. She wasn't the only one, male or female, with a bag or basket of skeins and some sort of needlework in their lap. Looms were taxed for whatever they produced; knitting and crocheting were not.

Sharing the guild bench—which in a Consulate of this size was a long, curved table set with several high-backed chairs—were the Grandmaster Gearman of the Heiastowne Consulate, his three master Gearmen scattered at the quarter points, and Rexei at the far left end. Next to the grandmaster sat the Captain of Heias Precinct. Chairs had been brought in and crowded around the table until one could scarcely move to get up, even by pushing a chair straight back from the table a body length. Rexei herself sat on a footstool dragged in from somewhere else, and she had only been accorded room because she could speak for those outside the immediate region.

The rest of those seats were filled with the Guild Masters of several guilds: Masons, Coalminers, Lumber, Ironworks, Steelworks, Hydraulics, Brassworks, Clockworks, Engines, Modellers, Munitions, Plumbers, Wheelwrights, and Luthiers, specifically those woodworkers and metalsmiths who specialized in making musical instruments. And, of course, Alonnen, representing the one Guild no one wanted to actually name. The grandmasters of the many other guilds were given preferential seating in the first three rows of pews facing the long, curved table, and the masters of those guilds with no one of higher rank in the area were right behind them.

Everyone else crowding the place was a nonrepresenting master, a journeyman, or a few rare apprentices of the various guilds— mostly from the Servers and the Hospitallers, distributing warmed drinks and small sweet biscuits. Such offerings were not uncommon; each time a Consulate gathering was held, a trio of Guilds was taxed to pay for refreshments.

A fresh cluster of people arrived. Two women detached themselves from the rest and were greeted by Grandmaster Toric. Rexei couldn't quite hear their titles over the general hubbub of the three or four hundred people crammed into the pews lining the rest of the hall, but she thought she heard the words *Actors* and *Lacemakers*.

Alonnen—who had donned a pair of blue-tinted viewing lenses once he had arrived—rose and hurried over to the side of the plumper of the two women, who was clad in a colorful knitted overdress patterned in shades of cream, beige, and russet from wool raised in the northernmost flocks. Nestled on her ample cleavage was the large oval gold-cast medallion of a Guild Master. From the masques engraved on it for its guild symbol, the woman had to be the head of all the Actors Guilds across Mekhana.

Rexei had never met her, but she had heard of Guild Master Saranei Grenfallow, one of the few female Guild Masters who was respected by the priesthood; she was that good an actor. Or had been before taking up the Guild Master's job. From what Rexei had observed in her many apprenticeships, it was difficult to lead a guild even as a mere grandmaster, never mind as the Guild Master for all the various chapters across the kingdom.

In contrast to all the Guild Masters who wore their palm-sized oval medallions with their symbols on both sides, Alonnen wore a large gold medallion that had been left polished but otherwise blank on the side currently facing outward. Rexei had seen the other face of it when he had taken off his coat upon their arrival; that side had been engraved with a striated triangle, with its point down. Only because she had *seen* the Vortex itself did she know what it represented, for it was not in the list of symbols Gearmen apprentices were supposed to memorize. Reassured by the sight of it that he *was* the Guild Master of Mages, she still marveled that he would actually dare to wear it in public, even with Mekha gone. *The man has far more bravery than me . . .*

While she watched and plied her hook, tugging out lengths of silvery spun wool every so often, the two Guild Masters engaged in an increasingly animated discussion. Then Guild Master Grenfallow turned and clapped her hands, gathering her entourage to her. More discussion followed. The grandmaster of the Servers Guild was called up from one of the front benches, and the matter, whatever it was, was discussed further.

Rexei didn't know and wasn't sure she wanted to know. As it was, she knew Alonnen intended to call upon her to discuss Guildra as their next Patron Deity and the formation of a new priesthood. It was taking most of her concentration to keep her crocheting stitches even, rather than small and tight with tension. Every few lengths, she looked up to gauge the mood of the room and the mood of the Guild Masters in particular, some of whom had been summoned from other cities.

Gabria Springreaver had done an excellent job of summoning everyone important within reasonable traveling distance; Heiastowne would not be the only Precinct represented here tonight. The Guild Master for Lacemakers had already been shown to the far end by a Gearman apprentice; from the looks of things, they were trying to determine if she could share the bench with the Master Gearman at that end or if she would have to displace him. If that happened, Rexei herself would be ousted from her own bench, to give Guild Master Grenfallow her seat.

"Are you Journeyman Rexei Longshanks?"

The question startled her. Quickly winding a span of wool around the tip of her hook to hold the yarn in place without slipping, Rexei stuffed it into her basket and gave the head of the Actors Guild her full attention. "Yes, Guild Master."

"Hm." The middle-aged redhead frowned at her. Behind her stood Alonnen, giving Rexei an encouraging look. He had removed his outer coat, revealing a dark, fine-spun wool waistcoat over his equally dark shirt. Grenfallow frowned at her, even as Alonnen smiled. "I'm told you changed your name after moving on from my guild. What name did you earn your journeyman rank under, and why did you quit the guild?"

Rexei glanced at Alonnen, who smiled at her. Confused and wary that he would have told this woman about her abrupt change in names as well as careers, she answered, "I used to be called Rexei Targeter . . . before I was harassed out of the Guild by a grabby woman who should've known that 'no thank you' *means* 'no thank you,' even when a lad is the one saying it. I moved on to Clockworks after that, among others."

"So I've heard. And tell me, where have you been apprenticed and working for the last two months?" Grenfallow asked her.

"Servers Guild. I was one of five who worked in the Heiastowne temple until yesterday," she admitted warily.

"So I've heard," the older woman murmured, before sharpening her tone into something very no-nonsense and direct. "Now, be honest with me, Journeyman Actor. Were you set to spy upon the temple inhabitants—the priests—for those two months?"

Alonnen nodded in encouragement, so Rexei admitted carefully, "Yes . . . as a Gearman investigating a claim of improper conduct by the temple inhabitants against members of the Servers Guild."

"Did they ever suspect you of being anything other than a Server?" Alonnen asked.

"Not while I was within their walls. If anything, the archbishop claimed I grew stupider every time he talked at me," Rexei admitted. "But . . . they may have overheard me speaking with some wit in the square yesterday, after they pushed us all out the doors. I do not know if they did, but the possibility is there."

Rather than speaking to her, the leader of the Actors Guild turned to her three companions, two men and another woman. All wore the large round medallions of grandmaster actors. Ovals were reserved for Guild Masters alone. "I believe Master Tall's assessment is accurate."

"Two months is an impressive time in the face of their understandable paranoia and skepticism," the older of the two male actors stated.

"One must subtract some of the points for that from their sheer arrogance, though," the younger blonde woman countered. "They do sometimes overlook things."

"Not for two whole months," the younger male argued.

Grenfallow raised her hand. "Value for value . . . would you agree with Master Tall's assessment?"

"Oh, yes."

"Of course."

"Definitely," the other three agreed.

"Then I'll take it up with the grandmaster." Nodding graciously to Alonnen, Grenfallow strode off. The others made their way toward the back of the room to look for any scrap of pew or bench unoccupied.

Rexei gave Alonnen a quizzical look. "What was that about?"

"Just a little bit of business I thought about on the way over here, after hearing who would be in attendance," he dismissed. He nodded to her and headed for the centermost seat to chat with Grandmaster Toric.

A sudden swell of sound from the back of the room caused heads to turn . . . and the sight of what caused it made everyone stop talking within seconds. Clad in snow-speckled velvet robes, Archbishop Elcarei of the Heiastowne Temple of Mekha strode into the Consulate meeting hall as if he owned the place, with three similarly dressed priests at his back. Their rich scarlet, emerald, and sapphire velvets looked very out of place among the plebian undyed wools most everyone wore—dyeing was also taxed, same as loomed cloth.

It was not the first time Rexei had seen priests enter a Consulate meeting with such arrogant airs of command. This time, however, the looks on the faces of the men and women seated on the pews were not expressions of fear and avoidance. Instead, they wore dark looks of irritation and resentment, even anger.

Before more than a few whispers and mutterings could begin, Grandmaster Toric picked up his stone-headed gavel and *cracked* it twice against its matching anvil. The sharp noise cut off all sound in the hall, beyond the sound of the priests' boots on the polished stone floor, and the movements of Alonnen and the leader of the Actors Guild moving off to the side to find their seats.

"This emergency Consulate meeting is reserved for Guild Masters, grandmasters, masters, and representative journeymen," the Gearman at the center of the table stated, his voice strong and steady despite the visible wrinkles of his years.

"And that is why I am here, Toric," Elcarei stated smoothly. "As Archbishop of Heiastowne—"

"As *nothing*," Captain Torhammer snapped, rising from his seat next to Toric, "you will be *silent*."

The archbishop stopped, eyes wide in shock. His face reddened, and he drew in a breath to argue. The Precinct captain cut him off.

"*You* are now a private citizen, Elcarei Tuddlehead," the captain asserted.

"*I* am the Archbishop of Heiast—"

"*Ex*-archbishop," Torhammer stated coldly, cutting him off mid-sentence again. "With the dissolution of Mekha and the removal of His Patronage, *there is no priesthood in this land*. Your own rank was dependent entirely upon the existence of the God you worshipped. With that God eliminated, by law, your guild no longer exists . . . and I will uphold the *law*, sir. Because you now lack any guild standing whatsoever, you are not invited to this meeting, Private Citizen Tuddlehead. You and your companions are thus asked to remove yourselves from this hall. It is reserved for Guild Masters, grandmasters, masters, and other representatives of the various Guilds in this land."

Elcarei blinked and stared. Rexei quickly scooted off the bench she was on, giving way for the Guild Master of the Actors Guild to take her place. Taking her project with her, she stuffed the wool into the bag and leaned against the back wall, since there were no more seats to be had.

Grandmaster Toric spoke. "As you can see, Milord Tuddlehead, we do not have enough room in this meeting for extraneous visitors at this time. Please remove yourself from the hall. I promise you, all decisions made by this Consulate this evening—if any— will be printed up within two days by the Binders Guild and posted on the reading boards at all city squares and in all public taverns."

Elcarei was made of sterner, and quicker-witted, stuff than that. He did not leave, but instead he lifted his chin. "Then I petition the right to represent all mages within Heias Precinct, as I am the most powerful, most highly trained mage present, *and* I have already held the rank of grandmaster in another guild, so that surely qualifies me for a high rank in the incipient Mages Guild."

Alonnen, again proving himself bolder than Rexei ever would have been, leaned forward and spoke bluntly, if with a smile on his spell-altered face. "Sorry, milord, but we already have one of those . . . and by the duly ratified Charter of the Mages Guild, *all* members of Mekha's priesthood, past, present, and future, have been banned in perpetuity from ever joining. I'm sure you'll realize *why*."

Two red blotches of color appeared on the ex-archbishop's face. They had nothing to do with the contrast between the snowstorm outside and hearth-heated air inside. Eyes wide, mouth tight with fury, Elcarei lifted his chin. "If you think *you* know anything about magic, you untrained, savage—"

"You're outnumbered." Rexei didn't know where this sense of rebellion in the last two days was coming from, but she swallowed and met Elcarei's gaze as the archbishop turned to face her. His eyes narrowed in recognition, but she lifted her chin anyway. "Remember? You set all your God-drained prisoners free. One hundred," she emphasized, pushing away from the wall to stalk slowly toward him, "and fifty-three. Some of them have recovered. Some of them *may* even be in this room right now, under disguise. And there are many more mages roaming this land, ones that you *never* captured.

"You are *outnumbered, ex*-priest . . . and you are a fool if you think you can just take anything from anyone ever again, by spell or by force." She stopped just beyond arm's reach and lifted her chin. "*If* that's what you think. So. Which *are* you? A wise man or a fool?"

His lip curled up in a sneer, and his gaze slid down over her body and back. "A fool, to have *been* fooled by the likes of you. Congratulations, boy. You had me actually believing you were a lackwit. Be grateful you aren't a mage. Mekha would have drained you dry the moment you crossed the temple threshold . . . and I would have done nothing to stop Him."

"We noticed," Toric stated dryly from his seat at the center of the table.

"I want my cap back," Rexei said, remembering the worries from yesterday that they could track her down by a stray hair caught in its wool. "And my jacket."

"Your cap and your jacket?" Elcarei asked, taken aback by her demand.

"Yes. If you haven't noticed, it's bloody cold outside, and I'd like my cap and my coat back. You shoved me out the temple door before I could fetch either," she reminded him. "The others in the Servers Guild lost theirs as well. You need to return them."

"And why should I?" the ex-priest challenged her. "You were in my temple under false pretenses."

"Wrong. I am a Gearman. I'm allowed to go anywhere under the direction of the Consulate. I was sent into the temple to investigate rumors of improper conduct against members of the Servers Guild," she explained. She glanced at the Precinct captain, then looked back at Elcarei. "I will confess that from what I saw, you haven't done anything wrong against the Servers, but if you keep my cap and coat, that's theft. For that matter, I *could* accuse Novice Stearlen of raping one of the women you were keeping below ground . . . since he was taking her without her consent *after* Mekha vanished, and that means *after* your guild was legally dissolved, taking with it your God-cursed right to do whatever you wished with non-priestly . . . mages."

"Stand down, Journeyman Longshanks," Grandmaster Toric stated. As Rexei backed up, striving to hide how her hands wanted to shake, he said, "Private Citizen Tuddlehead, you will return all such belongings still held within the temple's confines to the Consulate, with such notes as you can deliver regarding the names and identities of their owners. Doing so through this facility will protect your fellow ex-priests from any . . . upset feelings. You will have three days to comply. For now, you and your companions are dismissed from this Consulate meeting.

"Now please go. Your continued presence will only cause more problems at this point in time." Toric held Elcarei's gaze until the latter lifted his chin, turned on his heel, and strode for the doors, pushing past the other three priests with tightly contained anger. Aiming a dark look of his own at Rexei, Hansu turned and followed, as did the other two velvet-clad men.

Rexei waited for the doors to shut behind the priests, then waited a few seconds more for her knees to stop feeling like they were going to collapse. Only then did she move back to the wall. As she did so, Guild Master Grenfallow stood and cleared her throat.

Grandmaster Toric, as arbitrator of the Consulate meeting,

nodded to her. She sat down again, once acknowledged, and settled in to listen. Rexei leaned against the back wall, hand digging into her shoulder pouch in search of her crocheting needle.

"Right, then. I am Grandmaster Toric of the Gearmen's Guild, and leader of the Heias Precinct Consulate. This emergency meeting was called by one of the local Guild Masters to discuss the disappearance of the God of Engineering from Mekhana and what that means to the guilds of all regions near and far.

"Given the short notice of the meeting and the inclement weather, we are very honored to welcome the Guild Masters visiting from our neighboring Precincts of Tanis, Luxon, Velchei, Grandsong, and Hollowfeld." Several of the Guild Masters dipped their head at the introduction, including Grenfallow. "Your local guild chapters are pleased you could attend, and the rest of us are grateful you are willing to represent your people.

"Our first order of business is brought to us by Guild Master Saranei Grenfallow of the Actors Guild, as well as by a fellow Guild Master, who claims the following piece of business will have some impact on the rest of our discussions. Guild Master Grenfallow, please rise and state your business," Toric directed her.

The middle-aged redhead nodded graciously and rose. "It has been brought to my attention that a journeyman Actor in our midst has just spent the last two months *fooling* the priests of this town. After consulting with my guild's grandmasters, and hearing the, ah, freely expressed testimony of the ex-grandmaster of the former Priests Guild of Heiastowne confirming the deception . . . it is my pleasure to elevate Rexei Longshanks to the rank of Master Actor."

"Witnessed!" Alonnen called out from his seat among the other Guild Masters. A few others echoed him. Rexei, taken aback, forced herself to move toward Saranei Grenfallow, who was digging in a pouch at her waist.

The medallion dug out was slightly larger than the journeyman discs dangling from Rexei's necklace. On it was stamped the two masques of the Actors Guild, the crying face of Tragedy and the laughing face of Comedy. She had actually carved similar symbols during her apprenticeship and journeyman days in the Engravers Guild, though not the one that had been used to strike this particular disc.

Stringing it on a bit of crumpled ribbon also pulled from the depths of her pouch, the Guild Master draped the coin around Rexei's head. "Welcome to the rank of Master Actor, Longshanks. Remember that with this rank comes the responsibility to represent the Guild favorably and well, to teach your apprentices carefully, and to understand that, as in any craft, there is *always* room for improvement. Even at higher ranks."

"Thank you," Rexei murmured, clasping and shaking the hand the older woman offered her. "I, ah, wasn't expecting this, but thank you."

"You've earned it," Saranei told her. She turned, still holding Rexei's hand. "Grandmaster Toric, this young Master Actor is a journeyman Gearman. That means he is also a journeyman in two other guilds. But now that he has a master's rank . . . ?"

The grandmaster took the hint. "We have a motion to elevate Journeyman Rexei Longshanks to the rank of Master Gearman, and with it, the right to be listed as a permanent Sub-Consul capable of representing any unrepresented Guild wherever he may go, and the right to be granted the rank of Consul on a temporary basis as needed to represent those guilds which he has served in good standing," Toric stated dryly. "Any objections?"

"Yes, what's his age?" one of the Guild Masters near the far end of the table asked.

"Almost twenty-two," Alonnen answered for her. "And the 'lad' has served in thirty Guilds. Thirty-one, including my own." His words stirred murmurs of discussion among the audience and the Guild Masters alike. Raising his voice, Alonnen explained. "The priests kept stumbling across his . . . abilities . . . so he kept moving on to new venues and new identities."

Sometimes the priests, Rexei thought. *But sometimes the grabby hands of men and women who thought a young apprentice, or even a journeyman, could be taken advantage of . . . Not often, but it did happen occasionally. Each time I reported it to the next-highest guildmember and picked a new guild. Not an unfamiliar tune, though many would simply have picked a new master or grandmaster in the same guild to learn under in some other town. But mostly the priests, yes.*

"That is an understandable reason for switching careers. I am surprised that you managed to gain journey status in three different guilds, lad," Toric allowed, nodding his head at Rexei, "but if you can fool the . . . *ex*-priesthood for two months straight, you've clearly earned your Master Actor rank. Any objections? . . . None? Motion granted," he stated, cracking his mallet on its anvil once. "Journeyman Callis? There you are . . . Fetch a Master Gearman medallion from my office, if you please. Master Rexei, as you are from outside the Heias Precinct, you are invited to join the rest of us as a discussion arbiter. Good luck trying to find a seat, but do stay at that end of the table and help maintain order."

Bowing, Rexei settled in to stand behind Saranei Grenfallow. The leader of the Actors Guild sighed and patted the bench next to her, shifting just enough to make room for Rexei to sit. Grateful, she sank onto the bench next to the older woman . . . who leaned in and murmured in her ear.

"Good job on fooling everyone that you're a male, too," the Guild Master said quietly while the grandmaster paused for a moment or two of quiet discussion among the audience members. "You might want to consider hiding your throat as you get older; men usually have an apple-lump there, while women do not."

Since there wasn't much she could say to that, Rexei merely dipped her head.

"The next piece of business is a petition by Guild Master Tall. You also said this one will pertain heavily to the discussion of Mekha's removal and the fate of this kingdom as well?" Toric asked Alonnen.

"Yes, Grandmaster, although it is not actually my place to say. Master Longshanks has a presentation to make to all of us," Alonnen stated.

Rexei wished she could shoot him a dirty look. She had just sat down, she was still a bit wobbly from the shock and the honor of her rise in rank—double rise, Gearman as well as Actor—and now he wanted her to leap straight into the heart of their problems? She wanted to scowl and stick out her tongue. But as every Gearman apprentice was taught, one did not act rudely within a Consulate meeting. Particularly when one sat at the head table. Sighing instead, she dug into her messenger bag, down past the wool, and pulled out her notes.

"I can now see why you chose to urge a higher rank onto the young man," Grandmaster Toric stated dryly as she readied herself.

Alonnen shrugged, elbows braced on the table and hands clasped in front of his face. "I merely pointed out the extraordinary abilities which Longshanks has already displayed. Grand Master Grenfallow chose to enact the elevation under the standards and qualifications required by her guild."

"Very well. Rise, Master Longshanks, and make your presentation."

Catching the grandmaster's nod, Rexei rose, a small sheaf of papers in her hands. She tried not to let them tremble visibly. A bow, and she began.

"Thank you for your attention, Guild Masters, grandmasters, masters, journeymen, and apprentices." She paused, tightened her gut to speak a little louder so that all could hear, and checked the opening statements she had painstakingly organized on the top-most page. And, since she was an actor, she let her voice sharpen a little with emotion as she began. "As you may know by now, Mekha, the long-burdensome False God of Mekhana, so-called Patron of Engineering, is now gone.

"We have received word that the Convocation of Gods and Man has indeed been reinstated, and with the visible removal of His symbols and His powers from our land, this means that the promises pledged to us by Knight-Priestess Orana Niel have come true. She has confronted the Dead God and presented our blood-signed petitions, gathered over the generations, to have Mekha removed from our land as a False Patron. His powers, ambitions, and accursed hungers shall plague us no more, which is a cause for rejoicing.

"However . . . this leaves us without a Patron God or Goddess . . . and in this new era of the Convocation, any kingdom that *lacks* a Patron Deity is now at a severe political, economical, and theological disadvantage. Should our neighboring lands decide they wish to invade us, we will have no Divine energies to lend to our militia in thwarting any would-be conquerors. We shall have no voice at the Convocation and no representatives. We will be *nothing* . . . unless we select, as swiftly as possible, a *new* Patron Deity.

"I, therefore, wish to propose a new Patron *Goddess* to the people of . . . to the people of the Heias Precinct and to its nearest neighbors," she allowed, stopping herself from saying the kingdom's old name. She tipped her head respectfully toward the dozen or so Guild Masters summoned from cities within a few hours' travel of Heias. "The sooner we can unite ourselves behind a common faith which we can *all* agree upon, the sooner we can claim Patronage, and the sooner we can re-create ourselves formally as a new kingdom and not a lawless land ripe for anyone to harvest.

"So. Will you hear the details of my proposal?" she asked, lifting her gaze to the others in the hall.

Conversations broke out all over the room. Since they were neither loud nor heated, the head of the local Consulate allowed them to continue for a minute or so before tapping his gavel. Rexei remained on her feet as the crowd of men and women fell quiet again. "Your words of warning have merit, though I doubt we will come to a vote within a single evening, young Master Longshanks. But we will hear your petition . . . and any others that may come along."

"There really is only one choice, Grandmaster," Rexei stated earnestly. On this ground, she felt secure and calm, not nervous. Turning to face the crowd on the pews and benches, she addressed them. "I ask all of you, what is our *true* strength in this land? Is it our weapons? *No*, for magic can and has thwarted them. They have kept us from losing more than an inch of our kingdom in decades, but neither have we gained more than an inch. Is it our militia? *No*, for the same reasons, having gained or lost nothing. Was it our engineering skills, our grasp of construction and machinery?

"No . . . and it *should not* be such things, because these things are *nothing* without the framework that has kept us strong and kept us safe in *spite* of Mekha's accursed hunger. What kept *all* of us safe was not even the rule of law," she added, looking down the table to the midpoint, where the formidable Precinct captain sat. Somewhere out in the audience was his leftenant, Alonnen's brother, but she didn't look toward Rogen. "It was the system that *enforced* those laws. The *guilds* kept all of us safe.

"The guilds have organized our crafts, proposed and ratified laws, even tended to the sick and the injured. Each guild is not just an organization that teaches certain skills; each guild is a *family*, bound by ties of expectation and regulation, not by mere blood. So I propose that we consider turning our thoughts and our faith and our *strength* as a system of guilds into worshipping a force I have come to call Guildra, the Patron Goddess of Guilds."

"A Goddess?" The question came from one of the men seated near her. She didn't know his face or his name, but from the oval medallion he wore, he was the Guild Master of Clockworks. "Why a Goddess? Why not a God?"

"Forgive my bluntness, Guild Master," Rexei apologized, "but the women of this kingdom are sick and tired of being forced into lesser status and rank under the thumb of a *male* God run by a *male* priesthood. We are all tired of the False God, and we need something completely different from everything that Mekha was and everything that He stood for. Which includes everything that His priesthood stood for—everything you saw for yourself when they arrogantly tried to come in here and claim their old right to force their will upon us. Do you really want to follow in *their* footsteps by forcing women to continue to take a subservient role, or would you rather women stand as an equal at your side, something *they* would not have put up with?"

The head of Clockworks shook his head, lowering his gaze.

"The Goddess I envision welcomes both genders equally into Her service," Rexei explained. "More than that, Her priesthood should *not* be ranked higher than any other guild, but instead should be considered to be in the *service* of other guilds rather than be served by them. I propose that Her priesthood be drawn from women and men alike, so that everyone is represented equally. I propose that this new priesthood should also be like unto the Gearmen, in that anyone wishing to join should serve as an apprentice in at least three different guilds, so that Her priesthood *understands* the differences and the similarities in each and every guild.

"I do *not* propose that the Gearmen should become the new priesthood," she added quickly, catching sight of Toric's chest rising. She didn't want him to interrupt. "Members of the Gearmen's

Guild may be welcome to join—and they will certainly qualify—but no one should be forced to join. More importantly, the Gearmen already hold an important position, as adjudicators and arbiters of the law. That should not be changed.

"Instead, I propose that those who would become members of the new . . . the new Holy Guild, to label it as distinct and different from the old Priests Guild," she added, since she hadn't been able to come up with any better name for it, "those who wish to join should be required to *step down* from participation in the Consulate system, because while Gearmen have a proud tradition of serving more than one guild, priests should not have the right to rule over gatherings such as this.

"We have all had it up to *here*," she added, hand rising to smack the back of her fingers into the bottom of her chin, "with Mekha's priesthood *making* the laws. The Holy Guild should be no more important than the Actors Guild, or the Tillers, or the Cobblers and Cordwainers, who repair and make shoes—they should have *a* vote in a meeting like this but not *the* deciding vote. So I propose that the Holy Guild, and our Goddess, be very different from all that we used to know. We all deserve something completely different!"

Her words were having an impact, for more than one head bobbed in an agreeing nod. Many did, so she increased the fervor of her proposal, her argument.

"Our Goddess should be a gentle deity whose focus is the gathering of supplies, the drafting of designs, and the crafting of the things we need to live in peace and cooperation. We shouldn't give up the pursuit of mechanical understanding, but we should turn our weapons of war into tools for construction," Rexei stated fervently, putting into words more than what she had put onto paper. She put her belief, sprouted and nurtured over the eleven-plus years during which she had run from all the evil that Mekha and

His priesthood had inflicted upon her people. "Serving as an apprentice and a journeyman in numerous guilds, I have given the true nature of our culture many years of thought. I have even done my best to spread a *symbol* for this Goddess we need, so that we should have something to look forward to one day. And while I never thought to see this chance happen in *my* lifetime, this opportunity is upon us now.

"I'm sure you have all seen the symbol by now: The paintbrush, through which we design all that is best in our lives," she recited, looking up often from her notes to make sure she caught the eyes of a woman here, a man there. "The hammer, with which we craft all that is useful. The scythe, through which we feed and supply ourselves. Each of these forms the spokes for a gearwheel. Even the gearwheel of our engineering achievements should be accepted and welcomed, for it is by the clockworks and the engines and the pistons and the whatevers that we have improved our magicless lives. Guildra shall be a Goddess of creation, not destruction. Guildra is a Goddess of cooperation, not deceit.

"Guildra is, therefore, a manifestation of everything the guilds *already* stand for: law, order, creation, innovation, cooperation, peace, and rankings based not upon our ambitions but upon our qualifications. *That* is who and what we deserve as our Patron," she asserted, watching the sea of faces staring at her . . . and now staring past her. The hairs on the back of her neck prickled, but Rexei strove to continue. "We are *not* going to fall into lawlessness, because we have the Guild System in our blood and in our bones supporting these things, the ways and means of cooperation and organization.

"We don't have to invent any new concept to gain a true Patron of this land. Let our Patron be the Patron of the Guilds, and let Guildra be the Goddess of a new land. Let Mekhana dissolve along with its False God, and let *Guildara* rise and take its rightful place

in the world. Guildara, which means the Land of the Guilds, overseen and guarded by Guildra, the Goddess of Guilds," she finished, spreading her hands in the hopes of emphasizing her words
enough to recapture her audience's attention. "Because this is what
we *are* and have always been, even when crushed under the will of
the False God, Mekha."

It didn't work. They continued to stare past her shoulders,
though all she could sense magically was a cool, clean feeling, like
soaking hot, sore feet in a shaded, spring-fed pool in the
summertime—refreshing not shocking. But there wasn't supposed
to be anyone behind her. Uneasy, Rexei turned and peered over her
shoulder as well.

EIGHT

A woman, strangely familiar, had appeared between her and the stone wall, though she was no woman that Rexei could recall seeing before this moment. Rexei took in her light complexion, her long dark brown curls that gleamed like the richest silk framing the rectangular face of a native Mekhanan, and wondered who she was. She even wore a knitted overgown similar in shape to Grenfallow's, save that this one came in every natural shade of wool imaginable. From the creamiest white to the reddest auburn to the blackest of fleeces, it had been embroidered with a repeating motif.

That motif was the one which Rexei herself had created and described: a gear-toothed wheel with the spokes formed from the crossed shafts of a hammer, a scythe, and a narrow-tufted brush, one sized for either painting or writing. Machinery gears, farming tools, crafting tools, designing tools, all of those things decorated her gown . . . or rather, *Her* gown, for Her eyes gleamed with a light that made it impossible to say what hue those irises were; like

Her aura, Her eyes shimmered with the cool promise of water on a hot summer's day.

She looked only somewhat like Rexei had imagined Her, but it was clear who She was.

"*You have an immense strength to your faith, Rexei,*" Guildra stated in a soft, pleasant voice not much louder than a murmur.

A quick glance behind at the crowd showed Rexei how the murmur echoed through the great meeting hall, reaching every ear and widening every eye. Rexei faced Her again, speechless at what was happening.

"*Your words in expressing it are well-spoken. You have convinced many here that I should exist, enough for Me to briefly manifest. I am . . . grateful . . . for My birth, and I will be honored to guide and defend you all . . . but you will have a long road ahead before you can achieve your goals of banding together as a new form of kingdom . . . and four more years before I can be Named and so take My place among My Brethren. Should you succeed,*" Guildra added in soft, sober warning. "*Only the past is immutable; the future must be seized and shaped. What you believe, so shall I be.*" She smiled. "*I would prefer to be a Goddess of Peace and Prosperity, as well as your Patron of Guilds.*"

That radiant gaze shifted to the others. Released, Rexei discovered she had forgotten how to breathe while the Goddess, *her* Goddess, had spoken to her. Inhaling slowly, deeply, she tried not to shake too hard. No Mekhanan cared to have *any* deity's attention, particularly a mage . . . but at the same time, Rexei believed with all her heart that *this* deity was what they needed and wanted, and thus She could not ever possibly bring them harm.

For several seconds as She regarded the crowd, Guildra said nothing more, until Her gaze came back to Rexei's face. Lifting Her hand, She placed it on Rexei's brow. It felt warm and alive, but not entirely solid, leaving a hint of cool waterfall in the back of the young woman's mind.

"Your task is well begun, Rexei. I place My blessing upon you," She stated. Sparks of light trickled down from Her touch, solidifying around Rexei's neck as a heavy weight. *"Your belief, first and foremost, has created Me, so I name you the incipient Guild Master of My Holy Guild. Petition them for its entry, Guild Master. I shall return when your collective faith in Me as a new nation has grown substantially."*

Pinpoints of light shimmered through Her form, first as faint as starlight, then growing in brilliance until they flared and faded, leaving nothing behind. Nothing but that heavy weight on Rexei's chest. Glancing down, Rexei blinked at the new medallion on her chest. Not the ribbon-strung one that marked her as a Master Actor, which was roughly the length of her thumb in diameter. No, this one had been strung on sturdy gold links. It was a flat oval as long as her palm and stamped with an engraved image she had never dared to carve so large.

Slowly, Rexei turned first to face the other men and women seated at the Consulate bench, then to face the breathlessly curious crowds on the pews and benches of the hall. She held herself still, trying not to tremble, and let them look long and hard at the tool-spoked wheel symbolizing her faith in the guilds the others represented and the Goddess she had envisioned for them.

It was all she could do not to faint. From journeyman to Guild Master in less than a quarter hour . . . Giving up, Rexei sagged onto the bench next to Grenfallow . . . and a storm of conversation erupted. It seemed that everyone in the meeting hall just had to comment, discuss, and argue over what had happened. Rexei let it wash over her while she struggled with the idea, the concept, the *fact* that *she* was now responsible for the spirituality of her nation.

Everyone knew where the Gods came from: They literally came from the belief and faith of Their people. Culture dictated Their focus; for example, if a culture believed that horses were the most important things in the people's daily lives, they would have a Horse God or Goddess. Equally important, the more people worshipped that God or Goddess, the more who believed in Them, the more their collective willpower fed that deity, permitting Them to grow strong and powerful.

The most often cited examples were the Patron of Fortuna, the Threefold God of Fate, believed by everyone to be the oldest and most powerful deity of all, and the second-most powerful deity in the world, Menda, Goddess of Mendhi and Patron of Writing. It was said They could even act well outside Their normal homelands because of this pervasive, worldwide belief in Them, though such miracles and manifestations were still exceptionally rare.

The terrible corollary to this belief-equals-power had been the bane of Mekhana for far too long, for *fear* could also keep a God in power. Sitting there, trembling from the draining effects of manifesting an actual deity, Rexei felt ill. If the priesthood in that temple *worshipped* whatever great demon they summoned . . . that demon could become a dark and vicious God—one with a small following, but even a small amount of belief could wreak miracles, regardless of whether they were malicious or divine. With that thought preying on her mind, she swallowed against the nausea raised by the possibility and swallowed again from nerves while people shouted questions and demands and argued near the top of their lungs.

The heavy cracking of the stone-headed mallet against its equally hard base cut through all the noise. Grandmaster Toric smacked his gavel again, a trio of sharp raps that demanded order. Looking up, Rexei could see the Guild Master of Masons wincing. Having been a Mason apprentice for four months at one point, she knew the stone used for the Consulate gavels was strong enough to withstand a fair amount of punishment, but it made a painfully loud, hard-struck sound.

Toric whacked the stone anvil twice more, then set his gavel down as the crowd finally fell quiet. "Thank you. I have listened to the chaos of your words, and I have gleaned three important questions. First, was that a true manifestation of a deity? Second, is this Guildra the sort of Goddess we actually want? And third, is Master Gearman Longshanks' apparent elevation to Guild Master of the as yet unvalidated Holy Guild a *legitimate* elevation? These questions will be addressed by this Consulate meeting, but we will have *order* in this hall.

"Technically . . . there should be a fourth question in there," he added dryly, "of whether or not we *want* a Holy Guild. I admit I am personally of the mind that I would rather do *without* any priests or any God . . . but then I have lost seven extended family members to the predations of the last group, who were less-than-stellar examples of what every other nation calls a priesthood. I acknowledge my prejudice, and must recuse myself from participating in any deciding votes on the particular subject regarding the validation of any new priestly guild . . . though I will oversee any arbitration needed with absolute neutrality.

"Let us begin with the first question," Grandmaster Toric stated as everyone stayed respectfully quiet. The guilds depended heavily upon the Gearmen for that very neutrality and the fairness it carried, and were willing to listen to the debates. He dipped his head in appreciation of their respect and placed an hourglass—or rather, a two-minute glass, a standard length for timing short speeches in such meetings—prominently in front of himself. "So. *Was* that a true manifestation of a new deity?

"I will open the floor to short speeches of proof or disputation of the matter. Please raise your hand if you have something useful and unique to contribute. Remember, if anyone else has covered what you want to say, simply state that you agree with them and sit down, or move on to a new point to be discussed."

The apprentices came around with a second set of refreshments, moving as quietly and unobtrusively as they could. This time, Rexei accepted a mug of hot spiced cider and a wedge of cheese. It gave her something to do while one by one, various citizens of Heiastowne and the retinue of the visiting Guild Masters stood and gave their opinions on the matter. Most everyone was in at least tentative favor of it having been a true manifestation, save for one repeating question.

"Master Longshanks, as many have asked just now, answer us truthfully," Toric finally stated, making her head jerk up like a deer hearing a noise in the woods. "Did you yourself plan for or attempt anything which would have caused that apparition?"

Caught in the mass of stares aimed her way, she shook her head quickly. "No! I swear, I wasn't even expecting it. If you'll remember, I was looking at all of *you* and . . . and just speaking from my heart. The only thought in my head was to hopefully sway you by the logic of my words and by the truths which we all know."

Alonnen spoke up, addressing the grandmaster. "For my own part, Grandmaster, I believe I saw a near-manifestation several hours earlier while in a discussion with Longshanks about the sort of Patron we should have now that the, ah, False God is gone. Longshanks did not notice anything then, same as he did not notice just now until after She had manifested. But he was speaking from the heart, then as now. Given what my Guild manages, I can also say with strong certainty that there was no magic involved, either then or just now."

"Your word on this?" Toric asked him.

"I give my word," Alonnen confirmed, bowing his head. "It is for that reason, the earlier, barely discernible image of the same figure we all saw just now, that I requested Longshanks put his words and thoughts into a usable format, defining what sort of Patron we best need and what sort of Guild might serve as the facilitators for that Patron Deity."

"So this is basically *your* idea?" Captain Torhammer asked dryly.

"Organizing it as a discussion, yes. Defining it, no," he replied calmly. "That would be Master Longshanks' purview."

"Thank you. Given the general consensus of everyone present, I believe we can vote that this manifestation was a genuine Goddess event. Any dissenting votes?" Toric asked. A few hands rose, but out of the hundreds crammed into the hall, there were only four or five at most. "Any abstaining? Eight, right. Show of hands for agreement? . . . Five dissenters, eight abstentions, and over five hundred confirmations. Consensus confirmed. Moving on to question two, is a Goddess of Guilds, representing everything which we as members of many guilds believe the Guild System stands for, the sort of Patron Deity we might actually want?

"Again, please raise your hands only if you have something unique to contribute, or we'll be here all night. Remember, this is a *discussion* question and not an actual vote by the guilds to accept any Patron Deities at this time . . ."

This time, the debate ranged longer. Some of the men and women called upon to speak even tried to define a different God or Goddess . . . but however fervently they spoke, however much the speakers peered around, nothing happened. Grandmaster Toric eventually ruled after the sixth or seventh attempt that discussing a *different* Patron was not the topic at hand and would not be further discussed. That sped things up a bit, until the general consensus was agreed upon that a Patron Goddess of Guilds was something most everyone could get behind.

More gratifying for Rexei was how even those who had suggested alternatives agreed that a Goddess of the Guilds seemed a reasonable sort of Patron for their culture to have.

Once more under scrutiny, Rexei found herself grateful that Alonnen had insisted she put her ideas down on paper. It had allowed her to revisit and refresh her ideas on what a proper Patron Deity should be, and more specifically the Patron for her people.

By being prepared enough to answer their questions—even if she had to think of a couple replies on the spot—she sounded competent, even professional. An equal among Guild Masters, however young she might be. Rexei felt relief and gratitude for that.

The third question, whether or not Rexei was a legitimate Guild Master of the as-yet unapproved Holy Guild, quickly morphed into whether or not Rexei was an *appropriate* Guild Master for a brand-new priestly guild. As the Grandmaster Gearman pointed out, it was a question partially wrapped up in whether or not they *wanted* a new priestly guild, but as more than one person expressed from the audience, if they wanted to be an officially recognized kingdom, it would help to have an official Patron Deity. That was a discussion which Rexei could not sit out of and ignore, for many of the questions and comments were directed at her.

Yes, she believed in Guildra, Patron of Guilds. No, she would never worship or believe in anyone even remotely like Mekha. Yes, she would serve as a priest. No, she would not demand to remain the Guild Master if someone more suitable were found. Yes, she had a charter drawn up—a rough draft of a charter—as an apprentice dozens of times over, Rexei had seen and studied far too many not to know how to put one together, even if she hadn't ever apprenticed in the Law-Sayers Guild.

Yes, she was serious about requiring apprenticeship in at least three different guilds, because Guildra was the Goddess of Guilds, plural, so Her servants would have to understand the viewpoints and needs of multiple guilds as well. No, she had not been joking when she said she would expect Gearmen to retire or recuse themselves from that particular guild and its Consulate-associated duties if they joined the new Holy Guild, because during votes, they would have to represent only their own guild . . . or choose not to represent the Holy Guild in a vote when choosing to act as a Gearman representative for any other Guild. Yes, she was willing to consider other names, though Holy Guild was the simplest and most direct name for it, particularly if they were going to discard and disassociate themselves from the corrupt, Mekha-ruled version that had just been disbanded.

She had to consult her notes several times to get an answer culled from the ideas written down, but otherwise, she didn't have too much trouble. If Alonnen hadn't insisted she write her thoughts down, however, she would have faltered.

The hardest question to answer came from the Precinct captain. "*What*, exactly, do you envision to be the daily life role of you and your fellow . . . Holies, for lack of a better label? How will you fit into our lives when you claim to want to avoid everything that Mekha's priests have demanded and done?"

"We . . . will inspire, I guess," Rexei said. She had forgotten to include this possibility in her note-organizing that afternoon. "We'll inspire creativity and cooperation. Understanding, too. The guilds don't always talk to each other, and when they do, it's often by bringing a complaint to their local Consulate. The Holy Guild would try to foster understanding before misunderstandings become formal issues. Gearmen do some of this, but their main focus is their *own* guilds, specifically the ones they joined—even as a Gearman, while I can discuss a subject, I cannot legally represent the Lessors Guild for a vote because I have never owned land. I cannot represent the Butchers; I haven't even harmed anything bigger than a roach or a fly.

"The Holy Guild must come to an understanding of the needs of *all* guilds, to be able to be the lubrication between the guilds. We need to help point out the *similarities*, the things that make each organization strong, secure, and caring in regards to each member's needs.

"And . . . and if we can get over our *fear* of a deity," she added, trying to put into words what she knew in her head was right but what her heart still cowered away from, "then the Holy Guild will help pray to that deity for intercession—for rain when the Tillers need good crops, and for dry weather when the Roofers need to work, or for safe conditions when the Roadworks are trying to clear avalanches in the mountains. For protection and aid against any aggressive neighbors, and for calm minds and hearts so that we ourselves are never the aggressors. For inspiration with new ideas, and for the . . . the coming together of resources and ideas when creating new things which will be very beneficial for everyone.

"More than that, though, if the Convocation of Gods and Man *has* been reinstated," Rexei told the others, glancing briefly at Alonnen because she didn't dare mention the word *demon*, "then we *need* a Patron Deity, and the sooner, the better. We need to have one codified and accepted so that outsiders will think twice before bothering us, and lost ex-Mekhanans will see that *we* have order and peace and a Goddess who is a true Patron of this land. She can be Named at the next Convocation, but She needs to be worshipped *now*, so that She can go to work now. For us, instead of against us. That, above everything, will give us a measure of safety that will stretch far beyond the borders of Heias Precinct or Gren Precinct or even beyond the old borders of Mekhana, for all we will probably never march past those borders."

Grenfallow spoke up next to Rexei. She did so by holding her arm out over the table, fingers curled and thumb poking to the side. "We have a saying, 'by the pricking of my thumb,' and we all know its meaning: The desperate desire to get rid of Mekha. Well, now we are rid of the False God . . . and we have a chance at a true Goddess, one envisioned by a fellow sufferer. It is time now for us to do more than just sign our names in blood. We must add in our sweat . . . but we will need guidance. If we are to have a Patron of the Guilds, then we must all contribute, if not bodies willing to join the new priesthood, then understanding and acceptance for those who wish to serve . . . instead of those who demanded to *be* served."

"I'm sure we are all deeply grateful for whatever agent helped rid us of the last one, but we as a nation cannot stand alone," one of the master-ranked Gearmen at the far end of the table stated. "We do have neighbors. We have things we need to trade for that can *only* be found outside our own borders—good quality sand for the Glassworks Guild is one example, but it is just one of the many things we can only get by trade. If we don't have a Patron Deity, if we don't have a priesthood that *does* represent the interests of all the guilds of this land, then how can we talk to our neighbors and be assured they will listen? How can we keep them from invading us, unless we get *their own* Goddesses and Gods to agree to leave us alone? That requires representation at the Convocation. The alternative would mean war . . . and I for one do *not* want another Patron Deity of War, whatever else He may have claimed to be."

"I find myself having to agree," Captain Torhammer stated. That caused a few blinks, but he continued smoothly. "We do need holy representation to take our complaints and our needs to the whole world, and to be reassured that our concerns are respected and heard. That requires a God or Goddess, and a servant to stand as the representative between Them and the people. But I don't want to be ordered about by any more holy types. I've had enough of that already."

Rexei answered that one quickly. "I have the same problem as well, Captain Torhammer. I don't envision Guildra's servants as the sort to do any ordering around. Suggest, yes. Advise, yes. Command, no.

"I also don't imagine that we'd ever need all that many 'Holies,' as you name us," she added, unconsciously including herself in that lot, though this was far, far from anything she had ever imagined would happen to her. Rexei had conceived of the idea of Guildra but not of herself as a priestess. Nor could she imagine all that many others would be interested, though she didn't quite put it that way to the Consulate meeting. "There'd be no more than a couple per large city, and maybe one per smaller town. The little villages wouldn't even need that much, maybe a visiting holy guildsman on a touring circuit, sort of like a member of the Messengers Guild, dropping by every so many days.

"We wouldn't be the smallest of guilds out there, but our numbers would be far smaller than Mekha's priesthood ever was. With everyone believing in the Guild System, we wouldn't *need* the power of an overcrowded priesthood to raise power for our Goddess. Your belief in the guilds—which you already have, or you wouldn't be high-ranked members of such good standing—that belief would easily translate into a belief in Guildra as our holiest representative. What *you* want in a Goddess, She would become . . . and I think we can all safely say that She would *never* become like Mekha, because of that belief-equals-being. None of us wants that, so She will not be that. If anything, I should hope there would be others besides myself, people who are experienced in many guilds but firm in their conviction of being utterly unlike the last lot."

That seemed to satisfy most everyone. Seated at the head table, she didn't have to restrict her comments to two minutes, though taking too much time would cause the five-minute hourglass to come out. Rexei checked her notes discreetly but couldn't think of anything to add. Grandmaster Toric pointed at one of the hands raised on their side of the table. The question came from the local grandmaster of the Architects Guild.

"Master Longshanks, would you be taking over the temple at the heart of this city, then?" the elderly man asked her. "Presuming we could evict that nest of roaches currently living inside, of course."

Rexei shuddered. "No. Absolutely not . . . and I *must* recuse myself from further answers on this particular topic, as my personal opinion is that every Mekha-tainted temple should be destroyed down to its lowest levels, filled in, and paved over with as many tons of prayer-blessed salt as we can sow, to counteract its evils." She paused, then added honestly, "Though when I push past my revulsion for the place, I can acknowledge that no building, in and of itself, is evil and that someone might find a far better use for it.

"I *saw*, with my own eyes, all the marks of Mekha erased from every surface in that temple. It *is* nothing more than a building now . . . and as such, should probably be put to good use. Perhaps by the Hospitallers for an inn, or the Militia for an inner-city barracks." Mind racing, she shrugged and finished, "In fact, if anything, members of the Holy Guild should be based in the Consulate halls, so that everyone knows we're there to serve all the guilds."

"We'll take that suggestion under advisement," Toric returned dryly.

At that point, one of the lady Guild Masters whispered in the ear of one of the master-ranked Gearmen not quite on the far side of the table from Rexei. He in turn spoke up, calling for a vote on a brief intermission to stretch and use the refreshing rooms. It passed with alacrity.

Only her own multicity familiarity with the general construction of most Consulates, even large ones like this one, allowed Rexei to beat the others to the nearest one. When she emerged, the line stretched all the way back into the meeting hall. A few of the men and women waiting in the queue looked like they wanted to talk with her, but long-standing tradition said that what was discussed in the meeting hall stayed in the meeting hall during such intermissions. Only when the meeting ended could anything be discussed freely elsewhere.

Of course, that made Rexei reluctant to return to the meeting hall. Taking a detour around the outer corridors ringing the central chamber, Rexei finally found herself at the front entrance. Peering through one of the windows flanking the great double doors, she watched the lamplit flakes of snow swirling thickly down out of the dark sky. Enough had already fallen to coat every surface of the city street, various motorhorses, and more than one motorcart within viewing range by nearly two inches, with more yet to come.

She returned to the hall when her breath misted the glass panes too heavily to see through. Several minutes and another round of refreshments later, the meeting reconvened with a rap of the Consulate mallet. The discussions continued, dragging on for another hour plus, if not longer; somewhere in there, Rexei lost track of just how late it was, other than the realization that a second mug of mulled cider and a sweet biscuit on top of a bit of cheese was no substitute for a thoroughly missed supper.

The general consensus remained that Guildra's appearance was a genuine manifestation. The corollary to that was Guildra's desire that Rexei Longshanks be Her Guild Master, Her highest-ranked representative. But while the majority did admit that the concept of Guildra as Patron Goddess was a good idea, no one was willing to implement it just yet. The idea of renaming their kingdom—or at least this corner of it—as Guildara had some enthusiasm behind it as well, but like Guildra Herself, no one was quite ready to make it official.

Rexei knew it was partly because some people were worried that Mekha wasn't truly gone, even though by all evidence His symbols were gone even from the temple's outer walls and His victims had been set free by His own priests, who had only released corpses and infants before this day. But that was only a part of it. Mainly, they refrained because no one in the room felt qualified to make such a huge decision as just one town alone, however large or well-graced by resident and visiting Guild Masters the meeting was.

At least there was a consensus about *that* much, though it was clear there was still much to be discussed. Finally, when there were too many side conversations happening around the edges of the room, Grandmaster Toric rapped his gavel, collecting the respectful attention of everyone in the hall.

"Enough. It is late, and these things are too great to be settled easily, never mind immediately. Master Gearman Terostream has reminded me just now that in order to *be* a guild, there really should be more members than just the designated Guild Master. I am, therefore, recommending to Master Longshanks that he acquire three apprentices, each having had experience in the requisite minimum of three guilds as any Gearman requires, with the added caveat that each experience be of no less than three months in order to qualify.

"These discussions will be debated at a future date, as yet to be determined. In light of the undoubted jealousy and outrage the ex-priesthood will no doubt experience when they learn of these facts . . . it is strongly suggested that you do not gossip about the identity of the proposed Guild Master of the new Holy Guild . . . just as you would not discuss the identity of . . . mages," he made himself say. More than one person shuddered and glanced around warily. Gathering himself, the elderly Gearman continued, "The proposal to rename this kingdom as Guildara shall be rediscussed two weeks from today and shall include Consuls and Sub-Consuls selected from our nearest sister cities and related towns. We shall also debate further at that time whether or not to accept and spread the idea of this Guildra, a Goddess of Guilds, as our new Patron Deity. With that being said, I declare this meeting—"

"One more thing, Grandmaster Toric," Alonnen interjected, cutting him off.

"What *now*, Guild Master Tall?" Toric asked, rolling his eyes. "Or have you not realized you've proposed more than enough for this evening?"

"There is one more thing which needs to be discussed right *now*, Grandmaster, and that is the distribution and care of the ex-priesthood's former prisoners. In other words, the *mages* that have been released, now that Mekha is no longer draining them," Alonnen stressed. Unlike Toric, he didn't hesitate to say the *M* word.

Rexei had forgotten about them. She winced, berating herself silently for having forgotten the men and women who needed care and protection. Others around her winced as well, though more for the way he so openly said *mages* than for anything else. Using the word snared their attention, however, and she watched Alonnen firmly press the point.

"My Guild *cannot* take them in. Literally, we have not the room; we have not the food; we have not the clothing, nor anything else. We are already overflowing with people we *cannot* care for . . . and as soon as this snowstorm is over, I am going to have to send them *back* to your guilds, which means you, *all* of you, each and every other Guild out there, will have to care for, clothe, feed, and assist them in learning how to pick up their lives again."

That caused an even louder uproar than the debate over Rexei's manifestation of the Goddess and abrupt Guild Mastery. The uproar was so loud, it took Grandmaster Toric several smacks of his gavel to get everyone to quiet down again. Alonnen seized their reluctant quiet to assert his reasons, rising to his feet as he did so. He spoke sternly, staring down the men and women across from him, and the men and women seated to either side of him.

"This is *not* negotiable! Heiastowne *alone* released one hundred fifty-three prisoners, and every *other* Precinct with a temple that released its prisoners wants to send them to *my* guild. *We do not have the resources for that*. More than that," he stated, pulling out a sheet of paper from his coat. "*More* than that, I have here a document signed by our predecessor Guild Masters to *acknowledge* that *all* guildmembers of good standing, current or former, have the *right* to call upon every guild they ever served in for succor in times of great need, whether that's one guild or twenty, whether it's illness, injury, or whatever . . . and these men and women *have* been grievously injured.

"And of these prisoners who have been released?" Alonnen added tartly. "Of all of them that we've taken in so far, nearly a hundred that you've tried to foist off on me, when we have neither the room nor the supplies to care for them? Only *three* were actual, registered members of *my* guild. The rest were taken off the streets and out of their homes long before they could ever take refuge with my predecessors and me. The responsibility is *yours*, gentles."

Another session of outbursts and counterarguments echoed off the walls. Rexei, tired, overwrought, and now angry, shoved to her feet and smacked her fist onto the table with a *thunk*. "Enough!" she roared, her high tenor cutting through the babble. "Breaking them up into *small* numbers and spreading them out across *all* the guilds means that each guild with a large member base only has to support three or four people—which your guilds can do *easily*— and each guild with a small membership, save for the tiniest, can equally easily handle one or two.

"You will *not* abandon your responsibilities to your fellow guildmembers, is that clear?" Rexei demanded. She thumped the table with her fist again. "You will *not* abandon your responsibilities. You are the *guilds* of this land. You are the power, and the responsibility, that has kept the False God's priesthood in check. But even though the False God is now gone, you are *still* responsible for maintaining order, for abiding by your own charters!

"And if you try to *refuse* your rightful responsibilities, then to the Netherhells with you! You will *not* abandon these people, nor force one guild alone to take up the entire responsibility of helping these undoubted *thousands* of Mekha's victims learn how to live again!" She glared out across the stunned, silent crowd, then turned her furious stare on the Guild Masters seated elbow to elbow along the length of the curved table. "Because if that's how you feel, then take off your guild medallions and get out, right now! Get out of this land! You don't deserve to live here! Get *out!*"

Her other hand jabbed hard at the main doors into the meeting hall, the ones that led straight to the front doors of the Consulate building and the snow outside. No one moved, and no one spoke. She lowered her arm, giving everyone a hard look.

"Since you're one and all sitting there instead of leaving," Alonnen stated in the silence that followed her words, "I'll take that as unanimous consent that each and every guild *will* accept responsibility for however many ex-prisoner mages they can handle. As I said, *my* guild literally does not have the resources to host more than a bare handful, so the remainder will be sent *back* to Heiastowne and its guilds . . . and by your unanimous consent, you will all send word, particularly the Guild Masters, that it has been decided that all other towns shall retain and care for their own mage-prisoner populations, *and* protect them from the ex-priesthood still in our midst."

Rexei sat down as he spoke, leaving him to hold the floor, but he was not uncontested. One voice did speak up.

"You may have shamed them into silence, Guild Master Tall, but the two of you cannot unilaterally make *that* kind of decision for the entire span of Mekhana . . . even if Mekha *is* gone," Captain Torhammer stated. "I will continue to uphold the laws of this land for as long as I remain a Precinct captain. These contracts may be valid, but the scale of responsibility is far greater than anything we have ever seen as a nation, and the corresponding impact will be as great. The law states that any decision which affects the entire kingdom requires a quorum vote, the minimum for which is twenty Guild Masters. Even if we include Toric as a Grandmaster-ranked Gearman and myself as a Precinct captain, both of which do have full quorum-level votes at our ranks . . . we still have only nineteen assembled in this hall."

"Then *I* move that we vote to acknowledge Master Longshanks as Guild Master of the incipient Holy Guild." The man who spoke up had not said much, if anything, before now. Rexei had to squint to see the symbol on the Guild Master's medallion. It took her a few moments to realize it was a lute crossed with a flute, the mark of the Luthiers Guild, instrument makers.

Toric quickly smacked his gavel, cutting off the start of the next round of conversational chaos. "Order! Be seated and be silent. This proposal is valid *and* fair. Incipient guilds have one year and one day to prove themselves, up to and including gathering a sufficient body of apprentices to learn the specific craft of that new guild.

"Since we have acknowledged that the Goddess Guildra did manifest in conjunction with Longshanks' expressed beliefs in Her, and given we all witnessed Her giving Longshanks a Guild Master medallion, we shall take it as moot that She wishes Longshanks to be the Guild Master of Her Holy Guild. Whether or not *She* will be our Patron Goddess, and thus whether Longshanks shall be the permanent Guild Master of the new priestly order within the borders of our land, is a discussion for *another* day.

"We are restricted to voting to see if Master Rexei Longshanks will be acknowledged among us as the Guild Master of the Holy Guild, its incipiency to begin today. Guild Masters, grandmasters, and masters, if you are in favor of acknowledging Rexei Longshanks as Guild Master of the Holy Guild, raise your hands now."

A forest of arms lifted into the air. Some shot up immediately, while others rose at a slower rate. Rexei couldn't count them all from where she was seated, but it looked like she had a majority vote in her favor at both the head table and among the first five rows of the pews.

"Lower your arms. All opposed . . . ?" Toric asked. This time, the number of arms was easily countable, less than ten. "And those who abstain?" A few more arms raised. He gestured for the arms to drop, consulted under his breath with the Precinct captain, then nodded. "The number of votes for is over eighty, which is where I lost count because it's too late at night. The number of votes against is nine. The number abstaining is twelve. Motion passes. The Consulate of Heias Precinct grants you the title of Guild Master Rexei Longshanks of the incipient Holy Guild. Don't let it go to your head," the elderly Gearman warned her. "You are acknowledged a Guild Master, but you are young, and your Guild virtually nonexistent . . . not to mention not yet fully acknowledged."

Rexei bowed her head, acknowledging his point. He continued, addressing the others.

"Guild Masters. You have been apprised of your responsibilities locally for those prisoners released from the Heiastowne temple. You have been informed of the release of prisoners elsewhere in your homeland and the fact that the inhabitants of those other towns are attempting to absolve themselves of their chartered responsibility for all members, current and former, of good standing . . . and I shall remind you that being kidnapped by the False God's priesthood simply for the ability to . . . to cast magic does *not* make any guildmember a member in *bad* standing.

"As Guild Masters, you have the right to make unilateral decisions for all guildmembers within your purview. As we now have twenty present, we have a quorum for kingdom-wide decisions. Shall we return these . . . ex-prisoners . . . into your individual guilds' care in small groups? Or shall we place them all into the care of the one guild which even now none of us cares to formally name out loud?"

The men and women seated at the Consulate table exchanged wordless, wary looks. It was clear they weren't comfortable with the idea of taking back into their midst *known* mages, whom the priesthood could come back and grab at any point in time. Rexei wanted to say something, but she knew this wasn't her fight.

The one man who knew whose fight it was did not stand up again, but he did speak sharply.

"If they get shoved into *my* guild," Alonnen told the hall, "then I will demand tithes from each of *your* guilds to cover the costs of feeding, clothing, and giving each ex-prisoner adequate medical care and emotional support. And a stipend to cover all further expenses that may crop up . . . and if you will not give those supplies willingly, then I shall have no choice but to command my people to *take* those supplies, just to keep everyone from starving to death within the first week."

"*Thank* you, Guild Master Tall. I will presume that *you* vote to insist that every guild take up the care and responsibility for at least some of these ex-prisoners," Toric said dryly.

"Damn right, I do," Alonnen shot back. "We'll take in a few, but we can *only* afford to take in a few—there are five guilds in this town with less than a dozen members, from masters to apprentices, so we'll take in one for each of them, plus the three who were registered with us before their capture. Any others will require a full-support tithe, and the maximum we'll take in will be thirty . . . so twenty-two of them would require support tithes."

Rexei seized the pause that followed his words. "I also must insist that the guilds accept and manage their responsibilities toward each other in this matter."

"If we will continue from that end of the Consulate bench," Toric stated dryly, "I shall take that as *two* votes for multiguild management of the ex-prisoners. Guild Master of Actors?"

"*I* vote for each of the guilds to take in a few of the prisoners," the redhead stated firmly. "Regardless of the outcome, the Actors Guild will take in at least three. My fellow guildmembers can manage that much locally here in Heiastowne. In Luxon, the temple has yet to release its captives, but when it does, I know we can care for five or six in the larger arms of the Actors Guild there. *We* won't abandon anyone, though we, too, are limited in how many we can accept."

"Guild Master of Modellers?" Toric asked.

"It is all our responsibility, not just Guild Master Tall's. We can take in three here in Heiastowne without any strain to our resources. Hollowfeld to the south is a small town. We had only twelve prisoners released total," the male Guild Master stated, "but the Modellers Guild has a solid presence for its size, there. We, the Tillers, Woodwrights, and Hospitallers all took in the released mages pretty much immediately. We can even take in two more from this area, ship them to my fellow Modellers in Hollowfeld, and see that they receive proper care . . . and wherever possible, we will take in one or two elsewhere as well."

"Guild Master of Wheelrights?"

"We'll do it across the kingdom . . . and we'll take in five here in Heiastowne right away. Or at least when the weather improves," the rough-voiced man stated. "I saw the snow outside. We'll all have to take refuge in town tonight."

The vote continued down the line. Each man and woman questioned agreed to accept responsibility kingdom-wide, and most listed a number, small but significant, which they knew their nearest groups could take in immediately. Hearing so many accept their responsibilities, Rexei started to relax. However, she could see Alonnen tensing, no doubt worried that a single vote otherwise would throw his whole guild into turmoil.

Torhammer dipped his head slightly when it was his turn. "As Precinct captain, it is my responsibility to enforce the law. This I have done as firmly as I could. The *law* says that each guild owes a responsibility to all of its members, past and current, provided they are all of good standing. That means the orphans of lost guild-members can call upon their parents' guilds for support and protection. Injured members can request their guilds to pay for their apothecary expenses, and so forth. I am well aware that these ex-prisoners are orphaned and injured, as much or more inside their hearts and minds as in their bodies. My vote goes toward all guilds across the land accepting their share of responsibility.

"*However,* that being said . . . this and the other Precinct militias cannot accept the responsibility of any of these orphaned and injured mages into its ranks—let me *finish,*" he added sternly, raising a hand as several in the audience across from the head table started to protest. "Not because we do not care, but because we must manage the *Hunter Squads.* Some of which are still out there, hunting down mages because they may not yet realize that Mekha is indeed gone from everywhere, rendering their captives unnecessary. I have reached *some* of them via talker-box in the last day . . . but not all of them have reported in, yet."

"Mekha doesn't exist anymore!" one of the female Guild Masters asserted. "There's no *need* for them to keep and drain their prisoners."

"Mekha being gone simply means that there's nothing to stop these bastards from draining any captive mages for their *own* benefit," Alonnen growled. "It isn't quite blood magic, but it is still a form of rape most foul. I must agree with Captain Torhammer; his support of the law is deeply appreciated, and technically all Precinct militias are a form of guild, and all of captain or higher rank have a vote in this quorum . . . but I also must agree that his reason for abstaining from direct support is understandable in the light of his explanation.

"My guild will take in an additional five mages on top of the original eight in the militia's name. With supporting tithes from the militia, of course," he continued, his tone pointed and dry. "I trust, Captain Torhammer, that you will rein in the Hunter Squads within your jurisdiction and inform them in no uncertain terms that hunting for mages is now at an end? And that you will explain to the ex-priesthood in equally blunt terms that they are no longer allowed to imprison, torture, rape, and drain any mages ever again?" Alonnen asked. "You are renowned as the Hammer of Hei-astowne. Feel free to invoke that hammer in the name of the law."

"It would help, Guild Master Tall, if our very next vote after this one is an equally unanimous quorum on decreeing the imprisonment and draining of mages to be utterly illegal," Torhammer returned wryly.

Toric spoke up, regaining control without using the gavel stone. "That is the very next subject and shall be tabled until this vote is complete. As a grandmaster-ranked Gearman, I have the right to vote in this quorum . . . and I vote for the guilds to undertake their lawful responsibility as well," Toric asserted. "The Hei-astowne Consulate can manage to care for at least one ex-prisoner at this time. Not every Consulate is large enough for a permanent staff, but ours can manage that much."

Rexei focused on tidying up her papers and returning them to her bag while the vote continued to the far end of the table. By the time the last Guild Master voted, however . . . it was clearly unanimous not only in agreement, but in the voicing of how many freed mages each guild would take. A nonbinding show of hands was called for among the grandmasters and masters with no Guild Master representing them at the head table. Most raised their arms in favor, with only a few abstaining—mostly those with only master-rank members within the city's walls—and none voting otherwise. Many of them stood up, each in turn offering shelter for the ex-prisoners.

She felt deeply relieved for the sake of the Mages Guild and its rather finite resources at that last revelation. From the look on Alonnen's face when he glanced at her, he felt the same way. By the time the last guild offered, all one hundred fifty-three mages, and then some, were covered.

By comparison, the vote to render any further capture, torture, and power-draining of mages illegal was a simple yes/no vote. In fact, it passed so swiftly that it was anticlimactic. With one last admonishment for "Guild Master Longshanks" to finish polishing the new Holy Guild's charter for future ratification and to pick up at least three apprentices as soon as possible, Grandmaster Toric closed the meeting with a rhythmic rapping of his gavel on its matching stone anvil.

Immediately, Alonnen was up on his feet and crossing the distance between him and Rexei. Snagging her elbow, he murmured in her ear, "Let's go. Out the back, right away," he ordered, literally pulling her off her end of the bench. "If we don't get both of us out of here *now*, we'll not get free for two hours or more."

Snatching up her bag and grabbing her coat and cap from where she had rolled them up and tucked them under the bench seat, Rexei followed him. Several of the others tried to intercept both of them for questions, but both were quick and slim enough to squeeze through the barely open side door. Rexei pulled it shut behind her, slowing down their would-be interrogators. That gave them a few more seconds to dodge into the back corridors of the Consulate building.

Alonnen led her out into the alley, quickly shut the door, then pulled her across to a door placed almost directly opposite, and rapped on it in a hard, fast pattern not too dissimilar from the one the head of the Consulate had used to end the emergency session. Rexei had only a glimpse of the trampled snow of the alley, but it was enough to tell her that several people within the last hour had used this particular door, both coming and going.

It swung open within seconds. By the time the Consulate back door started to open, the door to the new building had swung shut. They were let into it by a vaguely familiar man.

"How many?" the middle-aged door guard asked without

preamble, watching them stamp off the three inches of snow they had waded through.

"Nine," Alonnen stated. "The others will come in soon."

Someone came down the nearby stairs, so heavily bundled up, swathed in coat, hat, scarf, and gloves, Rexei couldn't have sworn they were fully human, never mind their gender or anything else. From the way the figure avoided her gaze, she thought maybe they were trying to avoid being recognized. *Then again, he or she could just be wrapped up against all that snow outside, with a long walk to wherever they're headed home . . .*

"You only get three. Back stairs, rooms thirty-six through thirty-eight," the burly man stated, plucking a key from the wall by the door and handing it over without being asked or offered anything—and that was when Rexei recognized him by voice as well as face. He was the fellow who had bruised her shoulder just the day before. She kept her head ducked low, not even daring to peek at him. Thankfully, his attention had switched to letting the other person pass outside.

Relieved to have avoided another confrontation with the strong-fingered man, she mounted three sets of stairs in Alonnen's wake. The place was remarkably silent; even the stairs barely creaked as they made the climb, leaving her with nothing to do but follow her guide and eye the rich, brocaded gold and red cloth glued to the walls in place of mere painted plaster. The corridor at the top of the stairs was equally opulent, though up here the predominant colors were gold and lilac, even if the flowerlike pattern was the same. Even the doors were painted pale purple with decorative numbers and trim in polished brass . . . including the one, tucked into the corner of the L-shaped hall, that Alonnen opened.

Visual opulence wasn't the only overwhelming factor. The smells inhabiting both the corridor and the chamber behind that panel made her nose itch from the faint but cloying mix of perfume, musk, and . . . Stepping fully into the room, she rubbed at her nose and frowned at the floor, trying to figure out what that scent was. It took her a few moments to realize the smell underlying everything was not musk, as in the perfume; no, it was the scent of sex. She stopped mid nose-rub and blinked, then hurriedly glanced around. Closing the door behind her, Alonnen lifted one brow, catching her bewildered look.

Rexei focused on the room, not the man at her side; him, she trusted. This place was another matter. Golden wood covered the walls to about hip height and a fancy, carved rail board capped the vertical panels, and above that, yet more silk fabric, this time patterned with delicately woven flying birds, had been glued to the plaster-smooth walls. The front half of the room had a padded divan for seating, a small table with two dining chairs, and a side table hosting a collection of carafes no doubt filled with expensive beverages. A scale sat nearby, suggesting the price of the drinks contained within were gauged by the weight of whatever remained behind. She resolved not to touch a drop, since she didn't have much in the way of money on her.

A woodstove on the left and a pleated privacy screen on the right divided the front from the back. On the other side, the far wall hosted a huge bed flanked by quilt-curtained windows and mounded with what looked like freshly bleached sheets and a thick, down-stuffed quilt. To the right of it, partially shielded behind the privacy screen, lay a rounded alcove large enough to host a permanent, polished-copper bath in the middle. More quilted fabric panels had been pulled down over the windows, shutting out the lamplight of the city and cutting off some of the drafts, but from the smell and the furnishings and the shape of the room, Rexei knew what that alcove was. This was one of the famous "turret" rooms of Big Momma Bertha's Brothel.

She had heard about it within her first three days here in

Heiastowne, in fact. When Big Momma wanted to "advertise" her establishment's offerings, she instructed some of the ladies of her guild, and even a gentleman or two from time to time, to take a bath with those blinds rolled up out of the way, particularly on the second floor, which gave just enough of a view to titillate the people in the street. The basement hosted a gambling den, and the ground floor catered some of the better meals for sale in the city. The four floors above were all for rent, usually by the hour, and always for a fairly high price.

Rumor had it the time spent at Big Momma's establishment was worth it, though. Some of the younger men in the Servers Guild, and even two of the women, had spoken of saving up enough money to visit this place or boasted of having done so in the past. Of all the places Rexei had expected them to go for shelter during a snowstorm, however, this was not one of them. In fact, she had expected somewhere else would have been chosen first.

"If your mouth were as wide-open as your eyes," Alonnen quipped, removing his cap, "you'd be choking on a bullfrog, never mind a fly. *Relax*, Rexei. This is a bolt-hole, not an assignation."

Blinking, Rexei struggled to regain some of her sense of calm. She swallowed and cleared her throat. "So . . . uh . . . how long do we stay here?"

"Two good meals with a bit of sleep in between," he told her. "If it's three inches down here on the plains, the snow up by the dam is going to be eight or more deep until it's cleared, too deep to drive in safely with all those hill-hugging curves on the last stretch of the road. I wish the Wheelwrights would come up with a better method of traction in icy, slippery conditions, but until they do, we're safer spending the night here. In the meantime, I am hungry, and if you're not, you should be after all that talking. We can check the menu on the little table, there, to see what's being offered this week."

Unbuttoning her coat, she shrugged out of it, then pulled off her winter cap and set her messenger bag on the divan. Belatedly, she removed the heavy gold oval, dropping that into her bag for safekeeping. After adding the medallion-strung chain of her other guild associations, she joined him at the table. Someone had paid the Binders Guild for the use of one of their small printing presses. Made from four sheets folded in half and stitched together down the spine with a bit of ribbon, the menu included a wine list, finger foods, hearty dishes, sweet desserts . . . and a list of jams, jellies, syrups, and "a set of old sheets."

That last one puzzled her. "Uhh . . . Alonnen? Why do they offer a set of old sheets on the same list as a bunch of flavorings and preserves?"

"What? *Oh.*" His face turned red. It was still altered somewhat by a disguise spell, a little more tanned with not even the hint of a freckle, but the illusion did not hide the rush of blood to his cheeks. Clearing his throat, Alonnen explained delicately, "That's so you, ah, don't get the regular sheets stained. It's all boiled in hot water and bleached clean, but sometimes the fruit jams can still stain, you know."

"I still don't get it," she told him. "What have jams and jellies to do with old sheets? Or new?"

Still a bit flushed, he cleared his throat. "It's for those who like to strip their lover naked, lay them down on the old sheets, and then, uh, coat their curves with sweet preserves or, uh, drizzle them in things like butterscotch or caramel syrups . . . which they then lick off their lover's body. And, ah, hopefully have the same done to them in return."

Her mouth formed a wordless "*oh*" in reply. Reminding herself to breathe, that the man sharing this room with her didn't even seem to want her in the normal way—an oddly unsettling thought—Rexei turned her attention firmly to her empty stomach. "Ah, do you know what this stuff is? Natallian . . . pah-stah?"

"It's something made from finely ground wheat flour. It's molded into shapes that are boiled, then drained and drenched in various sauces. It's hard to explain," he added at her dubious look, "but it's just one of those things where once you've seen and tried it, you'll just know what it *is* from that point on, rather than trying to explain it. I like the Nutty Chicken dish with it. Two or three kinds of nuts, mostly hazelnut, a bit of hazelnut-flavored liqueur, plus a bit of cream simmered with some herbs for the sauce, and it's done."

One of her brows raised. "You've never apprenticed to a cook in the Hospitallers or the Bakers Guilds, have you? Because that was a very bland description."

"No, I haven't. I grew up in the Hydraulics and Mages Guilds, right here in Heias Precinct," Alonnen admitted. "I know I had a sheltered childhood compared to most mages elsewhere and that I haven't suffered nearly as many hazards, though I have seen them, and the results of them." He reached over and cupped his fingers over her hand. "You have my admiration for all you've survived, Rexei. You truly do."

She looked down at his hand, wondering once again at how he could be such a . . . a *touchy* person. Just as he started to pull his hand away, she released the menu booklet and turned her palm over, twining her fingers with his. She blushed as she did so, and she didn't quite meet his gaze, but she held his hand. "Thank you, Guild Master."

NINE

Alonnen felt his heart thump a little stronger. It was an odd sensation, but not entirely unexplained. Between her blush and the way she returned his touch, he wondered if she had unspoken feelings for him. The strings he had pulled during the Consulate meeting had been necessary in his view, because he believed she really was going to be a force to be reckoned with in relation to the coming demonic plague. He didn't know how, but he wanted to give her what advantages and recognitions he could in preparation for it.

This, however, was much more personal. He knew he tended to reach out physically to a lot of people; it no doubt sprang from growing up in a very loving, protected family. Because of his position, a lot of people did not reach back in equal measure. Those that did, he treasured. But this, the willingness of her hand entwined with his, touched him deeply. Instinct said that showing it, however, would do more to scare her away than keeping silent.

So he diffused the moment by focusing on something a bit more trivial, yet still important.

"Nonsense," he dismissed, waving his free hand. "You've never really been in my guild. At least, not very deeply into it. And look at you," he added, gently squeezing her fingers. "You're a Guild Master yourself! You're now my equal, and I'll have nothing less than that out of you. Call me Alonnen, as my equal. Or call me 'Tall' outside of sheltered zones."

She looked up and around at the sybaritic brothel room. "This isn't exactly a sheltered zone."

"Actually, it is," Alonnen said. He tapped the table. "My predecessors had the wisdom to invest in land in the Lessors Guild, and to involve themselves in the Architects and Masons Guilds, and with the Woodwrights. As a result, there are certain buildings—this being one of them—that are very carefully warded to hide all traces of magic taking place within. Moreover, *this* building—which has been a brothel for hundreds of years and has from time to time been the seat of the Guild Master for the Whores Guild—has had each of its rooms spell-warded for sound as well as magic.

"We're almost as safe here as we would be back at the dam, save that there aren't several layers of sentries on guard. Still, in exchange for keeping up the spells and the wards, this particular establishment lets us use these rooms as a temporary bolt-hole. Not often, and only for a few days or in a few rooms at a time, but that's the deal," he told her.

Rexei could see how that would be a good deal. Before she could say anything, however, her stomach gurgled. Alonnen smiled wryly.

"We don't get more than one meal a day for free, but the food's worth paying for. Let's order a Nutty Chicken and a Creamed Salmon," he proposed, squeezing and releasing her hand. "That way, if you don't like the one, you can try the other. They serve a really good barley soup, too, and there's a greenhouse on the roof so they have fresh greens to go with it. Big Momma *swears* by fresh greens for reinvigorating the libido in winter."

Rexei narrowed her eyes, watching him rise and head for what she realized was a small, wire-connected talker-box by the front door. Just like that, he had gone from being labeled nearly sexless to being very male once again in her mind. "And just how would *you* know what Grandmaster Bertha claims about . . . you know?"

Swinging around to face her, Alonnen sighed and rubbed the back of his neck. The movement ruffled the curls tied into a short tail at his nape. "You know, Longshanks, I've seen this in other female mages, and I can understand why so many think this way, but I was hoping *you* were smart enough to think past the fear. Rexei . . . there is a whole *spectrum* between gelded asexual male on the violet side of the rainbow, and bestial, brutal rapist on the red side.

"*Most* men are somewhere between yellow and blue. I'm about as green as they come—I have a libido, I have an interest in sex, and I find many women to be attractive. My brother happens to find both women *and* men attractive, but he's green in hue, too," Alonnen explained. "Neither of us are going to grab and violate any partner, but neither are we going to castrate ourselves, literally or otherwise, just to pretend our need to be touched, held, and pleasured doesn't exist. It does.

"*Your* needs exist, too," he said, pointing at her, wanting her to understand that, and that they weren't anything worth fearing. "They might be smothered by the many problems you have seen so far, but you have every right to know what it feels like to be hugged and held, to be kissed and . . . and so forth."

This time, he blushed, trailing off for a moment. Rexei didn't look very feminine, but then again, a lot of women around the Heias Dam tended to downplay their femininity, simply because it meant less hassle for them in the public areas whenever the priests came by to collect mandatory tithes and such. But there was something about her that . . . Sighing, he dragged his mind firmly back into safe territory.

"Unfortunately, this conversation is heading in a direction I don't believe you're ready to discuss in a calm state of mind," Alonnen said. "I do think you are cute as a button and as smart as a piston engine, but unless and until you should feel the same, whether it's with me or with anyone else, that's as far as it should go. I will repeat that you're as safe in my company as if . . . as if one of us were a pet dog, worthy of a few pats and a cuddle-hug and some positive attention, but that's it. And if you fear anything more than that, just say so. As it is, as soon as Gabria gets free of the Consulate and comes over, she'll swap places with me, and I'll share a room with one of the other lads."

Turning back to the door, he moved up to the talker-box and began turning the crank-handle to charge it.

Rexei watched him place their dinner order, face warm and mind racing over his words. She could not remember the last time she had been complimented by someone who knew she was female. A couple of times her gender had been uncovered, but the comments made during those moments of discovery had been insults, not compliments. Multiple times someone had complimented her as a male . . . but some of those had been just as awful in their own way. The rest of the time, she had ignored the good ones, since underneath her attitude and her disguises, she was still very much a female at the end of each day.

And here I am in a brothel with . . . with the first man I've been interested in, as *a man, woman to man, since . . .*

A knock on the door startled both of them. Caught in the act of hanging up the cone-shaped earpiece that allowed a talker-box operator to hear what the person on the other end was saying,

Alonnen fumbled it onto its hook, then glanced at her. He opened his mouth to say something, then the rhythmic rapping was repeated. Relaxing, he nodded.

"I didn't catch the pattern the first time. That'll be Gabria." A step to the right allowed him to grasp the doorknob and pull the solid panel open. The blonde woman smiled at him, opened her mouth to speak . . . and her gaze drifted to Rexei beyond his shoulder. She froze, eyes widening in fear.

It was the first time anyone had looked at Rexei in fear, and Rexei didn't know what to make of it.

"Is something wrong?" Alonnen asked his assistant. He glanced over his shoulder at Rexei and the rest of the room, but he couldn't find anything alarming in it. Looking back, he watched as Gabria shrunk in on herself, huddling in her knit tunic. "What's wrong?"

Swallowing, Gabria looked down the hall, as if she'd rather be anywhere else.

He stepped back from the door, giving her room to enter, guessing that she didn't want to talk about it in public. "Come inside."

That only made her eyes widen further. She shook her head and moved back. "Uh . . . I'll . . . just go find another room . . ."

Frowning, Alonnen stepped into the hall, letting the door almost close behind him. Mindful of the potential for eavesdroppers, he spoke under his breath. "Gabria, what's wrong? You're acting like you're afraid of Longshanks. You're supposed to be sharing this room with her tonight."

"She . . . she's with one of *them*," Gabria hissed, eyes still wide and wary.

On the other side of the door, inside the room, Rexei ghosted up to the panel as quietly as she could. She had seen the other woman's fearful stare and wanted to know why she was upset.

"What do you mean, one of *them*?" Alonnen asked.

"A *God*," Gabria hissed, shuddering inside her coat. "I can't even *think* about . . . about *Him*, and you want me to . . . to spend the night in a room with *her*?"

"Gabria . . ."

"No! I'm going to Marta's," his part-time assistant asserted. "I'll spend the night with her. Where I'll be safe!"

Movement by the stairwell resolved itself into the faces of two familiar men. Alonnen lifted his chin in brief greeting, but he kept most of his attention on the woman in front of him. "Gabria, Guildra isn't the same as Mekha."

"You don't *know* that. And frankly, I don't *want* to know. I'm going to Marta's, and that's *that*."

"Then at least let me and Ohso walk you there," Alonnen compromised, meaning one of the other men who had accompanied them to town. Hearing his name, the fellow raised his brows and headed their way.

"I don't need a keeper," Gabria retorted, folding her arms across her chest. "It's not *that* far to her tenement on the west side of town, and once I get there, her building is . . . you know. I'm not a sheep, needing to be shepherded every step of the way."

"I know you're not, but if you slip and fall in the snow, you could lie there all night with a broken leg, and nobody would know," he countered. "I'll not have you die of exposure. And he and I can keep an eye on each other on the way back."

"Actually, Mark and I can go with her," Ohso offered, coming close enough to hear Alonnen's words and to guess the rest. "There's a gaming house between here and the westside we were thinking of visiting anyway, so we might as well just walk her to her friend's place and hit it on the way back."

Alonnen suppressed a sigh. "Set aside money for your suppers and breakfasts, and don't bet anything more than what you actually carry. And don't get caught cheating if you use . . ." He wiggled his fingers to indicate magic. "Try not to cheat at all."

"Oh, c'mon," Ohso joked. "How else am I going to retire into a castle of my very own? Join the flippin' priesthood? That won't work anymore, you know."

Gabria's mouth twitched into a smile, but it was a weak one. Sighing out loud, Alonnen flipped his hand at the trio. "Off with you, then—when dawn comes or when the storm stops, ascertain if the streets are passable, and be here within an hour of that. Report in by talker-box if it takes more than a day. Other than that, have a good night."

Nodding in farewell, the pair departed to pick up Mark on their way out of the brothel. With a sigh, Alonnen closed the door. "Bloody hell . . ." He put his back to the door and leaned against it, eyeing Rexei. "How much did you hear?"

"Why is she afraid of me?" Rexei asked. Then winced, realizing it was a stupid question, given their whole culture.

Seeing her wince, Alonnen nodded. "Exactly. Gods. She doesn't trust any of 'em. She won't be the only one, either. I'd said a good sixty, seventy percent of most mages will look sideways at you, and a good chunk of the rest of the population will, too."

"Yes, but I am a . . . one of them," Rexei hedged, not quite willing to call herself a mage openly yet. "Anything I could believe into existence would by logic *have* to avoid all that holy manure we've been forced to swallow all these years. Guildra is not like that, because I, too, couldn't stand the thought of it being like that."

He reached up and rested his hand on her shoulder, giving it a supportive little squeeze. "I believe that, and you believe that . . . but some people, like Springreaver, just won't believe it until it's sunk into their very bones. And that can only take time to accomplish, Longshanks. Give 'er time. Spread the word of what Guildra stands for and what She stands against, and give it time."

"Well . . . sorry to chase away your girl," Rexei offered awkwardly.

Alonnen blinked at her. "My what?"

"You . . . and her aren't . . . ?" she asked tentatively.

"What? Oh no," he quickly denied. "Not in the least. I'm not her type, she's not mine, and I haven't dated anyone in a while. It's not a good idea for the Guild Master to court anyone within his or her own guild anyway. At most, it'd be someone on the periphery, and Gabria's been one of my close assistants for a few years now—inner-circle close, not intimate close," he clarified.

"Oh." She felt strangely relieved to hear that. Her face felt hot. Moving away from the door, she shrugged. "Well, I'm glad. I mean, that I didn't interrupt any plans the two of you may have had. Third wheel on a motorhorse, and all that."

She's blushing? Alonnen thought. *Why would she blush* after *I said it was alri—Oh.* Grateful her back was to him, he felt his own face heat a little. Carefully *not* clearing his throat, for he didn't want to sound awkward himself, he did his best to explain smoothly and simply his own reasons. "Well, as the Guild Master, it's important not to take advantage and important not to seem to be taking advantage. There are rules and all that. But . . . when I was still a journeyman, apprenticed to the previous Guild Master . . .

"Well, what I thought was my first serious romance turned out to be a case of social climbing," he stated wryly, wrinkling his nose. Rexei turned to look at him in inquiry. Alonnen nodded. "Yeah. Her name was Daralei, and she knew—everyone knew by then—that I was going to be the next Guardian of the Vortex, being the strongest in the Guild next to Millanei. Before that was settled, she was flirtin' with one of the other two candidates. Storshei. He's second-in-command of the dam works now. But back then, she glomped onto me, had my head spinning . . ."

"And?" Rexei asked, curious in spite of herself.

"He tried to convince me of what she was up to, then he went to Millanei, who contrived my 'fall from grace,'" Alonnen said, giving her a lopsided smile. "Dara tried getting me reinstated. A little too hard. So, suspicious, I told her I was happy to let Storshei be the next Guardian . . . and so she started flirting with him on the sly. I caught her at it so it wasn't just his word against hers, and Millanei kicked her outta the guild. Put her in Pistons far to the north."

"I'm sorry you had to suffer that," Rexei told him. She moved over to the couch and settled into the corner of it.

Following her, Alonnen claimed the other side. He pulled off his boots, then put a wool-covered foot on the cushions between them. "Better to find out before she leeched any real status, power, or wealth outta me. The next one . . . wasn't a mage."

"Next one?" Rexei raised her brows. "Uh . . . how old are you?"

"Thirty."

Her brows rose. That was a bit older than she had expected. "Thirty? Well . . . I suppose you act it, but you look more like you're twenty-five."

He grinned at the compliment and doffed his cap to her. Literally, pulled it off with a bow of his upper body. "Thank you, thank you . . . my dad could get mistaken for a twenty-five-year-old at the age of forty-one. Good bones, and all that. I take after him in all but . . . well, in all but the nose. More like my granddaddy in that."

The way he flicked up the tip of his longish nose with the side of one finger, teasing himself, made her chuckle and smile. "I'm not sure, since it's been so long, but . . . I think I have my father's chin. And his forehead. Everything in between was mum's."

Her gaze dipped down.

Not wanting her to grow sad, Alonnen changed the subject. "My mum calls me 'Al,' and some of the others, but I rather prefer my full name. A bit opposite—most children would rather their parents didn't call them by their full name. That, and there are three other Alonnens in the Precinct. I know of at least seven people named Rexei between here and Gren Precinct to the west, two of them girls here in Heiastowne. But one of them likes to be called 'Lani' for some reason. She's in the Bakers Guild. Do you have a nickname? Or did you?"

"No," she admitted, after giving it a few moments of thought. "Not unless you count things like 'sweetie' and 'kitten' when I was very little."

"I got saddled with 'dumpling,'" Alonnen found himself confessing—and grinned as she burst out laughing, then quickly covered her mouth, blushing. "No, it's okay. At least I'm not as round as one." He looped his arm around his knee, staring off past her shoulder. "If Millanei hadn't warned me, I wouldn't have realized that working magic burns the body's reserves as surely as working muscles. You won't see many plump mages in and around the dam, unless they're compulsive eaters.

"But, if you're ever tasked with setting warding amulets, you'll be set a diet of vegetables and greens to eat, not just things like potatoes, breads, and meat. We don't do as much of that in the winter, though," he said. "It's hard to get fresh greens. The few books on magic we have all agree that fresh plant-based food is good for a mage, since that's where magic comes from."

"It does?" Rexei asked, blinking. "I don't remember that. Mum said it comes from within people and is something I should never, ever let the priesthood find out about, because they'll steal it all away."

"Oh yes, it has a whole cycle, like rainwater," he told her. "Rain evaporates from the land and the lakes, goes up into the sky, condenses into clouds, falls as rain, evaporates again . . . Magic comes from plants and is absorbed by animals when we eat the plants—we humans are animals as surely as any donkey or cat, just a whole lot smarter. And we in turn shed magic, or rather, life-energy, which in turn the plants drink up and grow strong, feeding us again. The only exception is the Vortex, and similar fountains of energy."

"There are other places like the Vortex?" she asked.

"Yes—those Guardians you spoke with, they guard other, similar resources. Some are formal points in the world where magic spills in from the . . . well, it's not the Afterlife, but it's on the way to the Afterlife. The Darkhanans call it the Dark, and they base their religion around it. I think," he added, frowning slightly. "Priestess Saleria of the far-off Empire of Katan was explaining some of it to me, because she's being visited by a Darkhanan Witch—not Witch-Knight Orana Niel, but someone else. I've met her, you know. Our secret champion."

Rexei smiled at his lofty look. She held out her thumb sideways, the other fingers curled into her palm. "I've pricked this thing thirty times—thirty-and-one, if you count *your* guild—signing the petition books. I even met her once, in the Glassworks Guild. Though at the time, I had no clue who she was or what her significance was. I just knew everyone in that guild trusted her completely and that we were signing special books to get Mekha removed from the world. No one believed it'd happen in our lifetime, but . . . we clung to the hope."

"And here we are, with Him actually removed." He relaxed into the corner of the divan, then sighed. "Well, we won't know any details of how it all happened until after the Convocation ends and we can speak with everyone in Nightfall, but I'm confident Sir Orana carried through on all her promises. I hope she—they— weren't harmed doing it, but when *I* met her, she swore on a Truth Stone she'd brought that she'd lay down her life to get the job done."

"If she could . . . Is she really immortal?" Rexei asked. "That's what everyone was whispering."

Alonnen shrugged. "Millanei said the Witch-Knight hadn't

aged one bit from when *she* was a young apprentice, so she very well could be. But nobody knows how she did it."

Thinking about it, Rexei finally shrugged. "Maybe it's because she slew Mekha? Slay a God, gain immortality?"

A tip of his head acknowledged her point. "Yeah, but the buggering bastard didn't *stay* dead."

Her eyes widened at the epithet. She hadn't ever heard anyone apply it so casually, so *jokingly*, to the God that so many had feared for so long, mages and non-mages alike. "You don't *fear* Mekha, do you?"

"I *did*," Alonnen told her. "But after living here most of my life, seeing His magics *fail* to find the mages who fled to the dam even while being tracked by His dog-priests . . . no, I'm not afraid anymore. And even if He somehow did return, even some of His own priests won't worship him anymore." At her puzzled look, he reminded her, ". . . They let the mages go?"

"They let them go so that *we* wouldn't attack," Rexei reminded him cynically. "I sincerely doubt they'll let *any* scrap of power go, if they can help it. Being told by the Consulate that the priesthood is no longer an officially recognized guild is going to enrage them. Particularly the lot here in Heiastowne."

"Well, without Mekha to back them up with His God-power, they'll get a good shock if they try to go up against *us*. We may be half trained compared to mages elsewhere in the world, but we *know* how to counter the priest-mages," he asserted.

That assertion made Rexei frown. "Alonnen . . . if you can contact powerful mages via that mirror—mages outside Mekhana's borders—then why do you say you're half trained? Why can't you just get the training you need from them?"

Her words caught him off-guard. It was an honest question, though. Sighing, Alonnen swept his hand over his head . . . then picked the knot out of the ribbon binding his hair at the nape of his neck. The golden strands fluffed forward, spiral curls released like snapped springs, and he caught her amused smile. He returned it, then dragged his attention back to her question.

"It has to do with the oaths of the Guardian, and the fact that, just up until a few months ago, we didn't even *have* that particular scrying mirror. Just two precious ones that could only view things within the kingdom's boundaries, and only with great effort could I peer at anything beyond. Mekha kept a shield over the entire border," he explained. "Unless they were extremely powerful— maybe even shielded by another God—mages could not slip into the kingdom without being seen and tagged . . . and most mages on either side of that border could not scry past it. If I hadn't had the power of the Vortex backing me, I wouldn't have been able to try. So almost nobody could come to us to teach us without getting caught, and even Witch Orana couldn't stay."

"Then how did you get the mirror?" she asked. "You all acted like it had been working for some time."

"The Vortex is connected to the Fountainways, and the Fountainways aren't included in Mekha's spell. Or weren't," he clarified. "I only got that mirror a few months ago. As it is, the Fountainways before that were voice only . . . and rules of Guardianship state most firmly that I could not explain to anyone that my Guardianship was *within* Mekhana's borders. You took the oath; you know the spell."

Rexei nodded and recited the rules of the oathbinding she had taken. "I know. Anyone who tries to say to the priesthood of Mekha, either of their own free will or via coercive spells, *where* the Mages Guild is located—or its members or speaks of the Vortex and its powers—automatically and completely forgets the answers before they're revealed."

"Exactly. As the Guild Master, my oathbinding is a bit different because I *need* to be able to talk about magic and mages and such . . .

but as the Guardian, I am still bound by my oaths to keep the powers of the Vortex out of the hands of those who would abuse that power. And the one thing the priesthood of Mekha *never* learned—and never will—is that there *is* a Fountain, the Vortex, here in Heias Precinct. With the power of the Vortex at His fingertips, Mekha could've challenged a fellow God to His or Her face, even without needing the Convocation to meet them here in the mortal world."

"War in Heaven?" She shivered. "Is it really that powerful?"

He leveled her a look. "Rexei, the Vortex has kept a *God* from finding out about the home of the Mages Guild. Perhaps not the strongest of Gods out there, since hardly anyone wanted to worship Him beyond His priests, but still, a God—and a God who drained magic from mages, at that, adding to His power. Not that it makes *me* the equivalent of a God or anything," Alonnen added quickly. "But from what the other Guardians have said about such things, two or three of the Fountains combined might make a mage close to being a God, if that mage could handle the power. I can just handle the Vortex, but adding another would fry me alive. Giving it to a God? That's just a bad idea all around. I don't have to test the theory to know that much."

A knock interrupted them. Rising, Alonnen crossed to the door and cracked it open. The last clutch of the fellows he had brought along for their protection had arrived. Murmuring where Ohso, Gabria, and Mark had gone, he directed them to pick one of the other two rooms. Once the door was shut, Alonnen realized what that meant. Sighing, he turned back to Rexei.

"As much as I'd like to give you privacy tonight . . . I'm going to have to stay here. Guild policy, no one sleeps alone outside the Vortex. These rooms are sheltered against magic, both scryings and attacks, but not against nonmagical attacks," he told her.

She blushed, thinking about sharing the bed with him again. Rexei glanced at it, then managed a casual shrug when she looked back at him. "It's okay. I trust you." The way he relaxed at her words, the smile he gave her, warmed her. She returned it, ducking her head a little. "Besides, you didn't snore last night. I've no guarantee about sharing a bed with anyone else."

"You were out so hard, not even the dam breaking would've woken you," Alonnen retorted. He tapped the tip of his nose and pointed at her. "But you can't say I didn't warn you tonight."

That made her laugh heartily . . . and that made him feel the paradox of a sudden flush of heat coupled with a chilling realization. *I like her. A lot. Like I haven't . . . like I haven't* loved *anyone since Bethana . . .*

His first romantic interest had tried to use him for power and prestige. His second had been a good woman at heart, but she had died in an explosion at her munitions factory. After that, Alonnen had buried himself in his work, believing that Fate just didn't have a long-lasting love in mind for him. *So either Fate is teasing me a third time, or . . . well, Daralei didn't count since it wasn't mutual on her part, so Fate just might be giving me a second chance, not a third, at love . . .*

Sleeping chastely beside her might be awkward, now that he was aware of how much he really liked Rexei Longshanks. The couch was a little short for a full-length sprawl, but he'd manage if need be. Pushing away from the door, he lifted his chin. "Right, then. Let's get out some paper and a couple writing sticks, and start figuring out what, exactly, the role of the new Holy Guild will be. What you'll do, what you'll not do . . . You are the Guild Master, the very first one, and that means you're the one stuck with figuring out how your guild will be run."

With a groan and a roll of her eyes, she pushed off the divan and headed back to the table, grabbing her satchel on the way. "Which means I'll have to present a Guild Charter *and* figure out who to choose for my three apprentices, as soon as possible.

Because there was another reason for a Patron Goddess, one I didn't dare tell the others at the meeting."

"Oh? And what's that?" Alonnen asked her.

She gave him a level look. "A Goddess might be the only being strong enough to deal with any demon conjured by the former priesthood of Mekhana. But a Patron's strength depends heavily upon prayer and worship . . . when They're not siphoning magic like a bullying thief."

"Good point. You'll need those apprentices fast, then. Tomorrow morning, you can use the Consulate talker-box to network with the other Precincts. They're bound to know Gearmen who'd be willing to volunteer," he said. Joining her at the table, he helped by taking up one of the graphite sticks she had brought, her previous notes, and a few sheets of paper. His stomach rumbled, but he ignored it; their food wouldn't be brought up for a little while more. "First, though, let's see what you've got so far . . . and let's see if we can word a message to the other towns about just what sort of apprentices you'll need. Three guilds, three months each . . ."

"We'll need wording that won't scare everyone away from the thought of serving a Goddess," Rexei agreed, thinking of poor Gabria. She wasn't afraid, but then she *knew* . . . obviously . . . exactly what Guildra stood for, and stood against. "Even if it's for a completely different sort of deity, finding others who are willing to serve is the biggest obstacle I face."

If it weren't for the band wrapped around his brow, sweat would have long since stung Torven's eyes. He was peripherally aware of the agitated man pacing angrily in the corridor outside this outer cell room, too, but building permanent wards to contain a minor demon took time, patience, and attention to the tiniest detail, including being aware before beginning that his face would sweat from the sheer effort and concentration involved. Crouched over the smooth stone of the cell floor, he placed another painstakingly neat line of binding runes along the curve of the ward-within-a-ward circle that would protect him from what he was summoning.

Crowded into the doorway, three priest apprentices, novices, scribbled notes on everything he was doing. Behind them, the clucking of a chicken could be heard. Demons required food, same as any other being, but their nutritional needs were not the same as mortals. They were more akin to what Mekha had done in a way, save that where Mekha sucked up magic from mages like a man in a desert sucked up water, demons sucked up agony, fear, and other ephemeral energies. And blood, of course.

More blood would be needed for a permanent binding, but Torven wasn't going to tell these ex-Mekhanans that. For one, he wasn't going to draw these runes on the floor in spell-bound, metal-dusted blood when simple chalk would do for a temporary, demonstration-based summons. For another, he wasn't going to tell them just yet that to bind a truly powerful demon required the prolonged sacrifice of something intelligent, a fellow human. That was blood magic.

Torven knew of a couple loopholes, however. Self-sacrifice— preferably one of the novices or priests, not himself—was perfectly acceptable by all. Sacrificing a known murderer was borderline but acceptable as well if the energies were used to recompense for whatever had been destroyed by their actions. Someone who had tortured others could be used, though that might backfire upon this priesthood. And there was at least one case in ancient recorded history of a Goddess—in actuality a demon princess in disguise—"permitting" the ritual sacrifice of Her enemies to feed Her.

Her existence and Her ambitions had been thwarted at the next Convocation of Gods and Man, but only at the cost of another God's life. If the Convocations had indeed been renewed yesterday, as he suspected they had, and he and these priests could summon and bind a demon-God here and now, then that would give them four years to build up a power base of worship and sacrifices. Based on what he had read in the crumbling records of the Tower's oldest archives, the previous attempt had failed because the priesthood in question had only been active for a year or so and because the demoness had sought to destroy all the other Gods and Goddesses, rather than focus exclusively upon making herself a true deity.

"Isn't he done *yet*?" Torven heard Archbishop Elcarei snap impatiently. The chicken clucked and ruffled its feathers in its cage. Marking the last three runes with slow, exacting patience, Torven finally stood up.

"I am done with the rune-wardings, milord. Such things cannot be rushed and must be done with great care, unless you wish for the demon to break free and claw its way through the bodies of your fellow priests," he warned the somewhat older, irritated man. "Demons are not easily killed, and their capacity for wielding magic is unusually strong, so do not think your normal shields will spare you from their rage."

"If it's that dangerous, I should wish to set it loose on that damned Consulate meeting! And what was that *boy* doing at the head table?" Elcarei added, his brow furrowed in a scowl when Torven turned to eye him. "He's no master of any guild, let alone anything higher! Not when the boy can't even grow his own beard yet. *That* was a meeting of Guild Masters. It doesn't make sense!"

Torven had no idea what the man was ranting about, and didn't particularly care. He was tired from imbuing his considerable reserves into the spells embodied by those chalked runes, he still had the actual summoning and subsequent banishing to get through, and he was hungry.

"Pass me the chicken," he ordered one of the novices. Careful not to touch the chalk marks, he accepted the cage and placed it at his feet, well within the blank circle enclosing him. It wouldn't do to have a demon possess the body of a beast intended to be its sacrifice, and it definitely wouldn't do to give the demon anything before a bargain had been struck.

Like mages, demons could be oathbound by their very own magics. One had to be very, very careful in the wording of binding a demon—the ultimate in law-sayers, in many ways—but once bound, the demon stayed bound until a condition occurred which either set it free or sent it home. Usually the correct phrasing included a way to force the demon back into its own proper Netherhell realm.

Most of the day had been spent in lecturing all the priests and novices who cared to listen in on what demons could be expected to be like and exactly how to word the oaths to bind them into service. In a few more minutes, he would be able to . . .

The archbishop snapped his fingers and pointed at the cage. "That chicken!"

Torven eyed the somewhat older man warily. "What about it?"

"I've heard that demons like receiving a sacrifice in exchange for their services," Elcarei stated. "Does the size or the intelligence of the sacrifice matter?"

"Yes," the Aian mage allowed, still wary. "The true demon-princes, the greatest of their kind, would demand daily living sacrifices of our fellow humans. They would also be nearly impossible to bind because the strength they would derive from daily blood sacrifice could allow them to weaken and snap their bonds. Not to mention it would turn *every* hand in this world against us."

That made the archbishop scowl. He flicked his fingers, dismissing that idea. "No, not that! Not daily sacrifices. What size demon could we bind for draining with a single sacrifice? Because I have a target I would *love* to see drained and crushed into lifelessness. And if not by Mekha, who is gone, then by *something* equally sadistic, that I could then drain in turn, cushioning me from directly benefitting by the bastard boy's death."

If this man is that easily swayed by a bit of fooling from a lad half his age, then he'll not last long as the leader of these men. Not without his Patriarch or his ex-God to back him up, Torven thought, eyeing the archbishop. The possibilities were many, but he settled on the long-term plan. *I'd easily let him hang himself with his impetuousness . . . but not the rest of us, I think.*

"We would be far better served in our ambitions to sacrifice that life to bind a demon as a proto-God than waste it just to eke out a little more magic for our own use," he stated blandly.

Elcarei frowned in confusion. "Proto-God? You mean for us to worship a demon? I'm not about to go *that* far."

"Nor would I, and not quite that far," Torven soothed. Between his feet, the chicken in the cage clucked a little and tried pecking at the wicker bars. It didn't get anything, neither freedom nor a bug, so it gave up trying. Torven, on the other hand, was not going to give up that easily. "A proto-God demon is one who makes a pact with humans to actually *become* a God, according to the rules of the inviting universe.

"Rather than focusing on a manifestation of group consciousness, we put our faith in a powerful being and elevate that being to Godhood. It takes far less energy—a great deal, but far less—to elevate a demon than it does to elevate a mortal," the mage added dryly.

Elcarei quirked a brow. "Aren't there laws against that? Laws of God and Man?"

"No outworlder may trick or otherwise falsely convince the mortals of this realm to worship and elevate them to Godhood," Torven said. He smiled slightly, ignoring the softly clucking chicken. "But there is nothing against the rules if we, as fully

informed mortals, agree to worship and elevate an outworlder—
which technically includes demons—to a state of Godhood. The
trick is to do it slowly, taking our time, and *not* rushing the process."

A stern look covered the novices who were listening to his every
word. Youth invariably equaled impetuousness, with rare exception, in his experience. A glance up from their crouched, note-
scribbling forms showed the archbishop listening as well. "What's
to stop this elevated demon from reneging on its oaths once it's
a God?"

"A proto-God is bound by its oaths, even after attaining Godhood. The true control lies in the hands of the priesthood . . .
because we would be draining the proto-God's energy, same as in
the previous plan. The proto-God would not have full access to all
that incoming power."

Elcarei narrowed his dark eyes. He rubbed his chin thoughtfully, then lifted it at Torven. "First, you have to prove you can
bind, control, and siphon energy from a demon. Prove you know of
what you speak, and I'll see about having locator amulets made
from any stray hairs on that impertinent boy's coat and cap."

Giving the older man a slight bow, Torven complied. "Of
course. Students," he asserted, recapturing their attention, "we
now embark on the application of all the theory I gave you. At this
point, I will carefully reassess all the runes I have marked onto the
cell, double-check my own personal wards, and prepare the 'offering' to our incoming visitor.

"This will not be the weakest of demons, however," he warned
them. "No mere, dull-witted hellhound or poorly powered imp,
but rather, one of higher intelligence. Preferably high enough to be
able to tell me what I want to know."

"And that is?" Elcarei asked, interrupting Torven's speech.

Frowning briefly at the archbishop, Torven resumed his visual inspection of the runes. "One intelligent and connected enough to know what sort of greater beings are available in the particular Netherhell I will be breaching. Remember, it isn't just *any* Netherhell we're looking for. There are roughly a thousand of them within range of this universe; we want one where the residents will be amenable to our bargain, lawful and magical enough to be bound by oaths, and several more codicils," he stated, pulling a rolled-up sheet of paper from his pouch. "All of which I outlined during our earlier lessons.

"Just like randomly catching the arm of a person in a city and asking them if they know of so-and-so, this will be a random summoning of a demon to find out if it knows of the kind of creature we seek to bind. If this first portal attempt will not suffice, then perhaps the next on the list will. And remember, do *not* use mirror-Gates to reach into any Netherhell," Torven lectured sternly. "Demonic mages—and there are many—will detect and seize any such mirror. Once they do, they will use it to widen the frame and create a hole in the Veil between worlds that will be large enough for them to invade, which is something none of us want them to do."

"That would be bad, yes," Elcarei agreed dryly. "But doesn't a frameless Portal use most of a mage's strength?"

"A personally crafted Portal, built upon nothing but the aether itself, takes more than twelve times as much energy, yes, but it has the distinct advantage of collapsing like a popped soap bubble if anyone outside the crafting mage tries to seize control of it, never mind force it wider," the Aian mage pointed out. "Weak mages cannot summon demons—or disappointed peasants who are of little use beyond crafting ice in the summer months would have long since torn this world to shreds in petty attempts at vengeance for the poor lot they drew in life.

"However, by working together, weak mages, moderate, and

strong ones can summon and bind very powerful beings. But we need to *know* which one we want to make a bargain with. To do that will take time. This project will *not* be ruined by acting rashly or hastily. Now, keeping in mind everything I have imparted to you, watch carefully while I summon the first demon to be inter-rogated . . ."

TEN

❦

This time, when she surfaced from the depths of sleep, Rexei knew where she was, who she was with, and what position she had taken. Well, maybe not the latter. She remembered going to sleep *next* to Alonnen, each in their own half of the bed, and not snuggled with him in the middle of it, but she knew who he was and that they were in a bed in a room in the best brothel in Heias-towne.

They hadn't started out in bed together, but after listening to the head of the Mages Guild squirm and shift for roughly two hours on the not-quite-long-enough couch, Rexei had given up and ordered him to share the bed. She had pointed out that they were both in undershorts and shirts, that they were quite capable of sleeping chastely, and that she trusted him . . . and that he could trust her in return, " . . . honest!" That had provoked a chuckle from him and convinced him to join her on the feather-stuffed mattress.

It had not been meant as a ploy to get him snuggled up along her side, with that long nose of his pressed into the side of her neck . . . except . . . *Wait . . . did I pull him over to me? I think I did . . . Yeah, I did! He was snoring something awful,* Rexei recalled, staring up at the whitewashed ceiling over the bed. The air was cold on her face and head, but she wasn't quite ready to get up and tend the coals in the iron stove off to the side. *I remember I poked him, and he rolled toward me, and he* almost *shut up. So I poked him, he rolled back, it got worse . . . so I pulled him back over to me by his shirt. Yeah.*

So this is all my *fault.*

Staring up at the ceiling, she was very aware of how much of Alonnen's body touched hers. By luck and the grace of his position, her arm hadn't gone numb under the weight of his shoulder and cheek. One of his arms had wrapped around her ribs, with his fingers tucked under her back, no doubt enjoying the warmth of being draped between her flesh and the feather-stuffed mattress. His chest and stomach warmed her from ribs to hip. And his right thigh lay atop hers, almost wrapped around it.

That meant his groin was snugged against her hip, replete with the distinct lump of his masculinity. Rexei waited for the fear to rise and grip her with panic at that awareness . . . but . . . it didn't. Not more than the briefest of surprised twinges rose before fading within moments. *I'm not scared he'll . . . do things to me like those men did to Mum. I guess this means I trust him. My face is hot. Am I blushing? Why am I blushing? Maybe we're sharing too much body heat? I . . . he's waking up?*

Holding herself still, she waited for him to process where he was and who he was with, too. It didn't quite work out that way. He breathed deep, sighed, mumbled something, and snuggled closer. The lump against her hip hardened. Another breath, and his hand shifted. Feeling her blush deepen, Rexei cleared her throat. Loudly. Before those fingers could completely cover her breast.

He stilled, drew in a third breath, and cautiously lifted his head, pushing up a bit on his other elbow. "Uhh . . . sorry? I . . . *Gods*, that's cold!"

She had to agree; when Alonnen lifted himself up, that allowed a rush of cold air to fill in the gaping tunnel created by the change in position. Shivering, she reached up with her free arm and pulled the covers close. "I'd hope the fire hasn't gone out, but I fear it did."

Grateful she wasn't screaming at him, Alonnen cleared his throat. "I'll take care of that, then. Sorry about hugging you for warmth and . . . so forth. Should've stuck to the couch . . ."

"I still trust you." The words blurted out of her even as Rexei hugged the quilts to her chest. Not because she feared what might be exposed—she was wearing her linen undershirt, after all—but because the room *was* cold, and he was moving to get out of the bed, which meant cold air was moving to get in and take his place.

Alonnen stilled, pondered her words, then nodded slowly. "Good. I'll, ah, try to remain trustworthy . . . if I don't freeze to death. It's rather bright in here, isn't it?"

Craning her neck, Rexei peered at the windows beyond the bed frame. The curtains had been closed when they had entered and were still closed, but a great deal of light was seeping around their edges. A glance at the clock mounted on the wall showed it was only mid-morning.

"Well, it's daylight, but that is a lot of light. I'd say the storm broke," she offered, twisting to follow his movements as he padded to one of the windows. The maneuver had the added benefit of wrapping her up firmly in the bedding, cutting off further drafts.

Pushing the curtain aside, Alonnen squinted and shielded himself from the bright sunlight with a hand, then closed the curtain, found his tinted viewing lenses, and tried again. Squinting through the blue-hued glass, he peered at the world outside.

"We're not going anywhere for a while," he stated. Drawing the curtains shut again, he shook his head. "There's a full foot of snow outside, and no one's cleared the streets yet. No wonder it's bloody cold—keep my spot warm for me, will you?"

"If you insist," Rexei found herself teasing. "But I'll require a tithe in exchange for all this warmth. Once I figure out what that should be, I'll let you know."

Alonnen tried not to shiver. He hurried to the refreshing room and used it, since it was too cold not to feel the need, then returned to the stove. Peering inside, he jiggled the handle to sift the ash out of the bottom, and unburied a few peach-glowing embers. Heaving the coal bucket up to the door, he used a bit of magic to move the black lumps around, spreading them evenly over each other and the remnants of the fire. Once that was done, he hurried back to the bed.

"C'mon, give me some room. I'm not getting out of this bed again until it's bloody warm," he ordered, climbing in beside her.

She let him tug the covers over, but the cold air got to her, too. Scrambling free, she used the refreshing room as well, then hurried back. It was horribly cold in the room, not much different than her own bolt-hole would have been, but Rexei took great comfort in the fact that she didn't have to get up and go to work cleaning the many public rooms of the temple this morning.

"I am so very glad I got to quit the other day," she muttered, trying not to let her teeth chatter. Tugging the bedding a little higher, she gave up trying to be polite about sharing the warmth and just rolled herself right up against the older mage's side. "I don't have t-to try to slog through the snow to the temple, and I don't have to scrub any stone floors in f-freezing-cold temperatures."

Alonnen twisted onto his side, wrapping her in his arms as well as the blankets and quilts. Their knees bumped, tangled, then intertwined when he pulled her close enough to rub her upper arm and her back for warmth. "Neither of us *have* to go anywhere. Not

until the roads are cleared. And as neither of us is in the Roadworks Guild . . ."

"I was. When I was fifteen," she added.

"Oh, right, the brickwork medallion," he muttered, remembering that one. "It's hard to keep track of all the discs you're entitled
to wear . . . ah. Sorry about that," he added, blushing and scooting
his hips back a bit. "It has a mind of its own in the mornings."

"It's, um . . ." She blushed herself. At his inquiring look, she
blushed harder, struggling to come to grips with the odd thoughts
flitting through her head. For the first time in her life—or at least
what felt like it—she finally understood the "fuss" everyone made
of moments like this. The pleasant sort of fuss, that was. "It's okay.
I'm not offended."

The way she snuck a peek up at his face made Alonnen wince a
little. "Please don't look at me like that."

"Like what?" she asked.

"Like you want me to kiss you," he told her candidly. "Because
if you don—"

She kissed him. It was awkward, it was short, the tip of his nose
bumped her cheekbone, and it ended within just a few seconds.
Feeling like she was blushing all over, Rexei cleared her throat.
"I-It's okay. I told you I trust you."

Groaning, he squeezed his eyes shut. "Rexei, *don't* tell a man
that. Not when I'm trying to respect you."

"I can't help it!" she argued defensively. "I don't know how all
of this is supposed to work. The only thing I know how to do is
either lie or tell the truth, and since I feel like it'd be wrong to lie
to you, I'm telling you the truth. I . . . like you. A lot."

Closing his eyes, he sighed heavily but hugged her close. A kiss
on her short-cropped hair, and Alonnen returned the sentiment. "I
like you, too. A lot. But we're going to go slow and get to know
each other."

"Well, I wasn't going to go stomping full on the galloper-pedal on this motorhorse, when I feel like I barely know how to steer it just yet," she muttered into his shoulder. Then mumbled, "I don't know what romance is like. Not from the inside."

An odd thought made him chuckle. When she shifted in his arms, Alonnen explained it. "I can see why you picked a Goddess of Guilds, instead of a Goddess of Romance, then."

That got him a pinch on his ribs, which got her a yelp in her ear. They tussled for a moment, until the covers shifted, sending cold air between their bodies. Shivering, both yanked up the bedding at the same time, cuddled close, and behaved themselves while the coals slowly caught in the stove and worked on heating the room.

At some point, Rexei drifted off to sleep again, but Alonnen stayed awake for a while. He thought about what she had said, about what had happened the previous night, and tried to figure out how all these disparate pieces would fit together in a way that would stop a demonic invasion. Thinking about demons was far safer than thinking about the fact that she wanted to kiss him, after all.

"Oh! Uh . . . sorry," Rexei stammered, taken aback by the sight of a woman in the Consulate's talker-box room. "I thought this was empty."

"I take it you need it?" the older woman asked, swiveling to face the door. She started to say more, then held up her finger, listening to the cone held to her ear. Turning back to the machine, she spoke into it, some sort of confirmation and a request for more people.

Rexei wondered idly if the woman's conversation had to do with last night's meeting. Possibly, from the sound of things. She studied the other woman, taking in the dark wool trousers and thick-knitted sweater, not much different from Rexei's own, save for a subtle pattern down the front and along the neck and cuffs. The smaller rooms of the Consulate were heated by those new boiler-fed pipes, so the woman wasn't wearing a cap or bundled up in a coat. Her ash-brown hair had been pulled up into a bun; from the size of the knot, it looked like it would be fairly long when unwound.

Absently rubbing her own short, dark locks, Rexei wondered if she'd ever get a chance to grow them out without fear. *Probably not for a long while. Not until we're so firmly a new kind of kingdom and Guildra is so firmly our Goddess, that She has the power to flick away the old priesthood like I'd flick a bug off a fence rail.*

". . . There we go. Do you know how to operate a talker-box?" the woman asked, turning back to her.

Nodding, Rexei pulled out her necklace of discs and sorted out one of the three medium-sized coins. The other woman raised her brows at the sight of so many coins, then slowly nodded.

"I see. So, *you're* Master Longshanks. Or rather, Guild Master Longshanks. Gabria told me about you last night." The woman smiled with one side of her mouth and held out her hand. "I'm Marta Grenspun, Clockworks Guild and Precinct clerk. Today's my rest day, so I came here. I was going to use the Precinct's talker-box to start making calls on behalf of this new kingdom idea you've tossed out there, but the Hammer of Heiastowne put his foot down." Her half smile gained a wry wince to it. "It's not Precinct militia business, so out I had to go.

"So. Here I am, networking with my fellow clerks and kinsmen, trying to spread the word of Guildra and Guildara. On your behalf," she added, pointing a finger at Rexei.

That took the younger woman aback. Blinking, Rexei asked, "You're not afraid of . . . of Guildra's manifestation? Or of me, for summoning a Goddess?"

The smile Marta gave Rexei was wry, and only on one side of her mouth. "I'm not Gabria. In the 'm' sense, as well as by personality—she's my dearest friend, don't get me wrong, but she's the shy, creative type, while I'm a natural-born organizer. And you, young lad—or lady, whichever you prefer—need organizing."

Rexei blanched. She quickly shut the door to the talker-box room, hissing, "She *told* you that?"

Marta blinked. "What? Oh no! Gabria would never betray anyone else," she denied firmly. "No, I figured it out for myself, the moment I saw you just now. I've met many women who dress as men, particularly those who work in the factories and among the militia ranks. In fact, I tend to do it myself. It makes dealing with the men in the Precinct offices easier. Speaking of which, what sort of militia-based role do you see women accepting? Strictly clerical and other forms of support, or do you picture them taking up arms and defending this new nation of Guildara?"

Caught on the spot, Rexei stammered. "I . . . that is . . . uh . . . I-I don't think a . . . a member of the Holy Guild should . . ."

"*I* think you should think about these things. Remember, we suffered in part because what the deity is all about, the kingdom *becomes*," Marta told her. "Now, since I have personally seen it, I know that women can be just as effective as men in combat, *if* they are given training appropriate to their strengths and their reflexes."

"But women aren't as strong as men," Rexei stated, bemused by the turn of conversation. She had come in here to use the talker-box to contact other Consulates to find Gearmen apprentices willing to serve in the new Holy Guild, and . . . Marta was shaking her head. "What?"

"Longshanks, Mekha gave us all that mechanical knowledge to *augment* our abilities. It honestly does not matter if it's a man or a woman steering a motorhorse. It does not matter if it's a man or a woman maneuvering around in a motorman suit. Both can do so equally well. It doesn't even matter all that much if it's a man or a woman operating a cannon, save that it may take two women to easily load the munitions into the chamber, versus one man with a bit of effort or one woman having to struggle hard. But they can all load the cannon and fire it. Not that I advocate going to war, but I do strongly suggest we prepare ourselves to defend against it."

"Well . . . good," Rexei agreed, seizing on that. "Because my Goddess does not *want* to go to war. We'll stand ready to defend against it, but . . . but we'll only take on those who *want* to join us. None of this forcing ourselves on others. That's nonsense and does nothing to ensure that our Patron will be a strong one, capable of standing strong in the face of anything. The False God certainly wasn't strong. We'll accept only those cities who want Her, because we won't be like Him."

That half smile came back, this time more amused than wry. Marta lounged back against the talker-box desk. "He wasn't very strong, was He? What made you think up that antiwar policy?"

"Because . . . well, because He was all about war and conquest, yet we'd not managed to make our borders budge any bigger," Rexei said. "We're lucky the Arbrans and the Aurulans and the Sundarans haven't been interested in claiming a single inch more for their own lands. And we're lucky the northeastern barbarians haven't enough organization, magic, or militia to do more than hold their borders."

Marta winced. "Please, that's not the diplomatic way to address them. They're hardly barbarians. They're just small, clan-organized, city-sized kingdoms, each with a God or Goddess no more powerful than Mekha was. Now, what do you think about setting up a new capital city? Should we do it in the same place as the old one?"

"Where the Patriarch lives?" Rexei asked, quirking her brows.

"Are you crazy? We'll have enough problems from Archbishop Elcarei. The old capital is full of the Patriarch's lackeys and yes-men. Besides, they only have five or seven or something Guild Masters. Heiastowne has twelve. The capital of *Guildara* should be located wherever the guilds are strongest, wouldn't you think?"

Both corners of Marta's mouth curled up, and her blue-gray eyes gleamed with good humor. It transformed her face from pleasant and full of character to actually beautiful. Rexei hoped the woman had never smiled like that around members of the priesthood.

"Heiastowne has *thirteen* Guild Masters," the older woman corrected her. Not much older, not by more than a decade at most, and probably only her late twenties, if Rexei was any judge. "At least, while you reside in the Precinct. Oh, the leftenant sent his congratulations on your triple elevation," she added. "Master Actor, Master Gearman, and Guild Master. Quite an achievement in just one night. Everyone will be expecting great things from you as a consequence."

Those words wilted her. Abandoning the door, Rexei pulled out the other chair at the talker-box table and slumped into it. "I don't know if I can *handle* this . . . I mean, I *believe* I've picked the right sort of Patron Deity for us—I truly do, and it's quite obvious, or it was last night, but . . ." She tried to gather her thoughts instead of letting them ramble. "Miss Grenspun . . ."

"Marta, please," the other woman said.

"Marta . . . I have no idea what I'm doing, beyond blind faith. Master Tall set me the task of writing out ideas, but . . . I'm just one person," she confessed. "I've had training as a Gearman and as a Sub-Consul, I've seen the workings of literally dozens of guilds, and . . . Well, you're asking me things I don't know if I should be discussing! Mekha's priesthood stuck their greedy, gouging fingers into *everything*. I don't want my Holy Guild to be anything like that. *They* were political. *I* think the priesthood should stay out of politics, save to try to bring opposing sides to some sort of understanding, in the hopes of them reconciling through . . . through *logic* and calmed emotions. By remembering our similarities. That's hardly the formula for creating a kingdom, I should think."

"It's a far better start than some," Marta countered. Reaching for a bound notepad, she pulled it over and flipped through several pages of neatly written notes to the beginning. "Now, after listening to Gabria talking last night—ranting and wibbling, rather—I got up early this morning and wrote down several ideas I had. I *like* the idea of a new kingdom based on the faith we all have in the Guild System. There are many laws we should retain, and we'll have to take some time to sort through all of them to see which ones were imposed by the priesthood for their own benefit rather than the benefit of all. But since you have the clearest idea—obviously—of what Guildra stands for, I was hoping to run a few preliminary ideas past you.

"If we—you and I and anyone else so inclined—all agree on what the differences should be, then we can start implementing them right away. I figured, since I *am* so good at organizing and thinking of little details, I could come and help you figure out all of the things that will need to be settled soon," she explained. "So. First thought: What sort of cultural gesture or ritual should we use to invoke the thought, presence, or spirit of Guildra?"

"I . . . don't know." Rexei hadn't given that any thought. Glancing down at her hands, which were knotted together, she spotted her thumb. Frowning softly, she lifted it, fingers curled in and thumb poked out sideways. "We used *this* symbol as a way to imagine a day when we wouldn't have Mekha around. The thumb that we pricked our blood to sign all those petition books. Maybe we'll keep this one? I mean, it wouldn't do to *forget* where we came from, because if we forget what we suffered, we might find ourselves straying into the wrong paths again."

"That's not a bad idea," Marta agreed, bending over her notes to mark an additional comment with a couple of underlines. "What about invoking the Goddess by name? Any specific ideas for prayers? Benedictions? Blessings?"

"'In the guilds we trust,' perhaps?" Rexei offered, shrugging. "And, uh . . . 'May Guildra guide you in your tasks' . . . ?"

"Good! Short, to the point, and easily memorized. Okay, what about the role of women in this new society? Are you going to go with an all-female priesthood?" Marta asked next, lifting one brow.

That was an easy one to answer. Rexei shook her head. "Definitely not. That'd lead to the temptation of treating men the way the old priesthood treated women. It should be a mix of both. Equals all the way.

"We may have a Goddess, but anyone can serve Her if they believe—actually, I should change my ruling that an apprentice in my guild has to *first* serve in three others," she added, sitting forward as she warmed to the subject. "Rather, to advance to the rank of journeyman of the Holy Guild, he or she should agree to co-serve in at least three guilds. To be an apprentice, they just have to serve in at least two guilds.

"And to be journeyman rank, their service should preferably be from at least two different types of guilds. From among those that design and inspire, those that craft and fix, those that tend and provide, and those that advance the quality and ease of our lives— the brush, the hammer, the scythe, and the gear," she said. "And then those of master rank should serve in at least five guilds, with one in each of the four categories, and be of at least journeyman rank or higher in two of them. . . and grandmasters should have so many years and so many guilds, with such-and-such rank . . . Sorry, I'm getting off subject, aren't I?"

"Not to worry, I'll just make a note of it so we can come back to it later . . ." Flipping to a new page, Marta wrote that down as well. "Right. It might be a better idea to start the apprentices with just two guilds' worth of experiences instead of three, since you'll have a harder time getting anyone from the more limited pool of the Gearmen's Guild. But it's wise to have that cross-guild understanding of how the various crafts and skills work. So. On to the next question . . ."

"*You.*"

Waiting in the front hall for Alonnen to finish checking via talker-box on the condition of the roads, Rexei flinched inside at the sound of the archbishop's voice. Silently in the back of her mind, she started humming hard; she hadn't done much of it during her long conversation with Marta Grenspun because the subject had been too fascinating for her to concentrate, but now, she needed her protective meditations.

Turning to face the middle-aged man, she gave him a bland look. "Yes, Mister Tuddlehead?"

From the narrowing of his eyes, he didn't like being addressed as anything less than *Your Holiness* or *Archbishop*. Still, he merely gestured sharply with a slash of his hand that ran from his assistant to her. The novice at his side stepped forward and drew a coat and cap out of the cloth bags he carried. Rexei took her cap, quirked her brows at the light brown wool of the coat, then shook her head. Flushing, the young man dug deeper. Two coats later, she nodded and held out her hand for the correct one.

"Thank you," she stated as calmly as she could. The wool jacket, she draped over her left arm; the cap, she shoved into one of its pockets. A subtle glance to the side showed that the apprentice

Gearman who had been mopping melted snow off the stone floor was trying not to move, so as not to draw attention to his brown-clad self. She couldn't blame him for not wanting to draw the ex-priest's attention.

She wasn't sure what to make of the archbishop personally coming along to deliver her and the other Servers' belongings. *For all I know, he's placed some sort of tracing spell on this coat. He was quite upset with me last night.* As much as she wanted to curse him and kick him out of the land, Rexei's rather lengthy chat with Marta had included a few questions about how she, the head of the new Holy Guild, should behave. *Which means I need to be gracious and forgiving . . . ugh.*

Taking a deep breath, she pictured her anger and her fear, imagining them as heavy bucket handles. In her mind, she opened her hands—though she kept humming to disguise her magic and hide herself from any magical traps or tracking spells—and let go of her burdens. Unbidden, words rose up within her, gracious words. She hoped Guildra would be proud of her for speaking them.

"May Guildra guide you onto a path of remorse and reparation in the days to come, Mister Tuddlehead," she told the ex-priest. "Returning our things is an encouraging first step. One, I hope, of many that will lead you to a much more worthy and well-deserved life."

"May who, what?" Elcarei asked, frowning in confusion.

The same quirk of courage from before made her flash him a brief smile. "Guildra. Goddess of Guilds, Protector of Heias-towne . . . and soon to be our new Patron Deity, the Goddess of Guildara. The kingdom that is about to rise from the ashes of Mekha's many mistakes."

Elcarei reddened at her claim. "Listen, *boy*—"

"*Master*," she countered flatly. "It's *Master* Longshanks." Another tight smile, and she dipped her head. "I have you to thank for my elevation to the rank of Master Actor last night. Which also elevated me to the rank of Master Gearman. So I thank you."

"Thank me, for *fooling* me?" he asked, his own mouth twisting into an equally tight but far less pleasant smile.

She softened hers. "Yes. You must remember that everyone here had regarded you, the Archbishop of Heiastowne, as a very astute, keen-eyed, sharp-witted man. You served a cruel, hated, and utterly *unwanted* master in the False God . . . but aside from that one particular flaw, no one in this town ever considered you a fool. And again, I remind you I went into the temple to investigate allegations of abuse against the members of the Servers Guild . . . and in two months found none. Not unless you count verbal abuse."

Elcarei folded his arms across his chest. "Every master has the right to castigate an apprentice. Regardless of guild affiliation."

"It can be carried to an irresponsible extreme," Rexei admitted, thinking of the foulmouthed, foul-minded bastard in the Roofers Guild she had fled from after only two months of his version of verbal abuse. "But in your case, it was more a matter of dismissive arrogance than destructive vitriol. I saw no reason to mention it as a flaw in my report to the Consulate."

Elcarei stepped forward, brows drawing together. "You dare *judge* me? You? A *boy* too young to grow a beard?"

Instinct warred with experience. Instinct said she needed to avert his wrath and avoid his attention. Years of ducking and hiding said she should apologize, grovel, and extract herself as quickly as possible from his attention. The Consulate apprentice did just that, quickly taking himself out through a side door so that he could escape further notice. She hoped he had also fled to report to one of his superiors, but she wasn't going to hold her breath.

Experience, however, told instinct to shove off. Similar moments in her past had taught her that one should never back down from a bully. Particularly when one was in the right, and definitely when in a place with plenty of witnesses. Even if the apprentice had fled, off to one side, she spotted a familiar long-nosed, scarf-wrapped face coming down the hall, hair re-illusioned to look nut brown instead of ginger red.

Encouraged, she lifted her chin slightly, not budging an inch. "Physical age is no obstacle to maturity, Mister Tuddlehead. And yes, I dared to judge you. I was doing my *job*. By the laws under which Mekha oppressed us . . . you did an excellent job as archbishop. Do keep in mind, however, that some of those laws have now *changed* . . . and were changed last night by a full quorum of Guild Masters."

He frowned, looking somewhere past her shoulder as he silently counted in his head. "I know all the Gearmen, save yourself, that were at that table. Subtracting them, the count should have been short of a full quorum."

"That's because we appointed a new Guild Master last night, of a new guild," Alonnen stated, joining Rexei. He looked remarkably relaxed, for the one mage the priesthood would have cheerfully killed to get their hands on just three days before, had they known of his strength and his existence.

"What new guild?" Elcarei asked, glancing between the two of them.

"The Holy Guild. The new priesthood," Rexei answered. It was her place to do so, though she certainly wasn't going to tell this velvet-clad bastard *who* the new Guild Master was. "Those who serve Guildra, Goddess of Guilds, shall also serve the people of this land. Rather than try to bully and abuse them."

He sucked in a sharp breath . . . but said nothing to her for her impertinence. Turning instead to his novice, he pointed at the reception desk. "Leave the rest for the ingrates to pick up. We have better things to do with our time."

Nodding, the young man fished out the various coats, hats, and scarves from his bag and dropped them on the currently unoccupied desk. Flattening the bags, he rolled them up and stuffed them into the pockets of his long velvet overcoat, not quite as luxurious as the ex-archbishop's but still clearly a cut above the average Mekhanan's woolens.

"Hey, Elcarei," Alonnen called out as the two headed for the front door. "Don't do it."

One hand on the door, pushing it just open enough to let in a spill of bright sunlight and cold air, the ex-priest frowned back at the long-nosed redhead. "Don't do what?"

"Don't summon what you're planning to summon. Don't betray humanity," Alonnen warned him.

Rexei flinched under the swift, sharp look the ex-archbishop flicked her way. She frowned at Alonnen, but he kept his gaze on the middle-aged priest. Not wanting to make any movement that would draw more attention to herself, Rexei bit her tongue to keep silent.

"I don't know what you're talking about," Elcarei finally stated, lifting his chin just enough to look down his nose at the shorter man.

"Don't do it. Or I swear, in Guildra's name," Alonnen promised, "you will be thrown out of this land and hunted through every other nation across the face of this world until you come to your end."

Elcarei raked his gaze down over Alonnen's plain, somewhat worn gray woolens, his slim frame, and unintimidating height. "What, should I be afraid of *you*? Your threats are meaningless."

"Not mine," Alonnen warned him. "Prophecy will be your downfall."

"*Prophecy* is a bunch of Gods-spewed shit, *boy*, designed to herd us onto a path of Their choosing," he told Alonnen, who was clearly old enough to grow a beard, given the hint of ginger stubble along his jaw. Elcarei pushed the door wide. "But They *also* gave us free will . . . or haven't you heard?"

"Then don't summon the demons They predicted you would," Alonnen said, his tone calm and matter-of-fact.

For a few seconds, the ex-archbishop lingered in the doorway, backlit by the white of the sun on snow and framed by a gust of icy wind that ruffled his robes. Then his mouth twisted in a sneer, and he turned away, striding down the clean-swept steps. The door swung shut in the wake of the novice, extinguishing the excess light and leaving Rexei and Alonnen for a moment in what felt like darkness, despite the glow pouring in from the narrow windows to either side of the double-wide entrance.

"I really wish you hadn't done that," Rexei finally muttered.

Alonnen looked at her. "Hadn't done what? Given him a warning? Hoped against hope that he might change his mind? I have an obligation to *stop* him, you know."

She sighed and rubbed at the tension in her forehead. "Not that. I meant, told him in the first place that you know about the demon-summoning thing. Because that put his attention on *me*. I may not be Gabria, shrinking from even the thought of a God or Goddess getting anywhere near me, but I am *not* comfortable catching the scrutiny of a bunch of men whose sole job in life—for generations!—was to capture and torture and suck the *life-energy* out of our people."

She said the last in a hiss, because she wasn't comfortable with the thought of anyone else overhearing even that much. The look he gave her was rueful and apologetic, enough to mollify some of her stress. Not all of it, but some of it.

"Sorry, Rexei," Alonnen muttered. "I guess . . . I guess I'm so energized by the thought of finally being *rid* of the threat of Mekha over our heads, I forgot the men who followed Him are still quite dangerous, even if they don't have His foul power to back their efforts anymore."

"Just . . . try to remember that," she sighed, for a moment letting go of her humming as she rubbed again at her forehead.

"Well, if it's any consolation," he told her, "you do have the top dozen most dangerous men and women in the whole world at your back. I told them you're the Gearman of the prophecy, and they'll do whatever it takes to help keep your strength up."

"Oh, *that* makes me feel better," she muttered. "I just wanted to avoid the priesthood, live my life, and . . . and *maybe* find what's left of my lost family. I miss my brothers and father, especially now that we're almost completely free."

"We'll look for them, too." He rubbed her arms through the oversized coat he had scrounged for her, urging her toward the back of the Consulate. "Come on, put on your coat. The roads are clear all the way home, so we're headed back there now. I need to consult with my colleagues on a safe way to spy on the idiots from a distance, like you suggested. Since I'm certain they'll decide to continue being complete and utter imbeciles, in spite of my warning."

Debating, Rexei decided not to put on her returned clothes. Not until the others in the Mages Guild had checked them for tracking spells. And for binding spells; she didn't want to be found *or* rendered helpless simply from being careless. When they returned to the formidable protections of the Vortex, she would find someone who could examine her coat and hat for spells, and then break any if need be.

For the time being, all she could do was hum her anti-magic songs and push the field outward, enveloping not only herself but Alonnen, and when they reached it, the motorcart. The others were already bundled in the back and waiting, while the driver kept one foot on the galloper to warm up the engine and the other foot on the stopper pedal to hold the vehicle in place until they were ready to go.

" ◆ ◆ ◆ *Live my life, and . . . and maybe find what's left of my lost family. I miss my brothers and father, especially now that we're almost completely free.*"

Elcarei nodded to himself, seizing on that piece of information. If that Aian mage was right, they might want several sacrifices, mage and non-mage, to bind a truly powerful demon to their cause—and to a Netherhell with that long-nosed fellow's warnings. Elcarei didn't even believe in Seers; there hadn't been a single one born within Mekhana's borders for over four hundred years, and all the fancy predictions of that freak of a Seer-King to the east hadn't lost them an inch of Mekhanan soil in hundreds of years.

The enchantments on the cap and coat were doing their job. He listened as the other man spoke. "*We'll look for them, too,*" the deeper voice stated. "*Come, put on your coat. The roads are clear all the way home, so we're headed back there now.*"

Elcarei wished he knew the man's name; he knew the fellow was a visiting Guild Master simply because he'd been one of the unfamiliar faces at the head table last night. Then again, the ex-priest wished he knew who the head of the so-called Mages Guild was. *Or the head of that so-called Holy Guild . . . what a piece of effrontery!*

"*I need to consult with my colleagues on a safe way to spy on the idiots from a distance, like you suggested. Since I'm certain they'll decide to continue being complete and utter imbeciles, in spite of my warning.*"

The cheek of the man! Elcarei took special care in cracking and grinding the ice of a puddle under his boot heel as he strode back toward the temple. *I'll show him who the imbecile is. But not hastily, no,* he reminded himself, recalling Torven's warnings on the matter. *No. Slowly, carefully, and with such subtlety that they will never realize my vengeance is cold but fully matured, until it is too late to stop their prolonged suffering.*

He kept the seeker amulet pressed to his ear, enchanted not only to track down the boy, Longshanks, but to listen in on the youth's conversations via the metaphysical link between discarded hair and head . . . but didn't hear anything more. Which was odd. He *knew* the amulet was enchanted correctly. It had taken him quite a bit of his own personal energy to craft the spell and imbue it with enough power to work over a distance of fifty full miles, all of it linked to the precious, short, dark hairs liberated from the boy's winter coat and knitted cap. But Elcarei wasn't hearing a peep now. Not a word, not a footstep, not even a hint of the boy breathing.

Did he . . . ? No, he couldn't have been a mage. Not inside the temple itself! Definitely not under Mekha's watchful, ever-hungering eye. Even when we had over half the cells full, Mekha was always subtly probing everyone, even us, trying to sup a little bit of magic from His own priesthood. He would have noticed *if the boy was a mage! No . . . oh, no, no, no,* Elcarei realized, eyes widening. He stepped into the relative dimness of the temple. *Not the boy! That man, the one with the sharp nose.* That *one spoke of a Mages Guild with the kind of assurance that spoke of personal experience with it, and he was seated as an equal among Guild Masters.* That *was the head of the Mages' Guild!*

Mekha! If only I'd known!

Ignoring the novice who had accompanied him, Elcarei strode for the stairs and his office. The apprentice could wander off and hide somewhere if he wanted, to avoid the extra chores invoked by the dismissal of the Servers guildmembers. Elcarei had a lot of far more important thinking and planning to do.

Somehow they've found a way to block our best scrying spells . . .

impudent bastards. But I heard enough to lure that boy into a trap. And given how thick-as-thieves the pair looked to be, if I lure the youth into a cage, the elder will no doubt come along in an attempt to set him free. Then I'll have both a sacrifice for a demonic proto-God, and a mage to personally feed me.

And there's nothing *that says we cannot still drain mages for their energies . . . for surely any mage appointed to be Guild Master of the lot will be quite powerful, with plenty to share with us as well as whatever demon that Aian fellow might conjure.*

It seemed this week was not going to be a complete disaster.

ELEVEN

"**C**ome on . . . come on! Open the door, you stupid, lazy beasts," Alonnen muttered.

Seated at the table brought into his office to serve as her temporary desk, Rexei glanced up only briefly. Her work drafting the Holy Guild Charter, outlining all the various tasks, levels of responsibility and so forth, was something he had insisted he should oversee. Yet the moment Pelai of Mendhi had sent him sheets of paper enchanted with scrying spells and instructions on how to fold them into useful, mobile shapes, he had abandoned that task for this new one.

Not that she could blame him. Spying on demon summoners was more important than figuring out how to worship a brand-new Goddess, particularly one Rexei hadn't envisioned as impatient in any way. "They're not going to open the service door to the temple just because you're willing it from five-odd miles away."

"Every day they take out the trash at this hour for the Recyclers Guild to collect," he told her. "Rags and scraps of paper go to the

Binders for adding into the paper pulp, metal scraps go to the Blacksmiths for sorting and re-smelting, and even scraps of food and paper rubbish gets handed over to the Tillers for compos— Ah! Aha!" Alonnen exclaimed as the gray-weathered door in question did indeed swing open.

Two novices lumbered out, laden with baskets. Looking around to make sure there weren't any glaring, angry citizens nearby, the novices headed for the collection bins designated for compostables and non-compostables. Taking advantage of the open door, little paper bugs scuttled inside. The paper had been painted and enchanted with the lightest and least-detectable of illusion spells to look like the real thing. All but one got inside before the door could swing shut; the last one got a corner stuck in a crevice and was crumpled to death when the closing panel squished it flat.

That left nine instead of ten to do the spying work which Rexei was no longer able to perform for anyone. Not with the archbishop fully aware the "lad" was quite intelligent, and aware of what was happening inside the ex-temple. Thankfully, with the loss of Mekha, the shields and wardings on the temple had weakened. That meant Alonnen could now scry inside directly, albeit with a fuzzy view and no real hope of clear sound. On hearing that, Guardian-apprentice Pelai had suggested he could send in a whole series of clever, Mendhite-style scrying nodes.

Muttering under his breath at the loss of one of his paper spies, Alonnen focused on guiding the rest deeper into the temple. It required sliding the fingers of one hand over the crystalline tablet held in the other; each finger controlling a couple of bugs. They had a rudimentary sense of awareness built into their spell; all Alonnen had to do was guide them in a suggested direction. The rest they did for themselves as they climbed up walls, scurried along corners, and hid in the nearest cracks whenever someone came near, acting very much like the roaches they resembled.

"Which way is it to the dungeons, Rexei?" Alonnen called out. "I think I got turned around in here somewhere . . ."

Leaving her writing efforts behind, Rexei stood and crossed to the mirror. She had to frown and think. Without the original carvings on the walls, without the symbols of mighty Mekha conquering His enemies via piston and powder, engine and gear, it was hard to tell where the paper bugs were. Alonnen tapped through the different viewpoints available until she spotted a familiar pattern of two doors close together with a third offset just on the other side of the hall.

"Le—no, right," she corrected herself. "Back up to the right; when you turn around, it'll be on your left. That's the door to the forbidden basement. Yes, that one there," she confirmed as the bug currently showing the scrying view in the mirror scuttled toward the tall-by-comparison door.

There was just enough room underneath the thick, iron-reinforced wood for even the tallest of the paper roaches to crawl. Alonnen sent five that way. Someone was coming up the stairwell; he tucked them into the corners of the steps so that they wouldn't be easily noticed, and tapped in an order on the controlling tablet to have them sit and wait.

Switching to the others, he quickly guided three of the remaining four to hide until the novice had passed, then sent them off to invade the higher-ranked priests' studies, including the archbishop's. The fourth, he guided all the way to the dining hall, where he had it climb up and tuck itself into a high corner, resulting in a pretty good view of the whole chamber.

Once those were positioned in high crevices, Alonnen went back to the first five, sending them scurrying down the remainder of the steps. Here, Rexei wasn't quite as sure where to go, but that was alright; in the dungeons was where most of the temple's masculine inhabitants were found. Specifically, in the chamber at the heart of the great circular corridors. All three levels had doors that led into the room, or rather, onto terraced levels that had once probably held crystals on pillars, but which now held scattered cushions and the occasional chair and writing desk.

Some of those seats were occupied, but at least half the gathered priesthood stood on the main floor, watching as the tall, brown-haired foreigner coaxed the gray-haired Bishop Koler through the steps of conjuring a demon.

"... *don't forget to include the name of the recipient of the energies in question—remember, students,*" their erstwhile instructor stated, "*if you use this energy for yourself directly and solely, you could end up tainting yourself with the madness of the Netherhells. Instead, offer it as a gift to your brethren, with the purity of that intention at heart.*"

Rexei shivered at the not-quite-mocking way he said that. She didn't know much about magic, but she did know a little bit about blood magic, thanks to the instruction she had received in the outermost circle of the Vortex a few months back. It made a terrible sort of sense that giving the collected power to someone else to use would remove most of the Netherhell taint. That was, if draining magic from a demon was anything like spilling blood to raise power.

"*Are the runes correct, Master Torven?*" Bishop Koler asked politely, almost respectfully, letting Rexei know that the mage had come a long way from his status as a mere prisoner. She wrinkled her nose at the implications of that.

"*Torven?*" Alonnen repeated, staring at the face visible in his scrying mirror. The foreigner walked around the chalked lines scribed on the floor as Alonnen and Rexei watched. One good look at that distinctive Aian face, and he reared back. "Oh bloody Netherhells . . . it *is* him. I'd wondered if it was."

Rexei frowned. "You know him? But *how*, if he's a foreigner? I couldn't quite catch his name myself when he was being interrogated. I was forced to hide in the next room and had to strain my ears to hear."

Alonnen shrugged. "Late last summer I was contacted by Guardian Kerric. He wanted to exile a group of adventurers that had tried to wrest control of the Tower from him—this man being their leader," he added, lifting his chin at the Aian mage. "The worst of the lot. Cunning, ambitious, self-centered, greedy . . . but rather too self-controlled to destroy himself with his own mistakes. Unfortunately.

"Sir Vedell of Arbra wasn't at his Fountain at the time the deal was being made, so I stepped in and offered to dump them on the Arbran/Mekhanan border. On the Arbran side by a good thirty miles," he added at her swift, sharp look. "It was as far away as I could get the mirror-Gate to work in conjunction with the Fountainways used to transport them all the way from eastern Aiar. Even a would-be power thief didn't deserve capture by Mekha's troops, or so I thought . . . though now I'm regretting my kindness. If *he's* the one behind this Netherhell effort, then *he* is the one we have to take out. Remove him, and everything will collapse."

"Maybe not," Rexei cautioned him, recalling something. "The others . . . they sent word to the other temples. We don't know how many have agreed to follow his teachings. We don't know how easy it is to *teach* someone to conjure a demon. And we don't know whether or not removing this Torven fellow will prevent the invasion . . . or *cause* it to happen. What the others in your Guild told me when I first met them as a journeyman Messenger still applies."

Alonnen gave her a curious look. "What's that?"

"That a half-trained mage is more dangerous than we may realize." She gestured at the mirror, where Mage Torven was scowling and lecturing two of the novices about not attempting any of this on their own. The guilty flush of their cheeks and their lowered gazes showed how close a probability that had been.

"*. . . In fact, I don't want any of you to try this on your own, all the way up through to the archbishop himself,*" Torven added sternly. "*We* *still haven't found the right Netherhell, and we will not act precipitously. One false step, one overconfident step, and we are all dead. These aren't cowering civilians in the streets. These are monsters from our blackest nightmares, and they will seek any excuse to rip us to shreds and feast upon our remains. Some may even prefer to devour us one bite at a time while we're still alive and screaming."*

Rexei winced. So did Alonnen, she noticed. The Aian mage continued his lecturing as they secretly watched.

"There will be no rushing, no practicing unsupervised, and no mistakes allowed. Elcarei has arranged for your brethren who are interested in joining us to begin transporting themselves here to learn. Patience is our new holy motto," they heard him say as he paced slowly around the larger circle. *"Learn it . . . or I will ensure you die by your own hand, just to sate the demons' bloodlusts and seal whatever Gate you crack open by accident—and I'll remind you, unlike you, I am fully trained in three foreign methods. Not just of magic but of magical combat."*

A slash of his hand and a snap of his fingers jerked one of the two novices to his feet, even though the Aian man had his back to the velvet-clad ex-Mekhanan.

"I—I'm a little kettle, squat and broad!" the teenager stammered, eyes wide as his lips moved without his will. One hand flung itself up, the other hand thumped onto his hip in a fist. *"Here is my h-handle! Here i-is my spigot!"*

A second snap let the youth go. He staggered back, blinked a couple times in fear, then quickly sat himself down again.

"The poem rhymes in Aian," Torven stated, his dry words filling the confused silence. *"Suffice it to say, I am quite adept . . . but I am nothing compared to the wiles of a demon, should a brief moment of carelessness, of rushing things, allow one of them to get free."* He turned back to Koler and nodded at the chalked circle. *"Your containment runes are almost perfect, bishop."*

Koler smiled smugly. Torven did not smile back in return.

"Almost is not good enough. The circle has a small wobble in it, to your right. That's a point of weakness that is potentially exploitable. Perhaps a weak demon would not be able to break free, but we will learn to do everything correctly from the earliest stages onward. The Aians have a saying, 'Begin as you mean to go on.' So let us begin again, Koler," Torven directed, clapping his hand on the older mage's shoulder. *"You may use an erasing spell to fully clean the stone, and this time you may use a compass spell to ensure the innermost circle is smooth.*

"Drawing it by hand was a learning example, to show how even the smallest flaws can be a cause for concern. Your patience at this stage in the learning process, bishop, is deeply appreciated," he finished, before stepping back.

"Dammit," Alonnen muttered, watching the older priest comply. "This isn't right."

"What's wrong now?" Rexei asked him, confused. "Because of his thoroughness, it sounds as if we'll actually have time to figure out how to counter their intentions before they actually start summoning in earnest."

"He's being *too* cautious," he complained. "For a man of such overwhelming arrogance as I saw over the last few months, he should have some flaws—not that I'm complaining about having the time to study the problem and come up with something solid, but I suspect the only reason why we *can* scry is because he hasn't looked at the temple wardings. Now that Mekha isn't blocking us out, what protections are left aren't quite good enough to keep out a double-focus like this paper-bug-and-mirror system Pelai sent me.

"I suspect that'll end once they get around to reinforcing the shielding, particularly with this fellow's help. He's far too clever. Cautious and clever are great traits in an ally," Alonnen said, giving Rexei a brief smile. He then lifted his chin at the mirror, "But they're frustrating in an enemy."

"So he's arrogant, but he's not overconfident," she murmured. "And charming enough to have won over his former jailors."

"Exactly. Arrogance coupled with overconfidence was the flaw of many a priest . . . and I can see it is just about time for supper." Hearing Rexei sigh, he glanced at her. "What now?"

She turned to lean against the wall next to the mirror, folding her arms. "Gabria. And everyone who thinks like her. I went down for a cup of mulled cider earlier, and three of the people I passed gave me startled looks, two more wouldn't meet my eyes, and all five of them practically scuttled away like your little paper bugs, there. I *don't* like feeling like a . . . well, like I'm a stupid, arrogant Mekhanan priest."

"Time and patience will hopefully bring them around. In the meantime, the other mages have been moved back into town, so that means my brother's back in his own quarters," Alonnen told her. He focused on the crystal tablet in his hands, repositioning his paper spies. "I know you're supposed to be assigned a room . . . which you would have to share, since the inner circle is still pretty full . . . but you're welcome to take his spot on my sitting room couch."

She felt ambivalent over the offer. Gratitude for the fact he offered her a place in his sanctuary. Annoyance for the fact that place was on a *couch* of all things. Giving in to her sense of humor, Rexei quipped, "Oh, I see how it is. Even *you* are afraid to let me back into your bed, now that I've gone and summoned a Goddess."

He grinned and slanted her a mock-chiding look in between positioning his paper spies. "If I truly felt that way, I'd have made you sleep on the couch last night at Big Momma's. But, if you want . . . you *could* sleep in my bed. You'd have to share it with me, though. And I'll give you fair warning, Rexei Longshanks. I find you very appealing. I might ask for a kiss at some point."

Looking up from the task of guiding one of the folded-paper bugs across a set of steps, he tried to gauge how she felt about that.

From the blush on her cheeks and the shy way she bit her lower lip—darkness swept over the mirror, the image fuzzed, snapped, and shifted to another cockroach's view. Blinking, he tapped through to the next viewpoint . . . and saw a small smear of color on the steps. Specifically, a bit of squished paper in the wake of a novice coming down off the tiers ringing the chamber.

"Dammit, I just lost another one!" he complained. A muffled noise made him glance sharply at his companion. Eyes bright, cheeks pink, and bottom lip bitten by her teeth, Rexei tried not to laugh out loud . . . but it was obvious she was laughing. Unable to help it, Alonnen grinned back at her. Only for a moment, though. Turning back to the mirror, he sighed and sent one of the other paper roaches scuttling forward to scoop its mangled, lifeless brethren off the steps. "Right . . . dispose of this one, stash the others in good viewing angles . . . then contact my fellow Guardians to let them know it looks like we have a little breathing room."

"I'll get back to my Charter-drafting," Rexei agreed, her mirth subsiding. She raked a hand over her short, dark locks. "Part of me wishes I could still be a kid again, responsible only for myself and my own safety. But I'm an adult now, and that means being responsible, respectable, dependable . . ."

"Lots of words that end in 'ibble,' eh?" Alonnen asked, not without sympathy.

She nodded. Arms crossed on her chest, she stood there for a moment, feeling restless and unsure. An impulse crossed her mind, one that Rexei found herself blurting out, "I want a dress."

Alonnen blinked but otherwise showed little surprise. He thought about it, then tipped his head. "That can be arranged. And it's a good sign."

"It is? Of what?" Rexei asked him, unsure what he meant by that.

He smiled. "That you're feeling relaxed enough to *want* to wear a dress, rather than tromp around in trousers all the time. I'm glad you feel you can trust me, and everyone else here." He made a fluttering, shooing motion with his fingers. "Scuttling away notwithstanding."

She blushed and ducked her head a little, but otherwise, she didn't hide the shy smile that curved her lips. On impulse, he leaned in and kissed her cheek. Rexei raised her head a little, her eyes wide with wonder, not fear. Swaying close a second time, Alonnen kissed her on the lips. Soft and sweet, it felt just a little too brief and light for his tastes, but he pulled back anyway. Not far, just enough to break the kiss and look into her brown eyes, wondering how she would react.

Rexei wondered, too. This wasn't a stage kiss for some play, and she wasn't playing the part of a young man at the moment. Alonnen knew she was female, knew she was leery of . . . well, things completely unlike what he had just done, she realized. *He kissed me because he wants to kiss me. And he's . . . he's nice. A truly nice, good man.* Her gaze drifted down his long nose to his lips. *And I actually want* more.

Being kissed by him felt natural and right, not staged or forced. She wanted to ask—no, she *acted*, closing the gap between them without a word. Not just pressing her lips to his, but her chest to his, her arms around his shoulders, her fingers touching the soft ginger curls of his hair. She felt him inhale deeply, and felt the shift of his hands as they cupped her arms. Not to reject, but to accept her kiss, for those hands slipped down to her waist and around the small of her back, holding her closer.

Warm, hungry, satisfying, the kiss deepened and lengthened until somehow her hands wound up on his ribs underneath his sweater while his landed on her rump, both kneading every bit of flesh they could reach. One particular squeeze on his part lifted her up onto her toes and rubbed her groin up against his. For a moment, she shied from the hardness her body found, then Rexei relaxed into it, accepting his interest in her.

The chiming of his newest mirror dragged Alonnen back to his senses. It was not easy, not when his attraction to the woman in his arms was surprisingly strong. Until now, Alonnen had considered her appealing, but more for her inner qualities, her intelligence, her strength of mind, her manifested belief in a better way of life than everything they had known. Now, though, he knew the way she felt against him, the way she tasted in each kiss. The soft sounds she had made—curious, hungry, and interested in more— left him aching and heady, as if she were some undiscovered wine.

A wise mage avoided any excess of wine. A wise Guild Master attended to his duties, such as the mirror which chimed again, try- ing to get his attention. A wise man did not let his passions rule his life when there was still work to be done.

Alonnen kissed her again. Not for long, but enough to let both of them know just how much he wanted to continue. Lifting a fin- ger, he touched the corner of her mouth and smiled softly.

"This is a bookmark," he told her. "If you want me to con- tinue . . . kiss me here." He tapped the same corner of his own mouth—and got a peck of a kiss from her. Caught off-guard, he laughed, then hugged her. "Kiss me there *later*, love," he mock chided. The mirror chimed, and he sighed ruefully. "Unfortu- nately, duty calls."

Stepping away, he moved to grab the green pair from among his collection of viewing lenses and a scarf to wrap around his hair and chin, while Rexei moved back to her temporary desk. Once he was ready, he opened the connection. It was Tipa'thia; despite her rich, natural tan, her age-seamed face still looked a bit pale and puffy from her heart troubles. Her brown eyes were still sharp though, and her voice smooth as it came through the mirror, trans- lated by whatever magic Guardian Kerric had wrought in the mir- rors he had passed to everyone.

"Good evening, Guardian Alonnen," she told him.

"And a good morning to you, Guardian Tipa'thia. I'm surprised to see you tonight. I thought your apprentice, Pelai, said you were still too ill to participate."

She wrinkled her nose. "I am not doing well, but I have to do *something* to get the Hierarchy off my back regarding the Convocation fiasco. They know better than to castigate me, but they also will not be allowed to abuse my best Disciplinarian."

"Fiasco?" he asked, curious. "Disciplinarian?"

"Temple business. Suffice to say, with the Puhon brothers out of immediate reach, the Hierarchy is frothing at the mouth for *someone* to blame. It is an odd day when discussing demons is an adequate distraction. So. How are those paper spies doing, young man?" she asked him.

"They're doing fine for the most part, and thank you for sending them. Unfortunately, I lost two on the way in," he confessed, "but the rest are tucked into good scrying angles."

"Two? How?" the Mendhite Guardian asked.

"The door closed a bit fast on the last one scuttling into the building, and an unexpected shoe squashed the other a short while later," he told her. "I didn't move it fast enough across a set of steps."

"I sent you ten. Eight should still be more than enough . . . though I suppose it is too soon to have any word on what they are doing," the elderly mage muttered.

"Actually, I've already heard some relatively encouraging news. The downside is that it's Torven Shel Von who's guiding the ex-Mekhanan priests in their demon-summoning quest. That's the fellow Guardian Kerric originally kicked out of the Tower for trying to steal its Fountain," he added in an aside. "The one connected to Kerric's forescrying mirror and its demon sightings."

"So what is he doing, that this Torven fellow keeps stirring up intermittent Netherhell invasions?" Tipa'thia asked, frowning softly.

"I have no idea. Actually, it looks like he's trying to *prevent* a Netherhell invasion. He's being very insistent on methodical train- ing, discipline, and perfecting every safety precaution available." Alonnen folded his arms, then quickly readjusted the scarf as it threatened to slip and expose his jawline. He shrugged as he did so. "On the one hand, that should buy us a lot more time than I'd feared we would have before any summonings begin in earnest. On the other hand, that means when they do begin, it'll be hard to counter, since there'll be fewer errors being made."

"True. Well. Having extra time while they practice their pre- cautions is still good news. If you will tell everyone west of you—to the Guardians of Fortuna, Natallia, and so forth, I will pass along the news to the east myself, to Althinac, Senod-Gra, and beyond. Guardians Callaia, Koro, Kelezam, and Ilaiea can wait until morn- ing comes to their portion of the world," Tipa'thia added. "It is not an emergency, so there is no need to awaken them."

"Good news can wait, but bad news cannot, eh?" Alonnen quipped. He glanced briefly to the side, to where Rexei had reseated herself, her cheek on one fist, the other holding a graphite stick, back to marking down more Charter ideas for her incipient Holy Guild. Dragging his mind back to the problem at hand, he asked, "Do you have any spare recording crystals? What I have for the scrying paper bugs will last a couple days, but from the sounds of it, we may be monitoring their activities for at least a couple of weeks."

The elderly woman lifted her brows. "You do not have enough? What about just making your own?"

"We're on a tight budget here, and saving the world is expen- sive," he retorted lightly. The last thing he wanted to get into was an admission that he didn't know *how* to make the necessary crys- tals and probably did not have any of the right materials on hand. "Do you have any to spare or not?"

"You should contact Guardian Kerric. He has pledged the resources of the Tower to this cause, and I am certain they have many to spare."

Not caring much for her dismissive tone, Alonnen narrowed his eyes. "And what does Mendhi's Guardian pledge?"

"We *were* going to pledge the resources of the Convocation. But as that power has been wrenched from our control, then I suppose we will simply offer what we always have. Knowledge." Her smug look was spoiled by the sound of a voice somewhere on her side of the mirror connection, some sort of reminder. Guardian Tipa'thia lifted her chin. "I am needed elsewhere. Good evening to you, Guardian Alonnen."

"And good morning to you, Guardian Tipa'thia," Alonnen muttered. He reached up to tap the mirror into quiescence and blew out the breath he had been holding. "Annoying, smug, arrogant . . . I'll not ask *you* for any of the help we need," he added to his own reflection, though his thoughts were on the Mendhite Guardian. "I'd rather ask that apprentice of yours . . ."

"Muttering at an unconnected mirror isn't going to get you what you want," Rexei told him. She hadn't quite heard his words, but she understood his tone. "Either speak up or say nothing."

"Pelai seems like a *reasonable* sort, rather than superior-than-you," he clarified, unwinding the soft black scarf from his head and shoulders. Removing the green-tinted glasses as well, he rubbed briefly at his eyes and the bridge of his nose. "Call it my own pride acting up, because while I *know* we don't know nearly enough about magic here in ex-Mekhana, I'm not about to allow anyone with that much pride learn just how little we know. There are times when she seems approachable, even amiable, and times when she seems like a vulture waiting for its prey to stagger. I do know that she's trustworthy as a Guardian, but I don't know if she's trustworthy as a confidante."

An amused thought crossed Rexei's mind. "Do you trust her as far as you can throw her?"

"She does look skinny enough for me to throw . . . but I'm told Mendhites are taller than most people, so I'm not quite sure how far I could actually throw her," he allowed, scratching at his chin. "The height'll add more weight, plus the awkwardness of the length . . . and all that kicking and screaming, of course."

Rexei snorted with laughter. She clapped her hand over her nose and mouth, but it was too late; Alonnen heard it and grinned back at her.

A dozen nights of sleeping on the Guild Master's couch. That was her lot in life of late. No one wanted to share a room with a God summoner, though most of those living in the inner Vortex were polite to her. Nor were there any empty rooms to spare; a number of the freed mages had proven too scared of being recaptured and re-abused to be housed anywhere else, plus ones were coming in from far-flung regions which were now being torn apart by civil war. Heias Precinct was one of the few peaceful regions around, and the dam was its safest zone for mages needing to recover from the trauma of their capture. So Rexei camped each night on Alonnen's couch. At least it was broad and comfortable, with enough bedding to keep her feeling warm.

Except that kiss, and the four or five they had shared in quiet moments since, made everything feel different. Too warm, and too unsettling. Empty in a way. She couldn't stop thinking about it, and about him. Too restless to sleep, Rexei gave up and got up, slipping her feet into lamb's-wool-lined slippers borrowed from her host. By now, she could navigate her way through his suite reasonably well in the dim light provided by the barely glowing crystals in the ceiling. Only after she knocked on the door to his bedchamber did she realize she was wearing nothing more than a thin pair of sleeping trousers and a matching loose linen shirt.

He opened the door just as she started to turn away. "Rexei? Is something wrong?"

Blushing, she turned back to him and found her gaze arrested by the sight of his naked chest. His own sleeping trousers barely rested on his hips, and he had lamb's-wool slippers of his own on his feet, somewhat more battered and age-worn than the ones he had loaned her, but that was it for clothing. With that curtain of reddish curls just brushing his shoulders, with nothing between her and his navel but a little bit of reddish gold fuzz that led down into those sleeping pants, he looked very appealing.

He was not quite as muscular as someone who served in the militia ranks full-time, but there was little spare fat on his body, either. When he flexed an arm, lifting it to cup her shoulder, she followed the flex and play of his muscles in fascinated silence. At least until he spoke again.

"Are you okay? Is there something you need or want?" Alonnen asked her. Seeing her blush and blink, still staring at his flesh, he felt his own face heat a little. Clearing his throat, he tried to speak firmly. "Rexei, *speak*."

"I . . . I want another kiss." It took quite a lot of her inner bravery to admit that to his face, but she did, raising her gaze to his so that he could see she was sincere. Her cheeks warmed further, but she added, "I liked it. A lot."

She is going to kill me. Pleasantly, Alonnen acknowledged silently. He debated what to do about her request. He knew he wasn't going to refuse it, but the question of *where* was important: In his bedroom there was the threat of his bed luring them into going further than perhaps she intended, but it also carried the advantage that if she wanted to get away from him, she could literally leave his bedchamber at any time; conversely, the sitting room was less likely to be turned into something more than a mere kiss, but he would have to be the one to leave, since that was her sleeping chamber. *Which might be best, since if she asks me to leave, I need to* show *her I will.*

Smiling, he tipped his head in a little bow of acquiescence. "As you wish. Shall we go into the sitting room?"

"Uh, not the bedroom?" Rexei asked.

Folding his arms, he leaned on the doorframe and wrinkled his nose. "Do you really want to risk the chance of going all the way? If all you want is a kiss, the couch would be a better place for it."

"Uh, you . . . Um . . ." Clearing her throat, she tried again. "I mean, you don't *want* to, ah, go all the way? I mean—do you *want* to kiss me? Not just because I asked you and you're being nice, I mean."

Her stammered uncertainty charmed him. Smiling, Alonnen leaned in and rubbed the tip of his long, pointed nose against her shorter, rounder one. That made her laugh and pull back with a bemused look.

"What was that for?" she asked.

"Because I do want more, but I also only want what *you* want," he told her. Moving forward, he flicked one hand over the controls for the suncrystals, brightening the room just a little, and wrapped his other arm around her shoulders, guiding her back to the blanket-strewn couch.

Embarrassed that her bedding was a rumpled mess, Rexei hurried forward and quickly twitched everything smooth. Then turned and dropped onto the cushions with a nervous smile. Alonnen eyed her, then sighed and held out his hand. Confused, she stared at it, then accepted his help back onto her feet. "Is something wrong?"

"Nope. Just a different position is needed, that's all." Dropping onto the couch in her place, he caught her hands and gently tugged her over to his knees. "Come on, straddle me like I'm a motorhorse. Knees up on the cushions."

Rexei awkwardly climbed up and settled onto his thighs. His

hands shifted to her hips, then slid up to her waist and ribs. She squirmed a little, biting her lip against the sensation. Without her bindings, with just a thin linen shirt between her flesh and his fingers, she was surprised at how ticklish she was. *Or maybe it's just the circumstances. I've been in tickle fights with fellow apprentices, and my fellow actors weren't entirely shy about touching and teasing . . .*

He sat up, face lifted so that his nose almost brushed her lips. Lifting his chin, he looked straight at her, letting her see his willingness and the controlled hunger in his hazel green gaze. Such boldness, his forthrightness, gave her a bit of courage. For a moment, she lifted her chin, silently acknowledging the fact this moment was in her hands, under her control. Then she dipped her head, tipping it a little to avoid the point of his nose. He tilted his head as well.

The moment their mouths met, it just felt natural for her lips to part. So did his. Within two heartbeats, what was meant to be a tentative kiss deepened into something rich and succulent, with soft nips and suckling licks. Her fingers cradled his head, buried within his soft curls. His hands pulled at her back, pressing their chests together, then slid down to her hips, snugging their groins closer.

Dizzy with the thumping of her heart, heated by each sweeping clutch and caress of his palms, Rexei lifted her head in the effort to seek some air and some clarity. It didn't work; that just bared her throat to his hungry lips. Shifting on his lap, she found herself scooped closer by the grip of his hands on her rump. At the press of his groin against hers, at the realization he had hardened with desire, her blood rushed through her trembling limbs.

His lips nuzzled down along the neckline of her shirt, then pressed against her flesh through the age-worn fabric. The ticklishness from earlier came back in a new flush of sensation. But instead of the urge to laugh or squirm, Rexei heard herself moan softly. Her spine arched out on pure instinct as he did it again, trying to lift the modest curve of her breast up into his nuzzlings.

It wasn't enough. Flushed with desire, frustrated by the barrier of linen, she extracted her fingers from his hair and moved them down to the buttons of her sleeping shirt. The wooden discs slipped one, two, three, out of their holes. In order to undo them, her hands had to nudge his cheeks back from her torso. Glancing up at her, he watched her face, not her fingers. She blushed at her boldness, but that did not stop her from gently easing the material back to either side.

Keeping his gaze locked with hers, Alonnen leaned in again. He had to shift his arms a little higher to support her as she leaned back, but he never stopped looking at her. Not even when his chin brushed the peak of her left breast, then his nose tip and lips.

Rexei shuddered, caught off-guard by how sensual, how sensitive, such a light touch made her small breast feel. Her breathing faltered, then quickened. Pulling back, he searched her face for a clue as to her feelings. She clutched at his shoulders to anchor herself, then gathered her courage and slid her fingers back up into his hair. Dragging in a deeper breath, she guided his head back toward her breast. Eyelids drifting shut, he gave in with a groan, parting his lips around the sensitive, pink-tipped peak.

She had no clue that her breasts could be so sensitive, so sensual. Until now, they had just been lumps of flesh, awkward and inconveniently female. But under the nibbling of his lips, the hot, wet curl of his tongue—*Guildra!* The mental exclamation was half curse, half prayer. *I never knew that . . . oh Goddess . . . so sensitive!*

An unfamiliar heat twisted and threaded its way through her body, connecting her breasts—for he licked the right one as well—to her thighs and the heat building at their crux. To her arms and her toes, which curled in the slightly too large slippers threatening to dangle and drop from her feet. To her own lips, which wanted to return every touch. Except, she couldn't bring herself to pull away from those divine feelings.

"Alonnen . . ." His name was a whisper, an exhaled breath that ended in a groan. It spurred him into licking more, suckling stronger. She shuddered again under his hungry feasting, his passionate nuzzling. But when he lightly bit at one tip, she cried out, body quaking in response to the mild sting of pain and its strong thrill of pleasure. "*Ahh!*"

Her shout and jerk broke Alonnen out of his lustful trance. Releasing her breast from teeth and lips, he struggled to remember who he was, who *she* was, and how far they were *not* supposed to go. Not this soon. Not this fast. The next sound out of her, however, beyond her heavy breathing, was a needy little whimper half muffled by the way her teeth had sunk into her own bottom lip. Her next move was not to sit up and berate him, but rather to tighten the way her fingers had entwined through his hair, tugging him by his locks back to her breasts.

Willing to comply but much more mindful now of what he was doing, Alonnen heeded her silent demand for more. This time, he was aware of each quiver, each unsteady hitch in her breath. Of the straining tension in her muscles, trembling, even spasming, but not quite releasing when he lapped or suckled just right.

Bracing his left arm along her spine, he brought his right hand around to her stomach. Cupping the flat muscles for a moment, he slid his palm down, until his thumb slotted between her spread thighs. There, he pressed and rubbed lightly, inward and farther down. He had to ignore the rubbing of his hand against his own barely constrained flesh, but that was alright; Alonnen sensed immediately when the fire sparked by his goal, the little hardened nub of flesh between her cloth-covered netherfolds, jolted through her body. Fire, not just lightning, for it dragged a wave of rose-blushed heat through her flesh in its wake.

Her back arched, almost pulling his mouth off her right breast, then she straightened up a little, returning it to within reach.

Thumb rubbing, tongue fluttering and circling, he listened to her whimpers and gauged his efforts by the strain and spasm of her muscles. She was so beautiful in her mounting passion; he moaned and sucked harder, rubbed faster.

Rexei could feel it coming. She didn't know what it was, but she yearned for it, ached for it, needed it. Her head thrashed, trying to deny it, to clear her senses, yet at the same time she wanted to shove away all distractions so that she could focus, focus . . . She heard Alonnen moan, felt the tugging of his lips, the flicking of his thumb.

It all crashed together in a bolt of electrical energy that snapped through her body and rocked all her senses. It didn't end quickly, either, unlike a real discharge from some dynamo engine. It rolled and ricocheted through her, until she finally sagged in his grip, slick with sweat and breathing hard.

Somewhere beyond her blissful lassitude, she felt him shifting her weight in his arms. Even as he gathered her up, he twisted on the couch, turning to lay her down. She wiggled a little when he tugged at the bedding, pulling blankets and sheet out from under her lethargic, sated limbs. At the last moment, Rexei caught his hand, tugging it back to her long enough for a kiss. She smelled something rather musky yet sweet near his thumb, and blushed at the realization the smell came from her.

Touched by her kiss, Alonnen crouched carefully and pressed his lips to her forehead. "Sweet dreams, Rexei," he told her. "If you want to do this again, just let me know tomorrow night."

"Mmm . . . thank you. I, uh, I think I might," she mumbled, blushing. She heard him chuckle, then shuffle off toward his bed-chamber. As he left the sitting room, he swept his hand over the lights, dimming them down to near darkness. She realized her shirt was still unbuttoned and worked on fastening it with tired hands, then pulled the covers a little higher. Now that he wasn't making her hot with his touches, she could feel the nip of winter in the air. A satisfied sigh escaped her as she snuggled into the couch to sleep.

Alone in his bedroom, Alonnen leaned his shoulders against the quietly shut door and bit back a frustrated moan. Lifting his hands to his face, he started to scrub at his cheeks, trying to get over the throbbing, unsated ache in his groin. It was a mistake; his thumb still smelled like her passion, her satisfaction.

Giving up, he pushed his trousers down past his hips, baring himself. His fingers stroked and cupped his ready flesh for a few moments, then he brought his hand back up to his nose for another sniff. With the scent of her climax filling his nostrils, he stroked himself, hips flexing. Overheated by watching her achieve bliss in his arms, under his touch, Alonnen found it didn't take long to achieve his own climax. Warmth coated his hands and his shaft.

Slowly sagging into the door, he rested with his legs bracing his weight against the stout panel, then sighed. Straightening, he tugged up his sleeping trousers and headed for the attached refreshing room. His own bliss would lead to a sleepy lethargy in a few more moments, and he wanted to clean up before crawling back between his empty sheets.

Another time, he promised himself. *If she can still look me in the eye tomorrow morning, then there will probably be another time. And another and another . . . and maybe there'll be a wedding and a wedding night between us . . . because I'm falling in love with her, and I know she won't settle for anything less. And . . . and I'm very okay with that.*

The lack of contraceptive spells—he didn't trust the iffy potion the Alchemists Guild made—meant it was hard for couples to consummate their passions without running the risk of a pregnancy. Both of them had too much to do in the coming months to risk that. *But there is still a lot we can do without intercourse*, he thought, dampening a rag under the faucet of his sink. A thought made him lift his brows, then smirk to himself.

I did enjoy an occasional use of the crankman Bethana owned . . . and no one reclaimed it from me after she died. For a moment, he lost his smile, remembering her death, his grief . . . but he had mourned her and moved on a few years ago. He also knew that she would not be pleased if he refused to fall in love ever again. Bethana had helped show him that he was fully over the duplicitous Daralei and free to love again.

I think she'd like Rexei. They're different physically—Bethana was curvy and muscular, Rexei is lean and, well, not very curvy. Long blonde hair versus short brunette . . . But they're both strong, talented, smart women. And we're both mages, and both Guild Masters, even if Rexei's just starting her guild.

And I can't help it. I admire her. I'm falling in love with her. And . . . I need to stop this line of thought so I can get some sleep, he ordered himself, knowing that if he kept thinking along such lines, his loins would re-harden with interest. *So, let's think about the vote in two days to make us the nation of Guildara . . . No, work will only stress me further, since that'll lead right back to the demon problem, and I'll never get any sleep this way . . .*

I know—I'll think about holy days. That's a neutral yet interesting subject. Mekha only had one per season, but I think we should have one per month. Perhaps on the full of Brother Moon? That gives us twelve holy days in a year, and we do have a lot to celebrate . . . so . . . what aspects should be celebrated each month?

Perhaps I should figure out how to divide the guilds into twelve categories? It was an interesting line of thought, intriguing enough to keep his mind off sex yet calm enough to allow him to drop off to sleep.

TWELVE

The first thought on her mind when she awoke was pure happiness. Rexei could not remember the last time she had felt
such an unsullied contentment; usually, worry and stress plagued
her days. The suncrystals overhead were still somewhat dim, suggesting it was barely morning, so she knew she had the time to
spare for contemplating her happy state.

*Let's see . . . safe and sound within the wardings of the Vortex . . .
well rested after a really good night's sleep on Alonnen's . . .* Alonnen.

She blushed, remembering. His lips nibbling on hers, the suckling pull of his mouth on her nipple . . . the feel of those fingers
stroking and sliding the fabric of her sleeping trousers through her
folds. A shiver rippled through her muscles, bringing with it a flush
of renewed desire.

Along with memory came a realization. *He didn't . . . he didn't
get to have any fun himself, last night.* She blinked up at the ceiling,
then knuckled away the grit of sleep. *That isn't right. I should've . . .*

Well, it's a bit late for last night, but not too late for this morning, Rexei decided. She wasn't ignorant of the theory of how sexual urges worked in men, not after a decade of pretending to be "one of the boys." Right now, presuming he had enjoyed a good night's sleep, Alonnen would be feeling the first stirrings of morning pressure.

Before she could lose her courage and backpedal herself into thinking this was going to be a bad idea, Rexei got up and headed for the bedroom door. She did hesitate before touching the panel, but only because she wasn't sure whether to knock first or not. After a brief mental debate, she rapped lightly on the wood with a knuckle, then pushed on the handle.

A soft grunt met the opening of the door. She heard Alonnen trying again. "Mmfh . . . Rexei? Whazzit?"

He sounds rather cute like that, she decided, smiling shyly. "Shhh," she said, closing the door behind her. "I'm just . . . um . . . returning the favor."

"Huh?" Cloth rustled as he turned over and pushed up on one elbow.

Crossing to the bed, Rexei pulled up the covers on the left side and crawled under them. Her sleeping shirt and trousers weren't thick enough to be proof against the cold winter air, but that was alright. Once she got close enough, she could feel part of the warm spot he had been occupying before rolling onto his side, and quickly huddled into it. Tugging the covers up to her neck, she gave him a shy, somewhat nervous smile.

Bemused, Alonnen studied her. *Why would she come in here and crawl straight into my bed?* "Bad dream?"

Rexei shook her head quickly. "Um . . . no . . . I, uh . . ." Taking a deep breath, she forced the words into the open. "I *really* liked what you did to me last night and, um . . . wanted to return the favor. This morning. If you want?"

Alonnen stared at her, groaned under his breath, and flopped onto the bed. On his back, because his body was instantly enthusiastic. Edging toward rampant. She took it as tacit agreement, for a moment later, her hand slid under the covers, brushed against his cloth covered hip, then fumbled a little onto the top of his groin.

Mindful of her undoubted innocence, he covered her hand with his, assisting her in cupping his thickening flesh. She squeezed him a little, fingers moving in gentle, curious exploration . . . then she wiggled her hand free from his.

Before he could ask if she was okay, he felt her fingers seeking and dipping beneath the waistband of his sleeping trousers. Breath catching, he sucked in his stomach under that tickling, explorative touch, then arched his back, lifting his groin up into her fingertips. Her skin was a little cool, a sweet, startling contrast to the heat of his manhood. Dizzy with lust, Alonnen panted, struggled for thought, and finally squirmed, shoving his sleeping clothes down below his hips, baring himself under the bedding.

Rexei blushed and bit her bottom lip at her daring; his enthusiasm did encourage her to continue, though. Twisting onto her left side, she leaned on her elbow and shifted her right hand into a better angle. Gripping his shaft, she marveled at the heat of it, the velvety-soft skin and slight spongy feel when she experimentally squeezed. His groan let her know she was doing it right.

A hundred crude comments and a thousand jokes came back to her, shared with her by men who had thought she was "one of the lads" at the time. She had even learned to give back as good as she heard, but this was the first time she actually touched one—at least, when trying to give pleasure instead of squeezing hard just to cause enough pain so that she could escape some would-be bully's grip. This, however, was something she wanted to do right, with just enough pressure to stimulate and no more, with enough movement, enough . . . her palm stuck to his shaft, her skin a little damp from nerves.

He tolerated it for a few strokes, then nudged her gently.

"There's a jar of lotion on the nightstand, made from mint, for chapped lips and dry skin. You can use that."

Blushing, she twisted over, found it, fumbled the lid off, and scooped a bit up with her fingertips. Careful not to get any on the bedding, she curled her fingers into a loose fist and returned them to his hip. From there, she found her way to his shaft, then gently spread the slick, mint-scented stuff onto his skin, grateful he had pushed his sleepwear even lower while she had been turned away. Not that she could see it, but she could feel it.

It helped a lot. Within moments, her fingers were able to stroke from base to tip and back with definite ease. The ointment felt extra cool on her skin because of the mint; Rexei could only imagine how it felt to the man himself, though she could guess. From the soft, deep whimpering noises and the way he tipped his hips up into each downstroke, it probably felt pretty damn good.

Mindful that he had done more to her than just stroke her folds, she leaned over, ducked her head awkwardly under the covers, and kissed his chest. His breath caught, and his hands shifted. One tugged the covers up higher over both of them, then cupped the back of her head. The other twined his fingers with hers, showing her how to squeeze and stroke faster, harder. She followed his silent instructions as best she could, breathing in the mingling scents of wintermint and musky man.

Alonnen loved the feel of her mouth nipping and tasting the muscles of his chest. It connected the nerves of his torso with those of his hips, even his legs. Groin lifting in needy rhythm, breath panting, he strained toward his bliss. Those little finger twists at the top, however, the little pulsing squeezes at the base, those blew his mind.

"So good . . ." he panted. "So . . . good . . . How'd you . . . how'd you learn to . . . do this?"

She blushed and smiled against the crinkly little hairs dusting his chest. "Lads like to gossip. I may not have one myself, but I've heard enough about what many like to do with theirs." Nuzzling him, she felt something pebbled rubbing against her cheek and heard the hitch in his breath. Turning her head a little, she licked at his nipple and grinned at the way he spasmed. "Like that?"

"Slag, yes!" he gasped. She did it again and again, and his hips pistoned faster, pushing his shaft through her tightening grip. There was just enough lotion left to ease each rapid stroke, yet just enough drag to stimulate every last nerve. "R-Rexeeeei!"

Back arching, he came, hips jolting into the edge of her palm in several hard, unsteady thrusts. Hot dampness hit his chest, the sheet, and her fingers. He bucked a couple more times, then slumped, trembling. His fingers quickly covered hers, but she had already eased her movements. Settling instead on a gentle, slow-pulsing grip, his partner eased out the last few drops, then just cradled his softening shaft under her palm. Her lips dusted little kisses on his sweat-dampened skin, a tender touch that was not lost on his heart.

As soon as he had enough strength back, Alonnen tilted just enough to gather her in his arms, hugging her close. "Thank you," he murmured, in between pressing little kisses to her forehead. "Thank you very much . . . for such a wonderful gift."

A soft giggle escaped her. "You're welcome. And I learned it by listening to the 'other' men bragging about what they liked when their lady friends stroked them. Ummm . . . if you want to do the same tonight? You with me, and, um, me with you . . . ?"

He didn't have to give it more than two seconds' worth of thought. "Okay. But tomorrow, clear heads. We have to go into town for the new-kingdom vote, and everything else that will have cropped up."

Rexei nodded, her cheek nuzzling against his shoulder now that she wasn't half buried under the covers. "Mmhmm . . . but tomorrow *night* . . . are we going to be staying at Big Momma's again?"

His shaft twitched under her fingers. Just the *thought* of

everything they could do, with the brothel's supplies on hand, was stimulating. Unfortunately, now he needed the refreshing room, and he lacked a crucial piece of information on top of that. Kissing her forehead again, he started worming his way out of the bed to go clean up. "I think that could be managed . . . but the real question is, do you like strawberry jam, or would you prefer birch syrup?"

It took her a few moments to realize what he was talking about. When she did, Rexei blushed and blurted, "I'd want elderberry jelly. I think. Um . . . yeah. Elderberry."

Grinning—and trying not to wince as the cold morning air hit the streaks of seed and mint, chilling his skin—Alonnen padded for the refreshing room. "Then dessert shall literally be on me. *If* we end up staying that late. If not, we'll come back here, and I'll introduce you to all the fun things we can do with honey. Win or lose, we'll either celebrate or commiserate. But only if we concentrate, tomorrow. It's a very important vote."

Word had been spread, representatives picked and sent, but not everyone was coming. Part of it had to do with the weather; most of those who had arranged to travel to Heiastowne were from cities to the west and south, where the lands were less steep. To the north, a heavy snowstorm blocked travel, and farther north of that . . . many cities were now in full riot. Priests versus mages, militia versus citizens, old regime versus new would-be despots. The northlands were feeling the full brunt of the turmoil stirred up by Mekha's destruction. Not all Precinct captains were interested in upholding the law, not when so many of them had also benefitted from the priests bending it.

Rexei didn't know if it was due to her own words on the temple steps or to Captain Torhammer's word that order would be maintained, or some combination of both. Probably both, since her words had quelled the initial urges to riot, yes, but the captain's commands had ensured no others had a chance to start. She did know she was grateful that Heiastowne was not one of the cities embroiled in the horrors of a wintertime war.

She was also grateful the Consulate was toasty warm when she arrived through the back door, via the alley from Big Momma's. The skies outside were clear, thanks to a steady wind from the west, but the thin winter sun couldn't penetrate far enough to compensate for the sharp chill imbued in each frozen gust. Once safely inside, she focused on unwinding a layer at a time as she headed through the back halls toward the meeting chamber. First to come off was her scarf, then the long coat she had worn on the drive into town, then her gloves and cap, then . . .

"There you are!" Marta's cheerful greeting startled her.

Blinking, Rexei found the older woman smiling with both sides of her mouth, to the point of beaming at her. Disconcerted, Rexei looked over her shoulder at the others who had come in the back way with her, but Alonnen only shrugged and tugged his cap down over his dark-spelled hair.

"Guild Master Rexei Longshanks," Marta stated, turning partially to face two youths and an elderly gentleman, "I present to you your new apprentices in the Holy Guild. Pensen Tuckerhart, of Lumber, Springs, and Brewers Guilds," she introduced, and Rexei found herself facing a tall, lanky youth with reddish hair and light brown woolens that almost matched. He dipped his head in a little bow, then stepped back as Marta continued. "Alsei Cartwound, of Bakers, Binders, and Embroiderers Guilds," Marta introduced next, which meant a young blonde girl in a cream felted dress decorated with gray and black embroidered vines bobbed a curtsy. "And Master Gearman Jorro Foundertack of fifteen Guilds, so I shall only mention that he has master-rank in Mathematics, Exchequery, and Lessors Guilds."

The balding, gray-haired fellow, clad in gray wool with blue-dyed trim, dipped his head and lifted his palm toward her. She found herself clasping his ink-stained and pen-callused fingers, which were warm and firm. He gave her a slight smile as he shook hands and said, "I understand you have me beat with thirty guilds?"

"Beat in numbers, yes . . . but not in the wisdom of years, I should think," Rexei countered, forced to be honest in the face of such seniority. She offered her hand to Alsei and Pensen as well. "I'm rather surprised anyone could be found so quickly. I . . ." She trailed off, realizing only now that she didn't even have a way to pay them wages yet. She shrugged, feeling awkward, but knowing it would be better to be honest about just how disorganized things still were. "I'm afraid the Holy Guild is still trying to get started. I'm terribly sorry to say this, but I, ah, haven't even figured out how to create an income for the Holy Guild yet, so . . ."

"Actually, I have that covered for you," Marta informed her, pulling out a stiff-paper folio from the messenger-style bag slung over her shoulder. Blinking, Rexei found herself the owner of a sheaf of papers, and the advice to, "Just bring up the laws on the summary sheet and call for a vote to change them in the ways indicated, and you should be able to get a portion of the previous mandatory tithes to the Priests Guild transferred over to the Holy Guild in no time."

"Right. Thank you, Grenspun," she said, still a little off-balance by how efficient the woman was. Clearing her throat, Rexei gestured at the doors in the distance, ones that led into the meeting hall. "We should head on in and discuss what we can of your thoughts and expectations before the meeting begins."

"Will we get to see Her?" Alsei asked her. "Guildra?"

"I'm not sure when," Rexei said, feeling a bit odd as two youngsters and a man old enough to be her grandfather followed her to the meeting chamber. "I'm told that manifestations take a lot of, uh, faith-energy. She said She wouldn't appear again until things were more settled. By that, I suspect She meant a lot more people acknowledging and worshipping Her."

"Well, according to what I read in some of the old books in the Binders Guild," the younger woman said, "if we're going to vote to become a kingdom tonight, we're going to have to ring a sacred bell, and then prove we have a Patron Deity by manifesting said deity."

"Just so long as Mad Mekha doesn't pop back to life when we do so," Pensen muttered. "I'll take any God over Him again. Just about. Won't take a God or Goddess that's worse."

"Smart lad," Jorro stated.

Rexei let the other two enter the hall first, but paused the old man with a hand on his arm. "A moment, if you please. Master Jorro . . . why did you agree to be my apprentice? You're a master thrice over, highly ranked as a Gearman. Why join the Holy Guild? Someone who is young, I can understand being willing to try something new, but you've suffered for decades under the old system."

Her comment earned her a smile and a tap of his finger first on the tip of his own nose, then on the tip of hers. "That's it, exactly, young man," Jorro told her. "I *have* suffered under the old system. And what Mistress Grenspun described to me, what she recorded of your thoughts on the matter, is very much in line with my own thoughts over the years. I just wish I'd thought of a Patron of Guilds myself, since it's so suitable.

"Besides, you'll get the younger ones to follow you with young apprentices in tow, but to snare a master-rank in three disciplines of my years? That'll command the respect of the older set." He tapped her one last time on the nose, then on his own.

Rolling her eyes, Rexei lifted her finger and tapped the edge of it on his nose as well. "Mind your manners, *apprentice*, and have some respect for your Guild Master. No more nose bopping. I'll let those ones pass, but no more, or you'll be stuck with the scut work . . . if I ever have any that needs doing."

He chuckled, not in the least offended by her sass, daring to speak like a gray-bearded grandmaster to a man who looked old enough to be her grandfather. She couldn't even remember her grandparents, though. As it was, she could barely remember her two half brothers and her father.

The shock of seeing a man who looked very much like her eldest half brother, Lundrei, in the third row of the now very packed meeting room blew all other thoughts out of her head a few moments later. She stared, blinked, then shook it off. *It couldn't be him. He looks to be in his thirties . . . Oh. Right. He* would *be in his thirties*, she thought, sneaking another look. *Is that the badge of the Laticifers Guild on his shoulder? Yes, a tree branch with a drop falling off of it, representing the rubber sap that guild collects for things like tires and piston gaskets and such. It's probable that after Mother's disappearance, Father and my brothers split up and scattered. But that can't be Lundrei.*

"I suppose you want to know my reasons for joining?" Alsei asked her, distracting Rexei. At a nod, the younger woman launched into a tale about how she'd always felt sheltered by the Guild System, and . . . Rexei knew she should pay closer attention, but the man in the third row, with the master's medallion and the dark brown hair, with the little mole just in front of his right ear, really did look like her long-lost brother. ". . . So that's why I'm not afraid," the blond girl concluded. "And I want to prove right off the top that women can be priests . . . er, members of the Holy Guild, too."

Rexei nodded, pleased the girl had foreseen that need as well. "You have my complete support in that, and I'm glad you're so willing. Now, I have a quick task for you, while I chat with Pensen about his reasons. See that fellow in the third row?" she asked, nudging Alsei around and pointing at the man who looked so familiar. "Would you go ask him if his mother's name was Luwese, long, long ago? And if his next-mother's name was Yula?"

"Uh . . . sure. And if he says yes, or if he says no?" Alsei asked her.

"If he says yes or if he asks who wants to know, ask him to stay after the meeting so that the Guild Master of the Holy Guild can pass along a message. If he says no, then thank him for his time, and apologize for bothering him," she instructed.

Nodding, Alsei moved forward. Forcing her attention to the other youth, Rexei looked up at Pensen. "What about you? What are your reasons for apprenticing in the new Holy Guild?"

He shrugged. "Marta knows I'm a cousin of Master Tall's. A couple generations removed. Never had any affinity for . . . you know," he added, fluttering his fingers in a little ripple, the kind suggestive of spellcasting without actually saying the dreaded *M* word aloud. "I want to make sure the new guild's safe for 'em. That, and I qualify with three different guilds." He eyed her from his lofty full handspan of extra height and shrugged. "I would like to get paid, though."

"So would I," Rexei muttered, her gaze slipping to Alsei, who had reached her target. The man started, blinked, and searched the crowd. Following the pointing of her cream-clad arm, he stared at Alsei's target. Rexei stared back. It was rather disappointing to see no sign of recognition in the man's gaze, only confusion. Guessing that the answer was *no*, she sighed and turned toward the eldest of her trio. "I already know your reasons, Jorro, and I can appreciate them. Please find yourselves a seat, or a spot on a wall or the floor. I may or may not call you up for proof of apprenticeship, though I'll still need to get you some medallions made."

"I know some people in the Engravers Guild," Jorro offered.

She smiled. "I earned my second journeyman rank in the Engravers Guild. I just have to get my hands on some tools and materials."

"Do we have a place to stay tonight?" Pensen asked. "Because I've come from Luxon, and I only have so much money on me."

"I'll see what can be arranged," Rexei promised, hoping Alonnen would be willing to be generous toward her new apprentices. He had created more quarters in the outer circle of the Vortex, after all, so surely there might be some room there for them, even if it had to be shared. At least until she could figure out a safe place for everyone to stay that was still within reasonably close reach of her quarters in the inner circle of the Vortex. She didn't want to be without its protections, not until the demon summonings were completely thwarted and the last ambitions of the priesthood broken.

Alsei made her way back through the crowd to Rexei. She smiled. "He said yes to both, *and* he wanted to know why, so I told him you'd have a message for him after the meeting." Her shoulders shrugged. "He also wanted to know *how* you knew, but I didn't know, so he'll probably ask you that, too, when you give him whatever the message is. Unless you'd like me to pass it along now?"

The sound of stone striking stone cracked through the hall. Rexei shook her head. "Find a place to sit with your brother apprentices—and thank you for asking him that," she added. "I need to go join the other Guild Masters at the head table now."

Nodding, Alsei moved to join the other two in finding a place to settle and observe. The hall was absolutely packed, though; the trio ended up having to sit on the ground in front of the foremost row of pews, while Rexei found herself sharing the same bench not only with Guild Master Grenfallow but another woman. With Grenfallow taking up the middle, the two relegated to sitting on the ends of the bench could barely plant a single buttock on the padded top. Turning sideways allowed Rexei a more secure perch, but that left her facing the back wall, since the other woman was seated facing the front.

As Grandmaster Toric rapped for order, someone brought up a stool liberated from elsewhere in the building, which allowed the woman on the end to perch on it. Grenfallow slid over, and Rexei turned and accepted her share of the bench more fully, if on the other side of the curvy head of the Actors Guild from the previous time. That gave her a chance to put down Marta's papers and quickly peruse the top sheet.

The more she read, the more she had to admire Grenspun's ability to think of a million little details and organize them by importance, necessity, and urgency. *I wonder if I couldn't convince her to join my guild, just for her sheer organizational skills . . . or maybe not*, she thought. *Maybe I should point her in the direction of whatever sort of government we should have.*

Rule by committee is fine for some things, but only if we have the time for them. The Patriarch ruled in times of peace, and the Precinct generals in times of war . . . or at least areas of war, but even they reported back to the Patriarch. So we need a King or a Queen or something . . . but that would imply a hereditary rulership, and it's a very common Guild Charter law that no offspring is guaranteed any rank in a parent's guild beyond that of apprentice . . . and at that, for only one month. The rest, the child has to earn.

I have no idea how we're going to rule ourselves, she admitted, turning her thoughts toward the Heavens. *Gods and Goddesses . . . and in particular, my Goddess, Guildra . . . I hope You'll give us good, solid ideas on what to do in the coming weeks and months and years.*

Grandmaster Toric rapped his stone-tipped gavel one more time, this time in the pattern that invoked the Consulate meeting, and then there was no more time for idle speculation. Rexei was a Guild Master of a shattered nation that had to vote on whether or not to *be* a whole nation, or at least whatever parts of said nation cared to rejoin with its brethren. That would require concentration, even if the meeting threatened to run long.

It was only early afternoon, and it looked like the food was being supplied by the Hospitallers Guild this time; if the meeting ran to suppertime, there would undoubtedly be spicy and sweet pocket pies for everyone to eat, shipped in from the nearest taverns and inns. *Thank the Gods . . . Guildra, I mean*, she corrected herself. *Thank You for small, tasty favors.*

Alonnen did not like the way that sap master in the third row kept staring at the new head of the Holy Guild. It had taken him a good hour of covert study to realize the symbol on the other man's master's medallion was the branch and sap of the Laticifers Guild. There was no logical connection he could see between the makers of tree-sap rubber and Rexei's lengthy history . . . unless perhaps the man knew her from her short time in the Lumber Guild. A short time, however, would surely not have generated any of the intense looks aimed her way.

When Grandmaster Toric finally ended the meeting, Alonnen's mind was not on the laws that had been altered and passed. It wasn't on the extra budget allocated to his guild for paying for the rehabilitation and reintegration of the mages who *had* to be passed to the safety of the carefully unmentioned Vortex, because their personal shielding was nearly nonexistent after too many years of being locked in spell-controlled mindlessness. It wasn't on the fact that the Holy Guild now *had* a budget; one-third of the funds originally tithed to the Priests Guild were now allocated to her needs and the other two-thirds to a new-kingdom fund, but only those funds from all the cities which had attended and agreed to become a part of Guildra.

He wasn't even thinking about the fact that they still needed a blessed, sacred bell to formally ring and summon proof that they were their own kingdom, with a Patron and a voice and an identity, though they now had eight cities and villages firmly under the banner of Guildara, and seven more whose representatives needed confirmation from the folks back home that this was the right thing to do.

His thoughts arrowed in on the need to get Rexei away from that older man before . . . well, he didn't know *what* might happen. Rising from his seat the moment Toric set the mallet down, Alonnen hurried to the end of the table. Stooping over Rexei's shoulder, he reached for the papers in front of her. "Right, then. Time to go."

"I can't leave just yet," she murmured back, pressing the papers back down when he tried to lift them. "I have someone to talk to first. Plus my apprentices need a place to stay," she added. Looking up at Alonnen, she gave him a wry smile. "I'd prefer it if that were somewhere near my current residence, but if you'd rather not, then I can get them somewhere here in town. At least I have the funds to pay them some wages now."

"I'll see what rooms can be found for them. But we really have to go now," he warned her, seeing a certain dark-haired man working his way forward through the tide of bodies headed for the doors out of the meeting hall. Beside Rexei, Guild Master Grenfallow murmured a farewell and rose, her own notes cradled in her arms. Alonnen lifted his chin in reply, but he didn't look at Saranei. She wasn't the one who concerned him at this moment.

Rexei caught his stare and followed the line of his gaze. *So that's what this is about. He's trying to be protective of me.* She thought that was very nice, but unneeded at this point in time. Covering the hand still trying to pick up her papers, she smiled up at him. "It's okay. I *asked* him to come talk to me."

Alonnen frowned at that, but it was too late to question her. The dark-haired man made his way around the three Holy Guild apprentices, who were fielding questions from the others. Flicking a wary look at the green-spectacled Guild Master not quite looming over Rexei's shoulder, he braced his palms on the front of the table, leaned over the corner, and spoke in a low, urgent tone.

"I have several questions for you, lad," he asserted. A flick of his brown gaze at Alonnen's face and back, and he added, "So unless you want this aired in public, I suggest you point out some place private where we can talk."

"You'll speak with Master Longshanks in full view of everyone else," Alonnen told him, leaning half over Rexei's shoulder. "If you want it private, keep your voice down."

Eyeing the two men, both in their early thirties, both determined to have their way, Rexei sighed heavily. Scooting to her left on the bench into the fading warmth left behind by the head of the Actors Guild, she snapped her fingers under Alonnen's sharp nose to get his attention, then pointed at the spot she had just vacated.

"You. Sit. Behave," she added. Hesitating only a moment, Alonnen did as she bid. That freed her to face what she hoped was her half brother. "If your mum's name was Luwese and your next-mother's name was Yula . . . then you tell me the family name of Luwese, and I will tell you the family name of Yula."

"How do *you* know such things?" Lundrei asked, suspicion clear in the narrowing of his brown eyes and the crease that formed between his brows.

He didn't recognize her? Rexei had seen his long, hard looks all through the lengthy meeting, and she had hoped he had figured it out. *I guess I need to start spending more time trying to look and act like a girl. Wear a dress, grow out my hair . . . well, not a dress all the time.* Sighing, she fixed him with an honest, blunt look. "Because I earned a master rank in the Actors Guild?"

His brows lowered farther in confusion. She rolled her eyes. This close, she could feel his aura, though he wasn't technically a mage. There were hints of home, of baked breads and worn fabric, in its feel, but there was also something else, something like a cheese that had aged and grown more sharp. Rexei wasn't sure yet if she liked the new flavor of her brother. Or how long it was taking him to get her point.

"As a *lad*?" she emphasized carefully.

Comprehension dawned. Eyes widening and brows lifting in shock, he gaped at her for one moment, then lunged inward, arms wide—and got stopped by the slapping of Alonnen's palm on his chest, straight-arming him from behind Rexei's neck.

"Guild Master Longshanks asked you a *question*, Master Latici- fer," he growled, using the man's guild for lack of a family name. "You will answer it to *both* our satisfaction."

Lundrei pulled back, visibly affronted and tense with a pent-up retort. Rexei blushed a little, but she didn't counter or soften Alonnen's demand. Sharp brown eyes flicked between her face and her companion's before the man standing to her left did an odd thing.

He relaxed. He even lifted his chin at Alonnen, though he kept his gaze on Rexei's face. "You know, he's not worthy of you."

For a moment, she didn't know what Lundrei was talking about. Alonnen lowered his arm to her shoulders in what would look to anyone else like a casual touch, but which to her half brother would be a clear statement that Alonnen didn't give a damn what the other man thought of his presence in Rexei's life. It felt good to know that she only had to say the word, and Alonnen would fight at her side for whatever she wanted. She slipped her arm around his waist in return, a visible show of solidarity. It felt right to do so.

Still, a ghost of an old memory teased at her senses; the scent of the apple pocket pies the Hospitallers had served along with the mutton and beef pies brought back the memory of her father slid- ing an apple cobbler out of the brick oven in their little house and her two brothers teasing each other about whether or not some of the local girls were "worthy" of them . . . and then they'd turned on Rexei and teased her, too, until their father, Gorgas Porterhead, had asserted that *no* man would be "worthy" of his little girl.

That was when her mother—his second wife—had given her husband an arch look and a witty retort. Smirking, Rexei gave it right back to Lundrei, if worked around a little so that it fit the current circumstances better. "I don't know, *he* seems to have managed . . . just like Da did for Momma. But I'll have *your* mother's family name out of you."

"Springfan. Now give me yours," Lundrei ordered, lifting his chin.

"Dartingcam." That earned her a grin, which she returned. She wanted to rise and hug him until the break of dawn, but Alonnen's arm on her shoulders was a reminder that they were in a hall still partly filled with people, some of whom were close enough to maybe overhear and definitely see.

She also felt an uneasy distrust at how quickly she had found one of her long-lost brothers. *It could just be a decade-long habit of caution, or it could be a worry that somehow he's been converted by the priesthood, or it could be . . . I don't know. Guildra, I just don't know, other than I want to take things slowly.*

That, and Alonnen had promised her there would be more fondling and cuddling tonight, and she suspected he would need some soothing and reassuring after this unexpected encounter with her brother. Not to mention hunger now warred with her weariness, letting her know that retiring to Big Momma's would not be amiss for yet another reason.

Still, this was her long-lost brother. Contenting herself with a smile, she said, "I'll be here tomorrow morning to take care of some business. We'll have more time and privacy for talking then."

Lundrei frowned at that. "Why not tonight?"

"Because I am a Guild Master." Gathering her papers, Rexei stood. Alonnen rose with her, guarding her almost like a hound standing over a fallen bone. She would have to talk with him about that, but first she needed to deal with her brother. "I still have to find quarters tonight for my brand-new apprentices plus give them their initial instructions, and that takes precedence."

"But, I haven't seen you in ten years!" Lundrei protested. He had the courtesy to keep his voice low, but the intensity was still there. "What happened to you? Where have you been all this time? Don't you want to know about Father and Tandron and me? Where we've been and what happened to us? Don't you want to tell me what happened to *you*?"

"Of course I want to know. But I am not going to abandon my responsibilities. I am not a little . . . child anymore," she amended carefully, mindful of the others still in the meeting hall. "Now, what name are you known by, and where are you staying? Since, if you've paid attention to this meeting, you'll know my name by now."

"Lundrei Cogsprite. And I'm staying at the Fallen Timbers," he added, naming an inn she vaguely recalled being on the southeast side of town. "Rubber makers get a discount there, same as Lumber and Woodwrights."

"I'm glad you get a discount," Rexei told him. She wished she could just toss the papers out of her arms and hug her brother instead, but too many years of caution said be careful, be cautious, don't rush things. "If I don't see you here tomorrow morning, I'll leave word at the Fallen Timbers."

Grandmaster Toric approached along the curve of the head table. "Guild Master Longshanks, I know night has fallen, but if I could have an hour of your time, Grandmaster Della Grindhammer of the Exchequers Guild is willing to begin the paperwork assigning you . . . and your apprentices . . . the funds allocated to your guild during this meeting. The local grandmaster for the Mintners Guild is also willing to work on a suitable set of guild medallions for your, ah, growing numbers."

Since it was clear he wasn't going to get the freedom to speak with her tonight, Lundrei sighed, ran a hand over his dark hair, and gave Rexei a look that said they *would* have words later. "I can't believe *you* were appointed a Guild Master at your age."

"I am what I am . . . and I am not the only one who has to deal with what *is*, instead of how we all wanted things to be. A good evening to you, Master Cogsprite," she told him. "I look forward to catching up with you tomorrow morning. Tuckerhart, Cartwound, Foundertack, if you'll come with me, we'll see about getting our first stipend set up, then see if the Mintners have the tool-spoked gearwheel already among their designs, or if not them, then the local Engravers Guild. Master Tall, if you'd like to accompany us, I'd be grateful for your continued guidance."

Thankfully, Alonnen simply nodded, relieving Rexei that he wasn't going to cause further trouble.

Alonnen held his tongue until after they left the Shambling Mountain Inn, where Rexei had secured temporary rooms for her three apprentices. It was late, he was tired, he had been looking forward to fooling around with his Rexei . . . and he didn't know what to make of the turmoil of feelings he had at the thought of that man. Under the prodding of young Alsei during the walk to the inn, Rexei had confessed the gentleman from the Laticifers Guild was her half brother, and Alonnen had felt a bit of a fool over his reaction. Or rather, his overreaction. He still felt protective of her, but he should not have reacted so strongly.

The temperature had thawed a bit, melting most of the snow left over from that snowstorm, but the night was cold and damp from an intermittent drizzle. Since they had several blocks to go before reaching Big Momma's, he adjusted the scarf to cover his nose a bit more, caught her gloved hand in his, and tucked both

into the pocket of his leather motorhorse coat. Thankfully, she
didn't object. In fact, she huddled closer while they walked.

"Rexei . . . I'm sorry I got a bit jealous in the meeting hall over
your brother," he found himself confessing. "I'm not used to that.
I didn't know who he was, and I was a bit of a guard dog there,
but . . . you're not a bone for me to claim or fight over."

"I know," she murmured. Then clarified. "I mean, I know you
didn't mean it. I already know *you* know I'm not something to be
fought over. And I do appreciate that you are willing to help protect me. I'm feeling just as cautious, too—excited," she admitted.
"Part of me just wants to run to the Fallen Timbers and talk with
him all night long about . . . about everything. But part of me is
wondering, why is he here *now?* Is this some trick or trap of the
priests? Is it some subtle maneuvering of my Goddess, to try to
restore all that I've lost? Or is it pure coincidence only?"

"I don't know," he admitted. "If you like, we can swing by the
Consulate and I can put in a call for a scrying specialist to come
out tomorrow morning to examine him for priest-spells. We have
all manner of amulets and pendants for that sort of thing. I'd do it
myself, but it's not my specialty."

She nodded. "I think I'd like that. I mean, he *is* my brother. He
looks like him, he knows the family names, he . . . I don't like having to doubt."

"It's just the product of living too many years with a False
God," Alonnen teased lightly, nudging her with his elbow. "You'll
get over it. Now, since we can't do anything else about *that* until
tomorrow morning . . . do you remember what I promised and
what you offered yesterday?"

She blushed, cheeks heating despite the cold, damp wind curl-
ing through the streets. A particularly strong gust tried to extin-
guish the flicker of the gas lamps, but the glass panes kept most of
the breeze out. "I remember . . . and I think I'd like to try that big

bathing tub. That is, if it doesn't cost too much to fetch up hot water?"

"They have a big boiler in the attic," he told her. "Hot water on demand for every room, fed by the aqueducts from the Heias Dam. None of that tedious heating it by the kettleful, even if they don't have magical runes."

"Good. Then we'll get warm, and, um . . . yeah." She blushed again, but grinned, thinking of the possibilities inherent in old but clean sheets and elderberry jelly.

The rumble of several engines approached. Wary of the noise, the pair slowed and moved close to the side of the nearest building, where motorcarts and motorhorses would be less likely to pass. Sure enough, a full seven glass-enclosed motorcarts drove past. It wasn't the sight of so many expensive machines that made Alonnen and Rexei stare, however. It was a glimpse of the Priests Guild symbol enameled onto the side of one of the carts.

"Did you see . . . ?" Alonnen asked her.

"It . . . it looked like the Patriarch's seal," Rexei confirmed, eyes wide. "I had to study it when I joined the Engravers Guild."

"This isn't good. If that's the Patriarch . . ." Giving the last of the vehicles a worried look, Alonnen stepped up his pace, heading for the Consulate.

Several blocks, a bit of ringing and waiting for someone to answer, and a little bit of fast-talking later, Alonnen had the talker-box cranked up and working. ". . . Are you sure you cannot see anything, Gabria?"

"Yes, and I'm sorry, Master Tall," the young woman on the other end of the aether-connected machine stated in his ear. "But wherever they are . . . ah! Aha! I just checked the paper roach in the dining hall. They've been taken there, and . . . yes, here comes an apprentice priest with the first of what looks like plates. They're going to be fed after their long journey."

"It's rather late; I suppose food *would* be foremost on their minds, not business. What about the Patriarch?" he asked as Rexei listened in to his side of the conversation alone. "Can you see him?"

"Elderly, gray haired, long beard in the traditional braid, with the God's Sigil on his forehead? . . . Well, not that the symbol would be there, since it's vanished from everywhere," Gabria muttered. *"No, I cannot. I . . . oh, a name! Oh. Archbishop Gafford. And he looks like the descriptions I've heard. Tall, lean, thin mustache, soothing voice. That's . . . not good."*

"Archbishop Gafford? No, it isn't. That's the Patriarch's right-hand man," Alonnen agreed. "Are they saying anything about the reason why he's here in Heiastowne?"

"Wait . . . shh . . ." Several seconds of quiet passed, then Gabria spoke quickly. *"He's just given Archbishop Elcarei a setdown, saying he's too tired and irritated to speak of business matters until morning. He just wants food, a warm bed, and quarters for his entourage—heh,"* the mage-clerk giggled, surprising Alonnen. *"He's just, oh the naughty, insulting words he used, should Elcarei try to stick him in one of the former prisoner cells . . . I'm torn between being frightened at h-having the Patriarch's Chief Enforcer in town, and . . . He has a very inventive vocabulary."*

"Be calm, Gabria," Alonnen directed her. "Remember, you're in the safest place. *We're* the ones in potential danger. Arrange for surveillance through the night. Oh, and get some detection pendants sent out here with, um . . . Master Tildei. Or Master Julianna. Either of them are good at detecting and discerning priest-spells laid on people."

"Yes, sir," Gabria agreed. *"I wish I knew how to record these scrying images. Archbishop Elcarei just turned an interesting shade of purplish red . . . Oh! Here comes the Aian mage. Wait . . ."*

Curious, Alonnen waited. And waited. Rexei lifted her brows, so he cupped his hand over the cone of the mouthpiece and whispered to her what was happening. Finally, Gabria spoke once more through the earpiece.

"*Oh my . . . This Torven fellow just firmly put the Patriarch's right-hand man in his place. This is important, Alonnen,*" Gabria told him. "*Important and frightening. The Patriarch's man came here to wrest control of the . . . the demon summonings from this 'usurper,' and Torven Shel Von just thoroughly set him in his place as being half trained, shoddily warded . . . and enchanted the archbishop into standing and dancing around to prove it! If Gafford was intending to s-summon demons . . . I think I am now very, very grateful this foreigner is in charge, even if his efficiency and skills frighten me.*"

"So you're saying it looks like the Torven fellow is firmly in charge?" Alonnen asked.

"*Yes . . . yes, I do think so. The Archbishop Gafford isn't happy about it . . . but he's reseated himself and is no longer threatening or bluffing. What do we do about this?*"

There were several options, but Alonnen had to admit to himself that if Torven Shel Von *was* firmly in charge, even of the arrogant newcomers, then that meant they had more time to prepare. "Continue to monitor all roaches. Arrange for around-the-clock study of the scryings, and have everyone take copious notes. If this Torven fellow is indeed in charge, then we have time, since it's clear he won't allow any rash, hasty acts.

"I'll stay in town for now. Don't hesitate to call the Consulate to send me a message if you overhear something that needs me urgently. I'd come back, but if anything happens, it might be better for me to be here on hand than all the way back at home."

"*Right . . . Heavens, but I am very glad I'm all the way out here and nowhere near there.*"

"Goodnight, Gabria," he told her, and at her murmured reply, ended the connection by dropping the ear-cone back into its cradle. He gave the crank several turns to keep it charged, then faced

Rexei. "Looks like our Aian invader is containing and controlling the problem. For now. Eventually, he *will* conjure a powerful demon and . . . do something with it."

"Are you sure you don't need to return?" Rexei asked him, anxious at the thought of something slipping through their fingers, some opportunity or piece of news.

Alonnen shook his head. "There's not much more I could do there than I could do here. I can't watch all night long without exhausting myself, so I'd just have to make others do what they're already doing right now, watching and taking notes on everything. Gabria's been introduced as my Sub-Consul to a couple of the other Guardians, in case any of them call. And . . . I'm here with you.

"I don't know how much time we'll have before the muck hits the motor, but since we can't do anything until we know more, either of what they're up to or how to stop them for good . . . I'd rather spend my time with you," he admitted plainly, searching her brown eyes. "I don't know why it's you, but I know it's you, Rexei."

"You know it's me . . . what?" she asked, unsure what he meant.

He gave her a lopsided smile somewhat reminiscent of Marta. "I know it's you I want in my life . . . and in my bed. For more than just sleeping. Still willing to head to Big Momma's?"

She blushed and ducked her head, then nodded. Eyes bright, she smiled and helped him to his feet. "You, me . . . and elderberry jelly."

Grinning, he let her pull him out of the talker-box room.

THIRTEEN

Rexei wrinkled her nose. "It's kind of small."

Alonnen rolled his eyes. "You don't need *that* much."

"Well, I thought it'd be a lot larger," she protested, holding up the little jar of elderberry jelly, one barely half the size of her fist. The oil lamps lighting the brothel room—fourth floor, instead of third this time, but still a corner room—shone through both the glass of the jar and the deep purplish red preserves inside, but there was barely half a cup's worth. "For that much silver, I'd expect a full pint, is all I'm saying."

"Can you honestly eat an entire pint of elderberry jelly in a single sitting?" he challenged her. He reached for the jar, only to have her pull away. Undaunted, he cupped her arm instead, but she didn't move far. Moving up behind her, Alonnen wrapped his arms around her sweater-clad chest. "Well, can you?"

"With a big enough stack of toasted bread? Maaaybe," Rexei teased. Setting the jelly back down next to the other jar, she picked it up and squinted at the label. This jar had a rippled outside texture and a smooth oval for the glued-on label, which simply said, *Pomade*. The translucent white contents were a mystery. "What's this one for?"

"Well, after you've had your elderberry jelly mess, and we've had a chance to clean up in that nice big copper tub . . . I was hoping we could . . . you know," he coaxed, sliding one hand down to cup her backside.

She considered his words, conflicted. Alonnen was a good man, smart, funny, handsome, and appealing in many ways. He had a lot of love to give, from what Rexei had seen. In fact, she was sure he would make a wonderful parent. However . . . "Um . . . I'm not ready to be a mum. And the potion isn't one hundred percent perfect."

"It's not for *that*," he told her. She gave him a confused look. Plucking the jar from her fingers with one hand, he slid the fingers of the other down between her nethercheeks and spoke bluntly over her little squeak of surprise. "Pomade is used to grease the bottom for pistoning. I'd hope to be a good father, and I'm sure you'd be a good mother, but neither of us is in a position at this point in our lives where creating a child is a wise option."

"Ah. Right. And using the back door for pistoning avoids that as a complication," she agreed, remembering all the lurid gossip she'd listened to over the years in her guise as a boy. The fingers between her nethercurves had been a bit of a surprise at first, but . . . were kind of exciting now. Rexei had heard it was enjoyable for both genders, though apparently it took a bit more preparation and effort than the baby-making route. *And he's willing to be careful, and I know he cares enough to make sure I'd enjoy it* . . . A thrill of excitement wormed its way past her trepidation. "Okay . . . we'll do it."

Alonnen squeezed her waist and nibbled on the side of her neck in gratitude. "As much as I enjoy fondling and being fondled," he murmured, tracing a little circle on her skin with the tip of his long nose, "I also want to do much more with you."

Part of her was nervous at the thought of all they were about to do. Part was curious. The greatest part of Rexei's feelings, though, was very glad she was here in this room with *him*. Alonnen. Setting down the pomade jar, she turned in his arms, looped her own around his shoulders, and . . . they bumped noses awkwardly.

He ducked his head at the collision, mumbling an apology. Smiling, Rexei kissed the "offending" appendage. Several times, too, so that he knew she didn't care his nose was a bit longer than most. In fact, she peppered it with pecking kisses until he laughed and pulled back.

"Enough—enough! Leave my nose alone, woman, or I'll attack you with it!" Alonnen mock threatened, though it was spoiled by his grin.

Giggling, Rexei covered her mouth with both hands; giggling was a girlish thing, a habit she had mostly broken over the years. But the way he smiled at her, warm and accepting this side of her, all of her, made her relax. "And how would you attack me with it? I'll grant you it's long and sharp at the tip, but it's still made of flesh."

About to reply, Alonnen paused, thought, smirked, and stepped back, releasing her. Lifting his hands to his knitted top, he pulled it over his head. "Here, first get yourself naked," he said. "I'll do the same. Then I'll show you how a nose is used—a Tallnose nose," he amended, "in lovemaking. It's a skill not every man can train, you know, as most just don't have the proper appendage."

The way he lifted his head, tilting it in arrogant nasal display, made her giggle again. The way he stripped off the rest of the layers concealing his chest made her cover her blush and cover her mouth.

That hid most of the smile she simply could not stop from spreading across her lips the moment he bared his winter-pale skin.

"Come on," he ordered her, flipping a hand at her own garments. "Off with all of it! Not unless you want them stained with elderberry jelly."

"Uh, no." Focusing on her own clothes, Rexei worked to remove them in the face of her growing nervousness. She glanced at Alonnen. He stripped in a matter-of-fact manner and dropped his clothes onto one of the chairs next to the little table, completely unashamed of his nudity. It made her realize just how comfortable *she* was with him, given his visible comfortableness with her. "Right."

Moving over to the lounging couch, she stripped off her clothes and piled them on the cushions. Everything came off easily, except her breast bindings. The material had tangled somehow; between that and the cool draft she could feel against her naked hips, she was even more anxious to get it off.

"Shh, shh, I've got it. A few loose threads got bound up in the knot," Alonnen explained, soothing her. His fingers took over from hers on her left side, then he helped her unwind the long strip of linen. He let her drop the wadded material on the couch, but did not touch her. Instead, he merely observed, "You have a very cute bottom. You also have wider hips than one would think."

"It's, uh, the baggy tunics and sweaters and shirts I wear," Rexei said. Her skin itched, as it always did upon removing the wrappings. Normally she scrubbed at her skin for a minute or so to rid it of the sensation, but with him right behind her . . . The itch didn't go away. It grew, making her shift her weight and grimace.

"Is something wrong?" Alonnen asked.

"Ugh!" Giving in to her greatest urge, Rexei scrubbed her hands over her modest curves, scratching and rubbing at the reddish lines formed by the wrinkles in her breast-bindings. "So itchy!"

Chuckling, he placed his palms on her back and started scrubbing. "Here, let me help."

Startled at first, Rexei relaxed into his efforts with a soft moan of pleasure; it was the one spot she could never reach, and he was now soothing the madness that she had learned by necessity to ignore. "Oh, that feels so good . . ."

"My pleasure. I'm happy to assist," he reassured her. His nails scraped lightly for a few strokes, then he shifted his fingers to her ribs. Rexei squirmed a little, until he firmed his touch past the point of tickling. Another happy sigh escaped her, drawing a chuckle out of him. "Hedonist."

"Um, yes," she murmured, blushing. Then felt his hands slipping around to cup her breasts, making the skin of her face feel rather hot. Those fingers wiggled and stroked, making the flesh gently caged in his grip ache with needs she hadn't really known about before the last few nights. Remembering now how he had played with and kissed her curves, she sighed and leaned back against his naked frame. Only because it was him, Alonnen, did she feel comfortable enough to confess, "I like this part, too."

"Mmm, so do I," he agreed, plumping one small breast. "Barely a palmful, yet so wonderfully sensitive." He kissed the side of her neck, and played with her other modest curve.

Being passive wasn't in her nature. She might run and hide, or she might face down a foe and fight, but Rexei was still doing something about her situation when she did those things; standing still was just not in her nature. Taking care of herself, learning new guild skills, all of these things had taught her to step forward and grasp what she wanted.

She also wanted Alonnen, and she had the grace to admit that to herself.

Turning in his arms, Rexei slid her hands over his flesh, exploring every angle and curve. She nipped at his neck and licked along the raspy edge of his jawline, enjoying his musky scent. This felt right, and wonderful, and was exactly what she wanted. "*This* . . . is where I want to be. In your arms."

Alonnen felt it, too, in an upwelling of love, need, and a deep-rooted contentment. He hugged her close, chest to breasts, and just breathed in the soft, slightly spicy scent of the woman in his arms. But when she wrapped her fingers around the heat of his erection, he twitched backwards. It was too much, too intense on the heels of the emotions she had raised.

"Easy! Easy, I don't want this to end quickly," he murmured, soothing her brief frown of disappointment. Beyond her shoulder, he could see the jar of pomade and the jar of preserves. "Actually, now would be a good time to experiment with the elderberry, yes? Which would you rather do, lay out the old sheet or open the jar?"

"Lay out the sheet. I can act like a young man all day long," she added, stepping back so that she could pluck the folded linen off the table, "but my wrists aren't up to the actual task of it. How about on the lounging divan?"

"That'll do," Alonnen agreed, picking up the preserves. He started to twist the cap off easily . . . and failed. Gripping lid and jar more firmly, he grunted twice, trying to loosen the lid. Finally, he got it off but not before provoking a small giggle from his lover over the effort involved. "Oh, very funny. You and I both know the Threefold God of Fate *loves* a good ironically timed joke."

"Then I'm very glad we don't have the Threefold God as our Patron," Rexei soothed him, hugging him from behind. The more time she spent with him, the more that hugging—and touching, period—felt natural and normal to her. "Or it would happen much more often, I'm sure."

"That does bring up a good point," he said, turning to follow her back to the couch. "Does *Guildra* have a sense of humor, O High Priestess?"

"Guild Master, and of course She does," Rexei pointed out. "How could She not? She *is* the Patron Goddess of all the entertainment guilds, as well as all the rest. Actors, Bards, Writers, Poets . . ."

"And Patron Goddess of Brothels," Alonnen replied, lifting the opened jelly jar as if it were a glass for a toast. Lowering it, he tilted the mouth toward hers. "Would you like to break the wax and have the first scoop?"

"I don't have a spoon," she told him.

"You don't need a spoon. Use your fingers," he countered.

She wrinkled her nose and sat down. "But that'll be messy."

"That's the point," Alonnen said, and poked at the wax that had been poured on top of the preserve. Working out several chunks, he tossed them onto the small table, then offered her the dark red contents. "Scoop some out, pick a target on either your or my body, and apply it with your fingers—wait," he added quickly. Stepping closer, he carefully made sure his feet were on a corner of the sheet that had draped over the floor. "Okay, *now* do it. The point of the sheet is to catch anything that falls, after all."

"Right." She dug her fingers into the cool, firm, slightly grainy jelly. It squished between her fingertips, and a glob threatened to fall off when she scooped some out. Catching it with her other hand, she hesitated, then scooted forward on the sofa and smeared a bit on Alonnen's chest.

His muscles contracted under the cool, sticky stuff. Fascinated, she spread the jelly around a bit more, then awkwardly tried to lick it. Sitting, she was too short; standing, she was too tall. With a grin, Alonnen graciously sat down and let her settle next to him so that she could lean over his lap and lick.

The jelly was a bit strong. She loved it, but she usually ate it smeared thin on toasted bread, not gooped thick on, well, non-toasted man. Still, she tried a few more licks, then looked up at his face. "Is this . . . good for you? Are you enjoying it?"

He gave it a moment of thought, then shrugged and lifted his brows. "It's not bad. Are *you* having fun?"

She debated, then bit her bottom lip in a brief grimace. "It's a bit too tart, to be honest. Maybe I should've asked for the birch syrup—I'll pay you back for the elderberry jar."

"It wasn't that much," Alonnen pointed out. He nudged her into a normal sitting position, then he twisted to face her. "Here, let me try it." Scooping out a bit from the jar, he carefully daubed bits of jelly onto her nipple. "Let's see if you like being on the receiving end."

The first few tentative licks felt good. The way he swirled his tongue, too . . . but then he pulled back. Wrinkling his long, pointed nose, Alonnen grimaced.

"Yeah . . . the flavor's too tart for this. Let's clean up and share that tub," he offered instead.

Rexei sighed, but let him rise and head for the rounded alcove. "Sorry."

"Hey, not your fault," Alonnen said, shrugging and spreading his arms as he turned to face her while walking backward. "We try new things, and sometimes they work okay, sometimes they work great, and sometimes they fail. Hopefully not spectacularly—and this time wasn't a disaster—but you'll never know until you try. We can try the syrup another time, but for now . . . one hot bath, coming up."

Rexei rose and put the cap back on the jar; it was still perfectly good jelly, and she would be having toasted bread with her meal when breaking her fast tomorrow. Pulling the old sheet off the couch, she wiped the smear off her breast, then bundled up the fabric and set it on a chair. Big Momma's had members of the Launderers

Guild—a sub-chapter of the Servers Guild—on staff who would take the sheet and the other linens, bleach and scrub everything, and hand it all off to the room cleaners to remake the beds and so forth.

She had done something similar in the temple, stripping priests' beds and remaking them with fresh linens once a week, and dumping the dirty linens and velvet clothes into sacks to be taken to a nearby Laundry guildhouse. Here, though, she didn't have to do any of that if she didn't want; the staff were paid well, based on what the brothel owner charged for these rooms. Since this wasn't an emergency, Alonnen had elected to pay for an entire night in one of these rooms for the two of them back when they had arrived at midday.

Fresh linens, a hot bath, scented soaps . . . Joining him in the alcove, grateful the blinds had been pulled low, Rexei investigated the low table of soft soap pots. Picking one with a spicy smell to it, she added a fancy, soft sea sponge, and held them in one arm. The other, she used to test the water splashing from the faucet into the oversized copper basin. A nod let Alonnen know he had picked a good temperature. She offered him the jar for a sniff and received a nod in return.

Pleased at her choice, Alonnen let her set the jar and sponge on the broad flared rim at the head of the tub, then climbed in and assisted her over the edge. Both sank down into the heat with little hisses and contented sighs, one at each end of the oval basin. Eyeing her, he contemplated her relaxed nudity, then tapped her hand and flicked his fingers. "C'mere," he ordered, opening his arms. "Put your back to my chest, and let's cuddle."

Blushing, she smiled and moved. "You really are a very . . . touchy . . . person. As in, you like to touch people. Aren't you?"

"Very much so," he agreed, parting his legs to make room for her to settle between them. His chest was still a little bit sticky from the jelly attempt, but the basin was quite deep, allowing the water to rise up almost high enough to soak the elderberries away.

"I feel better when I'm touching someone I like. Happier. It's like . . . it's like making a wordless connection, deep with trust, and abiding in affection and caring.

"And when they touch me, when they reach out to me and I don't have to start it? Then I *know* they care about me." Gently wrapping his arms around her ribs, he nuzzled his jawline against her steam-dampened hair. "I love sex, don't get me wrong—and don't deny either of us the pleasure of it," he teased lightly, "but just a simple, honest, cuddlesome hug conveys as much love or more. Actually, *more*. I could get a dozen women to grease my piston with their hands, simply because of my rank and their own desire to rise in the ranks somehow. Hell, a dozen men. But a hug? That's something special."

Rexei grunted, dropping her head back onto his shoulder. "Ugh . . . why do you tell me this when I'm facing *away* from you? And in a bathtub? If I tried to turn around now to hug you, it'd be all awkward elbows and mangling knees and unwelcome bruises for both of us."

He chuckled and squeezed her. "We'll have plenty of time for hugs. Right now, I'm going to enjoy the heat of this bath a little bit more, then help you scrub the elderberry preserves off our hides. Then . . . I'm going to clean your cute little bottom."

"My bottom is not little," she muttered. "My hips are a little bit too wide for someone trying to pretend to be a boy. I have to wear long, baggy tops to hide it."

"The part I'm interested in is cute and little," he asserted, sliding a hand down to her hip. "These lush bits are lovely for grabbing on to, but it's the little cog-star between your cute nethercheeks to which I'm referring."

His words reminded her of what they were going to do. "I, uh . . . heard it can be painful. Um, using that one."

"It can be, if you don't go slowly, don't take time to gently loosen it, and definitely if you don't use any pomade or such," Alonnen admitted. "The other way is faster, easier, and better-feeling, but it carries the long-term risk of babies." Shifting his hand to her belly, he rested it there for a moment, then hugged her around the ribs. "As much as part of me wants a couple of little Rexeis running around—boy or girl, doesn't matter—the greater part of me knows we still have some serious problems to clear up before we can go that far."

She nodded, turning her head just enough so that her forehead caressed the side of his jaw. "You're right, we shouldn't. And . . . um . . . well, I trust you to take your time, go slow, and . . . um . . . pomade. We should have grabbed the jar of pomade."

"Yes and no; it might be helpful to clean up a little, first," he told her, and slipped his other hand between her nethercheeks for a subtle tickle.

Sucking in a startled breath, Rexei squirmed a little in surprise. She forced herself to stop and relax. "Wait . . . Is my shoulder blade *sticky?*"

"You're the one who leaned against me without cleaning off the jelly, first," he teased lightly.

"Fine. Just for that, *you* have to scrub my back," she mock ordered. "And anywhere else I want."

Without a word, he reached behind him, groped for the soft yet scratchy tuft of sea sponge, gently soaked it in the hot water—and applied the sopping thing against her head and face in several rapid, gentle pats, splattering water everywhere. Yelping and spluttering, Rexei twisted around and splashed at him in affront. Since he was laughing at the time, he coughed from a mouthful of liquid, but she didn't show much mercy when she splashed him again, so he splashed her back.

The water fight was somewhat short; very noisy with shrieks, shouts, and laughter; very wet; and glorious fun. When it ended, it did so because Rexei slipped and splashed face-first against him, breasts to chest, her legs straddling one of his. Just like that, the playful mood between them snapped amorous.

This time, she didn't wait for him to make the first move. Gripping the rim of the tub for leverage, Rexei pulled herself up the last two inches and claimed his mouth. The shift in position allowed his manhood to slide along her belly and nudge between her thighs. Aroused, she parted her legs and straddled his hips, never quite ending the kiss, though their lips parted for fractions of a second here and there.

Wrapping his arms around her, Alonnen held her close while they kissed. Eventually, he urged her higher. Nibbling on her neck, tasting the little water droplets that clung to her collarbone, he sunk just slow enough so that she straddled his waist, bringing her small breasts into the range of his lips.

As before—as with every time—the moment his mouth brushed her skin, she shivered. The moment he licked, she shuddered. And the moment he suckled, Rexei moaned, swamped by the pleasure his simple touch evoked. A shift of his hands curved them under her rump for support, allowing him to increase the lovemaking he applied to her chest.

Her breasts were so sensitive, she was flushed and panting with pleasure before she realized what his fingers were doing. When she did, Rexei gasped. Two of them—not just one, but two—had slipped into her . . . and they were . . . !

Before she could do more than tense, he pulled his mouth off her nipple with a smacking kiss and murmured, "There, all the jelly's gone. Or would you rather I used soap?"

His fingers wiggled impudently just inside her cog-star, ruining any chance of a coherent reply. Eyes wide, Rexei looked down at him. "That . . . That feels . . ."

"Yes?" Alonnen asked her, smirking. "It feels . . . how?"

"Disturbingly good," she confessed, blushing. It did. It was embarrassing, but it did. He had slipped two fingers into her netherhole, a spot on her body far more associated with refreshing rooms than bedrooms, and . . . and she was enjoying it. Rexei had heard from several sources over the years that it could be pleasurable, but she hadn't been completely sure it would indeed be so. Now, she knew.

"Well, the other way's even better, but we make do with what we have," Alonnen told her. "Now, if you can reach the soap behind my head and find the sponge, we'll continue cleaning up . . . and then have lots of fun getting dirty all over again."

His grin was difficult to resist. Complying, Rexei stretched past him . . . and found her nipple nibbled by his lips even as her fingers closed on the jar of lightly scented soft soap. It wasn't easy to concentrate, but she found the sponge as well, groping through the water. Applying one to the other, she . . . forgot what she was supposed to do when his free hand slipped between their bellies and stroked that little nub between her legs. Forgot in favor of trembling and moaning, overwrought by pleasure.

His chuckle grounded her. Remembering her task, Rexei started scrubbing his shoulders and chest with the soap . . . and when he wiggled his fingers in her fundament some more, swiped a blob of lather onto the tip of his long, pointed nose. She wasn't intimidated by the narrowing of those hazel eyes, however impudent her "attack" might have been . . . but the alcove soon rang with shrieks of laughter and the floor did get a bit wetter as he retaliated with tickling and splashing and snatching at the sponge to scrub her from nose to toes, too.

When it ended in breathless grins, they finished lathering a few missed spots, then rinsed carefully so they could climb out. Alonnen stopped Rexei from trying to use the damp toweling sheets to mop up the water on the floor, however. Instead, he held out one hand, flicked his fingers in a circle, and gathered up some of the dampness with a simple, wordless spell. Her look of surprise made him smile.

"You can't work in the Lubrication Guild without learning at least *something* about cleaning up liquid messes," he joked. A pass of his hand guided the bobbing, head-sized globule of liquid into the tub, where it joined the rest of the water in swirling down the drain. It wasn't the only puddle on the floor, but it was a good start.

The mention of his alternate guild's name made her blush. It also made her retort, "I'm not planning on spilling any of the pomade."

His eyes gleamed with wicked humor. "Neither am I. Go fetch it to the bed, will you? I'll join you as soon as I've cleaned this all up."

Nodding, she retreated to the larger portion of the room. She didn't go straight to the table, though; instead, she detoured to the iron stove and used the tongs to add a few more coals, ensuring the room wouldn't grow cold anytime soon. Only then did she move to fetch the jar. Unlike the jelly, the contents of the plain container were a lot more liquid than viscous. Curious as to what it smelled like, Rexei worked on twisting off the stiffly screwed-on lid. It didn't come off until after her fourth or fifth try, when she had reached the side of the largest piece of furniture in the room.

Like the previous brothel bed one floor below, this one had clean, bleached sheets, layers of blankets, and a mound of feather-stuffed pillows braced against the headboard. Sinking onto the edge of the equally feather-stuffed mattress, she carefully pulled off the metal cap and sniffed at the contents. The slightly oily smell, she expected. The hint of mint, however, she had not. Dabbing a fingertip in the translucent white liquid proved it to be quite slick, to the point that Rexei was not sure she wanted to touch the smooth glass with that hand again.

She looked around, but with no good place to wipe it off, she gave up and scrubbed it onto her stomach. Once her hand was clean, she was free to set down the jar and lid on the nightstand. Then she rose and pulled the covers back a bit, so that they would be on the soft linens instead of the scratchy woolens.

Only then did she notice that Alonnen had moved to rummage through the pack he had brought, now placed on the bench at the foot of the bed. But not to get out any spare clothes he had brought, no. Instead, she had a glimpse of something metallic and silvery. Noticing her curious look, he quickly tucked it behind his back and gave her a disarming smile.

"What are you hiding?" she asked, not fooled by his charm.

"A pleasant little surprise," he demurred, moving to join her. "You'll like it."

She arched an eyebrow at him. "What are you *hiding*, Alonnen?"

Sighing, Alonnen brought his arm back around. Clasped in his palm and resting along his forearm, the awkwardly shaped object took her a few moments to recognize. The long, gently tapered cylinder had a bent arm sticking out from the flat end, and a push button . . .

Oh. She knew very well what that was, even though she didn't own one herself. Cheeks hot, she blinked at it, then at him. "You bought a *crankman*?"

"It was my late fiancée's," he confessed, "and no one bothered to claim it after she passed, so it's now mine. I, uh, don't use it often, but . . . Um. Here, let me show you another bit of magic."

Muttering under his breath, he gripped the smooth cylinder in one hand, pressed the push-through button just below the crank with the other . . . and magic made the curved handle spin. She could hear the gear-teeth clattering faintly, rapidly inside the device as he wound its one-way spring, and she covered her over-heated cheeks. He was using a *spell* to wind the device. One clearly tailored to this specific object. *That* was what made her blush. Rexei felt downright inadequate in her knowledge of such things—she could hide herself from a *God* if need be, but . . . everyday uses for spells? And for this particular use?

The spinning handle gradually slowed down as the internal spring stiffened in its resistance. When it stopped, Alonnen carefully pushed the button to the midpoint before releasing his spell, so that the handle didn't spin the other way around in springwound release. Rexei blushed, knowing why he was being so careful; pushing the button all the way through its hole the other way would have sent the crankman rattling.

Setting it on one of the pillows so it would be within easy reach, he leaned over and kissed her. She kissed him back, liking this lovemaking stuff more and more. Conversations that had gone half over her head in the past now made much more sense. Though most everyone had assumed she was male and had discussed things with that viewpoint in mind, she remembered the things discussed from the other perspective. One of those things was something an actress had tried on her, thinking Rexei to be a boy.

The moment her lips nibbled on his ear, he twitched. A glide of her tongue along the slightly fuzzy curve made him pant. And suckling on the lobe evoked an outright growl. Overwrought, Alonnen dragged both of them fully onto the bed. The crankman slid off its pillow and thumped into her shoulder, but both ignored it for a long while in the passion of their kiss. Rexei tried nibbling on his ear again.

Frustrated with too much stimulation, Alonnen pulled free, grabbed the crankman, and brought the cool metal down to her breast. Her brows narrowed in confusion, but he couldn't smile. He just thumbed the button and pressed the rattling, buzzing, vibrating machine to her left nipple.

"Oh Holy *Goddess*!"

It was a good thing the room had been spell-warded against

sound, for her shout echoed off the decadently papered walls. Alonnen teased each sensitive breast, switching back and forth as she shouted and clutched at the covers, at his shoulders, at his wrist, half clinging to his arm, half pushing him away. Thumbing the button to neutral, he leaned in close, admiring the little beads of sweat raised on her flushed face. "*That*," he murmured, "is what it feels like to me when you nibble on my ears."

Her brown gaze, soft and unfocused as she struggled for breath, sharpened. Looking at him, she stared into his hazel green eyes, clearly thinking things through . . . then deliberately slid her gaze to the side of his face and licked her lips. Staring at his right ear. It amused him that this bright, talented, cunning woman would dare to *think* about licking his ear some more in the wake of his unspoken sensual threat.

He did not turn the crankman back on, though. Instead, he slid the curved metal tip down between her breasts, along the soft curves and planes of her stomach, and teased the dark brown curls of her mound. Those eyes unfocused again, and her dark-lashed lids drifted shut. Her lips parted a moment later. So did her knees, granting him access to her netherfolds. Aroused by her acceptance of this passion between them, Alonnen focused firmly on plying the rounded tip down into her folds, between her netherlips. He gently stroked and rocked the quiet device a few times, then pulled away.

It was gratifying to see her hips lift in the wake of the crankman's retreat, seeking more stimulation. The sight of her dew slicked over the polished metal made his hand tremble. He wanted to taste it, to toss aside the Clockworks toy and replace the cool metal shaft with the heat and the hunger of his mouth, and follow that with the heat and the hardness of his own shaft. Carefully, he refrained. Instead, he nudged her hand into taking the crankman from him, then helped roll her onto her side so that she faced away from him.

"Rub that between your legs," he coaxed, gliding his palm along the underside of her thigh until she lifted it up and braced her foot on the bed. "Don't turn it on, yet; just rub it against yourself."

"Mmm . . . o-okay," Rexei agreed. She was still a little rattled—pun inadvertently intended—by the way he had used the crankman, but she was willing to comply. Within reason.

The buzzing against her nipples had been unbelievably intense. Though the toy was purely mechanical, it felt as if sparks of electricity had arced down through her whole body, connecting her breasts to her belly, her loins, even her toes. She had no idea what would happen if she turned on the machine while pressing it to that little nubbin between her legs that felt so good whenever it was stroked.

She moved the metal against herself, while she felt him shift on the bed, no doubt fetching the jar of pomade. The metal, hard, unyielding, and polished nearly mirror smooth, felt good gliding between her folds. Pleasurable, mildly intense, and just enough of a distraction that she didn't mind what he was doing with his fingers, slick and mint scented, between her nethercheeks. She stroked a little faster, a little firmer, feeling the cool ointment, the gentle insistence of his fingers . . .

"Now, bring it back up to your breasts," Alonnen urged, hearing her breath quicken and seeing her skin beginning to flush with desire, ". . . and turn it on."

"Uhh . . ." Do that to *herself*? Could she? Dare she? An impudent wiggle of his fingers reminded her why: as a very pleasant distraction. Ignoring the slick moisture coating some of the shaft, she brought it up to her chest, braced herself . . . and thumbed the switch. The wrong way, whapping herself in the wrist with the crank. "Ow!"

Her lover had the grace to stay silent, rather than laugh aloud . . . though she felt him shake a little from suppressed mirth. Embarrassed but equally amused, she quickly pushed the button the other way. The crank immediately stopped pressing against her arm in the effort to unwind its internal springs, and the inner, rubber-wrapped hammers rattled to life. Bringing the device to her breast, she didn't tease the nipple directly, choosing instead to press and slide the buzzing, tapered tip along the gentle swell of her left breast, then the right.

The feel of his fingers probing and stretching her star, the occasional pomade-slick brush of his knuckles lightly, teasingly along her perineum, all of that made her blush and bite her lip against the urge to moan. *Now* she understood all the jokes in her boy-disguised presence about "a back door to the Heavens." Now she understood why so many couples used this route to avoid an unplanned pregnancy. Not because it was the only way to copulate without that great risk, but because it was also very, very pleasurable—and this was just his fingers.

In fact, it added a whole new layer of experience to her sense of sexuality . . . just as the crankman added something new. An addicting level of pleasure, because the more his fingers pumped in and out, the more the metal case buzzed and tickled her breasts, the more she wanted of both sensations. Panting, moaning between heavy breaths, she moved the machine up to her nipples in little teasing touches. The polished metal rarely lingered for long each time, since that would have been too intense all at once, but she did gradually increase the length of time each nipple was stimulated.

Pleasure in front, pleasure behind . . . *Guildra, tell me this is what lovers feel when reunited in the Heavens . . . !* Finally, his hand came over hers and shut the crankman off. Slick with pomade, his fingers were no longer prepping her body, but she could still feel something . . .

Oh. Oh my. He's inside me . . . She blushed hard, her eyes went wide, and she felt a small tremor of a climax ripple through her nerves. His touch had distracted her from the realization that his shaft had actually entered her, replacing those fingers with a thickness that satisfied instead of scared.

"You feel so *good*," Alonnen groaned, kissing her shoulder.

"A-Alonnen," she gasped as he moved his manhood a little.

He nipped at the muscles underneath her skin, then sucked on the sting he had made, soothing it with lips and tongue. Working his way up to her neck, he lapped at the lobe of her ear. "Do you like this?" he asked, pausing to suckle on the soft flesh. "Do you like me nibbling on your *ear*? Does it excite you like it does me? Or is all this trembling and moaning because I've put my piston in your beautiful cog of a bottom?"

He suckled again. She shivered, and her leg wanted to twitch. "A-Almost as much . . . and . . . and more," Rexei panted. "I want . . ."

"You want . . . ?" he growled, his tone conveying an unspoken promise to deliver on whatever she desired.

Swallowing, she confessed, "I want *more*."

He shuddered and held on to her for a few seconds. She could feel his heart beating through his chest pressed against her back, felt his shaft twitching and throbbing faintly in time to that beat. Ignoring the slippery stuff on his fingers, Rexei twined her own with his, barely holding on to the crankman. She needed to anchor herself in him, not some mere machine, however blissful.

Finally, he moved. Slowly, patiently, Alonnen pushed deeper inside her untried back door. Plenty of pomade had made the trouble of friction minimal; it was simply the tightness of that ring of muscles that required caution and care. She moaned, feeling the lightning currents rushing out through her limbs, and he groaned with her, moved faster, feeling it, too.

His hand covered hers, turning her grip so that the crankman pointed downward. The damp metal slid down her belly, over her mound, and came to a stop between her folds, making her shiver from the press of it against her clitoris. Then his thumb shifted, sought, and pressed . . . and the machine throbbed to life, snatching away rational thought in a deluge of overwhelming stimulation.

Pleasure escaped in a wordless holler. Rexei clawed sideways at the bedding. Bucked against him. That made her breath catch from a slight stinging stretch at the move, but Alonnen used it, rocking gently into her, delving deeper. Bracing his own foot on the bed, he abandoned her hand. That let her pull back on the crankman, easing the rattling press against her clitoris, but it was for a good cause.

Pulling her leg up over his to open her up more, Alonnen thrust deeply, if carefully. He had to grit his teeth against the urge to buck and pound in fast, holding back against the demanding needs of his own pleasure. Each inward stroke delved a little deeper. Once he was fully inside, he returned his hand to hers and pulled the buzzing crankman up to her breasts. Only then did he move, using her gasp and twitch to pull his shaft partway out, then he pressed back inside. That in turn pressed her forward, bringing her nipple once again into contact with the machine.

Rexei gave up control of the device. Gave up control of her pleasure. In absolute trust, she cried—with a spill of tears as well as with her sobbing voice—while he teased and tormented her nipples. He almost stopped, hearing her breath hitch in sobs, but she caught his wrist and held his hand close, then released it to reach back to his hip.

Relieved, Alonnen resumed making love to her, wanting her to forever associate pleasure with him, with this moment in his arms, rather than all the fears she had suffered while hiding for over a decade from the False God's minions.

He did his job well; Rexei pulled on the blankets and sheets when he tucked the tapered metal cylinder between her legs, but she knew better than to close her thighs against the vibrating invasion. And when he started thrusting in earnest, picking up speed in compliance with her broken pleas for more, more, *more*, she pushed back into every stroke, for it was just one more layer of deep, passionate stimulation in her mind-shattering pleasure.

Her writhing and trembling made it hard for him to keep the crankman positioned just right. During one of her thrashings, he tried a little too hard, bumped the tip past her sheath opening along the sensitive span of skin between it and her cog-star, and right up against his own flesh as he thrust. That not only stimulated the underside of his shaft, it also brought the buzzing metal up against his scrotum, vibrating straight through his flesh to his own perineum. Stars exploded behind his eyes.

Vaguely, he got the machine back into place; he knew he did because of the way she hollered and clenched up in pleasure with hands and toes and buttocks, limbs straightening and spine stiffening, but it was too late to stop his own eye-blinding, toe-curling bliss. His own body tensed, shuddered, then jolted like a bowstring snapping back and forth now that the arrows of his seed were being released. He shouted, too, a strangled sound that was too far gone to be her name, though he tried.

White-blinding bliss drained away rational thought. When it ended, he found himself shaking almost as hard as the still-rattling device. Carefully thumbing it off, he dropped it onto the bedding, then wrapped his arm around her waist. She, too, was still trembling hard from her own climax. Spooned together, still connected piston to cog, he held her while their hearts slowed and their breathing steadied. Every few seconds, her inner muscles clenched just a little in pure post-bliss reflex, making him bite his lip from the lingering pleasure of it.

Finally, the twitches ended, and Rexei could think again. Think and have enough energy to speak. "I . . . I don't know if I can . . . do that again . . ."

Alonnen lifted his head a little, alarmed. "You can't? Why not?"

"Because if this . . . if this is how the *back* door feels with you . . . I don't think I can survive the *front* door version," she half complained, half complimented him. "But . . . I, uh . . . think I'm insane enough to try. When I'm not a puddle of limp jelly, that is."

This time, the sound-masking spell was needed to hide his hearty laughter from the rest of the building.

FOURTEEN

othing seemed able to ruin his good mood, come morning. Not the drizzling rain on the way from Heiastowne to the dam, and not the information that his scrying spies had found no recording of what the Patriarch's right-hand man wanted from his fellow ex-priests in this corner of the land. Not even the frowns his mother gave him when he went down to the dining level to get something to eat at mid-morning could spoil his happy mood.

His brother Dolon came close to puncturing Alonnen's ebullient attitude. Having invaded the dining hall of the inner circle for much the same reason—oven-baked flatbread topped with slivers of onion and scattered with cheese—Dolon ate slowly, frowning several times at his older brother. Toward the end of the snack, he finally smiled. Grinned, rather, with the predatory look of a sibling who had figured something out.

"Why, Alonnen, I didn't know you liked *men*," Dolon teased slyly. Alonnen frowned in confusion. "What? Since when?"

"Since, oh, last night? When you took Master Rexei into town . . . and came home this morning sporting that unbelievably silly grin?" his brother said, pointing at Alonnen's lips. "You haven't done that since the last time you got to piston someone . . . or was *he* pistoning *you*? All those protests to the contrary . . . what a smoke screen! You should be nominated for an apprenticeship to the Actors Guild."

For a long moment, Alonnen did not feel like smiling. His brother's comments were crude, rude, and . . . well, typical hazing from a brother. This wasn't the first time either of them had tormented the other verbally. But it wasn't the teasing that bothered him; it was that as much as Alonnen wanted to correct his sibling's mistaken impression, he didn't know if he had the *right* to correct Dolon's view of Rexei as a male.

"Rexei" was not an unusual name for both boys and girls; just about any name ending in *ei* was gender neutral in Mekhana. Many parents used it to ensure a casual conversation would not give away a child's gender identity whenever a priest was around. His own name wasn't gender neutral, nor was Dolon's, but then their parents had raised them and their siblings mostly within the protections of the Vortex. But naming conventions were not the same as permission to speak.

Sighing, he settled on a different tactic. "Does it really *matter* whether or not the person I love is a male, a female, or . . . or some weird gender the Gods Themselves haven't yet invented?"

"Oh-ho!" Dolon crowed, distracted as Alonnen had planned for him to be. "So my middle brother is in *love*, is he?"

Alonnen narrowed his eyes and peered over the top of the green-lensed spectacles he had not bothered to remove. "Are you going to keep giving me grief about being in love, or are you going to go do something more productive, like actually *work*?"

Dolon mock swept his strawberry blond curls back from his

face, lifting his hawkish nose into the air. "I'll have you know I'm quite competent at doing *both*."

Alonnen relaxed. This was just typical teasing. "You have a low threshold for competency, I see." He started to say more, but the talker-box rang. He rose to go answer it, but Dolon beat him to the machine. "I was going to get that. It's probably for me."

"Hello, you've reached the inner dining hall," Dolon offered into the speaking cone, lifting the matching earpiece to his head. "What? . . . He's right here. I'll let him know."

The way his brother hung up the ear-cone, ending the conversation instead of offering the cable-connected device, annoyed Alonnen. "I could've spoke to them myself, you know."

"Yeah, but you'd just hear the exact same thing, and this'll get you upstairs faster," Dolon told him, shrugging. "The Guardians have called a conference, and they need you up there, since it's apparently about you."

Glad he had finished his flatbread snack, Alonnen pointed back at the table they had used, and the dirty dishes still sitting on the age-worn surface. "Just for that, *you* can take care of my cup and plate. Since it'll get me upstairs faster."

Ignoring the dirty look his younger sibling sent him, Alonnen headed for the stairs. It didn't take long to reach the top. Debating a moment, he touched the doorknob, chanted a brief set of spells to change the illusions cloaking his office, then stepped inside. What should have been a room with four or five people in it, examining the images captured by the spying roaches, had turned into an empty chamber with a single mirror on the wall.

Alonnen didn't understand how it worked; his magical education wasn't up to the task and wouldn't be for a long, long time even if he had a competent teacher who did understand. But he knew that he wasn't going to run over someone turned invisible, but not intangible, by some spell. The way Millanei had described it, this whole floor acted more like his office formed a giant ring around the heart of the Vortex, and he had simply spun the floor like a cogwheel, accessing a gear-tooth version that had no one currently in it. Or perhaps it was the others he had shifted out of his office into an alternate version somewhere around the ring.

Donning cap and scarf to augment his green-tinted, identity-hiding lenses, he touched the frame, shifting it from a pulsing blue field to a set of squares filled with faces. Given the number of Guardians assembled, this was to be a very important meeting. He recognized nearly every face, but two of the mirror-windows were different. Both Pelai and Tipa'thia occupied the same scrying frame, one with her tattoos creased and crinkled into near-illegibility by her age-lined face, the other with her smooth-inked features framed by dark hair instead of white. In the other frame, not one, not two, but five faces peered at the others.

In the center, in a window that occupied the span of four of the others, Guardian Kerric nodded a greeting for their newest conference member. "I'm very glad you could join us, Guardian Alonnen, because *we* have come up with a solution for *your* problem."

"A *temporary* solution," Guardian Tipa'thia interjected firmly. "The spells will only last about two years, then they won't be able to be reapplied for ten years. Keep that in mind, Guardians."

Amber eyes rolled, and a suntanned hand tugged on a pale blonde braid. Alonnen quirked a brow at Serina's image. She looked like she was not at all happy with whatever solution Kerric and Tipa'thia had in mind—irritated with it, even—but she didn't say anything. She just stood there next to Guardian Dominor, her husband. Witch-Knight Orana Niel stood to Serina's right, looking as calm and patient as ever.

To the left of Dominor stood some young man with ash-blond hair and aquamarine eyes. He was a bit thinner than Dominor but had the look of a kinsman to the dark-haired mage. To his left stood a woman with hair just a few shades lighter than Alonnen's own and a curious look in her eyes; those eyes were the same shade as the young man's, but other than that, the two had nothing in common regarding their looks. Certainly she didn't have the slightly slanted, almond-shaped eyes of a Katani. What she lacked in ethnic nationality, Alonnen realized was made up in the crown she wore: delicate-looking, it had been fashioned out of slender gold wires bent and joined together to look almost like a set of mountain peaks.

Given the location of the Fountain which Dominor guarded, Alonnen could guess who the crown wearer might be. "I take it you, milady, are the new ruler of Nightfall? If so, congratulations."

"Queen Kelly of Nightfall, hi there. Forgive me for barging into this, but after reading the prophecies in question, I realized I might be of some help, even if I'm no mage," she stated bluntly. "I also figured, given how secretive you Guardian types are of your magical whatsit-wells, it might help for you to have a front man, so to speak. You know, someone whom everyone could point to and say, 'She ordered it!' and thus send the stampede of questioners and complainers *my* way, to distract everyone from the truth and keep them from interrupting or interfering with your work."

Her blunt forthrightness made some of the others blink. For a moment, Alonnen couldn't think of why; her forthrightness simply reminded him of several other Guild Masters . . . and that was the reason why. For a queen, this Kelly woman did not act at all how the tales of outkingdom queens were reported to act. She even looked like a fellow ex-Mekhanan . . . like a Guildaran, given her buttoned shirt. Alonnen liked her immediately based on that. He suspected from Ilaiea's impatient look and Keleseth's frown that not everyone did.

"I think that's a good idea," he stated, before anyone else could speak. He might not know nearly as many spells as the other men and women in this scrycast conference, but Alonnen was not stupid.

He had given all the information gathered over the last few months a lot of thought. "Given the prophecies in question seem to suggest the Convocation is somehow involved, the queen of its host nation would indeed make a logical 'target' for all inquiring outsiders. And the 'Synod Gone' prophecy by the, uh . . . Seer Howpunay?"

"Howpanayah," the ash-blond man pronounced. "Only the Seer Haupanea goes by 'Hope' now . . . and she'll be joining us as soon as she gets out of the refreshing room."

"Uh . . . right," Alonnen said, thrown off-balance a little by the other man's assertion that a centuries-old Seer would be joining them in a few moments. He dragged the conversation back to the point he wanted to make. "That prophecy does say, '*Gone, all gone, the synod gone, brought back by exiled might; By second try, the fiends must die, uncovered by the blight.*' If the Synod is indeed the restored Convocation, as we suspect, then whatever is required to end the impending demonic invasion *will* happen within the kingdom of Nightfall, or at the very least, at the same time as your second Convocation ceremony, Guild Master Kelly . . . uh, sorry, is it Highness? I'm not used to addressing royalty."

"Just call me Kelly," the redhead soothed. "I don't stand on formality when it's not a formal occasion. I don't even sit on formality, unless there's an extra cushion or two," she added, as the men and women sharing Guardian Dominor's frame with her smiled in humor. So did some of the others, Sheren, Migel, Kelezam, Pelai, even the two stuffy Guardians of the Fountains in Fortuna. "And you had the very same thought I did, reading those two lines. Whatever happens, it *will* involve the Convocation in some way.

"The more I know right away on what your plans are, the more I can ensure that they get incorporated into my own plans for hosting the next Convocation. Which will be in four years, since that seems to be the long-standing tradition, and I won't object to the wait, since we still have a long way to go before Nightfall is fully functional as a kingdom and a hosting site. But enough about me; I'll just listen in and take notes while you get on with the solution you found. Serina?"

"Ughh," the younger of the two pale blonde women in view groaned, tugging again on her braid. "I don't like this . . ."

"Stop whining, love, and get it over with," Guardian Dominor told his wife.

"*Fine*. Okay, as many of you know, I've been working on the problem of the old mass Portals that used to span both continents and oceans, and how the Shattering of Aiar not only destroyed the heart of the old Empire up north and ended the last set of Convocations of Gods and Man, but it also shattered the aether, allowing said Portals to span the world. Well, between my efforts with the Fountain which Mother Naima has been sharing Guardianship of with me and the efforts of Priestess Saleria"—Serina nodded to the blonde priestess with the almond-shaped eyes and golden curls, who dipped her head in return—"we've managed to quell a strip of aether running from the center of Western Katan and the Fountain of the Grove all the way up to a stretch of kingdoms to the east of your, well, ex-kingdom and the region governed by Guardian Callaia."

"Sorry about that," Kelly muttered under her breath, giving Alonnen a somewhat guilty, apologetic wince.

"Don't be," he murmured back, wondering what the redhead had to do with the loss of Mekha. He returned his attention to Serina. "What does the restoration of Portal abilities have to do with the threat of a demonic invasion?"

Nose wrinkled in disgust, Guardian Ilaiea scoffed, "Are you really that *ignorant*, boy? Who in the name of the Netherhells made *you* a Guardian, if you're so stupid?"

Alonnen narrowed his eyes. "Excuse me for being uneducated, but if you haven't noticed, Mekhana has been a *death trap* for mages for the last four centuries, with damn few mages able to get in or out without getting captured. Forgive us for most of our highly educated mages having their will suppressed by magical shackles and the weight of an uncaring, ever-hungering False God, who destroyed their minds and drained their magics to the very last drop. Forgive us for losing a lot of knowledge over the centuries under the oppressive rule of a False God who was just two steps away from *being* a Netherhell demon. *Forgive* us for—"

"Wow. You have a temper worse than mine," Queen Kelly interjected, her brows lifted and her tone light, if pointed.

Forcing himself to relax, Alonnen muttered a very grudging, "Sorry."

It was a bit angry, but it did smooth over the moment. It helped that Tipa'thia spoke up, seizing the awkward silence. "Regardless of how well-trained you and your local mages might be, Guardian Alonnen, it would not matter. This will be a *new* spell for everyone . . . and we will all have to learn how to apply it. Half of it was researched by my apprentice, Pelai, from forgotten knowledge culled from scores of ancient grimoires. Half of it has been updated and integrated into the aether-cleansing magics which Guardian Serina has been tirelessly researching and striving to enact."

"Unfortunately, this will put *back* that aether quelling by at least two full years!" Serina argued.

Lost, Alonnen opened his mouth to ask what the two were talking about. Guardian Kerric got to it first, raising his hand. "Ladies, *please*. Guardian Serina, please cut through the side discussions and just outline what needs to be done and why, so that we all understand the *necessity* of it."

She tugged on her long braid again, then released it with a heavy sigh and a brief mutter. "I need more vases . . . As I was saying, instead of calming the aether to reestablish our ability to create Portals, we shall instead temporarily agitate the aether. The resonances of normal, world-crossing Portals are very similar to, but not exactly the same as, the resonance frequencies used by the shorter, merely region-crossing mirror-Gates which are still usable in most kingdoms.

"By the same token, if you push things up higher, you reach the resonance frequencies not only in the local aether, but in what we call the Veil between Worlds. Depending upon the exact resonances, you can pierce the Veil into other universes entirely, where the rules might be slightly different . . . or you can pierce the Veil into the region of the Netherhells," Serina explained. "Blood-based, violence-infused magic assists in piercing the Veil to the Netherhells, creating Portals to and from that realm. Mages can also use these resonances to summon and bind demons, which is what these ex-Mekhanan priests are attempting to do."

Alonnen nodded, glad he was able to follow along in spite of his . . . lack of a perfect magical education. He really did not like Ilaiea. He did like Serina, however, even though both women looked very similar to each other. Serina paused before continuing, glancing to her right. A curly haired woman with richly tanned skin moved into the scrying mirror's view, and the man with the ash-blond hair motioned for her to join him; when she did, he tucked his arm around her hourglass curves, snugging her against his side. For a moment, Alonnen wished Rexei were here instead of in town, meeting with her long-lost half brother, but this was more important than any spark of envy or undoubtedly misplaced mistrust.

"Everyone, this is Hope, my newest and last sister-in-law, who just married Morganen, there," Serina stated, introducing the newcomer. "Two hundred years ago, she was the Duchess Haupanea of Nightfall, a Holy Seer of Katan, but the destruction of the last Convocation caused a tear in the Veil between Worlds, which caused her to be cast into another universe at a different point in time. She met Kelly in that world, who came across to join us in this one in accordance with a series of prophecies made by several

Seers, not just herself. Hope, these are some of the various Guardians of the world."

Hope raised a hand and fluttered it. Like Kelly, she was wearing an almost Guildaran-style buttoned shirt instead of the more commonly seen tunic, robes, or dress of the others, albeit in a cheerful shade of pink that contrasted pleasantly with Kelly's light blue. "I was a poetic Seer, and according to the Gods of the Convocation, I'll still continue to be a Seer, so we're in the process of assigning a set of scribes to follow me around in case I start spouting pertinent bits of doggerel again. Based on what I've learned of recent history and what I found when I went through my old prophecy scrolls, it looks like there's at least seven or eight prophecies of mine alone which tie into this whole Netherhells mess . . . which scares the *willies* out of me, as Kelly's old people would say. But whatever the Gods send for me to say about this whole mess, I'll make sure you know it."

Alonnen decided he liked her, too.

"Welcome, Holy Seer," Guardian Marton of Fortune's Hall stated dryly. "I'm glad we have a scapegoat and a mouthpiece, but I want to know what, exactly, Guardian Serina has in mind regarding the resonances of the Veil and the Portals, and how it ties into thwarting the demonic invasion."

"Well, you're not going to like it," Serina returned bluntly. "I don't like it, either, since it sets back my work two-plus years. But we are going to have to agitate the layers of resonances involved in the deeper stretches of the Veil, where the borders between this world and the various Netherhells exists . . . and that *will* have an impact on the Portals that span the curve of this world."

Marton narrowed his hazel eyes. "How *much* of an impact? Fortune's Empire relies heavily on our intact Portals for cross-kingdom commerce and travel."

Serina winced, clearly not happy with having to answer that

question. "It'll cut their reach in half at best . . . on a really good aether day."

Both Fortunai Guardians, Marton and Suela, spat out near-identical, manure-based epithets, then started arguing about how this was *not* going to be well received by their governments, and how . . .

"*Enough!*" Alonnen's demand cut through their mounting tirades. "You are *Guardians*, and you are comparing the piddling problem of putting up with the inconvenience of having to take twice as many *luxurious* Portals—which the rest of us would have *killed* to have access to, particularly *my* people in order to escape being drained to death—you are comparing all of that, to the *destruction of this world*. Either step up to the prices and the pains of your responsibilities, or step *down* from your Guardianships!"

". . . Thank you for that rather blunt and tactless piece of truth," Kerric said dryly in the silence that followed Alonnen's shout. "But as it *is* the truth, we shall take it as a given that this *is* our responsibility, however much our various governments *and* our neighbors will complain about it. You may find your single, if vast, empire inconvenienced, Guardian Suela, Guardian Marton . . . but the reach of *my* Fountain covers fourteen kingdoms, five of which rely heavily upon mirror-Gate travel, and nine more of which rely modestly upon it. Gate travel which may *also* be affected, though at a lesser rate than the great Portals will be."

"*Most* of us are not accustomed to having those Portals, and so it will be a miniscule inconvenience for us to have that inability continue for a little while longer," Guardian Tuassan stated, his dark brow furrowed into a pointed look. "If you need something to say to your nation's people, Guardian Suela, then remind them it will be good for your nation's character to suffer a little in the name of helping save the entire world."

"Actually, I was going to suggest blaming *me*," Queen Kelly offered, raising her hand. "After all I, above and beyond all the rest of you, will suffer far more, because having these inter-dimensional Portals sealed by these spells means I will *not* be able to reach, contact, or even see the world where I was born. Yet I do grasp the absolute necessity of this. If we can use these vibration resonances to disrupt all cross-dimensional Portals, including to the Netherhells, then there is no way for these demons to invade. Problem solved."

"Not exactly, Kelly," Dominor told his queen. "As Guardian Tipa'thia pointed out, it's only a temporary solution. The aether will only be disrupted for about two years. But it *will* give us time to hunt down the would-be summoners and prevent them from ever trying again . . . one way or another."

Alonnen saw Ilaiea inhale and had the feeling from the arrogant look on her face that she was going to try to dump *that* responsibility strictly upon his lap. He spoke quickly, beating her to it. "As we *know* from the various prophecies involved, the ex-priests here in ex-Mekhana—which we're going to start calling Guildara— the ex-priests will probably flee this region once the aether-disrupting spells have been applied, and they have come to realize they cannot summon demons here. From my point of view, that is a very good thing."

"A *good* thing?" Ilaiea argued.

"*Yes*, a good thing," Guardian Saleria stated, quelling the older woman's outburst. Once she had Ilaiea's attention, the blonde Katani priestess looked like she was trying to meet the gaze of every other Guardian as well in the scrycasting link. "The Gods are constrained from intervening directly and have been ever since we evolved from animals into thinking beings. We have free will; therefore, *we* are responsible for doing whatever we can to alleviate the trials and troubles we must face. The Gods *cannot* wave a hand over every last one of our problems.

"*Some* of them, yes—and I am deeply grateful Holy Kata and Holy Jinga saw fit to smooth over *most* of the problems plaguing

Their Sacred Marital Grove here in Katan, which I guard . . . but They did not fix everything, and the other Gods and Goddesses *will not* fix everything for us. They may not even *have* that much power to spare. In the last two weeks," Saleria continued, pointing off to her side, "I have met priests and Gods from kingdoms that have held less than a hundred thousand people for their worship base, and thus their prayer-power base.

"There are very, very few kingdoms and empires that have millions of worshippers to support the miracles of their Patrons. But our many Patrons *can* give us clues as to how to fix these problems ourselves via the words They give Their Seers to pass along to us . . . and I, for one, am grateful for even the *littlest* piece of help They can give in the face of power constraints, free will, and what other problems there may be out there."

Alonnen liked her, too. *And I think I know why,* he realized, as Suela grudgingly asked Serina another question on the effects of the proposed Portal-disrupting spell. Since his people didn't use such things, and weren't going to complain about their lack, the answers were of no use to him. *There's something of that same . . . how to define it . . .*

Certainty of purpose, that's it. The same certainty of purpose with which Rexei speaks of her concept of Guildra. Only in Guardian Saleria, it's much more mature and refined. There were some priests after all, he realized, that he *did* like and trust. Not just Rexei, but this woman as well. Not because she was a Guardian, though that had gained his trust initially, but rather, *because* she was a priestess. A true holy servant. *Now if only our kingdom had known such goodness in its priests . . .*

A silly thought, he dismissed. *We wouldn't be suffering what we're suffering now, if it weren't for the selfish bastards we did end up having to deal with . . . and not even the Threefold God can turn back the clockworks of the universe itself just to rewrite the mistakes of the past.*

". . . Right, then. Back onto the topic of carrying this project through," Kerric directed the others. "We acknowledge that the people of . . . the region overseen by Guardian Alonnen are not equipped or trained to completely eradicate on their own the problem of demonic summoning as foreseen by forescrying mirror and Seer-based prophecies. We acknowledge that prophecy *does* indicate there is a way to eventually stop these people, and that we *should* seek to send them out of Mekhana's former borders, into territories that *do* have the necessary resources to whittle down their numbers. And we acknowledge—however much it may inconvenience *everybody*—that we *do* have a means of forcing that escape into more favorable lands and of buying all of us more time to find a better solution to this worldwide problem. Is everyone in agreement on these points, even with all the problems that still remain?"

Most of the Guardians nodded firmly. A couple—Ilaiea and Keleseth—rolled their eyes, plus an impatient look of "get on with it" came from Guardian Daemon, who looked sleepy, but it was enough for Kerric to continue.

"Very well, then. The spells have been carefully learned by Priestess Orana Niel, Pelai of Mendhi, and Morganen of Nightfall. Orana has business in former Mekhana, and Pelai is the foremost authority on the new spell, aside from Guardian Serina," Kerric said, "but as Serina is a new mother, we are not going to ask her to travel everywhere. Morganen may be newly wed, but with his wife's permission, he has agreed to journey in Serina's place. He will do so via the Fountainways to Guardian Shon Tastra in Darkhana, where he will begin instructing various Witches in how to cast aether-disruption spells."

The blue-and-black-robed Guardian bowed his head, acknowledging the plan being outlined. "We look forward to hosting him and will be happy to allow him to travel back and forth in this manner. It will be much more pleasant by comparison than the other method we Witches have at our disposal."

Kerric nodded, continuing. "Many of the Darkhanan Witches are still scattered around the globe in their efforts to assist in ensuring enough priests from all the Gods and Goddesses showed up at the Convocation, but they have some means of reaching each other and teaching each other despite the vast distances involved and the lack of easy mirror-based communications. Priestess Orana would normally be involved in this matter, but she tells me she has been pledged for centuries to return to ex-Mekhana to speak with its citizens on the matter of the dissolution of their ex–Patron God. She will travel to your location, Guardian Alonnen, as will Guardian Apprentice Pelai."

Alonnen wrinkled his long nose but dipped his head. "It normally would be against my Guardianship policy to allow anyone to use the Vortex Fountainway in such a manner, but . . . I will trust Guardian Tipa'thia's judgment of her apprentice."

The younger tattoo-covered woman lifted her brow. "You have no objection over this Darkhanan Witch traveling to the seat of your Guardianship, but you have one for me? Neither of us is a Guardian. Yet."

"Nothing personal, Apprentice Pelai," Alonnen said wryly, "but we of ex-Mekhana have known for generations of Knight-Priestess Orana Niel's many efforts to free us from Mekha's enslavement. We will need to spend at least a little time getting to know you to develop a solid level of trust . . . but it will happen in due time."

She tilted her head, acknowledging his point.

"Once they have instructed enough of the mages in Guardian Alonnen's region to set up the anti-Portal resonances, and he has tied them into the singularity he guards, Apprentice Pelai and Witch Ora will disperse to other locations to instruct others. Pelai will do so via the Fountainways, while Orana will use . . . whatever methods Darkhanans use," Kerric hedged. It was clear he didn't understand what those methods were but equally clear he was willing to trust her competency in using them. "This will add to the instructions being offered by Morganen of Nightfall and increase the spread of the effects."

"Keep in mind that this set of spells can only be applied once every decade," Tipa'thia asserted, her voice a little unsteady from age, but her gaze as sharp and level as her apprentice's. "To apply it a second time before the aether has healed and recovered would be to risk tearing open the Veil in uncontrolled rifts."

"I can vouch for that *not* being a good idea," Guardian Saleria interjected. "You don't want to know the damage that can be wrought by having three rifts in one location spewing unchecked, uncontrolled magic into the world. I'm dealing with constrained rifts, and they're bad enough."

"Quite," Kerric agreed. "We will begin by setting the first spell with the power of Guardian Alonnen's singularity. By Serina's calculations, that should blanket all of Mekhana, a fifth of Arbra along its eastern border, the western half of Aurul, a tenth of northern Sundara—it's a long country—the northeastern third of Haida, and some of the kingdoms to the northeast whose names I forget. From that point, every Guardian and mage involved will then examine their local aether and apply their own version so that it matches up to the edges of the previous applications but does not overlap."

"What of the oceans?" Guardian Sheren asked, speaking up for the first time this session. Alonnen recalled she was the Guardian of Menomon, which apparently was an underwater kingdom. "We can only cover so much, Migel and me."

Serina addressed her question. "There is no Portal which can be erected on a ship at sea; mirror-based Gates, yes, but not any grand Portals. The deck of a ship moves far too much and is far too distant from a solid chunk of ground—as in, a chunk of the planet we all live upon—for a Portal to be successfully opened. We need only cover the islands with civilized presences upon them."

"But what if they pick some uninhabited island somewhere in the middle of an ocean?" Ilaiea asked.

The question visibly worried the rest, furrowing brows and turning down mouths. Alonnen, however, thought he had a pretty sound counterpoint. "Guardian Ilaiea has a good question, but I know these priests. They are a very spoiled lot. As much as the Aian mage Torven might try to convince them otherwise, and as much as we will strive to end their ambitions one way or another, they will not be easily swayed into going to an isolated, uninhabited island with zero buildings, services, shops, supplies, and other trappings of civilized life. They will instead try to seek out a city or a well-managed kingdom, or even a remote but wealthy nobleman's estate—these are men used to taking whatever they want of the finest things in Mekhanan life, not laboriously creating it from scratch."

"We'll try our best to keep an eye on where they go and what they try to do," Kerric promised him. Or rather the others, for he added, "Just in case. Now, since this does have a bit of a priority on it, when will you ladies, and you sir, be ready to travel?"

The ash-blond man in the crowded mirror-window shrugged. "I can be packed within just a few hours."

Pelai smirked. "I already packed a couple bags in anticipation."

Orana Niel arched one brow, then stated serenely, topping both of them, "I am a Witch of Darkhana. My bags are *always* packed . . . and kept in the Dark."

Did she mean . . . ? Isn't the Dark the place where ghosts roam on their way to the Afterlife? Alonnen shivered at that thought. He'd heard rumors of her being able to magically summon or dismiss items from plain sight via that black-lined sleeved cloak of hers, and the thought of those things going into and coming out of the place where only the dead dared tread unnerved him. He trusted her—nothing about that had changed—but he wasn't about to *be* her, if he could help it.

Clearing his throat, he spoke up. "Well. If you ladies are ready to travel, then I shall need just a few minutes to set my Fountainways to accept and catch you gently upon your arrival."

"I'll need two minutes to pick up my bags," Pelai agreed. "But then I'll be ready to go."

"I'll let Guardians Dominor and Tipa'thia know when I'm ready to receive you," Alonnen agreed.

"Orana will have with her a set of Artifacts to gauge the effectiveness of the disruption spells," Serina told him. "If you could set up a feedback sub-channel through your Fountainways to Koraltai so that I can monitor everything, I'll be able to run calculations on exactly how much the disruptions will affect local Gates and regional Portals, and whether or not there's a risk of overlap tearing the Veil. Hopefully there shouldn't be, but monitoring will be a good safety net."

"I'll do my best," Alonnen said. Silently, he promised himself to contact Guardian Kerric privately for a lesson as soon as discreetly possible, since he was fairly sure the Master of Scrycasting would know how to do just that.

As irritating as Ilaiea's contempt was, Alonnen knew very well how little he and his fellow ex-Mekhanan mages knew, and he could admit it to himself, even if he didn't like his long nose rubbed in it. Admitting his ignorance was an irritation, but it was at least one he could do something about. Eventually. In his copious spare time, of course.

Her bottom ached. Not much, but there was definitely a sense of tenderness in that area. A certain lingering *awareness* of what she and Alonnen had done.

There had been ribald jokes about that, too, throughout her youth—jokes of cog-stars being widened, of "boring the hole wider," and more. Sore-bottom jokes, tender-bottom jokes . . .

Rexei hadn't realized just how many butt jokes she had absorbed in her guise as a young man over the years, but seated on one of the unpadded chairs in the Heiastowne Consulate Hall, she was recalling them now. Feeling them, too, every time she shifted the wrong way.

It was a good ache, though. It made her smile at random moments, even when it made her feel like wincing a little. She kept both the smiles and the flinches to a minimum. Instead of chatting with her brother, or even instructing her apprentices, Rexei had found herself corralled within minutes of entering the Consulate for a long discussion with a wide selection of townsfolk on the nature of Guildra, Patron Goddess of Guilds.

The astonishing thing was how they came to her to actually *learn*, not to rail against or deny or demand a completely different Patron concept. The more she talked with the men and the women, the elderly and the teenagers who wanted to understand, the more Rexei realized she *had* picked the right Goddess for her people. The guilds were something they intimately understood.

The Guild System was a concept every ex-Mekhanan could grasp. A Goddess of Guilds, patient, educated, disciplined, encouraging . . . these were characteristics utterly unlike the last God. That was the reason why her fellow citizens came to her in the dead of winter; they wanted *reassurance* that Guildra was indeed real and that She was going to be their new Patron . . . exactly as they wanted Her to be.

This was a gratifying and very humbling realization, on Rexei's part.

Her apprentices listened in, too, and spoke when she gestured for them to add to the conversation. Master Jorro, a fellow Gearman, was even able to speak for her when her voice started to grow rough around the edges from so much talking. When she realized he was indeed thinking along very similar lines, Rexei paused the conversation long enough to promote him to the rank of journeyman of the Holy Guild. She still didn't have any guild medallions just yet, but she knew the Mintners Guild was working on it for her, since she didn't have time to gather tools and start the work herself—there was so much to do, she just didn't know when she would fit it all in.

One bite at a time, she thought as lunch drew near and her stomach nudged her sense of time in pre-hunger warning. *Speaking of which . . .*

"Okay, people," she told the crowd of roughly two hundred gathered into the meeting hall, with herself and her apprentices occupying the center of the curved head table—which felt a bit weird with just the four of them up there. "As much as we could continue to expound and expand upon the nature of Guildra, it is almost time for luncheon . . . and every Guild charter I know of demands the right to a luncheon hour for its members. Mine shall be no exception."

Her dry-voiced reminder provoked a ripple of laughter in the men and women seated in the pews, thanks to the truth in her words.

"I thank you for coming, and I shall send word for the Binders to post the time and day for the next open meeting to discuss the nature of our new Patron and new Holy Guild. Feel free to discuss what we have talked about today with others; though if any of you have questions, I strongly encourage each person to come to the Consulate hall and leave a written question for my fellow guild-members and me to contemplate the answer. In the meantime . . . it is lunchtime. Have a good day."

Grasping the wooden handle of the stone mallet, she cracked granite against polished granite, ending the meeting. A young apprentice wearing the familiar medallion of the Messengers

Guild moved up to the head table, a folded paper outstretched in his hand. "Message for you, Guild Master Longshanks."

Nodding, Rexei dug into her pouch. All messages were prepaid for delivery, but it was courtesy to tip the apprentices for a job well-done; once a guildmember became a journeyman or higher, their pay was good enough—and presumably the service as well— to not need tips for encouragement. She handed over three square coppers and accepted the note. It wasn't sealed, just folded over, and was fairly simple.

Rex,

I twisted my ankle on the way out of the inn, and now cannot even hobble across the room, let alone halfway across town. I know you have meetings this morning, but if you could join me for the midday meal over here, I'll buy. Send word if you can't make it; send yourself if you can.

Lun

Rexei quirked her brows, looking up at the apprentice. "Why didn't you deliver this earlier?"

"He said before noon was fine, no big rush," the youth told her, shrugging. "I had a dozen others that were. Any return message?"

"No . . . I'll go myself. Thank you." Watching him walk off, she absently tucked her brother's note into her pouch. Rexei looked around for some of the other mages but couldn't see them. They were still nervously avoiding her. Her apprentices and journeyman had already vanished as well, taking off to find their own food sources, leaving her alone. Sighing, she acknowledged that she should leave a message for Alonnen, in case he was already on his way back from the Vortex to rejoin her here.

Using the pen and paper she had brought for this morning's meetings, she dipped the pen in the ink jar and wrote out a quick note explaining she had gone to the Fallen Timbers Inn for lunch with her brother. Rexei folded it up, writing *For Master Tall* on the outside. With that task done, she dropped the letter off at the front desk of the Consulate, belted her winter coat over her clothes, and headed into the damp and windy but no longer drizzling winter day.

The gusts increased as she turned down one of the main streets, heading for the Fallen Timbers. Leaning into the wind, she timed the pace of her steps to the songs that always hummed in the back of her head, masking her magical signature, warding her from detection, from attack, from—magic sizzled over her skin, disrupting that song. Just for a fraction of a moment, but it was enough to make her foot fumble.

The misstep drove her to the ground. Heart pounding, knee bruised, she twisted as she struggled back to her feet, looking all around for the source of the attack. Three men—strangers, none of them from the Heiastowne temple—converged on her from three different directions. The one on the far right scowled at her and flicked his hands. Panicking, she tried to shove to her feet, humming harder. The spell slapped into her with a jolt of pain.

For a moment, unable to see or move, she lost the thread of her protective meditations. One of the two remaining men grabbed her right elbow, saying gruffly, "Easy lad, you look ill."

The other grabbed her left arm and pressed something to her neck. It sealed to her skin with a sizzle of magic just as she got her humming back. The pain remained, blurring her vision . . . but . . . she could hum, and that meant she could think. It was hard; Rexei felt the energies in the spell trying to drown her thoughts. She fought it to the point of humming faintly under her breath, struggling to remember the melodies of her warding spells.

"Stand up, Longshanks," the man on her right ordered tersely. "You will act like we are helping you. Now, walk with us."

Physical pain and cognitive dullness warred with the need to struggle, to escape. Rexei found herself walking between the two men, who still had their arms tucked through her elbows.

"Looks like your left knee is twisted," one of them said aloud. Immediately her knee throbbed and her leg started limping in response.

Don't panic—don't panic—don't panic! That frightened thought chased itself in circles, ruining the rhythm of . . . *It* has *a rhythm! Don't panic, don't panic, don't panic, don't panic* . . . The warding harmonies came back, albeit at a faster, higher, more frantic pitch than usual. The more she concentrated, the clearer her thoughts felt, but at the cost of giving up some of the fight to control her body. *I can do this . . . I can do this. I just need to concentrate . . . stall for time . . . don't panic, don't panic, concentrate, stall for time . . .*

The words became a mantra, the mantra a melody. Her steps slowed with each fractional gain in her self-control.

"Walk faster," the man on her right ordered gruffly. Her half-limped steps quickened a little. "Walk *faster*."

"You twisted the boy's knee," the man on the left muttered. "Be thankful we need the limp as an excuse to take him off the streets, should anyone ask."

It's okay . . . I have time . . . and . . . and if they're taking me to the temple, the paper roaches will see me . . . I just have to figure out . . . figure out the weak points in this controlling spell. It's an amulet, not a collar, which means if I can somehow detach the adhesion spell, I can get rid of it and time my escape . . .

Time wasn't on her side; the Consulate was not that far from the back door to the temple. Giving up her resistance to the body commands, she focused on trying to feel the resonances, the vibrations of the spell. Two spells, rather, one to command and one to cling. One tingled all through her body, threatening to turn her flesh numb. The other itched against her skin.

Rexei already had a spell to counteract itching, a useful ward to know when traveling through some of the more bug-infested stretches of the land. With a bit of thought, she started weaving that song into her warding melody, the one that cut down all magic in her immediate vicinity, and tied it into a countermelody to the itch. It was a long shot since she didn't know if it would work—

Just as they reached the back door and the third man pulled it open, the stone popped off her throat. It dropped into the neckline of her winter coat. She faked a stumble the moment she felt it slithering down between the layers of wool, only to fall for real as all three men overreacted in their opposing efforts to get her steadied. Thankfully, their soft curses and grumblings hid the *clack* of the control stone hitting the paving stones of the alleyway. Rexei was free, yes, but only of the spell's effects. Elbows and knees bruised, she realized from the way they were grabbing her that physically she would not be able to get away, even if she was magically free.

A scrap of colorful paper caught her eye. Quickly, she passed her hand over the doorsill, scraping the crushed paper roach out of the crack where it had been squished and left behind. She wasn't sure if she could pull off a repair, but there was a way to transfer a bit of magic from one piece of paper to another . . . such as her brother's note. At least, she knew the theory of it. Vaguely.

Guildra, help me, she prayed earnestly as they hauled her back onto her feet and pushed her into the temple's back corridors. No one noticed the missing stone or the scrap of paper hidden in her hand.

Though the stone no longer forced her body into obeying their commands, she was still trapped. Two men, she could put to sleep with a spell. Three . . . four. *No, five . . . six . . . Gods!* Forcing her expression into the dulled look of one of the mages who had been collared, Rexei kept her fingers curled around the rumpled paper spy. *All these years, I escaped and escaped and escaped . . . but now that Mekha is gone, now is when I get trapped by the priests?*

Guildra . . . if this is a joke, it isn't funny. If it's a priestly test of my faith, that *would not be funny, either.*

Archbishop Elcarei stepped into view. Moving up to her, he grasped Rexei's jaw, lifting her head. She tried not to look too self-aware while he peered at her. His brown eyes were distant, almost clinical, then his lips moved. "Bend over and kiss my crotch."

The only thing that saved her was how her gaze instantly dropped. *Oh Netherhells . . . ! Guildra, you had* better *give me a chance to get free.* Stooping, she puckered up her lips, aiming for a spot below the belt of his blue velvet robes. *There has to be a point where they'll leave me alone . . . I hope . . .*

"Stop," he ordered sharply. Rexei froze, balancing as best she could on her toes. "Straighten up, Longshanks, and walk down to the holding pens. First ring, first door on the right. You remember it, don't you? The first prisoner you walked out of here? Go there, now. You, go with him. You, go fetch a control collar."

Yes, if they leave me alone . . . she thought, turning to walk toward the first set of stairs, the ones that led up to the forbidden door . . . *Gears!* Three *of them are still coming with me? Can't I get a break?*

Hands gripped her elbows. Fingers brushed back her scarf— *No, no, NO!* Panicked, Rexei quickly stepped up the state of her humming. Metal touched her neck, and for a while, the world went away, smothered in a fog of mental wool.

FIFTEEN

Both women alighted gently upon the balcony outside Alonnen's study, each wrapped in a bubble-shield to keep them from being harmed by either the waters or the magical energies of the Vortex.

Orana looked much the same as ever: a youngish woman in her early twenties, her blonde hair braided and wrapped around her head, with a deep-sleeved robe worn over trousers and a tunic in shades of blue and cut in some foreign but comfortable-looking style. The outer robe was half black and half white, each side marked with a tower keep embroidered in the opposite color; the inner lining, of course, was pitch-black, for it was a Darkhanan Witch-robe, the symbol and possible source of her priestly powers. Alonnen didn't know and didn't mind not knowing.

Pelai, on the other hand, had arrived in what she thought was adequate winter clothes, a long-sleeved shirt and vest over a strange, knee-length pleated skirt made from colorfully cross-striped linen.

Wool would have been much better, since she had only sandals to cover the rest of her tattoo-covered legs. Seeing the dark-haired woman shiver, Ora tucked her hands up her sleeves and pulled out a bundle of bluish green fabric.

"Here, Pelai," she stated, her words delivered in flawless Mekhanan. "The colors will clash with the red, gold, and black of your clothes, but these leggings should keep you warm, and that's the important part. Master Tall . . . I am pleased to meet you again. The Dark informs me that you now have a priesthood you can trust. Does this priesthood have a Guild Master?"

"Yes, but Guild Master Longshanks is in Heiastowne at the moment," he admitted, turning his back politely so that the Mendhite could slip out of her sandals and struggle into the leggings with a semblance of privacy. He didn't think the balcony overlooking the Vortex was all that cold, but then he was dressed for winter, with layers of wool over his linens. The scarf and cap had been set aside, leaving his lower face, throat, and carroty curls bare, but he also hadn't just come from a country located close to the Sun's Belt region of the world. "Why do you need to know the location of the head of our new Holy Guild, Orana?"

"I have information for the new high priest and for any followers," Ora explained. "I used the mirror on Nightfall Isle which connected to the Guardian of Koral-tai—bypassing the Fountainways of Nightfall, which were inaccessible due to the Convocation—and asked the nuns there to look up any holy spells or prayers which a true priest could use to banish and remove demons, plus prayer-spells to cleanse Netherhell-fouled ground. Mother Naima in turn passed along my request to Pelai, here, who has done some research of her own."

The Mendhite spoke up, grunting a little as she struggled into the leggings. "Stupid . . . too short . . . ah, there. Yes, I have a scroll with several such prayer-spells copied onto it, culled from the

Great Library. It's in the blue pack, there . . . and I wish I knew more tailoring spells," she added under her breath. "I need a hand-span more of cloth, or I'll be forced to waddle the moment these things start to slip . . ."

"Sorry, they were made for Sir Niel, my deceased Guide," Orana apologized, and held up her hand, palm out toward the woman beyond Alonnen's field of view. *"Basher louzaf cha-nell, k'ko . . .* There, that should do it. I've had plenty of time to study Fortunai spellweaving techniques. Niel is tall for an Arbran, but not quite as tall as a Mendhite, I'm afraid."

A soft sigh of happiness from Pelai made Alonnen curious, but he did not turn around. Instead, he waited until the tanned woman walked around him into his line of sight, looking pleased with her borrowed tights. They did clash a bit, but he knew she would be warmer.

"Welcome to Guildara, formerly Mekhana," he told her. "And welcome to a rather wet and chilly winter."

"I've seen Mekhana on the maps. You're not *that* far north," Pelai stated, folding her arms across her chest. Alonnen had the impression her arms were feeling cold despite the long sleeves of her shirt. "Why *is* it so cold?"

"We're not as far north as some kingdoms, true," Orana told the other woman. "This part of Mekhana is only a couple hundred miles from the northernmost point in Sundara. The land extends almost a thousand miles to the north before hitting the North Sea, where it can get quite cold in winter. However, we are high up in elevation, compared to Mendhi, and the higher one goes, the colder things get."

"Apprentice Pelai," Alonnen began, intending to return the subject to the reasons why both women were here.

"Doma Pelai," she corrected him. At his blank look, the Mendhite explained. "I am a Disciplinarian; males are called Domo, females are called Doma. It means 'controlled one' and the suffix at the end indicates gender. My status as a Doma outranks any apprenticeship. Though I suppose, as we are all working together as near equals, you may simply call me Pelai when titles are not needed."

". . . Right. Thank you, Pelai, for the courtesy of informality," Alonnen said. Regathering his thoughts, he returned to the subject at hand. "I'm afraid Master Rexei Longshanks is in Heiastowne at the moment, but if you like, I can call up the Consulate on the talker-box to see if Rexei is done with the morning's training sessions."

"Talker-box?" Pelai asked him.

Moving to the glazed doors, Alonnen murmured a command under his breath, waited until the image of the room beyond filled with a trio of people, then pushed the panel out of his way. "It's an engineering device that transmits silent aether-signals to a similar machine within a day's journey—Heiastowne lies well within its range. You listen with the cone on the cord held to your ear, and speak into the one on the metal armature, and the other person on the other end of the connection can do the same. I—"

"Master Tall! Thank goodness, you're back," Gabria called out to him. "We just saw something awful on one of the spying roaches. We think we saw Master Longshanks in the *temple!*"

Out of the corner of his eye, Alonnen saw Pelai giving Gabria an interested look. Beyond her, Orana merely lifted a brow, apparently not fazed by much despite not knowing what they were talking about, unlike Pelai. Hurrying forward, he reached the spare mirror and took the crystal tablet Gabria held out to him. She pointed over his shoulder, indicating which roach symbol was the one with the recording.

He had to pause and back up the image to find a good shot . . . but it was her. The sight of Rexei in her gray woolen coat, black scarf and cap, and the brown woolen trousers and darker leather boots from this morning was irrefutable. The curve of her cheek, a lock of thumb-length dark brown hair, the shape of her modest nose . . . and a dull look of horror in her eyes. Dull, that was, until he manipulated the controlling spells in the block of crystal, advancing the magic-captured images painting by painting, and saw her gaze dart around, then flick straight to the roach. She didn't lift her head, but she did shift her eyes straight to it for two full seconds, before she left its field of view.

That was the roach he had moved to sit in a corner of the curved corridor ceiling on the uppermost of the three imprisonment rings. It was supposed to count the comings and goings of all the temple residents, since it had been relocated from the power room to the hallway and had been angled with a good view of the doorway to the one stairwell that led to the outside. A man Alonnen dimly but imperfectly recognized had his arm tucked around hers, and he seemed to be guiding but not dragging her somewhere.

Orana's voice, normally smooth and calm, sharpened with anger. "What is that *thing* doing on her neck?"

"What thing?" Alonnen asked. He wasn't sure how the Darkhanan Witch knew what Rexei's gender was, until he realized that after two hundred years, he'd probably be very good at spotting such things, too. Orana's outrage confused him, however. "The scarf?"

"The control collar!" She pointed at the image on the mirror.

He snapped his gaze back to the mirror, reversing the image until he could see for a brief moment the rune-chased metal band clamped around Rexei's throat. Alonnen suspected he had blinked at just the wrong moment to have missed it before. "Dammit, they're not allowed to . . . Wait, that's right—they're *not* allowed. It's illegal, now!"

Shoving the tablet back into Gabria's hands, Alonnen strode for the talker-box attached to his office wall. The other two mages, Jenden and Pioton, gave him worried looks. Like many of their kind, both men had had friends and relatives who had vanished into the hands of Mekha's priesthood, never to be seen again until their body emerged in a black woolen bag, drained of all magic, all hope, and all life.

Not this time, Alonnen silently swore. Setting the resonance level to the one used by the militia, he cranked the handle rapidly and lifted the listening cone to his ear.

"You've reached the Heiastowne Militia Precinct," a female voice stated calmly on the line. He recognized it: Marta Grenspun, best friend of his best assistant, Gabria. *"What is your inquiry?"*

"Get me the captain, or the leftenant—anyone in charge," he ordered. He remembered now where he had seen two of those men accompanying Rexei, driving in the caravan of motorcarts yesterday. "Visiting priests from outside the Precinct have kidnapped Guild Master Longshanks with the intent to kill."

"Gears and Gods! Leftenant!" he heard her hollering. *"Leftenant Tallnose!"* A clatter accompanied the fading of her voice into the background.

Grimacing, Alonnen turned to face the others. "Dammit. I need to be here to help with the Vortex spells . . . and I *need* to go help rescue her. The militia has hand-cannons, but they're going up against well-trained priests, too many of them to get off more than a single volley before the mages start flinging spells—that's assuming the militia has the advantage of surprise, but I'll doubt it. Assuming they can get *inside*, since there'll be wards . . . but I have to stay here and . . . *Dammit!*"

"Anyone can apply the spells to the Vortex if they have permission to use its energies," Pelai pointed out calmly. "Appoint a temporary Guardian—under oath so as to ensure they give it back at the appointed time—and then you can go."

Alonnen gave her a sharp look. He kept the cone cupped to his ear, but he heard nothing other than the slight aetheric hiss that said the talker-box on the other end was still active. Unsure what to make of the foreigner's request, he lifted a brow.

She lifted her hand palm up in return, gesturing toward the inactive mirror, the one hung sideways instead of vertically. "Have we not seen over the last year how Guardian Serina exchanged places many times with Guardian Naima, the Mother-Superior of the Temple of Koral-Thai? Select your apprentice to handle the matter, and you can go."

"I don't have an apprentice," he dismissed. "Not one within reach. Storshei, Gavros, and I were apprenticed to Guardian Mil-lanei, but Gavros is up in the far north. Storshei normally works locally with the Hydraulics Guild, but *he* was sent to a dam a hun-dred miles north that was experiencing a problem with the sluice gates freezing shut just when they need to be opened to relieve some of the meltwater backing up in the reservoir up there." He scowled . . . then focused his gaze on Orana. "You. I trust *you*. I know you'll hand the Vortex back to me—"

"Whoa!" The Witch-Knight quickly held up both hands. "*Not* me. I was able to shield myself against the energies of the Foun-tains in order to travel here, but I *cannot* be allowed to touch any singularity. The energy contained is too much for me to handle."

That confused Alonnen. "But . . . you're the strongest mage we've ever heard of! All the stories passed down through the Mages Guild . . . How can a Fountain be too powerful for you to control?"

The blonde shrugged. "It tries to spill its energy straight into me, like a giant waterskin exploding in my grip—no control and too much for me to hold. I'm not the only one with this problem; Morganen of Nightfall also suffers from it. At most, all I could do would be to channel it for someone else. I cannot use it. I would *also* be of far more use accompanying you to the temple to help rescue Longshanks. There are very, very few spells out there for which I do not know a counter . . . and by myself I am a match for a dozen mages without breaking a sweat."

"Good. *You* can go," Gabria muttered, fingers still curled around the edges of the crystal scrying tablet. "I'm not going anywhere near that place—sorry, Alonnen, but I am *not* going anywhere near anything related to a God."

"It's okay," he reassured her. Part of him was disappointed she could not get over her fear, but a larger part did understand. He turned to the Painted Warrior in their midst. "You're Guardian Tipa'thia's apprentice. You said you'd swear an oath?"

She nodded her head. "I can have one written up in two minutes for your approval." Lifting a tanned hand, she tapped the side of her equally browned face, where a set of pale blue lines and swirls had been inked from the base of her throat up to her ear and around her right eye. "I have a translation tattoo which will allow me to write it in the local tongue for you."

"Do it. I'm going to the Vortex armory to get some weapons— Pioton, man the talker-box," he ordered.

"I was about to offer to go with you," the mage stated. "You'll need all the mages you can get, even with the Holy Knight's help." At his side Jenden nodded, including himself.

"I'll do that," Gabria offered immediately. "It's probably Marta on duty. I'll let her know you're on your way with mages to help, then I can go back to scrying for what's happening in the temple. I won't go *near* it, but I will watch what's happening and send word when I can."

"I'll give you a communications Artifact that will allow you to reach me immediately," Orana offered, moving to the younger woman's side as Gabria took over the earpiece from Alonnen. Once again, Ora's hands moved to the deep cuffs of her robes. "I've based it on an idea I saw while staying on Nightfall Isle . . ."

"The Vortex?" Pelai prompted Alonnen. "If these are the demon summoners, and you fear for the life of this Master Long-shanks, then if we can seal off the ability to cast Portals of any kind, we can prevent the summoning that is the *reason* for Long-shanks' capture. If nothing else, it should delay them as they check their warding runes to see why the summoning is not working."

"You know how to summon demons?" Alonnen asked, wary.

The tall woman gave him a pointed look, one hand going to her hip. "I also know exactly where to stab a human so that they bleed to death from one of their major arteries, either at throat, armpit, or groin. Do you see me stabbing anyone? Fetch me pen and paper, and I shall write an oathbinding that forswears my using your Fountain's powers for anything that would harm anyone you care about. That would limit my use very strictly to just implementing the aether disruptions, as that will not hurt anyone."

He had to trust her. Alonnen's older brother was very good at his job, but Rogen was no mage. No one in the militia was a mage. The more of those Alonnen had on his side when riding in to rescue Rexei, the safer everyone would be . . . and that meant leading *his* guild into battle. Gabria's reluctance to go anywhere near that temple was not a fear he himself could afford to display. So he had to trust Pelai of Mendhi.

Nodding sharply, he gestured at his desk. "There's a charcoal pencil on my desk and plenty of paper. Start writing your oath. I'll be back to witness it as soon as we've been to the armory. Pioton, Jenden, I'll handle the inner circle; the two of you divide up the middle ring and snag any mage willing to come fight."

"Barclei's off-duty and more than willing to face down the priests," Jenden told him. "He'll know the names of the others who are equally ready."

"None of us are ready," Alonnen muttered, grabbing his glasses and scarf from their resting places near the door. "We have less training, incomplete knowledge, limited numbers . . . The one thing we're *good* at is shielding and blocking spells. Orana Niel, I'm afraid you'll have to be our main cannon in this fight. Make every shot count."

Nodding with that same constant level of calm she had always displayed for as long as he could remember, the Darkhanan Witch followed Alonnen and the other two Guildarans out the door. Behind them, Gabria listened at the talker-box, craning her neck to stare at the mirrors every few seconds, while Pelai crossed to the desk and sat down.

They left Rexei in one of the cells with the order to, "Sit down," but no other commands. So she sat on the edge of the cot and waited, bottom still feeling a little sore. The strangers left the cell room first, while Archbishop Elcarei glared down at her. Rexei kept her gaze unfocused and aimed across the room, as if unaware of his presence, though her peripheral vision strained, as did her ears, for any sign she was in immediate danger from the middle-aged man.

Finally, he left, doing nothing more dangerous than closing the door. A key *ka-chunked* in the lock a few seconds later, and a hint of magic shimmered across the door, sealing her inside. Rexei slowly counted to ten, ears straining for any sounds. There was a bit of muffled talking right outside her door, but she couldn't make sense of it. After a few moments, the noises went away.

Humming hard in her mind, she tested the spell on the collar. She already knew her legs could move. Her arms could move. She could even twist as she sat on the bed, and she was able to set down the carefully cradled, half-smashed paper cockroach . . . but getting up off the wool-draped pallet was not easy. In fact, it triggered a painful shower of sparks through the backs of her eyes. Dizzy from the moment she reached her feet, she had to brace one hand on the wall. She *could* move, but only slowly, gingerly feeling her way; the pain interfered with her sense of balance.

She almost tripped over the refresher, and she bruised her hip on the sink, but she made a full circuit of the crystal-lit cell. She could see better, and it was getting easier to move with each hummed bar of her warding spell, each second she stood and walked instead of sat, but it did exhaust her. Sinking back onto the bed let the pain fade, but it also made her leg muscles tremble from the effort.

So I can move, though it's a struggle to fight the spell. Thank the Gods that Mekha isn't around anymore, she thought, rubbing her hands over her face. *I don't know how many other mages have meditations they could have done—probably not many, beyond my mother—but even without His will enforcing the spell, I can see why those first well-trained mages found it impossible to resist and escape once the drainings had begun.*

It was not a pleasant thought; in fact, it churned her stomach. Rexei forced herself off the cot and over to the refresher, bracing one hand on the glazed rim of the sink. That made her think of another need, one starting to grow urgent in spite of the blinding headache the *Sit down* command had given her. Taking advantage of her moment of privacy taught her that *any* seat would do, to the point that standing up again was not pleasant on several levels. The bed, however, was a far safer seat to be found at than the porcelain one.

She had no idea when they'd come for her or when they'd discover she was a female not a male. Nor did she know what was involved in a demonic summoning, nor how long she had left to live. But Rexei did know she wasn't going to wait to be killed. Nor could she be sure that anyone had seen her on her walk through the temple. The first step was to try to get the others to see her, despite being locked in a room without a functional paper roach.

Turning to the crushed, folded bug on the mattress, she picked it up and started gently pulling it back into a puffed-out shape, in the hopes that that was all it would need to work.

How did they know I'd be coming out of the Consulate by the front door and headed that way? she wondered, thinking about her half brother's note. She pulled it out. *Is . . . is this even Lundrei's handwriting? I don't remember. I don't remember what any of their handwriting looked like, save for I think I remember Mum's handwriting on the jars of preserves we made together.*

A sick feeling churned in her gut. *Did he do this? Lundrei, my own kin? I'd like to think he wouldn't have done it of his own free will . . . but there are nearly twelve years between the half brother I knew when I was ten years old and the man I met last night.* She swallowed down the uncomfortable thought and felt her throat muscles pressing against the metal circling her neck. *Of course, I could be mentally accusing him of the wrong things.*

I know the priests had their hands on my cap and coat for a while. Long enough to find hairs. And I've heard rumors of mage-kin being tracked down despite changing their names, identities, regions . . . They might have used a location spell on him, something the Hunter Squads use. And if they caught up with him last night and slapped one of these collars around his neck . . . wait, would *anyone hunt down one of my kin just to . . . ?*

She all but slapped herself on the forehead; only the delicate, half-crumpled paper bug in her fingers kept her from doing so. *Of course they would,* Rexei thought, wincing. *I made a fool of the Archbishop of Heiastowne. And not only did I make a fool of him for two months,* and *gain a Guild rank elevation out of it, I'm now the head of the Holy Guild, utterly supplanting everything he and his cronies enjoyed, stood for, and gloated about for the whole length of their perverted, power-hungry lives.*

I'm more surprised he hasn't personally carved me up yet, now that I think about it.

The paper roach shimmered and moved. Freaked, Rexei

jumped. The good thing was, she confined the urge to scream into a throttled-down squeak. The bad thing was, the enchanted cockroach—which now looked disturbingly real—moved again, making her instinctively fling it away from her. It hit the ground with the faintest *papf* sound as one of the fluffed-out bits crumpled . . . and the roach stopped moving again, turning back into mere, if colorful, paper.

Panting, she forced herself to calm down. *Just a spell . . . just a spell . . . Guildra*, she prayed, staring wide-eyed at the enchanted paper on the stone floor, *help me to get out of here! I don't want my nerves to break . . .*

It took her a few more moments to calm her racing heart. "Come on, Rexei," she whispered to herself, knowing that standing up and fetching the paper back would hurt. "Come on . . . stand up and get it back . . ."

Bracing herself with a deep breath, she pushed to her feet . . . and felt no pain. That startled her into freezing—and that was when the pain started to creep into range, pushing her limbs forward. Toward the paper spy on the ground.

Oh! Ohhhh . . . I'm already touching the collar, and my mind isn't so deeply sunk under the weight of Mekha's will that I cannot even think . . . so I can give myself orders that the collar forces me to obey? Oh, thank you, *Guildra!*

For a moment, she thought she heard the faintest whisper of, *You're welcome*, but the pain was getting in the way. Letting it go, Rexei stooped and carefully plucked the roach from the ground then returned to the bed. The new order cancelled the compulsion to *sit down*, but if she didn't sit, she might get caught *not* sitting, since there was no telling when the priests would come back.

And if I can think . . . Oh yes. I never apprenticed to the Locksmiths or the Law-Sayers, but I know exactly what to do. Thinking swiftly as she gingerly re-plucked at the corners and curves of the paper bug, she stated aloud, "I am to completely ignore any and all spell-based compulsions forced upon me by this collar, following the completion of this order. I will be free to act in any way I desire, or not act, and I command myself to use the power of any reinforcing spells on any other commands to instead reinforce this order: I will have complete and total free will from this point forward. This is the only order that will apply to me from this point forward."

There, she thought, smiling. *That takes care of that. Now to pick this open again . . . and . . . almost got it . . . eurghh, it's moving—ick!* she thought, wrinkling her nose at the lifelike roach now perched on her hand. From a scrying mirror, they had looked a lot more paperlike, but she supposed that was just the scrying spell's method of letting a mage know which cockroaches were the paper ones without tipping off the people being spied upon to the reality underlying the carefully folded, mobile illusions. *This reminds me of those tenements back when I was in the Cobblers Guild, learning how to repair shoes . . .*

I had to get a room in the "young apprentice" building in that town. I appreciated the adults who kept an eye on us, making sure we had food and such, but the other kids didn't always know how to seal up food inside jars and things to keep the roach population at a minimum. Of course, I'd trade a room infested with roaches and other bugs any day over this priest-infested Netherhell-hole.

Unfortunately, if she couldn't figure out how to communicate with the mages back at the Vortex via this illusionary bug, she'd find herself quite dead inside a real Netherhell soon.

The sound of a key in the lock gave her a few seconds of warning. Tossing the roach onto the corner of the cot, where it would hopefully pass unnoticed, she quickly shifted into an approximation of the pose Elcarei had last seen her in, with her hands on her thighs and her gaze unfocused across the room. Out of the corner of her eye, she watched the door open, admitting an apprentice with a cup in one hand and a bowl in the other; the handle of a spoon and a bit of steam rose above the rim of the bowl. She hadn't interacted much with the lattermost male, but she thought his name might be Kurt or something like that.

Behind him entered Archbishop Elcarei, and behind *him* was the foreign mage, Torven. Stepping up to her, Elcarei leaned over and touched her collar; the other touches had been given by the men holding her arms, outside her field of view. This time, she saw it coming. "When we are done questioning you, you will take this bowl and eat the food in it, drink water to keep yourself hydrated, use the refresher and the sink to ensure you stay clean and healthy, and when you are tired, you will sleep in this bed. You will drink a few sips of the water now, then you will answer our questions."

The apprentice priest—not the one who had been violating that one woman mage, thankfully—held out the cup. Rexei felt her arm moving before she could even think of doing so deliberately. The moment she instinctively tried to resist, testing the horrible theory racing through her thoughts . . . the pain came back in a prickle that forced her fingers to open, then close around the curve of the ceramic cup. That same spell-command forced her to bring the goblet to her lips and drink.

One, two, three . . . she tried for a fourth sip to stretch out the command and stall for time, but the spell apparently considered that more than the commanded "few" sips and stopped her. Giving up, she held on to the cup and waited. *At least I can think . . . and the roach is now repaired. Someone's bound to see me when the mages Alonnen set to watching the scryings 'round the clock see a new set of images in the mirror in his office. The roach is even pointed the right way, more or less; I'm sure I'm in its field of vision . . .*

"You are the new Guild Master of the so-called Holy Guild, is this correct?" Elcarei drawled.

Her mouth opened, words forcing their way out of her. She could delay them for a few seconds, but only a few. "That is correct."

"And your name is Rexei Longshanks?"

"It is," she admitted. Again, a slight delay before she was forced to speak the truth. *Maybe I can adjust what I say—keeping it the truth but only the portion of the truth I want them to know?*

"Do you really think your strumpet of a Goddess will ever be able to supplant the rightful place of Mekha in this world?" Elcarei sneered.

"No," Rexei managed to say. Elcarei's brows lifted, a look of surprise and delight in those brown eyes. The spell forced her to clarify that *no*, because without clarification, it could not be true. But she was able to say it in her own way. "Guildra is not a strumpet, and there is no need for Her to strive to supplant the False God in the future, because She has already done so."

"Bastard!" Elcarei's hand lashed out, backhanding Rexei. Her body swayed and her cheek throbbed, but the pain wasn't too bad. It helped that the Aian mage, Torven, snatched at the archbishop's wrist.

"Do *not* hurt the sacrifice!" he ordered sternly. "The more powerful a demon is, the more they will want to wreck their prey themselves. That sort of bloodlust can be useful during the binding process. Control your *own* bloodlust, Archbishop Elcarei."

A shiver swept over Rexci's skin. Resisting the urge to rub her arms, she hoped they didn't notice the goose-prickles. *It's true, they're going to kill me just to summon a demon. Guildra, I wish I knew how to use my priestly strengths to thwart them. Alonnen and I were waiting for the priests among the other Guardians to pass along what they knew or could find.*

"Ask your questions. Learn what you need to know. And be *grateful* the boy is so easily compelled that he tells you the full truth. Even if it isn't a truth you want to hear," Torven added, staring down the slightly older man.

Elcarei stared back, then let out a heavy breath and lowered his arm. Torven released his wrist. "Be glad I am the one doing this interrogation. If Archbishop Gafford were doing it, the boy would be bleeding in seven spots by now."

"The archbishop has his own assignment. Stick to yours, as we planned last night."

Planned last night? Planned what? Were the other cockroaches able to spy on them last night, while Alonnen and I were—?

"Tell me about Master Tall," Elcarei ordered her.

The collar prodded her into speaking, but the pain was weak. Unfocused. Rexei, therefore, said the first thing on her mind. "Master Tall is short. Or at least average in height."

She fell silent the moment the compulsion to reply ended. Elcarei covered his forehead with one hand, the other bracing his elbow. Dragging his palm down to his mouth, he stared down at her, in her coat, cap, trousers, and boots. One finger tapped the side of his cheek, then he pulled his arm down across his chest. "Is Master Tall the Guild Master of the Mages Guild?"

"I . . . don't know." Rexei blinked up at him, feeling a tingle wash through her mind, almost as if the inside of her skull itched. She honestly didn't know, and she didn't like the way her answer made the archbishop scowl.

Elcarei glared at her and growled under his breath. "Gods-be-damned amnesia spells . . . You're lucky I thought of an alternate way to ask. Describe the location or locations you have visited in the last week."

"Buildings made out of stone, wood, plaster, and tile. Streets and roads covered in snow or damp with winter rains . . ." Outwardly, she strove to give him a blank look. Inwardly, she felt a twinge of fear. *The oath I swore . . . I think it made me forget something important, just now. Something very, very important. Guildra, what did I just forget?*

He almost lunged forward and slapped her. Checking himself

at the last minute just as Torven caught his wrist again, Elcarei dragged in a deep breath. Composing himself, he tried again. "Each time you left the city in the last two weeks, which road or roads did you take?"

"The north and east ones," she said. Again, her head felt like it was itching deep under her scalp. Rexei felt another surge of fear.

"Were you on foot, or did you take a vehicle of some sort, and if so, what kind?"

"A . . . a motorhorse . . . and a motorcart . . ." Since she hadn't been forbidden from moving her arms, she lifted the one not holding the cup and scratched, dislodging the cap perched on her short, dark locks. She wanted to unbutton her coat, too, since she was now growing a bit warm down here, out of the cold, damp winter air.

"How far would you say you traveled each time, in terms of either distance or time?"

"I . . . don't remember." She didn't, and that worried her.

Growling, he grabbed her by the upper arms, pulling her up off the bed. "*Where* is the Mages Guild located?!"

"I d-don't know!" she stammered as he shook her. "I don't know of any Mages Guild!"

"*Bah!*" Thrusting her away from him, he let her drop back down onto the thin, wool-stuffed pallet that served as the cot's mattress. "You're pistoning useless—you're not even good *for* a pistoning, you useless little pile of goat manure—sit here, eat your food, and obey the rest of my orders from earlier," Elcarei snapped, gesturing for the silently watching apprentice to hand her the bowl. "You will keep yourself healthy and well until we're ready to sacrifice you. Stupid Gods-be-damned renegade mages . . ."

Forced to accept the bowl, Rexei watched the archbishop storm out of the cell. With a heavy sigh, Torven followed, and the dark-haired apprentice, the one whose name she couldn't remember, followed. She remembered her time in the Servers Guild spying on these priests, but not all of them had served in the public areas where guildmembers were allowed to go . . . and she couldn't remember *why* she had gotten a job cleaning the temple.

She couldn't remember why she couldn't remember, either, which was unnerving. Rexei remembered most of her life in great detail, but this? There were now gaps in her brain and an ache in her heart. And in her bottom. She didn't know why she had a sore bottom, yet could not remember being violated in any way by the priests, beyond being captured, dragged down here, and slapped by the ex–Archbishop of Heiastowne.

Why is my bottom feeling a little tender? Did I eat the wrong food at some point? That thought brought her back to the compulsion laid upon her. Stooping, she set the cup on the ground, then gripped the handle of the spoon and dug into what she thought was a stew. It wasn't, at least not in the traditional sense. Stews had vegetables and gravy, sometimes some grain, and meat. This glop, from what she could tell, was all meat in a bit of rich gravy. *That's odd. Why would they serve me something as expensive as meat? I'd think the mage-prisoners would be fed on cheap grain and vegetable pottage with only a little bit of meat now and then, not pure meat. Why would they feed a demonic sacrifice meat?*

There were too many things about the world, about magic, and about monsters which she simply did not know, but the collar compelled her to put the first spoonful into her mouth and chew anyway. Rexei was hungry; she remembered she hadn't had her midday meal yet. Doing what Archbishop Elcarei wanted did not make her happy, though at least it was something she *could* do.

There was nothing in this room to distract her from her predicament but the cot, a chair directly under the suncrystals in the corner—she didn't remember where she had learned what they were called, but that was what they were—the refresher, the sink, and her cup and bowl. And a cockroach sitting on the corner of her current bed.

It wiggled an antenna at her. She resisted the urge to squish it, feeling surprisingly sympathetic toward the repulsive little scavenger. Mainly because she would have traded just about anything to have been a Cobblers Guild apprentice once again, dealing with roaches by the dozens. Resolving to ignore the bug, she kept feeding herself what tasted like a mix of beef and ham stew. There were hints of pepper for seasoning, but mostly it was a rich reduced broth coating fall-apart-tender meat.

Her thoughts whirled with the need to figure out how to escape and regret she hadn't brought someone else along to meet her brother, or at least had them follow at a discreet distance since she would not have wished a second capture on anyone else. And despite the flavorful, expensive-for-a-captive meal, her stomach felt sour with the sinking feeling she had forgotten something very, very important just now. Something very specific, because there were fuzzy spots in her memory of the archbishop's interrogation and of several other points in her recent past. That worried her deeply.

SIXTEEN

The linens room on the bottom-most level was large, but the presence of one Aian mage and fourteen ex-Mekhanan priests, most ranked bishop or higher, made it feel crowded.

Torven shook his head. "I'm sorry, but I still cannot find the source of those scrying-spell auras. Some sort of blurring spell makes it vanish the moment I try to focus on more than one quarter of a room where they are. They move occasionally; they don't just sit still. And *yes*, I have checked for spells placed on insects. Nothing alive shows any signs of magic, and when I applied a toxic gas spell to a warded area, I found bugs and even one mouse dead when it was through, but the scryings have continued. We are just going to have to accept that we are being spied upon, save in this location, or by relocating."

"We cannot relocate quickly, and if we do, we will be vulnerable," Archbishop Elcarei stated. "I have Hunter Squad members still loyal to the priesthood trying to find traces of this 'Master

Tall' but we may just have to be content with ridding the world of
this stupid youth who dares call himself Guild Master of the 'Holy'
Guild—he should be enough of a sacrifice. Don't demons enjoy
defiling the pure?"

"Some do. Others prefer to have them pre-defiled by the persons offering them," Torven admitted. "Based on what we have
discerned through interrogating the lesser residents, this 'Lesser-
Prince Demon Nurem' of the seventh Netherhell we contacted
prefers to defile his victims himself. I wouldn't even have suggested
feeding the boy meat, save it will depress the ability every peasant
yokel has to cast a last-moment curse. If we try to move to a
scrying-free location, we run the risk of being stopped."

"Then we need to act fast," Archbishop Gafford said. His voice
was smooth, his words reasonable, his appearance almost charming. The men in the linen closet with him knew of his ruthless
reputation, however. "If we act now, we can sacrifice, bind, and
have a major power in our back pockets within the hour. From
there, we can cross-bind lesser demonic powers with ease. With
our sanctum secured with that much might, we can work in safety
on turning this Nurem into a chained God bound to our will and
rule once more. Build the fortress, gentlemen, and *then* you can
send out raiding parties. With this Lesser-Prince under our
thumb, your 'Master Tall' will be rendered impotent, which means
he will be easily caught, caged, drained, and gutted. Does anyone
disagree?"

Gafford and Elcarei looked to Torven while the other twelve
men exchanged glances and shook their heads. The Aian mage
rubbed his chin in thought.

"I think we should set up just a few extra precautions, before we
begin," he finally said. "I've made you those casks of Gating powder—
strictly for travel within this world, not cross-dimensionally. I know
it's a risk to bring them into the power room, but I cannot help but

think of all those horrid adventure tales from the Tower wherein the heroes arrived *just* in the nick of time to ruin their enemies' plans."

"I see," Archbishop Gafford said, raising his brows in mild respect for the foreigner. "We're supposed to be spaced out around the wardings to help contain the demon with our powers. If we position mirrors around the chamber, with little pots of Gating powder, anyone breaking in would not be able to stop all of us from escaping."

"Yes, but escaping to what?" the bald-headed Bishop Hansu asked. At the confused frowns of his compatriots, he explained. "It's all well and good to leap out of a burning building to save our lives, but are we leaping into an equally flaming haystack, into a dockside river, or into a pile of rusty farming equipment? I, for one, would rather have a landing that would put out the fire in my clothes and carry me downstream, far away from trouble. *Where* are we to direct our mirror-Gates? As far as I know, one can only direct them to a place one actually knows, and *then* adjust the view to somewhere within a mile or two of that starting point."

"He's right. You're the only one with solid knowledge of what the world looks like beyond Mekhana's borders," Elcarei agreed.

"I suggest, gentlemen," Gafford interjected, "that we don't *care* about where the mirror-Gates are aimed, so long as they are aimed somewhere that we can safely escape to. *Afterward*, we can journey to a predesignated meeting place."

"In that case, I suggest picking spots ahead of time where we can toss through some wealth to await our escape if needed," Torven said. "I've been cast once before through something like a Gate with just the items I wore . . . and I would far rather not have to start from scratch like that again. If there is no need to flee, then we can use levitation spells to bring the goods back through our mirror-Gates once the Lesser-Prince is bound. If there is, then we will have already set the mirrors to scry upon a safe location, we will have funds, and we can escape as we go."

"What's to prevent the others from following us?" Brother Grell asked. The young man was not yet a bishop in rank, and until they regained power probably never would be, but he was one of the stronger mages within the temple grounds and thus had to be included in this shelving-flanked planning session. "If we all go through, the mirror-Gates would remain open for anyone to pursue—and don't say one of us will have to sacrifice himself to remain behind. The power room is too huge to have one man go around casting the powder upon each mirror in turn to seal it shut again, never mind the time it would take to shift the scrying image."

"We just need time-delayed destruction spells," Torven stated. "Break the frame, and you shatter the opening. While the rest of you double-check the main warding circles against the diagram I made, I can make enchanted sheets of paper to be laid at the base of each mirror. Stomp on it as you go through, and it'll explode after ten heartbeats have passed. If anyone tries to follow, it'll be just one or two at most, and they might even be caught midway through and cut in half."

"Clever. Do it. But first . . . *where* should we meet up again?" Gafford asked, his voice taking on a pointed edge. "I know the lands to the north of here far better than anything close by. I'd be relatively safe because I'd be hundreds of miles away. If you stick strictly to what *you* know locally, the locals might realize where you have gone and send their version of Hunter Squads after you, and you'll be besieged within the hour if you stay wherever you go."

"Outkingdom," Koler grunted. The others looked at him, and he repeated himself. "We head outkingdom. Mekhana is falling apart, and from what you told us, young man," he added, eyeing Gafford, who bristled at the patronizing words, "the Patriarch is none too happy about the idea of binding and draining demons for power, so don't be too sure of your 'hundreds of miles away' protecting you. It takes less than ten minutes to transmit a short message from one end of Mekhana to the other via talker-box, after all."

"It is gratifying to see that each of us *can* think, when we put our minds to it," Torven stated dryly. "If we cannot bind a demon tonight, we head out of the kingdom. I suggest we pick a place that is not in the next kingdom over, for that matter; your neighbors would not be pleased with you if they realized you were ex-priests of their former divine enemy."

"We each have the spells in our books—or should—that teach us how to make translation pendants for interrogating captured foreign mages," Gafford said. "So traveling to another nation should not pose a language problem. But there is the concern that other, farther-flung lands might think a foreigner with an accent from Mekhana would be suspicious, and not want foreign priests congregating in their lands. I suggest we change professions if we have to flee."

"To what?" Elcarei asked his former superior. "Excepting the Aian, we were all raised and trained to be priests, not journeymen of the Tinkers Guild or whatever."

"Scholars," the green-clad archbishop said. "We are scholars, and we will be traveling to the one place where a foreigner would not be amiss: The Great Library of Mendham, in the kingdom of Mendhi."

"Good," Bishop Koler grunted. "I approve."

"Looking forward to new books to peruse, Brother Koler?" one of the other priests asked him.

He shook his head slightly, fingers first scratching at his chin, then combing through his long, streaked beard. "No, looking forward to somewhere *warm* for a change."

"I certainly cannot disagree to that," Torven said. Even Elcarei let his mouth curl up on one side in humor. "Any opposed? No?

Motion passes. Let us move the mirrors, find and secure our retreating sites as quickly as possible, and begin the binding ritual. And *not a word* to anyone else. Take what apprentices and journeymen you can—make sure they know that only the last one through is to stomp on the paper—but only tell them *where* we will be headed *after* the mirror is destroyed."

"How will we know when the mirror is destroyed on the other side?" Priest Grell asked.

"Bits of debris will come through the opening, before the Gate collapses and is sealed," Gafford told him. "Make sure to shield yourselves as you count to ten, and then check the floor behind you. If something has fallen through, grab your goods and retreat from the region, in case they recognized where you went through. If nothing glasslike has fallen . . . then flee even faster."

"Today, I serve Guildra, Goddess of Guilds, Patron of this land."

The motorwagon jolted over a rut in the road. Alonnen clenched his jaw and continued loading his hand-cannon. Like most of the weapons developed in secret by the Munitions Guild for the Mages Guild, it was not a standard cannon. He didn't have to measure the munitions powder and pack it into the barrel; he didn't have to drop in the flannel charcloth or the lead ball and ram it down into place. Nor did he have to grease the openings to keep any moisture from reaching the powder and ruining it before the sparking gear could ignite it.

"Today, I shall be a warrior of the Light of Heaven, striving to defend the innocent and protect this land from the profane."

Some clever soul with a secondary status in the Brassworks Guild had come up with clever little capsules with the powder tucked behind the payload. In Alonnen's case, the missile being fired out of the short, heavy barrel was not one large ball, but rather, many smaller beads. The range was short, but that was fine with him; Alonnen was headed into the stone-walled confines of a temple, not facing down a foe from the far side of a battlefield. These "buck beads" might not go through a man unless fired from up close, but they would turn a chest, an arm, a leg, whatever got in their way into painfully shredded meat.

"Today, I ask my Goddess to forgive my flaws, and grant me the purified instincts to do what is right and just with my foes."

He had the faces of Torven Shel Von and Archbishop Elcarei firmly in mind. He wasn't entirely sure if firing a hand-cannon into their faces was going to be right or just; he only knew he'd feel safer without them in the world. Still, he tried to focus on the fact he was going to the temple to rescue the woman he loved and not to kill the most dangerous, annoying men in the world.

"Today, I, Orana Niel, dedicate myself to the works of Heaven in my efforts to defend and cleanse this world of evil."

"Today, I, Alonnen Tallnose, dedicate myself . . ." he recited along with the other mages accompanying them into town, just as he had recited every other line given to them. They hit a pothole, and he almost lost the last two brass capsules. Catching them against the felted-wool coat of the man seated on the floor between his feet at the back of the wagon, he muttered an apology and pushed the little brass cylinders into the holes in the firing cogwheel.

Orana paused, squinting a little at each man and woman crowded into the back of the wagon, then nodded. "Good. Your auras are suitably sanctified. Keep this feeling in mind, and remember to focus your thoughts upon Guildra as you enter the former temple. Picture the various guild symbols, and imagine a woman whom you trust, respect, and think of as strong marching in there beside you, ready to help you kick out all that is evil. Remember: What we think, our Gods become.

"True, you lost control of the previous one, and you sank into hopelessness and despair as the priests seized control and power. That weight is gone. You face priest-mages who are still somewhat strong, but who are no longer backed by a False God who fed upon stolen powers. You have your own powers, and you know how to shield each other. More than that, it is *you* who have the power of the Heavens on your side this time. You are free to worship again . . . and you *know* what your Guilds honor, what cornerstones and foundation blocks underlie your best way of life.

"Put those feelings into your Goddess, and She will manifest in ways both subtle and sublime."

The motorwagon swayed around a corner and lurched to a stop with a yelp from the driver, who had stomped on the stopper pedal. "Oy! Grinding idiots! They blocked the road."

Craning his neck, Alonnen stared at the scene. Several other motorcarts, motorwagons, and motorhorses blocked the street, all of them marked with the hammer-on-shield of the Precinct militia. Whoever had parked them here had turned this well-traveled thoroughfare into one long, open-air parking stall, with no regard for how anyone else would get through.

When he realized there wasn't even foot traffic in sight, Alonnen felt a stab of alarm. Scrambling out of the back of the wagon, he muttered a spell-ward around his hand-cannon before shoving it through his belt. The ward would keep it from discharging into his leg, or worse, but would only take the briefest of thought to dispel. Hopefully . . . hopefully his brother and the other officers in the Precinct militia had not just ordered their men to charge into the temple without waiting for magical protection.

Behind him, he heard a few mutterings of confusion, then the sounds of the others dropping out of the vehicle. The air was crisp and cold, and it reeked slightly of motorcart fuel and cooling metal. They were still two blocks and a side street from the temple, but it looked like the Militia had arrived in full force. That also explained why no one else was moving by vehicle in this part of town; no one could remember the last time Captain Torhammer had mobilized so much of the Precinct's forces outside of the old parade days.

"Oy! Tall! Over here," a voice called out from a shop door, speaking just loud enough to get Alonnen's attention.

Glancing that way, Alonnen frowned, then widened his eyes, recognizing one of his brother's under-officers. The man beckoned Alonnen over, then pulled back into the shop, giving him room to step inside. Yet more leather-and-metal clad bodies shifted and shuffled, giving him room to work his way deeper into the shop.

"There you are, Master Tall," Rogen said, working his way through what had been a textiles shop. At the moment the bolts of fabric on the tables were covered with what looked like maps of the temple. Alonnen hadn't even known such maps existed.

Gathering his wits, he addressed his brother. "I've brought fifteen mages with me. Including our champion."

Turning, Alonnen looked toward the shop windows, only to see Orana right behind him. She smiled slightly, her robe pulled fully shut. Her frame looked a little odd, shoulders wider and bulkier than usual. Alonnen didn't know what to make of that, since on the ride to the city she had seemed slender and normal.

"Ahh . . . right. Leftenant Rogen Tallnose, this is Witch-Knight Orana Niel," he introduced politely.

His introduction immediately stirred a flurry of whispers around the men crowded into the shop. "*Orana Niel!*"

"*Orana . . .*"

"*The Holy Knight is here?*"

"*Praise the Gods!*"

"*I got my cousin back, thanks to her!*"

"Enough!" Rogen called out as a few started to shift forward.

"You can thank her later. We have the new Guild Master of the Holy Guild to rescue, and we need to do it before these bastard ex-priests sacrifice Master Longshanks to some dredged-up demon from the Netherhells. Master Tall, I've a portable talker-box operator coordinating with Captain Torhammer on the other side of town. What in the way of illusions can your people cast around the temple so that they don't see us coming?"

"Not many. I'm . . . not in charge of the main source for such things at the moment," Alonnen was forced to admit. He had the unique experience of watching his unflappable brother's jaw drop, and Alonnen quickly held up a hand. "It's being used for the far *greater* need of sealing off the entire region from the ability to create cross-universe Portals, which will prevent more demons from being summoned. What we can do is shield you and your men. The rest will be up to Witch Orana."

"I can toss up a static illusion if all the streets are empty of people," Orana offered. "But there cannot be any people moving around, if you want my attention free to be able to go with you into the temple itself."

"*I* vote bringing the only *highly trained* mage we have in the area into the temple with us," Alonnen interjected before his eldest brother could do more than open his mouth to speak. "But what do I know? I'm just the Guild Master."

"Don't be a piston," Rogen muttered back, giving him a dark look. "I'd agree to the same. What I was *about* to say is that we've already sent out an order to clear the streets. You can cast the spell as soon as you've ascertained it's clear. I'll assign you a squad to move you around between the shops and streets unseen."

"No need. I have a scrying mirror with me." Pulling it out of her copious sleeves, Ora moved over to the table with the maps.

Rogen leaned in close to his brother, speaking under his breath. "How did she get here just when we needed her?"

"My guild has its ways," Alonnen murmured back. "Now that Mekha is gone, we can import teachers across the borders by land as well as other means . . . if we *have* stable borders. There's peace around Heiastowne and some of its immediate neighbors, but not everyone has it or wants it." He shifted, impatient with the preparations despite knowing they were necessary. "I don't like waiting. I want to go in now."

"You never served in the Militia," Rogen reminded his brother. "Far more battles are lost through lack of care and planning than are won. What seems like a sudden ambush is often the product of hours and days, even weeks of preparation."

"We don't have hours, never mind days and weeks," Alonnen countered.

"We'll do our best," Rogen said. "But I will not send my people into a slaughter, and I will not send yours, either."

"And I don't want to send them, either," Alonnen agreed. "I'm just . . . I'm afraid they'll interrogate her," he muttered. "If they do . . . she'll forget everything about the guild. She'll forget *me*."

"Try praying to that Goddess of hers," the leftenant offered dryly. "Ask Her to intercede. That's supposedly why Patron Deities exist, isn't it? To pull off miracles and make amends when mortals cannot manage?"

"Yeah, but . . ."

"No buts. Start praying," Rogen ordered him. Lifting a hand, Rogen poked his sibling in his wool-covered chest. "One more thing. Just in case she *has* been interrogated and has forgotten you, *don't* run up and hug her. I know you. I know that's what you'll do. But if you do that, she won't realize why this complete stranger is trying to embrace her, and she may panic. She might even think she's being attacked . . . and if she calls out for help, I am duty bound to have to arrest you."

Alonnen gave him a disbelieving look. Rogen lifted his brows in pointed, silent reply. Scowling, Alonnen folded his arms across his chest.

Rogen shrugged and folded his own arms as well, echoing his sibling's disgruntled pose. "If I don't do it, Captain Torhammer will, and *he* won't care about your reasons why or your past relationship with her. All he'll see is a frightened woman thinking she's being mugged by a stranger, not just hugged. Sorry, Brother, but if she has been spell-bound to forget you, then . . . well . . . you'll just have to start courting her all over again. From day one. Start with words, not touches."

As much as he wanted to argue the point, Alonnen knew his elder brother was right. He hated it, but Rogen was right.

"It is done," the Witch in their midst announced. She turned to face the leftenant, and the edge of her robe parted, showing a glint of rune-chased metal. That was what she had under her Witch-robe: armor, undoubtedly infused with spells both offensive and defensive. Some property of the sleeved, hooded cloak had hidden the aura of its magic before the folds parted, but Alonnen could see it now.

I'll have to speak with her about how to imbue metal with various spells. We could seriously use them on things like the motorhorses and motormen, should we ever have to go to battle. There's no guaranteeing the northern precincts won't stop just at their own borders in their effort to throw off the old shackles and impose a new set of leaders and a new set of rules.

"Right, then," Rogen stated, raising his voice so everyone in the shop could hear. "Master Tall, break off your . . . guildmembers into six groups. I'll pair five sets of them with a scout to take them straight to the other groups around the perimeter. Your job, m . . . mages," he added, stumbling a little over the dreaded *M* word, "is to shield our forces from any spells being cast. One of the favorite tricks of the priesthood is a sleeping spell that will hit an area around you. Another is a gluelike spell that will knock you down and lock your body to the floor . . ."

Alonnen wasn't the only mage in the shop who nodded; they were familiar with such things and knew a few counters for them. *And some of those counters aren't even spells*, he thought grimly, fingers going to the grip of his hand-cannon. *Hurt a priest badly enough, and they won't be able to concentrate to cast any spells.*

"One warning," Ora called out as Rogen came to the end of his list of known spells to counter. She flicked her hand, and a hovering illusion of a single man appeared in the air over their heads. It made the non-mages gasp and shift back, and the mages sway forward in envy at her skill. "This man, Torven Shel Von, *must not die*. Do not kill him."

Dammit, Alonnen swore, wincing as he realized where her speech was headed. *Gods in Heaven, You are just bound and determined to mock me, aren't You?*

"We have determined that *this* mage is the reason why these other priests have not unleashed *unchecked* demons upon this world. He is an Aian, so you will know him by the differences in his features from the common ex-Mekhanan, as you can see. He *must* be allowed to live and to escape, so that the various prophecies will come true regarding the successful thwarting of these demon summoners' ambitions. Mark his face and learn it well.

"I may even have to *save* him," she added grimly. It was the first time Alonnen had seen the normally serene woman unhappy. "But I have learned from personal experience that either you work *with* a set of prophecies to make them come true in a way that benefits you . . . or you'll find out just how badly they can piston you from behind. *Without* pomade."

Reminded abruptly of last night's activities, Alonnen felt his cheeks burn. Rogen slanted him a bemused look, but thankfully did not ask why his middle brother had turned so red in the face.

Hopefully the other men and women in the shop would think it was simply from Orana's crude mention of a topic best reserved for the privacy of a bedroom or a brothel visit. *And, dammit to a Nether-hell, we won't be able to do* any *of last night's activities for however long it takes me to get her to fall in love again!*

Focus, Alonnen, he ordered himself in the next breath. *That's a petty whine about a sprained finger, when the world might have all of its bones broken within the hour. Do your job, and help your brother to do his.* Clearing his throat, Alonnen addressed the dozens crowded into the shop. "You heard our champion, people. Let's go save Rexei and, hopefully, the rest of the world."

The key in the enchanted lock warned her someone was coming. Rexei tensed, prepared to zap whoever it was with a sleep spell if they were alone. The door swung inward, revealing a clutch of five apprentices. She checked the change in her inner melody before it could actually start, and forced herself to continue humming the tunes that kept her mind clear and her body able to act, if at a price.

Moving up to her side, the foremost of the five apprentice priests, Apprentice Stearlen, poked his finger against her control collar. "On your feet, boy."

She didn't feel any prickling compulsion to move. Rexei had a split second to realize why, then she quickly jerked herself up off the cot. By calling her *boy* when she was actually a female, he had robbed the collar of its depth of control. She couldn't let any of the apprentices know that. Not when trapped in a room with four of them blocking her only escape route.

His next order didn't come with a wrong-gendered epithet, however. Ordered to follow the one who had poked her collar, she debated trying to escape the moment she reached the hallway. The others flanked her, clearly unwilling to take chances. Neither was she, save for one thing: they were clearly herding her toward the nearest entrance to the power room, where Mekha had once sat and drained His victims. Chanting, filled with syllables and sounds that made her stomach feel queasy, echoed from within the chamber.

Now or never! Letting her body walk forward under the spell's compulsion, Rexei hummed out loud—softly but with every bit of intent she could muster. Two of the apprentices let out soft but audible sighs before crumpling. Their bodies hit the floor with soft thumps and velvet-draped rustles, turning the other three around. While the young men narrowed their eyes, Rexei gathered her energies for a second strike.

She hummed aloud again—and Stearlen cut her off with a grab of her throat and a sharp, "*Stop* that!"

One of the apprentices fell; the other staggered into the wall and braced himself, but managed to stay awake. Unable to run because she was being held up onto her toes by the taller youth's grip, Rexei was forced to grab at his fingers in the effort to pry them off her neck. The metal collar prevented only two of his fingers from squeezing painfully into her throat; the rest dug in deep enough to choke.

Stearlen shook her even as he tightened his grip, growling, "Don't you dare try any more spells! You will come with me and stand where I tell you, and you will *not* move from that spot until we tell you what to do, you little grease stain!"

Dragging her forward, he didn't wait for the last apprentice to finish shaking off the dizziness imparted by her spell. Forced to stumble in his wake, Rexei continued to try to pry his fingers from her neck. It hurt to keep humming the warding spells in the back of her mind, but she was so close to escape, she *had* to get them back up and running strong so that she could . . . step out between the slanted steps of the tiers ringing the power room, endure another shake from the novice, and be ordered to stand still and be silent.

Yanking his hand off her throat, Stearlen stepped away, leaving her with an unobstructed view of the power room. Instead of crystals topping spikelike pedestals, all surrounding a huge throne at the very center, the power room had been smoothed flat and painted with ring within ring of runes and wards, symbols and sigils. Painted, not just chalked, in several hues. The foreign mage had been busy in the intervening days; if she hadn't realized within seconds that this piece of spell-crafted artistry was going to be the source of her demise and the center of a plan to throw the world down into chaos and despair with a Netherhell invasion, she would have admired the jewel-tone lines and pastel swirls.

There were more details to see, all of which she took in quickly as Stearlen moved a few steps away. Most of the apprentices and lesser-ranked priests were scattered around the room in random clumps. Those who had strong magic, fourteen of them, had been spaced around the chamber at regular intervals, while the Aian mage who had started this mess stood in one of the cleared circles painted on the floor. Spaced between pairs of chanting mage-priests were mirrors.

They did not reflect the power room, however, but rather peered into other, mostly unfamiliar locations. For a moment, she thought she recognized one as the courtyard of a high-ranked priest's manor which she had once upon a time delivered a sack of scrolls and letters to as a journeyman in the Messengers Guild. She only had time for a brief, angled glimpse of that mirror, though. The novice standing nearest her drew in a deep breath.

"Grandmaster Torvan!" Stearlen called out, his voice cutting through the chanting, though not stopping it. "He's a *mage!*"

Rexei paled and closed her eyes, humming hard. Stearlen had said any *more* spells, but the ones she was using to thwart the compulsion, those technically weren't more, they were simply the same ones as before. The hard part lay in changing their melody enough to break the controlling magics, not just shove them aside, without triggering a blinding headache.

The Aian male turned, one of the few in the chamber not chanting. "*What* did you say?"

"I said, he's a *mage*. He knocked out Ervei, Talos, and Doric with some sort of sleeping spell," the apprentice priest added. "Almost got Frankei, too. He's shaking it off outside, still."

Stepping over the painted lines, his face a pale, tight mask of fury, Torven stalked up to Rexei. Just as Stearlen had, he grabbed the wool-clad captive by the throat. "What *else* do we not know about you, boy?"

His magic flowed into the collar, reinforcing its obedience spells. Rexei snapped her eyes open, compelled to speak . . . but she could still direct what she had to say. "Almost my whole *life*?"

For a moment, his fingers tightened, hurting her throat even more than the apprentice had. With the physical force came a rush of magical energy, too. It was brief, though; just as she reached up to try to pry his fingers off, maybe even break his thumb, Torven shoved her back far enough that she swayed and staggered. Rexei winced in pain as the compulsion to stay in one place attacked her nerves for daring to move half a step back. She quickly stepped forward again.

Torven grimaced, mind spinning rapidly through the choices. "Light blue paint!" he snapped at Stearlen—then jabbed a finger at their captive's metal-banded throat. "*You*, Rexei Longshanks, or whatever you call yourself, will stay right here until one of us commands you to move. You will obey our commands, and you will do *nothing* to disrupt this ritual.

"I *said*, get me the light blue paint," he repeated impatiently, whirling on Stearlen. "I have to add in the fact that this idiot is a mage and reword the oathbinding contract to account for anything *else* this idiot is that we do not yet know and don't have the time to find out—*now*, or I'll sacrifice *you* to bind Nurem, instead!"

The only relief Rexei had from the despair of her situation was the abrupt shift from gloating to pallid fear on the apprentice's face. He stumbled backward, then turned and dashed for a collection of pots and jars located on one of the lower tier risers a third of the way across the room. The Aian followed him at a more normal pace, hands fisted at his sides. Rexei struggled with her countering harmonies, trying to restrengthen them, but the mage had imbued extra energy into her collar, making it hard to concentrate.

The priests spaced around the edges of the room continued to gather energies via chants and gestures that were at odds with the horror of the moment, given how graceful the slow swoop and scoop of their hands and arms looked. They collected those energies into crystals vaguely similar to the ones she had seen when getting the prisoners out of this horrid place. Using some sort of hovering spell, Torven Shel Von floated above the painted runes lining the smooth stone of the floor and carefully applied new symbols around the edge of a medium-sized circle set right next to the edge of the largest one in the center.

As much as she did not want to be surprised by what was coming, Rexei forced herself to close her eyes and concentrate. Humming the base melody under her breath, adding in the harmonies in her mind, she struggled to break the collar. A slight shift of her weight, half a foot's length back . . . another foot . . . Her head ached, but she—bumped into someone.

"So you *can* cast in spite of that thing," a male voice said.

She belatedly recognized the quiet murmur as Frankei's voice, the novice she had not successfully put to sleep with her second spell. She hadn't had much contact with him during her Servers Guild efforts, but she did know him as one of the quieter priest apprentices. Now she felt his hand on the back of her neck, sending a shiver of fear down her spine as he spoke.

"Cast and move . . . despite being told not to go anywhere." He did not throttle her from behind, but he did do something that nudged at the side of her throat. "Don't shout, and don't fight," he ordered softly . . . and eased away the collar. His hand gripped her shoulder, holding her still even as hope exploded upward in her heart. "You'll still need a huge distraction to get out of here . . . and from what these men have planned, you're going to need a friend hidden among them. Frankei Strongclip. That's my name. Remember it."

She didn't turn, didn't look at him. Not that she needed to; Frankei was one of those young men who had a bland, ordinary, forgettable face, with the typical rectangular face and dark brown hair of most southern-born Mekhanans. Even his dark brown eyes weren't too unusual, though they were several shades darker than her own. But she did whisper, "*Why?*"

"I served because it was either serve or be drained. But that was the coward's way," she heard him confess just behind her right ear, his words barely audible over the chanting of the rest. It looked like the apprentices were spacing themselves out to guard the various openings to the three layers of the outer rings where the cells were. Since there was a doorway tunnel behind her, it probably looked to the others like Frankei was guarding this one. He continued after a pause, and a sigh. "I stayed because it was either flee and be at fault for what these men want to do to the world—cowardice again—or find out what their plans are and find a way to thwart them.

"Now stay here. I need to go get a jug of paint thinner, and I want you to hide the fact I'm not still—"

His light blue artistry done, Torven gestured with a fist. Magic closed around Rexei's body, yanking her up off her feet. "You will stand in *this* circle, Longshanks. You, Stearlen, get this pot and paintbrush out of here. *Pay attention*, everyone!" he called out sharply. "We are about to begin. No more delays!"

Freed of the collar, but trapped within the circle painted in shades of pale blue, bright yellow, dark red, and more, Rexei struggled to free herself from the Aian's magic with her meditation songs. She could slip free of just about any spell, given time. Unfortunately . . . he was strong. Very strong, enough that she wasn't sure if she *had* enough time, because this wasn't a collar she had grown used to over the last little while; this was a completely new warding spell. It gripped and held her body still as the chanting shifted in tone, though at least she could still breathe, blink, and see.

She saw Torven, the Aian mage, walking about a foot off the ground on a patch of misty-looking air, chanting something and scattering some sort of gritty powder in a very carefully laid circle within the greatest circle drawn on the floor. As soon as the powder circle was complete, he retreated to a heavily rune-warded ring a quarter of the way around the chamber from her.

The chanting of the others changed, and now light streamed in from every crystal held by one of the fourteen priests and bishops, and even two archbishops positioned around the room, gauging from the size of the medallions displayed on their velvet-covered chests. Despite the weight and warmth of her woolen clothes, Rexei shivered. It was clear the ex-priests had practiced in the two-plus weeks since the Aian had offered them an alternative source of power. It was enough that their chant—a short, repetitive, almost brutal set of notes and words—threatened to overwhelm her own inner melodies.

Her ears weren't the only thing under assault; the glow of energy pouring into the painted circles and runes filled her eyes with aetheric glimpses of great domes rising up from each circle, of shimmering walls of force emerging from each symbol and set of mystical words. Squinting to enhance her view of the energies, she realized these were not domes but were actually bubbles, with hidden halves sinking down into the bedrock far enough to seal it off from the rest of the world.

On the bright side, no demon could dig down through the floor and escape the wards that way. On the dark side . . . I haven't nearly enough energy of my own to counter this and esca—

Torven shouted in a voice that thundered louder than any munitions-packed cannon, making Rexei shout and clamp her hands over her ears. The others winced, but the priests kept chanting and the apprentices—minus Frankei—kept watch with one eye on the ritual and one eye on the passages into this giant round chamber, each determined to do their part. Squinting against the rolling, echoing, overwhelming words, Rexei realized Torven no longer held her bodily in place. Only the ward-spheres did that.

The shouting ended. Stepping forward, she lifted her hand to the edge of the transparent sphere. It was and was not there; her fingers met firm resistance, but she could feel a slight draft cutting through the room at the same time, proof she would not suffocate. She could, however, *feel* the magic, like resting one's fingers lightly on the belly of a resonant instrument. It was the same short brute of a tune the priests had just finished chanting.

"Every piece of magic has a voice, Rexei," she remembered her mother saying. *"Every spell, every ward, every spark of energy. It all sings its own song. Learn to match the song, and you can learn to mimic the song. Mimic the song, and you can* hide *in that song . . ."*

So let's see if I can match and hide in this *song, Mum.*

To do so, she had to turn around and move to the back of the circle holding her prisoner, so that she had the shortest distance to push through the rest of the painted runes and whatever spells they held. To do that, she had to open her eyes first so that she could see where to go . . . and that meant she saw the black mist spewing out from a tiny spark of nothingness about knee-high in the center of the largest dust-ringed circle.

Between one breath and the next, that spark snapped wide, spewing forth a hot wind of sulphurous, acidic hatred in a ring— no, a sphere, that should not have been there. Something defined by that line of dust poured onto the ground. Within its confines, within a soap bubble of an innermost ward, a veil between sanity and that burning, dark-shrouded Netherhell, a Monster stood in towering view. Terrified, Rexei dropped to her knees.

Blackened, scale-plated skin, burning fire for eyes, long claws upon which something torn and bloody had been snagged . . . the demon stared through the sphere connecting the two realms . . . licked its lips with a long, forked tongue . . . and transformed.

"*Hhhhumannnsss,*" the monster hissed, shrinking down from something that filled the sphere to something that was merely half its size, if half again as large as any actual human in the chamber. Pale pink skin took the place of some of those scales, and the demon morphed from a monstrous bulk of muscles to a well-toned chest, normal-seeming arms, and hands that . . . were still long clawed and bloodied. The waist and legs were still black scaled, with twin tails, and spikes growing out of the man-thing's black mane. He almost looked handsome . . . but the eyes were still afire. That mouth, sensuous and shiveringly cruel, quirked up on one side in amusement. "*You ssseeek to bind me?*"

Goddess . . . ! Guildra, help *me!* Rexei pleaded, praying as she had never prayed in her life. *If they turn this . . . this* thing *into a God . . . Help me! How do I stop this from happening?*

. . . Patience . . .

Guildra? Rexei blinked, but darting her gaze around showed no female other than her disguised self in the chamber. No divine Patron to protect her.

"Nurem. You are summoned to the Veil to be oathbound to our

service. We offer you this boy for you to do with as you wish, body and soul, in return for your utter obedience and, through it, your elevation to bonded, subservient, but extremely powerful God-hood," Torven stated.

Nurem's flaming eyes shifted, and his head turned, taking in the various figures in sight. He returned his attention to Torven. *"Whhhich boy?"*

"That boy," Torven stated, pointing at Rexei. "That young man, who goes by the name of Rexei Longshanks. He is a mage, among other things—whatever he is, we offer him to you if you will offer yourself in total obedience to us . . . with myself as your master, and my fellow binders your controllers. Those who oppose us, we will feed to you or slay in your name, and in turn you will give your powers to us to reshape this world for our needs . . . and your occa-sional pleasures."

Rexei shuddered as those burning streaks of fire were turned toward her. *"Thissss . . . boy? You give thissss boy to me?"* The other side of Nurem's mouth quirked up in humor. *"I acsssept."*

Reveal yourself! Now!

SEVENTEEN

The shout, in Guildra's voice, spurred Rexei into pushing to her feet. For a moment, she didn't know what to say, then seized on the word *boy*. "I'm *not* a boy! I'm not a *young man*, either," she added firmly as Torven scowled at her. She didn't know why her Goddess wanted her to do this, but she quickly worked on the buttons of her trousers as she continued. "I've never *been* a male—all this time, you've been duped by a *woman!*"

Whirling around, she dropped her trousers, pulling down her undershorts as well, and mooned Torven, the demon, and over half of the ex-priests. The look on Elcarei's shocked face was worth the fear that she would be brutalized for her revelation, but it was the demon's response that caught everyone's attention. Nurem snarled, hissing at her with jaws that gaped four times as wide as any human's, revealing nested rows of too-sharp teeth lining that unhinged jaw. He clawed at the bubble-sphere separating his universe from theirs and glared at her as she hastily yanked her pants up and faced him again, fumbling to get everything buttoned back in place.

Beyond him to the left, she could see Torven, his palm scraping slowly down a face screwed up in a grimace of rage. "Stupid . . . moronic . . . ! Why didn't anyone *check* to make sure she wasn't a *she*?!"

"What does it matter?" Elcarei called out. "Feed *her* to the demon!"

"The demon has already accepted a *male* sacrifice, that's why!" Torven yelled back, whirling to face the middle-aged, blue-robed priest. "If we feed her to him *now*, he'll be able to break the bindings and escape our contr—"

BANG bam POW! Tufts of munitions smoke puffed out from the passageways. Priests and apprentices cried out in pain, some dropping with hands clasped to reddish stains, others whirling to confront this new danger.

"Torhammer!" Elcarei snarled, spotting the captain of the Precinct. Rexei remembered the face of Captain Torhammer from the Consulate meetings, and she felt both worry and relief. The captain was more than competent as a warrior, as were his men, but none of them were mages like the priests in this chamber.

"*You!*" Bishop Hansu accused, pointing at a younger man with brown curls, green viewing lenses, and a distinctive pointed nose, one which Rexei knew she would've remembered if she had ever seen him lurking around the temple. She wondered who he was, if Hansu could be so upset at his presence among all others.

Others appeared all around; she recognized the chief leftenant, Rogen Tallnose, but most of the others she didn't know. She loved them, however, for most had hand-cannons pointed at the priests, and hopefully some hadn't wasted their only shot. The ones who weren't in leather-and-plate-armored coats were somehow casting energies from their hands, some of them female like her.

"Retreat!" Archbishop Gafford shouted. "Full retreat!"

Those that could still move whirled and ran for the mirrors displaying those odd views. Inside his bubble-sphere, Nurem hissed and clawed at the membrane separating their worlds; he lost the shape of his semi-handsome form, resuming the same horrific monster visage as before. Backing up from that side of her own bubble-ward, Rexei turned and pressed her hands against the shield, striving to *hear* the tones it made so that she could match them and slip through.

Before her hands could do more than sink wrist deep into the shield, a woman in steel armor and an open, black-lined cloak cleaved through the air between herself and Rexei with a mirror-bright sword. Though her long blade cut nothing, touched nothing but air, entire sections of paint were somehow flung off the stone floor. Rexei knew the woman. Knew her name was Orana . . . something. Orana Niel. But Rexei had *no* context as to how she knew the other woman, other than having seen her face some-where. Whatever spell had been used to cut out chunks of her memory had been very concise in some areas and a bit vague in what it removed from others. The demons, she knew about; her chosen Goddess, she had always known. But . . .

"You! Longshanks! *You* planned this!" Torven accused, making Rexei turn around to see what he was up to. He was doing some-thing with a small sack of powder pulled from the pouch strung on his belt. Scattering it in a circle, he called out over his shoulder. "Well, guess what, *Guild Master* of the new priesthood? I'm leav-ing this mess for *you* to clean up! *Bazher faroudoel!*"

Light flared up from the powder and the mage somehow dropped down out of sight.

She has the words. You have the will.

Rexei *knew* that was a message from her Goddess, but she didn't know *what* sort of a message it was. The sphere trapping Nurem inside the ward-circle was starting to bulge; he had somehow regained the half-handsome, half-humanoid shape from before, but his claws were pushing against the soap bubble of the Veil, deforming it in an effort to tear through. Another slash of the sword behind her popped the bubble capturing and confining Rexei . . . just as three of the mirrors exploded, making people yelp.

"Champion!" Captain Torhammer called out. Two more mirrors popped. "What's going on?"

"They're destroying the mirror-Gates!" Orana called back. "And with the primary demon summoner gone, it's going to be difficult to get the Veil resealed."

". . . Guildra said *you* have the words," Rexei said, turning to face Orana. The last two mirrors exploded as well. She flinched but continued, "And that *I* have the strength. But I don't know *what* words."

"Ah. Just a moment . . ." She shifted her two-fisted grip on the sword and dug one gauntlet-covered hand into the robe's sleeve. "Where is it . . . where is it . . ."

A sickening *pop* behind them made Rexei whirl around. The Veil-bubble was gone. For a moment, the demon-Monster returned, swelling to fill the containment sphere, then Nurem controlled himself, shrinking down to merely twice as tall as a human this time. "*I willl have my sssacrificssse, sssweetling,*" he hissed, and *liiiicked* the transparent magic that was all that held him in place. "*The agreement wassss made.*"

"Bullshit," Ora muttered. She pulled out a scroll and pushed it at Rexei, who fumbled to take it and untie the ribbons holding the aged parchment and sticks together.

"*Priessstling withhh a sssword, are you?*" Nurem hissed, looking more amused than enraged. "*You thhhink you can sssstop me?*"

The containment wards started to stretch. Below them, the lines of paint started to bulge and move. Rexei gulped and yanked at the ribbon holding the scroll shut. Orana stepped up next to

Rexei, sword now resting on her shoulder, her free hand on her armor-plated hip. She gave the demon a contemptuous look. "I have slain a *God*, little beast. The former God of *this* land. I will slay *you* if need be . . . but your demise will be swifter and more final at the hands of a *true* priestess of this land."

Rexei managed to get the scroll the right way up, skimmed quickly over the instructions at the top, and started chanting. "I summon the spirit of my God . . . dess," she called out, quickly adjusting the lines to better match this moment. She also tightened her gut in the way the Actors Guild recommended for making sure audience members in the farthest rows would always be able to hear. "*I summon the will of my people's Patron!*"

"I summon the spirit of my Goddess!" she heard someone shout, echoing her words. A quick glance up showed it was the brunette with the green viewing crystals perched on his nose. He quickly circled his hand, looking at the others, the ones who had come to rescue her. "Come on—*help* her! Give the Gearman your strength! I *summon* the spirit of my Goddess!"

The others quickly if raggedly repeated his words, then continued with her second line. ". . . I summon the will of my people's Patron!"

Quickly looking back down at the scroll in her hands, Rexei read off the rest of the lines, pausing between each one for the others to recite them in her wake. With each verse asserted, she could feel something welling up within her, and she clung to it, along with her image, her belief, in her Goddess.

> "*I bless this land in the name of my Goddess . . .*
> *I bring the Goodness of the Heavens and their power to smite!*
> *I sanctify this ground as holy in the name of Guildra,*
> *And I purify the air, the rain, the day, and the night!*
> *I am a believer with faith in my Goddess;*

I believe with all my strength that She will protect us.
I bless this place in the name of Holy Guildra
And in the name of the Guilds and the values by which She exists.
I cast back into the Nethers all demonic intrusions,
And by my faith and by Her Great Blessings,
I seal now the Veil, cutting off all darkness and blight!"

Nurem screamed and clawed hard at the trembling, visibly weakening wards. Rexei felt only the tiniest tremor of fear, though. With the invocation's assertions had come an answering, controlled anger. All the pain of having lost her mother and having to flee her family, all the stubborn determination to survive despite being so terribly young and alone, all the maturity she had learned and the lessons she had absorbed in how to listen and heed, obey and learn, how to create and *believe* first and foremost in herself, and now . . . and now, to believe in her Goddess . . . who stood *with* her, behind her, supporting her . . .

This demon was *not* going to win.

"I call upon Guildra, my Patron, my Goddess
To cast you back into the Netherhell from whence you came,
And to seal forever this ground as Holy, not profane!
Be gone in the Name of Guildra!
Be gone in the Name of the Heavens!
Be gone in the Name of the people of Guildara!
Be! You! Gone!"

She flung up her arm, shoving her palm heel-first through the air. *Something* coalesced inside of her as she did so, and thrust outward with the force of her arm. A golden spark, shimmering with hope and faith and trust, seared straight for the weakest point in that claw-stretched, cracking ward—and slammed Nurem the

Monster back down through his bubble, down through the half-seen hole in the world, all the way down into the Netherhells. Golden sparks—smaller and less powerful, but appearing in the dozens, the scores—flung themselves inward from her fellow Guildarans, each a tiny spark of faith that caged the darkness, squeezed it down, down, down . . .

"*Be Thou Gone from this Blessed Place!*" Rexei asserted, putting every last inch of her life and her will, her magic, her music, and her faith, into her command.

A final, fat spark shot forward, expanded, devoured . . . and erased the dark stain of a sparklike rift from their side of existence. The contracting bubble of Light burst outward in a bright spray of harmless pale gold sparks. Where they fell, they erased all traces of paint, scrubbing away most of the runes on the ground.

"*Well* done, Gearman," the woman at her side praised. She rested her gauntlet-covered hand on Rexei's shoulder. "Well done, and well managed for prophecy's sake."

"Prophecy, hell!" Captain Torhammer snapped. "I recognized five of those places in those mirrors. We need to get after them!"

"No." Rexei hadn't realized she was going to speak, but the mention of prophecy . . . she could not remember the time or the place, but she *knew* that this was important. "No. Let them go. They will be dealt with. We have our *own* messes to manage."

"That's not your call to make—" Torhammer started to argue.

A chime rang softly right next to her ear, startling a yelp from Rexei and a visible twitch from the captain. Orana gave both of them a sheepish look. She tucked her sword inside her robe and pulled it shut, making the blade somehow vanish, then stuck her hands into her sleeves. When she pulled them out, the left one had no gauntlet on it, nor a vambrace, though it did have a bracelet with a strange hinged top. Flipping it up, she moved away a few steps as she spoke. "Yes, Pelai . . . ?"

Pelai . . . why is that name familiar? Rexei wondered. The others were picking their way down toward the two of them, foremost the sharp-nosed, green-lensed fellow with the curly hair. At first it had been brown, but now . . . it was reddish gold? *When did that happen? It must've been an illusion spell. A smart choice around priest-mages . . .*

"Rexei, are you okay?" he asked her, stepping through the gaps in the speckled remnants of paint, the ones which the swordswoman had made. "Do you . . . do you remember who I am?"

She nodded her head, then shook it, wrinkling her nose. "Um . . . sorry, no. I'm okay now, but . . ." Pausing, she looked at him. He was only a few inches taller than she, and she knew she had never seen him before, but . . . Awkward silence stretched between them as something in his gaze turned sad and regretful. It hurt her to see it, hurt her deep down inside in the same place where she could feel Guildra residing. "I . . . don't know if this is going to sound really strange or creepy or . . . or like I've slipped a cog and broken some gear teeth, here, but . . ."

". . . But?" he asked, brows raising in encouragement for her to continue.

"But . . . I feel like I know you," Rexei forced herself to admit. "I know I *don't*, but . . . I feel like I *know* you, and . . . like . . . I feel like I care for you . . . which is really silly and stupid, because we obviously haven't ever—"

His fingers covered her lips, even as his own mouth curved in a smile. "You *do* know me. Or you did. We knew and liked each other a lot. Unfortunately, you had to take a magically binding spell to *forget* all about me, and everything around me, so you wouldn't betray me to the ex-priests who just fled here."

"I *do* know you? And you know me?" Rexei repeated. He nodded, and a strange but utterly welcome sense of relief flooded her. "Good. Good . . . because I really thought I was stripping some gears here, thinking either it was, uh, me going crazy or . . . you know . . ."

"Love at first sight?" he asked, giving her a shy smile. His hand reached out and clasped hers, the one not holding on to the scroll. "More like you were a combination of highly wary and a bit belligerent that very first time, out of what you thought was a need for self-defense. I wish I knew how to *reverse* the oathbinding, but . . ."

An indelicate snort interrupted their conversation. Both glanced at Orana, whose bulk of armor had somehow vanished from beneath her robe without her actually needing to disrobe. "It's an *oathbinding*. Just have her swear an oath to *remember* again. If she does it of her own free will, without coercion, then she'll re-remember everything—you people seriously need some training," the Darkhanan woman added. "I can spare a couple months to teach you the basics of magic, but as soon as spring has thawed its way up toward the northern coast, Niel and I really need to get back to our home."

Rexei knew that Niel was the unseen soul of Orana's Host, residing somewhere inside the blonde woman's body via the holy powers of Darkhanan Witch-craft. As much as she wanted to ask questions about the woman, about her life, about what had happened at the Convocation of Gods and Man—Rexei could not *remember* how she knew anything about a resumed Convocation of Gods and Man.

Guildra . . . will you help me with my oath? she asked silently. A pulse of something warm rose up from within, a sense of love, support, and acceptance. Nodding to herself, Rexei carefully phrased what she wanted to say in her thoughts. She was no apprentice in the Law-Sayers Guild, but she knew what an oathbinding was.

"I, Rexei, bind unto my powers the following vow: I will remember everything I have forgotten at the end of this vow, including any memories purged from my mind by oathbinding, and I will remember all these things with calm clarity. So swear I, Rexei . . . High Priestess of Guildra, and Guild Master of the Guildaran Holy Guild."

A bright, bubbly tingling feeling swept down over her body from the crown of her head to the tips of her toes in her winter boots. It felt far cleaner than any of the other magics she had been touched by in the last hour—at least until the last few minutes or so—and in its wake . . . she remembered. Remembered why her bottom was sore and what it felt like to sleep trustingly next to the man with the green lenses, Alonnen Tallnose, head of the carefully hidden Mages Guild. She remembered how he had teased her, shared with her, and believed in her. Remembered every warm, welcoming, friendly touch, and remembered their first kiss.

More than that, she remembered other things. It was a good thing she had asserted that she would remember them with *calm* clarity, because she remembered forgotten horrors of being groped and cursed, bullied and badgered. Remembered all the *good* things that had happened to her, too. And she remembered . . . Frowning softly, Rexei quirked her brows. "I even remember how to make pickled beets? I didn't realize I even knew how, let alone that I'd forgotten that . . . I couldn't have been more than *three* when Mum made pickled beets . . ."

Watching the expressions play across her face, in her eyes, Alonnen was caught off-guard by that non sequitur. Chuckling, he dared to lean forward and wrap his arms around her. To his everlasting relief, she immediately snuggled close, hugging him right back. "I'm sorry everyone knows what your gender is now, with Orana calling you priestess and all that."

Rexei snorted. "I revealed it myself to the ex-priests in order to get that Aian fellow, Torven, to call a halt to the summoning ritual. He offered me as a *male* sacrifice . . . and I dropped my trousers and mooned him to get him to stop."

"You . . . what?" Alonnen asked her, brows raising in shock. "I, ah . . ."

Orana shrugged. "A bold, yet unconventional choice. Your

mistaken gender identity would have invalidated the binding, allowing the demon to cross the barrier with impunity, had you been fully handed over for sacrifice."

Recovering from his shock, Alonnen realized Captain Torhammer and his brother were approaching. Alonnen switched to hugging his love with just one arm. "Definitely unconventional, but undoubtedly the best proof possible. We should be very grateful that this Torven Shel Von fellow is such a stickler for getting the demonic bindings perfectly right."

"Master Tall. We need your people to help us track down the escaped mages," the captain said once he was within polite conversation distance. Polite, but assertive.

"Actually, no, we don't," Alonnen corrected.

His brother frowned at him. "This isn't your call to make, Master Tall. Nor is it hers."

"Neither is it *yours*," Orana returned calmly. "Prophecy is involved . . . and prophecy has already let us know where they'll be confronted next. Torven was ejected from the Tower's vicinity in Aiar. High Priestess Saleria and her 'servant'—a fellow Darkhanan Witch—have saved the Sacred Grove of Katan . . . and now the Gearman's Strength which Master Rexei just displayed is going to help the Guilds' defender cast them out. Master Tall, I'm afraid that Pelai is having . . . difficulties . . . adjusting to the way your, ah, guardianship is managed. She'll need you to return immediately and perform the aetheric spells yourself."

"Aetheric?" Rexei asked, wondering what she had missed.

"We're going to disrupt the aether for the next two years," Alonnen told her, "and do it in such a way that the Netherhells will not be accessible. Not here and not in any other land we can reach and cover. Captain Torhammer, my guild will want to get our hands on any books left behind by the ex-priests. The rest of the wealth confiscated should be split into quarters, shared between the Holy Guild, the Militia, the Mages Guild, and the new government. Orana, if you would assist them in looking for any magical 'surprises' that might have been left behind . . . ?"

Rexei liked how he had divided the wealth; Alonnen had more years of experience as a Guild Master than she, and this was yet another good idea she had seen from him. She nodded when Captain Torhammer and Leftenant Tallnose each flicked a querying glance her way.

Orana bowed, acquiescing. "With the local land well sealed against demonic energies by Her Holiness, the rest should be mere nuisances to me, for all they might be dangerous to you."

"Let's just hope we don't have to do that again," Rexei said. She offered the scroll to Orana, who shook her head.

"Keep it. All priesthoods should have a copy of how to bless away demon taint and reseal the land . . . and I fear many more lands will need their own copies."

Nodding, Rexei nudged Alonnen into moving toward the exit. His brother followed them, muttering as soon as they reached the rounded corridor. "I can't believe you're just *letting* them flee."

Alonnen rolled his eyes. "Stuff it, Rogen. The next place they're going is Mendhi. Prophecy says as much, and that means it'll be up to the priests and the Painted Warriors of that land to manage what happens next. *We* have a lot of work to do if we're going to have any hope of stabilizing ex-Mekhana into a new nation and figuring out where we want this new Guildara to go."

"Alonnen," Rogen warned him.

"We don't even know *how* we're going to rule over ourselves," Alonnen pointed out, flicking a palm at his brother. "We don't want a Matriarch or a Patriarch—"

"I *certainly* wouldn't agree to that," Rexei interjected firmly, and received a loving squeeze from Alonnen's other arm.

"See?" Alonnen asked rhetorically. "There you go. And we

cannot be successfully ruled by Consulate committee. Nor by any one guild, unless you want inter-guild politics to be our next big enemy."

"Marta Grenspun might have some ideas," Rexei found herself offering. "She's ruthless as an organizer, and she has managed to find great people for my guild. She's not the only one we can ask, too . . . Oh. Lundrei," she whispered, seeing her half brother through an open cell door. Two militia members were working on the collar binding his throat, trying to pick it open. "So they *did* coerce him into writing that note."

"Probably," Alonnen said. "Orana promised to give us a few Truth Stones and leave a list of instructions on how to make them. We can question him with that to be absolutely sure."

"Truth Stones are going to completely revise the way the law is handled in this land," Rogen observed dryly. He let his mouth curve into a wry smile. "I think I'm actually looking forward to those kinds of headaches, instead of the ongoing fears of Mekha and His priesthood."

Alonnen frowned, then stopped, bringing Rexei to a halt as well. "Oy . . . I just realized something."

"What?" Rexei asked.

"Well, I love you, you see," he said, making her blink and raise a hand to cover her mouth. He quickly patted her forearm in reassurance. "And I know you love me, right?"

She couldn't speak, but she could nod. Vigorously. Nod and blink back the tears of emotion welling up inside of her.

"Well, then . . . how in the name of your Goddess are we going to get married?" he asked. "I'm not in the mood to put up with that Mekhanan-style nonsense of women pledging to be subordinate to men, but we're too young as a new land to have any formal ceremonies written up, yet. And *you*, Master Longshanks, are the highest ranked member of the new priesthood. Who'll bless our union, if and when we marry? *If* we marry," he added, allowing for some wiggle room on her behalf with a tip of his head.

"*When.* And I'll write it up so that anyone can get married by Holy or Gearman witness. And I'll be known as a priestess, as well as the Guild Master," she stated, making up her mind. "I'll grow my hair out and wear skirts from time to time and *not* be afraid of anyone finding out I'm actually a female."

"Well, no. Not after baring your bottom and mooning the worst bastards to ever be born in this land, as it'd be a bit too late to erase *that* particular image, even if I had an oathbinding big enough to help with that task," Alonnen said mock mildly . . . and grinned when she mock whapped him for teasing her. He leaned in and kissed the tip of her nose.

Rexei kissed him back on the tip of his. Their noses bumped together, then they were kissing, swept along by the sheer relief of having won the day with neither harmed. It would have continued and deepened, except Alonnen felt his brother rapping his knuckles on the top of his head. Not painfully, just annoyingly. Pulling back, he eyed his brother.

"Stow the passion, brother," Rogen chided him. "Don't you have to get back to seal off those Portal-whatsits?"

"Right. Yes. Very important. By the way, I'm stealing one of your militia motorhorses," Alonnen added, nudging Rexei toward the stairs. After losing her to her kidnappers, he did not feel comfortable leaving her behind, prophecy or no.

"You're what?" Rogen asked, frowning at him. "You are not!"

"*You* and your men blocked every street leading to this place," Alonnen countered. "Only a motorhorse is going to get the two of us free of the tangle of vehicles before the rest of you are ready to leave, and I am not taking the motorwagon. It will still be needed to transport all the other mages back home. So, I'm taking a motorhorse, and Rexei is riding it with me . . . right?"

"I have no plans of forgetting you anytime soon," she told him, guessing why he wanted her to go with him. She felt the same way and wanted both men to know. "I'm glad to see that not even the tightest of oathbindings could keep me from the memory that I love you. But *I'll* be the one to drive the motorhorse."

"You? Why you?" he asked.

There were several answers she could have claimed: that as a member of the Messengers Guild, she had been trained to handle a motorhorse in all forms of weather. That she knew she was a slightly better guider of the vehicle. But the real reason, she told him bluntly. "Because I love it when you hug me, and I want you to hug me all the way back home, and that means you have to sit *behind* me, which means *I'll* have to guide the thing."

He considered her words, then dipped his head. "I must admit, that is the most logical excuse for a miles-long hug I have ever heard. I'd be delighted to hold you as long as I can, too. Shall we plan on a nice long ride all the way to the northern shore for our wedding trip?"

"Ugh. Just get yourselves out of here, before I start thinking *I* need to settle down, too," Rogen muttered. "I don't need Mum making any more 'I want grandchildren' noises in my direction. And refill the tank, brother! You'll return the motorhorse in perfect condition to Precinct headquarters with a full tank of engine potion tomorrow and no extra scratches, or I'll tell Torhammer I *didn't* authorize it, and he'll make you slave away for a month or more in the quarries."

"Ah, the joys of civilized, law-abiding life . . ." Alonnen muttered. "*Yes*, Brother."

"It beats the alternative," Rexei reminded him, walking with him away from the room where her half brother was still being held. "I'll visit with Lundrei tomorrow. I just want to get out of here and back into the safety of . . . you-know-where."

The sight of three slumped, snoring bodies on the floor slowed their steps. Alonnen lifted one brow, but Rexei shook her head and nudged him onward. The novices would either be handled by Torhammer's men, or awaken and flee to wherever. She wondered what had happened to Frankei and resolved to see if he had escaped, or if he had been caught. There was no telling if the notoriously strict captain would go easy on him for helping rid her of that horrid collar, but if he was still around, Rexei knew she had to try.

She was done running from trouble. Done hiding from threats and from responsibilities. Done with flitting from guild to guild whenever things got tough.

That's my Guild Master, she heard in the back of her mind. *Keep up your inner strength, continue spreading the word, and I'll have enough faith to manifest and help make this land a true kingdom, soon . . .*

"Copper for your thoughts?" Alonnen asked her.

"Guildra's faith . . . this demonic mess . . . I'd rather think about why my bottom is still a little sore and what we can do to make it feel better," she admitted under her breath, blushing.

"Well, my brother once told me the militia has a saying about the things that make you sore," he said.

"Oh?" Rexei asked.

He leaned in close enough to rub the pointed tip of his long, tall nose against her cheek, tickling and teasing her. "The only cure for what made you sore, Master Longshanks, is *more* of what made you sore. I'm ready whenever you are . . . after I take care of the aether, of course."

She blushed . . . and pinched his bottom, making him jump a little. "Careful, Master Tall, or I might grab the pomade and the crankman once you're done with casting out any chance of more demonic summonings, and show *you* how good it feels to be so sore."

Blushing, he cleared his throat and said no more . . . though he certainly smiled.

Song of the Guardians of Destiny

When serpent crept into their hall:
Danger waits for all who board,
Trying to steal that hidden tone.
Painted Lady saves the lord;
Tower's master's not alone.

Calm the magics caught in thrall:
Put your faith in strangers' pleas,
Keeper, Witch, and treasure trove;
Ride the wave to calm the trees,
Servant saves the sacred Grove.

Cult's awareness, it shall rise:
Hidden people, gather now;
Fight the demons, fight your doubt.
Gearman's strength shall then endow,
When Guilds' defender casts them out.

Synod gathers, tell them lies:
Efforts gathered in your pride
Lost beneath the granite face.
Painted Lord, stand by her side;
Repentance is the Temple's grace.

Brave the dangers once again:
Quarrels lost to time's own pace
Set aside in danger's face.
Save your state; go make your choice
When Dragon bows unto the Voice.

Sybaritic good shall reign:
Island city, all alone
Set your leader on his throne
Virtue's knowledge gives the most,
Aiding sanctions by the Host.

Faith shall now be mended whole:
Soothing songs kept beasts at bay
But sorrow's song led King astray.
Demon's songs shall bring out worse
Until the Harper ends your curse.

Save the world is Guardians' goal:
Groom's mistake and bride's setback
Aids the foe in its attack.
Save the day is Jinx's task,
Hidden in the royal Masque.

~BY SEER HAUPANEA